The Japan Conspiracy

This Large Print Book carries the
Seal of Approval of N.A.V.H.

The Japan Conspiracy

JACK ANDERSON

Thorndike Press • Thorndike, Maine

LT
F
ANDERSON

Published in 1994 by arrangement with Zebra Books,
an imprint of Kensington Publishing Corporation.

Thorndike Large Print ® General Series.

The tree indicium is a trademark of Thorndike Press.

The text of this Large Print edition is unabridged.
Other aspects of the book may vary from the original edition.

Set in 16 pt. News Plantin by Juanita Macdonald.

Printed in the United States on acid-free, high opacity paper. ∞

Library of Congress Cataloging in Publication Data

Anderson, Jack, 1922–
    The Japan conspiracy / Jack Anderson.
        p.   cm.
    ISBN 0-7862-0110-X (alk. paper : lg. print)
    1. Corporations, Japanese — United States — Fiction.
2. Commercial crimes — United States — Fiction.
3. Commercial crimes — Japan — Fiction.
4. Lawyers — United States — Fiction.
5. Large type books. I. Title.
[PS355 1.N365J36   1994]
813'.54—dc20   93-39748

The Japan Conspiracy

Prologue

1945

Richard Zehlke heard the swell of angry voices before he felt the wave of hot, humid air as the door of the C-54 transport plane swung open. Out on the tarmac, thousands of Filipinos surged against a sagging chainlink fence, while a small band of military police nervously swept the fence line with their silent M-1 carbines.

Stepping back into the plane, Zehlke raised his palm like a traffic cop to keep his human cargo from the door. The gesture wasn't necessary. No one was moving. The sixteen Japanese soldiers and diplomats sat impassively, staring straight ahead. They could not help but hear the tumult outside, but they refused to acknowledge it. Zehlke dropped his hand, surveyed the scene outside the door, and nodded to a U.S. Army colonel on the ground below.

The senior Japanese officer, Lieutenant

General Torashiro Kawabe, rose first from his seat and stepped forward into the searing light of the doorway. He looked out on Nichols Field, the Allied air base in Manila, and down the stairs at the unsmiling face of Colonel Sidney Mashbir.

Kawabe descended the metal stairs, followed by his entourage, and extended his right hand Western-style to Mashbir. The colonel deflected the hand with a curt gesture for the Japanese delegation to keep on moving. The crowd roared its approval at the rebuke. Six months earlier, in February 1945, the Japanese had abandoned their brutal occupation of the Philippines. Now this group of sixteen was back to negotiate a surrender, and neither the Filipinos nor the Americans were in the mood for gentlemanly courtesies.

Kawabe was a minor player, pressed into service as a negotiator when General Yoshijiro Umezu, the Japanese army chief of staff, refused to go. Even after Hiroshima, even after Nagasaki, General Umezu was still pressing Emperor Hirohito to fight on.

Richard Zehlke wasn't impressed with Kawabe. He kept his eye instead on a Japanese officer who melted unobtrusively into the delegation. An OSS operative, Zehlke had been ordered to accompany the Japanese delegation to the Philippines on August 19 to prepare the terms for a formal surrender to take place on the USS *Missouri* two weeks later. He had done his homework. The dossier that interested him was the file on Lieutenant Colonel Masahiko Takeshita.

Zehlke thought it was a mistake to allow Takeshita to participate in the negotiations. The details were still sketchy, but Zehlke had heard from sources in Tokyo that this little man with the Hitleresque mustache had to be dragged kicking and screaming into surrender. When, on August 14, 1945, Hirohito announced his intention to capitulate, Takeshita rallied other officers to resist. He even sent out a bogus cable under the name of his brother-in-law, War Minister Korechika Anami, ordering the army to fight on. Anami was dead now. Five days earlier, unable to bear the shame of defeat, he had plunged a dagger into his gut.

Plenty of Japanese officers and diplomats were taking the *seppuku* option that month, but Anami was the most prominent. Zehlke was fixated on a curiosity. An OSS source in Tokyo swore to him that Takeshita had been present when his brother-in-law killed himself. That when Takeshita offered to die with him, Anami had ordered him to live and continue the fight.

Now, as Takeshita stepped onto the tarmac, bringing up the rear of the Japanese delegation, he muttered under his breath, "We surrender only the first battle of the hundred-years war. There are still ninety-six years to fight."

He was unaware that Zehlke understood Japanese.

The Japanese surrender took Richard Zehlke out of action. He wound up behind a desk in the Army of the Occupation. The seasoned field agent despised the role. The paperwork in his office at SCAP Finance Division was humdrum. The Supreme Command Allied Powers, under the direction of General Douglas MacArthur, was rebuilding Japan brick by brick. Documenting that achievement was tedious work to a man who would rather be diving out of airplanes or skulking through the back alleys of the Ginza. Zehlke would have settled for a stateside transfer, except that he had no one there who cared if he came home. His choice of career hadn't leant itself to permanent attachments.

Six months into the Occupation, the pace had picked up. Acting on a tip that came across Zehlke's desk, General MacArthur ordered Tokyo Harbor dredged. The salvage crews pulled up what was officially said to be $2 billion in gold bars — the spoils of war dumped into the harbor by the Japanese when defeat was inevitable. The gold was deposited in Japan's Central Bank. It provided the funding SCAP desperately needed to carry out General MacArthur's grand plan for the new Japan. MacArthur, ever sensitive to Japanese pride, linked up with a business consortium, the Sonno Group, which was given the responsibility for parceling the money out for rebuilding.

One thing bothered Zehlke. The accounting for the Sonno Group's investments in the reconstruction went through his office, and the numbers didn't add up. The supply of gold appeared to be limitless.

Another thought persistently played in the back of his mind. The same Japanese who had vowed they would rather die than surrender seemed to settle comfortably into the submissive role of the occupied. Even the rebel Masahiko Takeshita became a general in the Ground Self-Defense Force, working cheerfully under MacArthur's thumb.

It struck Zehlke as a curious way to carry on a hundred-years war.

One

The Present

Toshio Miyaki, patriarch of Miyaki Industries
and one of Japan's wealthiest men, tapped on
the window that separated the rear seat of the
white Mercedes limousine from Kato, the
driver. An abrupt hand signal directed Kato
to pull over and stop. Soundlessly the vehicle
eased toward the curb in front of a small
pachinko parlor whose facade blazed and
winked in gaudy neon colors, like one of the
1950s American jukeboxes that Miyaki collected. The old man — small, slender, frail-
appearing — stepped from the hushed privacy
of the Mercedes into the noisy blare and glitter
of the Ginza. For a moment he stood blinking,
as if stunned by the raucous life that swirled
around him.

He was, in fact, immobilized by the assault
of memories.

Over the past half century he had taken this
journey innumerable times, passing through

12

or near the Ginza on his way to his offices in Nihonbashi, Tokyo's financial district, traveling at first on foot or pedaling a bicycle, later taking the subway train, driving his own car or, finally, riding in his chauffeured limousine. This morning's trip, however, was different. In a sense it was the culmination of all those many journeys. He had at last come full circle.

Pausing at a busy intersection, he stared at the uniformed, white-gloved policeman directing traffic with the self-conscious flamboyance of the conductor of an orchestra. The narrow street was jammed with vehicles moving only a few feet at a time. Crowds of tourists and young Japanese overflowed the sidewalks. A group of the latter jostled Miyaki as they flowed around him — a small rock in the center of a turbulent stream. The girls had faces painted into ghastly masks with Western makeup. Some of them — young men as well as women — wore streaks of green or red in their long black hair. All were decked out in the latest symbols of American rebellion — jeans, leather jackets, studded boots, T-shirts. If he had not known better, Miyaki would have viewed the spectacle with dismay, an image of a society disintegrating into anarchy. But Japanese youths, he knew, only mimicked the defiant posturing that, in

America and Europe, was all too real. Within a few years these same youngsters would be taking their places in factories and insurance offices, wearing acceptably conservative dress, finding models in their older peers rather than American rebels. Like their parents they were conformists at heart.

Miyaki gave them only passing notice. Amid the Ginza's neon glitz he was remembering a time not long after a young Japanese soldier had returned from China to his homeland. A darker time. The first time Miyaki had passed this way, on a morning in 1946 that was to determine his destiny.

It had been raining earlier that morning, and the sky was still overcast and gloomy. The Ginza was a devastated place, surrounded by gutted, bombed-out stores. Miyaki was a skinny young man, half-starved like most of the city's population in that postwar period of humiliation, wearing a hand-me-down suit from his father that, because the elder Miyaki was a heavier, taller man, hung loosely from Toshio's small frame. Most of the Ginza was dark in spite of the time of day. The throngs in the streets that day were not shoppers but sidewalk peddlers trying to ward off starvation for themselves and their families. The traffic lights did not function, and an American mil-

14

itary policeman in his crisp khaki uniform, wearing a white helmet — tall, handsome, attracting the sidelong glances of the young Japanese girls who shuffled past him with their heads bowed — directed what little vehicular traffic there was, mostly American military vehicles and dignitaries' cars. Miyaki, who had spent seven years during the war in Manchuria fighting the Chinese, shared the bitter burden of defeat and despair that gripped his people.

His future appeared bleak. Before the war his family had been wealthy, with income from rubber plantations in Indochina. He had attended the best schools. He had been groomed for his family's business. His marriage had been arranged to the daughter of a banker in Osaka. Now the rubber plantations, along with the family fortune, were gone. Jobs were virtually nonexistent. He had no money, no prospects, not even enough rice and fish scraps to put in front of his wife and two children. He had but one tenuous hope, his father's remote connection to one of the old *zaibatsu* — the family-based and elaborately linked business and financial conglomerates that traced their power back over centuries. They had controlled prewar Japan. It was this hope that brought Miyaki to the Ginza that morning, and from there to the financial district near the brackish Kanda River.

From the Ginza he walked the whole way to Kabutocho, Tokyo's Wall Street, on the paper-thin soles of borrowed shoes. He hurried over the last mile, terrified he would be late. Arriving at the unmarked building while the last minute ticked down toward eleven o'clock, he stood irresolute on the deserted street. Had he got the directions wrong? Would men so wealthy and powerful secrete themselves behind so unpretentious a facade?

The teak door set into the recessed entry opened slightly. A man of his own age peered out at him, stared for a moment, and bowed. *"Hajimemashite, Miyaki-san. Dozo yoroshiku."*

Miyaki bowed in turn and entered. He was expected.

The elevator did not function — not surprising that year in Tokyo, where few facilities were immune to the general breakdown of machinery and services. Miyaki walked up four flights of stairs to a large, tatami-floored room divided by thin partitions into several private rooms. The young man, who did not speak after the initial greeting, led him through to another room, open and spacious, furnished with a dozen black-lacquered chairs arranged in a semicircle. A single mat had been placed on the floor facing the arc of chairs, each of which was occupied by a man wearing

16

a gray or black business suit. Their faces were impassive, the eyes hooded, offering no welcome.

Humbly, Toshio Miyaki bowed and took his place, sitting cross-legged on the mat to face his inquisitors.

The questioning was harsh, even hostile. Had he been cowardly in battle as a soldier? Had he fled from the enemy? How was it possible that he had fought for the emperor honorably for seven years without receiving a single wound, not so much as a scratch?

Frightened, his voice trembling, Miyaki answered as well as he could. He hardly dared to lift his head to meet the accusing eyes of his scowling interrogators. He was demoralizingly aware of the ill-fitting suit that bagged around his arms and feet, of the tremor in his voice.

"Miyaki-san! Do you give honor to your emperor?"

Startled, Miyaki looked up. *"Mochiron."*

"Do you accept defeat? Do you recognize our inferiority to the American conquerors?"

He hesitated, not sure what answer was expected. He took his cue from the bitterness in the eyes of his questioner, a compact man of about fifty years with steel-gray hair and a heavy mouth pulled down at both corners. "It's true we have lost the war," he said care-

17

fully. "America is very powerful, its industries more advanced than our own. This much has been proved. It may be that the time to fight such a war was not right for Japan."

"Do you believe our cause was unjust?" another man demanded.

"Hontō de wa arimasen." Toshio remembered what his father had told him about the men he was to meet this morning, men who called themselves the Sonno Group. Their motto, taken from a popular nineteenth century slogan, was *Sonno joi* — "Honor the emperor, expel the barbarians!"

"Asia must be for Asians," he continued, choosing his words thoughtfully. "Not for Western barbarians. Our destiny must be of our own choosing." His listeners were silent, staring at him. The tremor left his voice as his confidence grew. "We must question the wisdom of our actions, but that doesn't mean they were unjust. It's true we have been defeated. That must be accepted, but . . ."

"But this is not the end?"

The gray-haired man with the bitter mouth spoke softly, leaning forward. Later Miyaki would learn that his name was Nashimoto, and that he was at that time the leader of the Sonno council. He was a man who traced his ancestry directly to samurai warriors in the province of Hidako.

18

Miyaki stared back at him, as if the question itself were a revelation. After a moment's silence he said, "No. It must not be the end."

After that exchange the tone of the questioning changed. He was asked about his parents, his wife and family, his schooling, any mechanical or other skills he had acquired, why he had dropped out of engineering college. ("To serve the emperor in China," he answered simply.) There was particular interest in his work helping to build and repair bridges in China during the war — a major reason, he was tempted to point out, that he had never been wounded in battle.

At a signal from Nashimoto the questioning ended abruptly. As Miyaki was sent from the room, misgivings assaulted him. For a half-hour he waited in one of the adjoining rooms, his despair mounting. How could such men respect anyone whose voice trembled like a guilty child's? Why had he not remained silent and humble? What did such men care for his real opinions? The smell of fish and a fragrant sauce caused his empty stomach to growl painfully.

As curtly as he had been dismissed he was called back to the conference room. There, sitting once more before the circle of men he had begun to think of as his judges, the young Miyaki learned to his astonishment that he was to start his own business in Osaka. All necessary financing would be provided. Connections with suppliers would be arranged. Permits would be secured, and any other requirements of the occupying American military authorities would be met. General MacArthur, he was told, had decreed that the traditional *zaibatsu* concentrations of businesses were to be broken up and disbursed. Stock in the many smaller companies that resulted from the breakup would eventually be sold on the open market for the first time, as part of the democratization of Japan.

"We will support this new path for the Japanese people," Nashimoto told him. For the first time that day he smiled. "When the elephant pulls, the mouse does not foolishly pull the other way."

With Sonno Group support behind the scenes, Miyaki would become the president of a small construction company. He would be responsible for hiring and training his workers, as well as for finding customers. In the war-ravaged country, this would not be difficult.

"I know nothing of this business," Miyaki stammered.

"You will learn."

He quickly discovered that there would be no need to walk the streets of Osaka to create business for his new firm. The influence of his backers was pervasive. There would be more work than he could handle.

Even on that first day, half a lifetime ago, the young Toshio Miyaki had understood that he was to be a front for the Sonno Group, a way for its members to circumvent the American attempt to break up their power and influence. He did not question the arrangement. He had come to Kabutocho that morning a beggar. He had walked out, on shaking legs, with his future assured.

Blinking away the memories, the old man looked about him, searching for the white Mercedes limousine that had been discreetly creeping along the street behind him. He raised his hand and the long vehicle surged toward him.

At precisely eleven o'clock, retracing the journey he had made nearly fifty years ago, Toshio Miyaki stepped from his limousine onto the street before a seventeen-story steel-and-glass building whose entry was adorned by a small brass plaque that identified THE SONNO GROUP. The modern building had been erected on the site of the old one, where he had had his first interview, that structure having been damaged by an earthquake in 1952. Once a month for the past twenty-three

21

years — since his success had earned him the invitation — he had come here to dine with fellow members of the Sonno Group. The luncheons always took place on the last Friday of the month. Normally these meetings, with their tacit acknowledgement that he was accepted among the most influential power brokers in Japan, were a source of quiet pride for Miyaki. This morning, however, he paused before the polished teak entranceway, which had been saved when the original building was demolished. Entering, his steps were those of an older man — small, cautious, reluctant.

He rode the elevator to the seventeenth floor, which was reserved exclusively for members of the Sonno Group. A pretty receptionist in traditional dress recognized him instantly, rose and bowed to the waist. She led him with mincing steps across the inch-thick smoke-gray carpet toward the main dining room.

Miyaki paused in the wide entry, taking in the scene at a glance. The room was large, modern and open, with a sweep of paneled walls leading the eye toward a dramatic, semi-circular arc of floor-to-ceiling glass that embraced the room. Beyond it soared the peaks and towers of the Tokyo skyline. Off to the right was a glimpse of the river far below, twisting and darting among the skyscraper walls as if it were at the bottom of a deep canyon.

There were about thirty dark-suited men in the room. All turned toward him as he paused, causing a momentary dip in the steady murmur of conversation. He was aware of the respectful lull, and of the haze of blue smoke in the room. Most older Japanese men still smoked heavily; nearly all of the men in the room were fifty years of age or more. It usually took that long to be admitted to the closely guarded membership of the group. There were no women.

Several men hurried forward. They had been waiting for him. Formal greetings were extended. Saduharo Okuda, the former prime minister, welcomed him warmly. The current minister of finance, Nakafumi Tokito, inquired about the health of his family. Toshio Miyaki moved easily among the assembly of rich and powerful figures, recognizing the head of Nippon Securities, one of Japan's largest brokerage firms, who was a close friend, the president of the nation's second largest bank, the chairman of one of the most powerful industrial *keiretsu*. The talk that swirled around him was confined to jokes, pleasantries, idle gossip.

"Miyaki-san!" A heavy hand slammed

against Miyaki's shoulder. "So — you have decided to join us?"

Miyaki looked into the cold black eyes of Yashi Nogama. A broad grin split the square face with its heavy features, but Miyaki was not deceived. They were not friends. A blocky, powerfully built, barrel-chested man whose heavy shoulders and biceps strained the fabric of his black silk suit, Nogama was a member of the *yakuza,* Japan's version of the Mafia. Beginning with intimidation and extortion, the *yakuza* had forced their way into many legitimate businesses. As their wealth and power grew, they had bought respectability, but Miyaki still regarded them as thugs. He had opposed Nogama's membership in the Sonno Group, and he suspected that the man knew it. Nogama had a nature and sensibility as coarse as his features. He was also, Miyaki suspected, a very dangerous man.

"I would not miss our luncheons," Miyaki said. He knew that Nogama's question had been double-edged, but he ignored the implications.

"Ah, but it is more than sushi we have come to dissect, eh?"

Miyaki's expression was impassive, concealing his distaste. "There is much to consider," he said. Business would be discussed after the relaxed meal, not before. Nogama's probing was typical of the man's blunt, bulldozing personality.

Miyaki was seated at the head table between Keone Tanaka, a vice minister of MITI, the Ministry of International Trade and Industry, and Shinji Sakai, an old friend and business associate, current *kaichō*, or chairman, of the Sonno Council, the equivalent of a board of directors. Miyaki ate sparingly, although the food, as usual, was delicious. Sakai, a man of great charm and intelligence, maintained a congenial discourse throughout the meal, as if he did not notice Miyaki's silence.

Finally the luncheon was over. The men settled back in their chairs, their attention turning toward the head table. Waiters cleared the tables discreetly. Drinks were brought for those who desired them. A glass of Hennessy brandy, which Miyaki was known to favor, appeared on the table before him. Dozens of cigarettes were lit, and the room began to grow hazy with the veil of smoke that drifted toward the high ceiling.

Shinji Sakai welcomed the members and thanked them for their attendance. He spoke briefly of the formalities of business carried over from the last meeting. As the words droned on Toshio Miyaki sensed the growing tension in the room. He knew that the men gathered here today were not interested in routine business. They were waiting for his response to their recent request. When he had first come to this site so many years ago, penniless and frightened, he had known such men only through rumor and gossip. Today they were all familiar to him. His personal wealth rivaled that of anyone in the group. He was one of the oldest in years, if not in membership, and he was accorded great respect. And with his successful businesses, his extensive American and European holdings and his wide range of investments, Miyaki's cooperation was essential to the Sonno Group's bold plans.

He was aware that Sakai had fallen silent. The chairman was looking down at Miyaki, seated beside him, with an expectant smile. The room was quiet. Miyaki realized that, without a question being asked, the others were waiting for his answer.

Inwardly the old man sighed. He had serious misgivings about what the group had planned, though his expression revealed no uncertainty. Long ago this moment was presaged. A debt had been incurred. It was time to repay.

Toshio Miyaki's answer was the briefest of nods. No words were necessary.

Throughout the room there was a detectable ripple of emotion, followed by a hush, as if all were suddenly conscious of the enormity of the decision reached in that moment.

At last Nakafumi Tokito spoke. The minister of finance said, "It has been a long wait."

Shinji Saku answered quietly, "We are good at waiting."

Two

Kevin Daulton covertly watched Alison Carey, one of the summer interns, leave the conference room during a break and head for the nearby kitchen. He was on his feet before her long legs scissored out of sight around the corner.

The kitchen on the forty-fourth floor of Pacific Plaza West was well stocked with snacks. Enright & Sons, Inc., a financial printer, was reputed to provide the best food in the printing business. Deli sandwiches from Langer's, steaks from Pacific Dining Car and Thai pizzas from one of the patio restaurants off the plaza far below. Daulton came up behind the blond intern, admiring the well-cut short hair, the blue silk-and-linen suit, those slender legs with their tapering calves. She flicked a glance at him, eyes as blue as her suit. Eyes dismissing him? No, he wouldn't accept that.

Why not? a small voice whispered in his ear.

Spear-carriers don't get the girl.

As long as he could remember, certainly since he was a teenager, Kevin Daulton had been forced to listen to this mocking voice that seemed to come from somewhere over his left shoulder. It was a disparaging, belittling, cynical voice. When he was trying out for the high school baseball team, the voice scoffed, *You'll never make it. You don't even spit well.* He made the team, but as a reserve outfielder. The inner voice said, *I told you so.*

The voice was there, ready with negative input, when Kevin dated the girl he had a crush on in his sophomore year at Penn State. *Why would she want to go to bed with you? Have you lost your mind?*

Kevin's greatest triumphs were those occasions when he had silenced that derisive voice. The girl did go to bed with him, even though the event was a fiasco he didn't care to dwell upon. He did finish law school. He passed the bar exam to resounding silence. The voice wasn't fooled. It knew he was a fraud.

Kevin fished a handful of nuts from a bowl and said, "Alison Carey, right?"

She looked at him as if he were a clever child. "That's right."

"Kevin Daulton. I'm an associate."

"I know."

"You do?" Quick elation. She had noticed him.

"I was given a working group list. I like to know who I'm working with."

"Oh, yes . . . well, would you like a Coke?" Mr. Eloquent. "Dr. Pepper, maybe?"

Alison Carey shook her head. The cap of wavy blond hair whipped back and forth like a model's hair in a television commercial. "Thanks anyway."

She was gone before he could think of another reason to delay her. He tried to remember what she had taken to snack on. A handful of M&Ms? He had been too distracted to notice.

Back in the long conference room Alison Carey took her place near the far end of the conference table, a thirty-foot-long blond oak table in a surfboard shape (this was California, after all) with a dozen chairs grouped on either side. A single chair at one end was occupied by Dexter Hilliard, the working group leader. When Kevin returned to the room Alison was once more buried in the pages of the Tyler Holdings Registration Statement and Prospectus. Except for being dressed in a suit instead of jeans and a Banana Republic safari shirt, she resembled any law school student hitting the books in the library before an exam. Which wasn't far from the truth. Alison Carey was one of five recent law school graduates brought in by Bryant Forbes Lederer & Wyman this summer for its intern program. Kevin Daulton called it the summer league tryout camp. One or two, at most, would be offered jobs as associates at the end of the program. Two of the five were women, one was a Hispanic male. A notoriously WASP firm, Bryant Forbes Lederer & Wyman was sucking it up and preparing to join the 1990s.

"Daulton? Did you hear me?"

"Huh? Yes, sure, Dex . . ." Dexter Hilliard was glaring at him with that faintly superior smile on his thin lips. What had he been saying? Dammit, Kevin, pay attention!

"Then I take it you don't mind working with Ms. Carey."

"What? Oh! . . . no, not at all."

"You can use the small conference room across the hall. Just go over the Management's Discussion and Analysis section for style errors, okay? When you're done with that, check out the global on flopping the periods outside quotes. The printer's supposed to have covered that, but do a spot check."

"Got it."

Hilliard turned his attention back to the other shirtsleeved lawyers sprawled in assorted poses along both sides of the table. "Let's get back to square one on the Risk Factors section. It sounds like Tyler is some savings-and-loan about to be taken over by the OTS. This is going to be the biggest stock offering the Street has ever seen, bigger than GM's by a ton. Let's make sure it sounds like it."

Kevin Daulton was struggling to keep the grin from spreading over his face. He felt as if he had just had a phone call from the *Reader's Digest*. *"Congratulations, Mr. Daulton of West Los Angeles. You've just won the $5 million Grand Prize. How would you like the check delivered?"*

"We'll do our best," he said.

Hilliard was no longer listening.

"What did Mr. Hilliard mean about the Risk Factors section they're working on?" asked Alison Carey. "Is there a problem?"

"No more than usual." Alison Carey had taken a seat on the opposite side of a small conference table from him, but Kevin wasn't about to complain. It was a small room, even intimate, he thought. "Any time you have a stock offering, you have to tell potential buyers the possible risks to their investment. SEC rules and regulations. There's some risk in buying any stock, of course, some more than others. The regulations are supposed to give buyers fair warning of any problems with the company, its products or prospects, its financial condition and debt, the competition it faces in its market, legal actions pending, and so on."

"Does Tyler Holdings have any suits pending?"

"Better believe it." Kevin was warming to his role as guide and mentor. "Any large company is always being sued for one thing or another. Keeps us lawyers in our BMWs. Environmental impact suits, product liability, patent infringement, whatever. Tyler's been a controversial, highly leveraged operation through the 1980s and 1990s. Reynolds Tyler hit on a lot of companies. He swallowed some of them whole. With others he spit out the parts he didn't like, or he just took all the meat and walked away from the bones. He did a lot of damage, made some enemies. I hear he also has environmental problems with seepage from some oil and gas fields in Mississippi. A writer is suing Tyler and Century Pictures, claiming plagiarism of his screenplay for a $300 million blockbuster. What you try to do in the prospectus is show that the suits have no legal merit or, if they do, that they won't have a material adverse effect upon the company or its financial condition." He grinned. "That's legal talk."

"I'd never have guessed."

Daulton considered his summary, and Alison Carey's close attention, with satisfaction. "It's routine stuff in any prospectus. What you're doing, basically, is selling stock."

"I thought we were supposed to be lawyers."

"Lawyers are like bank robbers. They go where the money is."

Alison looked thoughtful. Cute little frown, Kevin thought. Maybe she needed glasses.

"How come Hilliard was coming on so strong?"

"Someone higher up is unhappy with the preliminary. The SEC picked on it."

"Are we going to be doing any rewriting on our section?"

Kevin laughed. "You kidding? We're the keepers of the comma. Guardians of the grammar."

"What's that supposed to mean?" Alison sounded annoyed, which sobered Kevin instantly. He had decided he didn't want her annoyed with him.

"Hilliard spotted you as a wordsmith. That's the good part and the bad part. We don't rewrite anything. We're just going over the material for any errors or deviations from the underwriter's style. Our colleagues across the hall will make any real changes."

"What about this global search? Did I hear

right? It's about flopping periods?"

She asked a lot of questions, Kevin thought. An eager beaver. He tried not to give the reflection any sexual connotation. "We go through the whole document," he explained. "Wherever there's a period or comma with quotation marks, normal style is to put the comma or period inside the quotes. That's the way it was done on the preliminary prospectus. Now we're changing all of them the other way."

Alison Carey stared at him in disbelief. "I went to three years of law school for this?"

"Commas are important," Kevin said soberly. "Take our firm's name — Bryant Forbes Lederer & Wyman. No commas between the names. Don't ever forget that. Hilliard goes bananas. It's like . . . Salomon Brothers Inc — that's their style, no comma and no period after the *Inc.*"

"Didn't you say every change to a document costs a bundle?"

"Sure."

"Who pays?"

Kevin Daulton shrugged. "In the long run, it's Joe Stockholder who pays. The printers sock it to us, we charge it to the client, it all becomes a part of the cost of the offering. You're talking 50 million shares here, at around sixty-two dollars a share, that's a $3.1

billion offering, the biggest single stock of-fering ever. And Tyler will be going back to the market for more before the year's over. From what I've heard his goal is $6 billion by year's end. What the printer charges, and even what we charge, is peanuts."

"But there are twenty lawyers here to-night!" For the first time Alison Carey lost a little of her cool.

"That's right." Kevin grinned. "Billing at an average of, say, two hundred dollars an hour per lawyer. That's four thousand dol-lars an hour in billings. We've been here close to four hours now. I'd guess we have another six or seven hours to go for this ses-sion. That's . . . what? Close to fifty thousand for one work session. And we've been stroking this prospectus for a couple of months at least, with more to come. Don't forget the supple-ments."

"Most of the last four hours in there" — Alison nodded in the direction of the main conference room — "they've been complain-ing about how the Dodgers and Angels are doing."

"It's part of the game."

"It sounds like an old-fashioned hustle."

Kevin grinned, enjoying himself.

When Alison Carey had reported for work

that morning at the law offices of Bryant Forbes Lederer & Wyman, she was wearing her best three-hundred dollar Jones of New York, silk-and-linen blue suit with a white Egyptian cotton blouse and the ninety-dollar pumps she had snatched up on sale at Nordstrom's. She felt good about herself. She was on her way to being a real live lawyer. For the past month she had been assigned to the firm's library along with the paralegals. Today she was joining one of the working groups.

Thrown in with a team of the firm's male lawyers, a bevy of peacocks, she felt almost dowdy. Her prize outfit was Budget City. There was an obvious competition among the men to maintain the firm's high sartorial standard. The twelve-hundred-dollar Italian worsted or pure silk suits were blue or gray pinstripes, the shirts were custom made, the silk ties were splashy. The standard was set, she discovered, by the firm's senior partner and chief executive officer, Calvin Lederer. Though he had a winter home in Palm Springs, Lederer was seldom seen at the Los Angeles offices. He was at the firm's headquarters in Washington, D.C. But his power and influence were pervasive.

By ten o'clock that night, back in the main conference room after what Kevin Daulton was now calling the Attack of the Killer Commas, Alison was feeling about as fresh and glamorous as a wet dishrag.

The lawyers with the working group were taking another break. They had broken up into small cliques. At one end of the room an eager circle surrounded Dexter Hilliard. Only Kevin Daulton, Alison noted, was sitting by himself, a faint smile suggesting secret amusement. He didn't seem to take himself or his work very seriously, she thought with vague disapproval. His amusement was a kind of rebuke.

From the forty-fourth floor of Pacific Plaza West, Alison stared out of the floor-to-ceiling windows at the glittering city below. Off to the west the spill of lights washed up against the Hollywood Hills. To the south the landing lights of an airliner traced its long, slanting descent toward LAX. Night gave the city a sheen of glamour. It hid the ranks of homeless panhandlers between her parking garage and Pacific Plaza, where a pair of smoked-glass high-rises towered over Los Angeles' financial district.

A stirring at the far end of the conference room caught her attention. One of the younger associates burst into the room and headed straight for the cluster around Hilliard. Even Hilliard was suddenly animated. The men began snatching up their suit jackets from the backs of their chairs. Shirt collars were buttoned, ties straightened out. One lawyer anxiously polished his shoes against the backs of his pant legs. Alison wondered what was up. Ending the long session would be a relief, but . . .

One of the printer's customer service representatives appeared. Two men followed him. The rep acted like a flustered headwaiter leading Very Important Persons to their choice table. And they *were* VIPs. If Alison had had any doubt, it was erased by Dexter Hilliard, who spurted toward the door like a watermelon seed taking flight.

Kevin Daulton appeared at Alison's elbow, between her and a tall potted rubber plant.

Alison stared at the new arrivals. Hilliard was greeting them fawningly, while the other lawyers jockeyed for position. "Who — ?"

"Silver hair is Calvin Lederer, of course. Our boss. And you must recognize the other guy."

"I recognize both of them," Alison said in a tone of wonder.

Calvin Lederer was a six-footer, trim, elegantly dressed in an impeccably tailored gray silk suit with a white-on-white shirt, blue-and-silver tie, mirror-bright black shoes. His thin, patrician features were smooth, unlined, although Alison knew from his biography that he was about sixty. He had appeared taller the only other time she had seen him, surrounded then by short Japanese men.

The second man was carelessly dressed, but he quickly dominated the room by force of personality. Reynolds Tyler had close-cropped sandy hair, a brush mustache of the same color, snapping blue eyes, a deep tan. He wore a rumpled cashmere jacket over white jeans and pointy-toed Tony Lama boots.

Tyler moved from lawyer to lawyer, dispensing quick handshakes and platitudes like a priest offering communion. Great job! Good work! Glad to meet you! Keep it up! His eyes lit up when he took Alison's hand and squeezed it. His grip was rough, hard, strong. She tried not to wince. "You dog, Lederer! Where do you find them?"

The two men swept on. It was a command performance. It was also very brief. In one door, a few nods, smiles, brief handshakes, compliments, working the room. Then out the other door.

Staring after Tyler, Alison thought, *These peacocks aren't glamorous, but he is.*

In her childhood, bouncing around from foster homes to group homes, she had had a recurring fantasy. An older man, handsome, charismatic, would push through the crowd of well-wishers after her triumphant concert, her victory in the 400-meter Olympic trials, or, later, the unexpected verdict in her favor after a headline-grabbing trial. She would notice the man at once, and feel a nervous tingling. In the crowd of admirers he would have trouble reaching her. When he did their eyes would meet, and there would be no need for words. She would *know* her father.

Later, as they talked, he would intuitively understand her anger and bitterness. "I was a soldier," he would explain quietly. "I was taken prisoner. I spent twelve years in a cage, treated like an animal."

"We never knew."

"There was no way you could know. When I finally escaped, and came back to find you, your mother was gone, and you and Kim . . . well you were girls then, not babies, happy in your foster home —"

"We weren't happy! You should have come for us!"

"I thought it best for you. I was still a soldier. They were sending me overseas again. I couldn't walk into your lives and then desert you again. . . ."

Neither she nor the imaginary father would mention the mother who had set her two daughters down in a Reading, Pennsylvania Greyhound bus station, and walked away.

Alison grimaced, annoyed with the resur-

41

facing of childish dreams. Reynolds Tyler was impressive enough — rough-edged and charismatic. But he had nothing to do with her.

Kevin Daulton was watching her quizzically. "I thought you said you'd never seen Lederer."

"I did . . . say that, I mean. But I've seen him."

"I suppose there's a perfectly reasonable explanation coming."

"I don't see why."

"Answer the question, counselor, or I'll tell Hilliard how good you are at flopping periods and quotes."

He had a nice grin. For a bottom-rung associate, that is. Not half bad looking either, except that he wore his black hair too long, crawling over the neck of his shirt collar. Short hair was the rule among all the other young lawyers. He had good shoulders, warm brown eyes, a sense of humor. But there was something missing. An eagerness. A desire to impress. She guessed that Daulton's suit was C & R rather than original designer label. "I saw Lederer earlier this summer."

"You were in Washington?"

"No. On Guam."

Daulton shook his head. "Now you've lost me."

"I was visiting my sister after graduation

— she lives there. Her husband teaches at the university. I saw Lederer at one of the beach hotels. I didn't know who he was then, but I couldn't help noticing him. It was Lederer, all right. He was with a bunch of high-powered Japanese business types. They looked like bankers, but that doesn't mean much. All Japanese businessmen seem to dress like bankers."

"You mistook Lederer for someone else."

"I know who I saw," Alison insisted.

"No way. Sorry, Carey, but this time you flunk Executive Recognition."

"What makes you so damned sure? I'm telling you, Daulton, I saw that man, Silver Hair, as you call him, Calvin Lederer, at the Guam Hilton in the first week of June."

"Impossible," Daulton said with infuriating confidence. "Two good reasons. One, Lederer won't touch the Japanese with a ten-foot pole because of Tyler. Tyler hates the way the Japanese have taken over this country. Hates the way they refuse to give quid pro quo when we deal with them. He's made it part of his whole corporate philosophy, America for Americans, won't deal with foreign suppliers, and so on. You must have read how he went to the mat to beat the Japanese out of Century Pictures. They say he didn't really want a motion picture studio, he just couldn't stand seeing Japan's Sakai Group get it."

"What's the other reason?"

"We had meetings in late May and early June on the Tyler preliminary prospectus. Lederer was in our Washington offices, running the whole show. We had two tele-conferences the first week of June and Lederer was in on them. I'm not the only one who saw him. Ask anyone in this room. It was our TV highlight of the summer!"

Three

The secretary of state had emerged in recent years as the dominant figure in the Administration. He was also a man with a sharp mind, strong convictions, and no small amount of ego. He was popular both on Capitol Hill and with the media, having made himself available to both more agreeably than any predecessor of recent memory. The president, more concerned with image and popularity polls than specific policies, was content to let Edward Grabow carry the ball.

President James Arthur Walton was fond of sports and related metaphors. He thought of himself as the quarterback of the team, handing off to his secretary of state, and piling up yardage because Ed Grabow was a good hard-nosed runner who almost never fumbled. When the opposition closed in to stop his ground game, Walton dropped back and tossed a long pass to Sylvester Runnels, the secretary of defense, a speedster with good moves who was very elusive in a press conference. And he relied on Gus Bonelli, the Administration's Italian Stallion and the president's chief of staff and principal adviser, to hold off the opposition from his offensive-guard position. An intensely loyal man with a nose for dirty politics, Bonelli had few scruples. He would grab or hold or use whatever tactics might be necessary. His role, Gus acknowledged with a grin, was to make sure the boss's uniform never got dirty.

Grabow, Runnels and Bonelli were the president's chief confidants. They had been with him from the beginning. They played golf and poker together, went to the Redskins games together.

Ed Grabow was effective on the Hill. He came prepared, and he never shot from the hip. He answered questions slowly, thoughtfully, without visible rancor. If he had one weakness it was that he was so self-assured and dispassionate that listeners had trouble warming to him. Or trusting him.

Senator Elinor Woods was one of the skeptics. "Let me understand this, Mr. Secretary. You're saying the proposed Pacific Rim economic summit is a *Japanese* initiative?"

"Absolutely, Senator. We consider that a very good sign."

"I would consider it a little unbelievable. Particularly in light of what we've been reading, and watching on our television screens, about the rising anti-Americanism in Japan. We've all been treated to almost daily demonstrations there, and even a student riot in front of the American Embassy in Tokyo. There seems to have been minimal effort on the part of the Japanese government to prevent the escalation. And very little response from the United States. Is that because you don't want to upset the summit plans?"

"The president believes it's very important to respond positively to the Japanese government's initiative, Senator. And we have made our concern about the demonstrations known through the proper diplomatic channels. It would have been easy to make headlines with some convenient Japan bashing. That is seldom the most effective approach."

"I was under the impression the Osaka summit is all about headlines."

"That's a provocative statement, Senator."

"It was meant to be realistic, Mr. Secretary, in view of our current trade deficit with Japan, and the economic malaise that is scaring the pants off the American people."

"The United States is still the most powerful nation in the world," Ed Grabow said crisply. "Perhaps the Japanese government's urgent

47

interest in an economic summit meeting simply recognizes that fact, even if the United States Senate is reluctant to do so."

"Now see here, Mr. Secretary!" Joshua Bodine, the chairman of the Senate Finance Committee, which is responsible for trade legislation, came awake with a bang. Bodine was a large, florid man with deceptively sleepy eyes hidden behind folds of flesh. His hair was pure white and thick. When roused, his voice gathered momentum like gravel pouring down a chute. "The chairman of this here committee yields to no man in his pride in this great country. But I do believe my distinguished colleague, the junior senator from California, has a point." Elinor Woods did not miss the chairman's emphasis on the word *junior*. "We're kind of goin' into this here summit hat in hand, the way I see it, and no American is going to take much pride in that."

"I can assure you emphatically that is not the president's approach to the economic summit. He has made it very clear that the summit has to address some very specific problems. One is opening up international service industry markets, including those in Japan. Another is a more equitable technology transfer in superconductivity and fiber optics, to name just two."

"Well, now, that'd be welcome, Mr. Secretary. But it seems to us that whenever we have these trade negotiations with the folks from Japan, we hear the same empty promises. They been sellin' us the same horse every year or so for the past twenty years, and it keeps gettin' older but we never get to look at its teeth."

Ed Grabow smiled. "Your point is well taken, Mr. Chairman. But I can assure you that the president is well aware of the difficulty of pinning the Japanese down to specific commitments. He is determined that this summit conference will be different."

"What I hear from the folks in Georgia," said Bodine, "is they're worried about their jobs. That is, if they still have 'em. Seems to me I recollect another president goin' off to a meetin' with the Japanese and sayin' it was about jobs, jobs, jobs. Near as I can see, very few of those jobs ended up in this country. Is this president talkin' to the Japanese about American jobs?"

"The Japanese government assures us that very specific steps are being taken to encourage more Japanese investment in American-based production and development." Grabow glanced toward Senator Woods, an unpredictable factor in the Senate since her appointment to fill the seat vacated when her predecessor died of a heart attack. "One of those enterprises is in your home state of California, Senator, where the Sakai Group have proposed building a new automobile production plant. That plant will eventually employ about five thousand American workers."

"I'd like to address that, Mr. Chairman," Woods said quickly. Bodine nodded. She spoke so quietly, her listeners strained to hear. "You're right, Mr. Secretary, Sakai is planning to open a new plant near Fresno. That plant, if it is built, will be constructed by Kirabashi Corporation, a Japanese company. The computer technology would be from Miyaki Industries of Japan. Most of the suppliers will be Japanese companies, members of Sakai's Japanese *keiretsu*. A Japanese-owned tire company is also planning a facility outside Fresno to supply tires for Sakai. The tire company is affiliated with the Sakai Group. What it seems to come down to, Mr. Secretary, is that Sakai is exporting its *keiretsu* to Fresno, California. That will bring some jobs to the area. But, it will create even more jobs in Japan. I would hope this administration is not going to use Sakai as a model for economic recovery in the United States."

There was a spattering of applause from the spectators in the hearing room. The chairman banged his gavel, and glowered at Woods. *This chairman yields to no man — or woman*

— *in bashing Japan!* his glare seemed to say. But Bodine's growl was almost amiable. "I thank the senator from California for her comments." He turned back to the patiently waiting secretary of state. "I believe this committee is concerned, Mr. Secretary, and the American people are concerned, that this summit isn't just another dog-and-pony show. We have a deficit in this country close to half a trillion dollars. We have unemployment at a godawful 8.5 percent and stubbornly stayin' there. We've got the stock market jitters, and worst of all we have a loss of confidence in our future."

Ed Grabow shifted in his chair, which was behind a long table facing the subcommittee. He glanced at the man beside him, an attorney attached to the White House staff who reported directly to Gus Bonelli. The lawyer shrugged almost imperceptibly. A certain amount of showboating was to be expected from the senators. No harm done? Grabow wasn't so sure. The media might pick up on some of Senator Woods's comments.

"You may rest assured, Mr. Chairman," he said carefully, "that the president is well aware of your concerns, and the very real concerns of the American people. That is precisely why this meeting of minds at Osaka in September is essential. Up until now, trade between our two nations has been primarily a one-way street. That has to change. But I needn't remind you that free trade is the lifeblood of the Japanese economy. I'm sure I don't have to remind the Japanese Minister of International Trade and Industry. So the president is not going to Osaka hat in hand. He is going with a very specific agenda, and that is a mandate from the American people to make certain that American and Japanese workers are playing by the same rules. The president is not about to allow the United States to become an economic colony of Japan!"

Behind the long committee table, Joshua Bodine smiled benignly, his eyes almost disappearing into their deep pouches.

"You made some powerful points there, Senator," Bodine said as the committee members began to exchange political gossip and jokes, and their aides gathered up the notes and records of the day's hearing.

"Thank you, Senator."

"You're new here. May I pass along an old pol's humble words of so-called wisdom?"

"I'd appreciate it." Elinor Woods tried not to smile at the idea of Bodine's humility.

"First thing a member of the U.S. Congress has to learn is, it's important to get along. And it might not be a good idea to be in too much of a hurry." Up close, it struck Elinor Woods that Bodine's aura of power and force of personality made him seem larger than life, a kind of irresistible force. It was easy to believe all the stories she had heard about cloakroom arm-twisting. "You understand what I'm sayin', Senator?"

"I believe I do, Mr. Chairman."

Bodine smiled. He had to look up slightly to meet her direct gaze. She was a tall, slender woman in her early forties, short blond hair showing the first hints of natural gray. She looked more like a Hollywood actress than the economics professor she had been before her appointment. "Away from the podium, call me Josh, Senator, call me Josh."

"I'm not trying to be pushy, Josh, or to get ahead of myself. I know I have to pay my dues. But I felt it was important today to say something about this economic summit. Something about it makes me uneasy. Maybe it's the odd timing of it. Congress does a little Japan bashing for the evening news, but nobody's raising any serious questions about what we're getting into. The question is, are the Japanese our friends?"

"You wouldn't be tryin' to tell this committee how to go about its business, would you, Senator?" The chairman's blue eyes twinkled, with all the warmth of Arctic ice.

"Not at all, Mr. Chairman. I'm sorry if I've given that impression. But frankly, I'm worried about Japanese intentions. What are they after? Why a meeting now? I hope our committee can address those questions, and I hope you'll lead the way." She rewarded Bodine with a dazzling smile. "You made some powerful points there yourself, Senator. I have an idea we're not so far apart in our thinking."

"Well, now, that may be, that may just be." Bodine's expression was benign again, indulgent of his younger colleague's enthusiasm. "But it isn't always the best thing to let folks know everythin' you're thinkin'. Save some of this fire, Senator. You don't want it to burn out too soon. By the way, did you happen to notice, the chief of the Japanese delegation for the presummit negotiations was in the room today?"

Elinor Woods was startled. "No, I . . . are you sure?"

"You go soundin' off, ma'am, it's always a good idea to know who's listenin'."

Bodine patted Elinor Woods on the shoulder and moved off. Waves of aides and spectators parted before him. Staring after him, Elinor knew she had just been given a warning.

Four

For a week after her initial ten-hour work session on the Tyler Holdings prospectus, Alison Carey was kept busy in the corporate section of Bryant Forbes Lederer & Wyman, learning the firm's computerized file system. It wouldn't be long, she concluded, before you wouldn't need a lawyer to research a brief, you would only need a clerk linked by computer to the law libraries at UCLA or Loyola. She also learned that she would be given all the time she needed to prepare for the California bar exam. The test, Kevin Daulton assured her, was a bitch. When she pointed out the remark was sexist, Daulton seemed suitably chastened. She liked that in a man.

Saturday was gloomy. "Early morning low clouds and overcast near the beach" was the definition of Southern California weather, but this was August and the clouds were supposed to burn off by noon. Alison had been hoping for a session of sun and sand, in defiance of all the magazine articles about the dangers of skin cancer and premature aging. But the cloud layer remained thick. By late morning it was evident this wasn't a day for the beach.

She had bought a car the week after arriving in Los Angeles — a used Honda one of the associate's daughters was selling to make way for the Mazda Miata Daddy was buying for her. Everyone told Alison she couldn't survive in Los Angeles without a car. The notion was strange to her, but she soon recognized its wisdom. L.A. was a sprawling city. The long-planned subway was little more than a local shuttle. Bus transportation was dubious at best, in some areas impossible. From Manhattan Beach, where she had rented an apartment, public transportation was almost nonexistent, especially late in the evening — and she would often be working late. The associates at Bryant Forbes Lederer & Wyman routinely put in eighty- to a hundred-hour weeks. Without a car she would have trouble going anywhere. Only the beach was within walking distance.

Alison drove downtown and parked in the nine-story garage beneath Pacific Plaza. She emerged at roof level onto Hope Street. Los Angeles' financial district spread over what had once been Bunker Hill, an area of quaint Victorian houses fallen upon hard times, reached by a tram called Angel's Flight that climbed up the slope from Hill Street. The houses were all gone now. A few had been preserved and moved to other locations; most had been demolished to make way for the high-rise office buildings and apartment complexes. Kevin Daulton had told a joke about the swarms of rats who, displaced when the old houses were razed, donned designer suits and reappeared as phalanxes of lawyers. There was a movement afoot, Alison had heard, to rescue the old Angel's Flight tram and install it approximately where it had once made a real connection between the city and residents on the hill. Now it would be a tourist attraction.

Meanwhile, there were the steps. They would never make anyone forget Rome's Spanish Steps, but a series of flights, broken up by landings and fountains and flanked by escalators, offered a pleasant access from Bunker Hill to Fifth Street. There the newly opened Central Library was Alison's goal. She counted the steps on her way down, passing out a couple of quarters along the way to the ever-present homeless people who inhabited the hill and its environs. One hundred and two steps. She decided she would appreciate the escalators going back up.

Los Angeles' Central Library had been

torched by an arsonist some years before and extensively remodeled. The character of the original architecture had been retained, making the building something of an anachronism amidst the towering new steel-and-glass cubes and cylinders that surrounded it. Alison found the Newspapers & Periodicals room. With nothing else to occupy a cool, cloudy Saturday afternoon, she had decided to satisfy some of her curiosity about Reynolds Tyler.

There was little about him before the mid-1980s. Then the stories became more and more frequent — in the *Los Angeles Times*, *Fortune*, *Time*, *U.S. News & World Report*, and finally, indicating that Tyler had arrived not only as an entrepreneur but as a celebrity, *People* magazine.

It was a familiar story from the era dubbed the decade of greed. Born into a working-class family, Reynolds Tyler played upon the theme of the self-made millionaire. He had parlayed a salesman's gifts and an early partnership with a brilliant young designer of computer applications programs into his first million. The details of the breakup of that partnership were vague, but Tyler was the partner who survived and prospered. He first made national news with a highly leveraged takeover of Milford Publications, a newspaper and magazine chain based in the Midwest. Typically, Tyler spun off or dumped some of the older, cash-rich but no longer productive publications. He used the infusion of cash not to improve the remaining publications but for other acquisitions, adding major newspapers in the prospering Southwest, acquiring a half-dozen television stations, branching out into cable TV.

Through the 1980s Reynolds Tyler made few headlines, unlike a Michael Milken or Donald Trump. Overnight millionaires weren't news. Lesser players in Milken's junk bond frenzy were banking $50 million a year and fretting that they were being left behind in the race to acquire the most toys. Corporate raiders chortled as Ronald Reagan, with naive aplomb, gutted the power of the nation's labor unions and still kept the working man's vote, while giving the raiders free reign. CEOs taking their companies private to fight a takeover discovered golden parachutes, along with creative ways to manipulate stock prices to run up the value of the inflated stock options they had granted themselves. With so many lining up at the trough, at the annual predators' balls in Beverly Hills, Reynolds Tyler didn't even make the "A" guest list.

That began to change with the market crash in October of 1987. With uncommon prescience, Tyler had abruptly stepped away from the runaway market in midsummer. Betting heavily in futures, he risked everything on his hunch that the free ride was just about over. He won. And in the next few years, as over-leveraged companies all over the country started to topple, Tyler Holdings Inc. snapped up one prize after another for the price equivalent of a package of Crackerjacks. The more troubled the economy, the bigger his winnings.

In 1991 Tyler had his first profile in *Fortune*. In the same year he was on the cover of *Time* for the first time. He acquired more publications, with their supporting casts of radio, television, cable, magazine and book publishing interests. Lumber and paper mills followed. His initial ventures into television and movie production. Oil and gas companies in Texas, Oklahoma and Mississippi at bargain basement prices. A city block in downtown Houston and an imposing lineup of high-rises in Houston, Phoenix, Denver, Cleveland, New York — wherever speculation-driven overdevelopment had left the developers desperate to unload at any price.

No less ruthless or attentive to the bottom line than any other pirate of his times, Tyler somehow or other escaped any negative attention to his maneuverings. Several of the major mutual and insurance funds saw him as safe and reliable. Both Standard & Poor's and Moody's awarded Tyler Holdings AAA ratings. Wall Street judged him to be a commendably tough, pragmatic achiever. Newspaper and television pundits couldn't say enough good things about him. David Brinkley and Ted Koppel called.

And that was before Reynolds Tyler took on Japan. Once again the white knight riding to the rescue, this time not to save a desperate company from a hostile takeover but to defend an equally troubled economy. Tyler did it first in a series of speeches to friendly audiences of investors and businessmen. The time had come, he said, to take the gloves off. America was beating herself. She was letting the Japanese change the rules of acceptable international behavior. Japan was telling America, he said in one memorable speech, to just lie back and enjoy it. Japan would take care of her when it was all over. Well, to hell with that! Reynolds Tyler urged. Increasingly militant women would no longer accept that kind of denigration. Neither should America!

Setting aside the *Newsweek* coverage of Tyler's speech — he delivered the same message with increasing frequency to ever more enthusiastic audiences — Alison tried to measure the emerging portrait of a dynamic financial and entrepreneurial titan against the man who had accompanied Calvin Lederer on their visit to the financial printer's offices. Seeing them together, you'd have taken the elegant lawyer with his styled silver hair as the corporate prince, Tyler as one of his sycophants trailing eagerly behind his master, smiling readily and making observers wonder why, if he was successful enough to mingle with the rich and powerful, he had never done anything about those buck teeth. Alison found herself admiring his style. He wasn't all surface gloss, she thought. Did that mean there was substance there?

She picked up the last of the magazines she had summoned from the archives. There were only a scattered few people at the other long wooden tables around her. The room was quieter. It was late afternoon, she realized. In law school it was commonplace to lose entire afternoons and evenings in the library. She hadn't realized how long she had been working her way into Reynolds Tyler's world.

The last of her magazines was another edition of *Time*. Reynolds Tyler's second cover, which put him up there with several presidents and dictators and movie stars. Not inappropriately, Alison thought. Tyler was now a star. The story detailed Tyler's all-out battle with a Japanese rival, the Sakai Group, for control of Century Pictures, the last of the great major studios, like 20th-Century-Fox, Goldwyn, MGM and Paramount, that had once dominated motion picture production. Century Pictures was still a contender, but a series of box office disasters had exhausted its liquidity, burdened the studio with debt, scared off investors and left the venerable Hollywood giant vulnerable.

Sakai was seeking a stake in international movie production to match that of its Japanese rival Sony, which had taken over Columbia Pictures. After acquiring a base of 15 percent of the shares of Century Pictures, Sakai made a tender offer for the company that, it seemed, its shareholders couldn't refuse. At the last minute Reynolds Tyler came to bat, like a pinch hitter emerging from the dugout in the bottom of the ninth. Working through a labyrinth of subsidiaries and arbitrageurs, Tyler had quietly been accumulating Century Pictures stock. Now he proposed a high stakes battle for control of the company. And he employed one weapon the rival from the land of the Rising Sun couldn't match: the growing opposition in the United States to the Japanese corporate takeover of America.

It was a battle suitable for a Japanese motion picture epic. King Kong versus Godzilla. Reynolds Tyler had meant what he said about taking off the gloves. He made Japan bashing an issue more important than statements of cash flows or assets and liabilities. Century Pictures was not just another company. It was part of the voice of America. It was a window on our world. It was a microcosm of America besieged. Tyler trotted out portions of his popular Chamber of Commerce speech and trumpeted its message in full page ads in the *Los Angeles Times*, *Chicago Tribune*, *New York Times*, *Washington Post* and *Wall Street Journal*. Century Pictures was a grand old lady. The Sakai Group was telling her that, like any compliant whore, she should just lie back and enjoy it. Sakai would leave its fee on the dresser.

The Japanese were outraged. There were anti-American speeches in the Diet. Student demonstrations at Tokyo University. In Washington, where a new round of negotiations had begun, looking forward to more equitable trade agreements between Japan and the United States, there was considerable behind-the-scenes anger. But Reynolds Tyler had tapped into a strong current of distrust Americans were feeling about Japan.

Alison closed the magazine. She had been making notes on a yellow legal pad. Her ballpoint pen beat a tattoo on the lined yellow paper.

It was late afternoon when Alison left the

library. She took the escalator, rising slowly above the traffic on Fifth Street toward the silent towers of the financial district.

Back at the guarded entrance to the parking garage Alison glanced up at the twin towers of Pacific Plaza. Dark glass looked back at her, impenetrable. She thought of the stories she had heard about Los Angeles being a dangerous place, world leader in murders per capita, and about the fact that she didn't carry Mace in her purse and wouldn't know how to use it if she did. "But I do belong here," she told herself. "Nobody's going to scare me off."

She thought of Reynolds Tyler and all she had learned about him that afternoon, and all she hadn't learned. He had no real childhood, she realized. There was nothing about his parents in the stories about him, no brothers or sisters, no schoolteachers who remembered what he was like at ten or twelve years of age, no classmates who had gone on to become barbers or dentists or salesmen. In that he was a lot like her.

She rode the elevator down three levels to her car, frowning thoughtfully. In spite of his very public life in recent years, Reynolds Tyler was invisible. His maneuverings were on display, not the man.

And she remained more puzzled than before

about the question that had brought her downtown on a Saturday to the library.

If Tyler was so anti-Japanese, and Bryant Forbes Lederer & Wyman were major instruments in his ongoing battle to save America from the Yellow Horde, then what had Calvin Lederer been doing on Guam this summer, meeting with a bunch of Japanese dark suits?

Alison Carey called Kim that night, partly because it was Saturday and the rates were cheaper, and AT&T had a special going for transcontinental calls, and partly because she wanted someone to talk to. She thought of calling Alan Gillespie, who had been, progressively, professor, mentor, friend and lover while she was at the Barnett School of Law. Gillespie, after all, had been instrumental in her getting the summer internship at Bryant Forbes Lederer & Wyman. She decided against it.

It was morning in Guam, hot and humid as it always was. Kim had been chasing bugs. She had one cockroach, she said, that she was thinking of putting a collar on and taking to obedience school. Jenny was through with the terrible two's, and was now giving new meaning to the tempestuous three's. Tim was fine, teaching at the university and really looking forward to his sabbatical year. All three of them were leaving for England toward the end of August. Kim's husband was an amiable, indulgent spouse who lived somewhere in the land of logarithms and thought Kim was a combination of Mother Teresa and Madonna, a description Alison found fairly accurate.

"That sounds like fun."

"Fun! It's thrilling! You know what I like about it? They say it's always cold in England, or almost always."

"I thought you liked the climate on Guam."

"I like sex too, but not twenty-four hours a day, 365 days a year."

"You must be getting old."

They chatted cheerfully for a few minutes. Then Alison told her sister about her first month as an intern at Bryant Forbes Lederer & Wyman, and concluded with an account of her day at the library.

"There is one funny thing. Funny peculiar, I mean. You remember those American businessmen we saw in the Guam Hilton when I was there? When you took me to that conference at the hotel?"

"The ones who were meeting the Japanese big shots? That whole scout troop wearing their dark suits outside when it was ninety degrees and humid enough for land swimming? How could I forget?"

"One of the Americans is my boss." Alison

told about Calvin Lederer's surprise appearance at the work session with Reynolds Tyler in tow. "Lederer works out of the firm's Washington offices. Kevin Daulton says it's just a fluke that I ever got to see him in person."

"Mmm. Who's Kevin Daulton? Is he someone I should know about?"

"He's just another one of the young lawyers I work with in corporate."

"Corporate, huh? I take it that's legal lingo, right? What's Kevin like?"

"He's all right. He's funny, actually."

"Take it from me, sis, funny is important. If I was filling out one of those quizzes in *Cosmopolitan* on what qualities I would look for in a man, funny would be maybe number two on the list."

"I'll try to guess number one later. Anyway, forget it, Kim. What I was talking about was Mr. Lederer being in Guam. Everyone keeps trying to convince me he was never there."

"You're sure it was him?"

"It was him, all right." Alison scratched her ankle thoughtfully, the telephone propped between ear and collarbone. "Didn't you take some snapshots there at the hotel? I remember you saying something about all those black suits against the palm trees and bikinis making a good picture. Maybe Lederer is in one of those pictures."

"I forgot about that roll of film! It's still in the camera. I'm glad you reminded me. I should finish up the roll and get it developed before the film melts in this heat."

"Let me know what comes out. If you got any of those hotel pictures with the Japanese in them. And send me any good ones of Jenny."

"They're all good pictures of Jenny."

After they hung up, Alison walked to the window of her apartment and peered out. Not much of a view. Her tiny balcony overlooked a side street, the roofs of parked cars, the blank facade of another apartment complex across the way. Front units in her building had a glimpse of the ocean, but they cost two hundred a month more. Maybe next year. Associates at Bryant Forbes Lederer & Wyman were offered sixty-five thousand a year to start. Everyone began at the same place, Dexter Hilliard had told her at her interview. A level playing field, as Reynolds Tyler had said, complaining about Japanese trade tactics. Where you went from there was up to you.

Fair enough, she thought. Then she remembered something else Hilliard had said, about the importance of being a team player. Not rocking the boat. Everyone pulling at the same oar. So what did it matter how Calvin Lederer spent his summer vacation?

Five

That Saturday evening, three days after Edward Grabow's appearance before the subcommittee hearings of the Senate Finance Committee on the Japanese initiative, Elinor Woods returned after dinner to her office in the Everett M. Dirksen Senate Office Building. She was restless, dissatisfied. The hearings were to conclude on Monday, after which the Senate was scheduled to recess until early September. By then President Walton would be en route to Osaka.

On a Saturday night in August the Capitol had a deserted air, like a compound already abandoned by all of its inhabitants, leaving only a flock of curious tourists. Elinor expected the Senate office building to be empty, but there were lights in her own office suite.

David Perez was at his desk. On it was a sack from McDonald's, a cardboard container of french fries and the remains of a milk shake.

The television set in a corner of the office was turned on, the sound muted. A baseball game flickered in pantomime.

Senator Woods's chief aide was a young man who, at the age of twenty-nine, had already acquired a remarkable knowledge of the Hill, much of it gained during a summer intern program with the office of the late senator from California whose shoes Elinor Woods now filled. David Perez was also bright, personable and loyal. He had won scholarships for undergraduate study at Stanford and law studies at Harvard. Elinor, who had inherited him from her predecessor's staff, considered herself lucky to have him. On the Hill, she had observed, David's relative youth had an unexpected bonus: it caused a great many people to underestimate him.

Perez's feet came off the desk and hit the floor. "Senator! What are you doing here on a Saturday night?"

"Just what I was going to ask you, David. Don't tell me you're working."

He gestured dismissively at the clutter on his desk. "Cleaning up some odds and ends. You can see what a great job I'm doing."

"No date?" David was handsome as well as personable. The problem, as far as female members of her staff were concerned, was that he was also ambitious and driven. He didn't have time to play.

"I couldn't talk anyone into helping me shuffle the letters from your constituents."

"I can't imagine why," Elinor said dryly. She moved past him into her own office. She wasn't much better than David, she thought. She'd come back to get her briefcase, which was filled with files and memos relating to the hearings that were to conclude on Monday. Ed Grabow was scheduled to be on *Meet the Press* Sunday before returning to the Senate for a final appearance before the subcommittee. Elinor guessed that the secretary of state would present the president's agenda on television, neatly preempting the final day of hearings.

David Perez grinned when he spotted her briefcase in her hand. "No date, Senator Woods?"

"I do, as a matter of fact. My husband is flying in from San Francisco tonight. We're going to the concert at Wolf Trap tomorrow."

"But you're taking work home tonight."

Elinor sighed. "It's not exactly a Monday-to-Friday job, David. You should know." She paused beside his desk. "Anything I should know about before I go?"

"There is something . . ." He pawed through a stack of correspondence, searching. With a triumphant flourish he snatched one letter from the pile. "Might not amount to anything, but . . . I don't know. When I read it I felt that funny tingle at the back of my neck, as if the hairs were standing up." He held the single sheet of paper toward her. "I think it's the letterhead that's the grabber."

Standing near the wooden counter, still holding her briefcase, Elinor Woods took the sheet of cream-colored stationery in her free hand. The letterhead did get your attention, as David said: Central Intelligence Agency.

The letter was addressed to her. It was hand written in a sprawling, shaky hand. There was no signature. She scanned the brief message, then reread it more slowly. "Dear Senator Woods — Ask him about the 'O' Fund."

She glanced up at David. "That's it?"

Perez made a face. "Sometimes you have to go by your gut instincts . . ."

"I know all about that tingle of yours, David." She had also learned to take it seriously.

She inspected the letter again. The use of the CIA letterhead had been calculated, she thought. The writer had wanted to make sure his note wasn't dismissed out of hand. It was also, perhaps, a kind of bona fide. Here are my credentials.

"Who do you think he means?"

"Ed Grabow, of course."

She was startled. "Why 'of course'?"

"Who else are you going to be asking questions? I mean, who is coming before the committee important enough our friend wouldn't have to name him? It's got to be Grabow."

"How do you know it has anything to do with the hearings?"

"It figures, that's all. I think this letter is a response to the way you went after Grabow on Wednesday. Nobody else wanted to ask him anything but puff questions."

"I don't know, David . . . it's pretty thin."

"I checked out the letterhead. It's for real. We have some friendlies at Langley, but they claim there's nothing in the files about an O Fund. Same at the Library of Congress. Nada."

"So? I need more than an unsigned letter, David."

"I know, I know. I made some calls."

"You really do take this seriously, don't you?"

"I think our CIA friend, whoever he is, is a serious man."

"You believe he's with the Agency?"

"He was able to put his hands on the letterhead. He used it to get our attention."

Elinor Woods's briefcase was becoming heavy. She set it on a corner of the counter.

"Is there any way of finding out who he might be?"

"Not if he doesn't want us to know. We can hardly send that note over to Langley and ask someone to identify the handwriting."

Elinor Woods was silent a moment. David's tingle didn't have to be infallible, she thought. "I still don't see why you think this might be important."

"It's . . . a feeling. Even the things the guy leaves unsaid speak volumes."

"What other calls did you make?"

David Perez shifted in his tiltback desk chair, for the first time a little uncomfortable. "I called some media friends. Nobody could tell me anything. One old-timer at the *Post* thinks he's heard of an O Fund, and thinks it does have something to do with Japan. So . . ."

"You might as well tell me, David."

"I got lucky. I was able to catch Dennis Loughery. He'd just got off a plane."

"Oh no!" Elinor Woods cried. "Not Dennis the Menace!"

Dennis Loughery had been a fixture inside the Beltway for a quarter century, a nationally syndicated columnist for at least twenty of those years. He had a well-earned reputation for sniffing out political dirt and puncturing inflated reputations.

"Hey, he's been around, Senator. He knows where the skeletons are hidden."

"Dammit, David. I don't want a furor over an anonymous letter on the last day of the hearings! Joshua Bodine will think I set it up."

"I never mentioned the letter. I just played dumb, asked Loughery if he'd ever heard of the O Fund."

Elinor Woods waited a moment, cooling off. "And?"

"It gets interesting," Perez said. "Loughery was the first one who didn't act surprised. He had heard of it. It goes way back, apparently, to the American postwar occupation of Japan. According to Loughery, whispers about a special fund have kept surfacing for the last four decades, but no one's ever been able to nail them down. Or at least to prove the fund exists, or establish who controls it and what it's for."

"Why should I ask Ed Grabow about it?"

Perez considered the question thoughtfully. He stuffed the last french fry into his mouth after dipping it into a pool of ketchup. The office reeked of the smell of Big Mac and fries — America's smell. "Because our anonymous friend thinks you should. And because Grabow's been around the block. He's been in four of the last five administrations. He was a junior staff man in the Nixon White House, too low on the pole to get himself arrested. He was with the National Security Council under Reagan, an undersecretary of state under Bush. Now . . . he's point man for the Osaka summit. State wants an agreement badly. They're in bed with the Pentagon, and both believe our national security depends on Japanese bases and Japanese goodwill. It's the Commerce Department — and some members of Congress — that's worried."

"Apparently not as worried as I am," Senator Woods said. "There's been surprisingly little opposition to the summit."

"Yeah."

"Yeah? What's 'yeah' mean, David?"

"It means the Japanese lobby has been working overtime, calling in markers, twisting a few arms. Telling Washington what to think."

"Oh, come on, David! It's not as bad as that. Nobody's been trying to twist my arm or brainwash me."

"No . . . but Senator Bodine did give you a hint he might take you behind the woodshed if you made too much noise at these hearings."

"Bodine doesn't like anyone to steal the spotlight. It's his committee, David. These are his hearings. His reaction the other day was understandable. Besides, he's such an egotistical old bastard, and so entrenched, I just don't buy that he's dancing to MITI's tune."

David Perez didn't argue. There was a moment's silence. Elinor Woods picked up her briefcase. "Go home, David. Get some rest."

"Are you going to ask Grabow the mystery question Monday?"

"I don't know."

"Maybe it's important. You think we're walking into this summit blindfolded, don't you? That we could get chopped off at the knees before we know what's hit us."

The senator sighed. "It worries me, yes."

"Our letter writer is hinting there are things we ought to know. Maybe the O Fund is some kind of key. If it is, and Grabow knows about it, you could open things up."

"And if he says he never heard of it? What will that tell us?"

"Well . . . it'll tell us one thing."

"What?"

"That he's lying."

Elinor stared at him. She knew she would spend the next forty-eight hours weighing the consequences of blindsiding Joshua Bodine with a question he wasn't prepared for. The Georgia senator would boil over. He could be vindictive, and he had the power to back up his warning that she should bide her time. She was a first term senator, appointed rather than elected, she had no established political base, she wasn't part of the Senate's old boys' club. Joshua Bodine, she thought, could go a long way toward making sure she wasn't elected to her own term next year.

"All right, David," she said. "You can keep digging. But be discreet. Keep it low key, okay? Don't link the O Fund with Monday's hearings. That'll be *my* decision."

David Perez grinned. "See you Monday . . . and enjoy the concert."

Six

On Sunday Kevin Daulton drove down to San Diego to see his father. The elder Daulton was attending a reunion with some of his World War II navy buddies at the old Del Coronado Hotel. Robert Daulton was sixty-eight. At each annual reunion the roll call of the missing was a little longer. He had come to feel an increasing urgency about not skipping one of the gatherings.

Kevin drove down the coastal highway from San Clemente, past the ominous domes of the San Onofre nuclear power plant, past miles of shoreline empty except for the parking lot ranks of weekend campers and motor homes, past the marine base at Camp Pendleton, through Oceanside and Carlsbad and Del Mar, where Bing Crosby and his pals had created a race track in the heart of an empty coastal valley back in the 1930s. It was a lovely morning for a drive. The air was clear, the sky nearly cloudless. The ocean was a poster-paint blue. White sails ran before the wind. Kevin Daulton was hardly aware of the background. He was preoccupied with the tantalizing scenery that had filled his thoughts for the past week: blond hair, challenging blue eyes, drop-dead legs.

The night before, after dining alone at a Mexican restaurant in Venice, he had indulged the kind of impulse he hadn't yielded to since his early college days. Driving south after eating, he told himself that he might stop at one of the comedy clubs that had sprung up in the beach cities. Instead, in Manhattan Beach, he turned west toward the ocean.

I don't believe this, the voice whispered at his shoulder.

"Mind your own business," Kevin muttered.

Bryant Forbes Lederer & Wyman printed a small, in-house booklet for each working group involved in preparing a major financial document. Members of the group were on call at any time. Alison Carey's address and phone number had been added to the working group list for the Tyler Holdings stock offering.

She had rented an apartment in Manhattan Beach. 2305 Ocean Vista, a few blocks from the center of the beach community and within walking distance of the ocean. Apartment 4C.

Once a funky beach town, Manhattan Beach had grown into a yuppie haven of six-hundred-thousand-dollar homes and three-hundred-thousand-dollar condominiums. Boxy apartment buildings jammed the narrow streets near the beachfront. They were popular with singles, airline flight attendants, young professional couples and live-togethers. On Saturday night the streets were crowded. The restaurants, some of which had sidewalk tables, offered standing room only. The bars were sardine cans.

2305 Ocean Vista was a corner building. The front units had a wedge of ocean view. Apartment 4C faced the side street. No view, Kevin noted.

What if she sees you? the cynical voice jeered. *How are you gonna explain that view?*

He drove on by, feeling foolish. It was time to head back to his own empty apartment in West Los Angeles.

There were lights in her apartment. The sliding door to a tiny balcony was open to admit the cool ocean breeze. What was she doing alone on Saturday night? She wasn't married — no ring, and nothing had been said about a husband. She'd been in L.A. less than two months. Kevin wondered if there was a man back east. In Philadelphia, maybe, where she'd gone to law school. The law students

Kevin had known would have camped outside her door. Just as he was now.

Circling the block, he found a rare parking place just vacated. He sat in the car, feeling stupid and adolescent, refusing to listen to the mocking inner voice. The cops would be along soon to ask him what he was doing there. "Spying on a girl," he could say. Kiss goodbye to the budding career. The possibility did not bring the dismay it should have.

He got out of his car and walked down toward the beach. At a crowded bar he bought a beer and stood alone in the hubbub, staring at a boxing match on a large television screen. He thought about the second work session on the Tyler prospectus. The group, only ten of them this time, had trooped over to the financial printer's offices in the evening, at the end of the normal ten-hour day at the law firm. Dexter Hilliard had been in charge, and this time Kevin hadn't lucked out. Hilliard had monopolized Alison Carey.

Kevin had had one brief moment alone with her. She'd startled him by bringing up his assertion that Calvin Lederer had never left the country that summer. "I checked out what you said. Everyone agrees with you."

"Lederer's kind of hard to miss."

She didn't argue, but Kevin knew that she was unconvinced. His rebuttal was silent. *Look*

84

at the evidence, Counselor. Look at the number of witnesses.

Alison Carey was stubborn, Kevin thought, but that wasn't necessarily a fatal flaw. Stubborn with thick ankles and a gloomy disposition would have been fatal. This reflection was so obviously shallow and sexist that it was accompanied by a twinge of guilt. Since Alison's arrival at Bryant Forbes Lederer & Wyman, Kevin had become very aware of the need to have his consciousness raised.

He finished his beer and walked back to his car. He tried to show how mature and in control he was by refraining from driving past Alison Carey's apartment building a second time.

Heading north on Sepulveda, he wished he hadn't been so mature. The inner voice consoled him. *You're pathetic.*

The Del Coronado dated back to the late nineteenth century. It was a huge, old-fashioned frame hotel on the beach on Coronado Island. It had been a celebrity hotel for generations. A photo arcade on the lower level documented the comings and goings of the rich and famous over the years, including a gallery of presidents and business tycoons of the first half of the twentieth century. The young Prince of Wales had first met his future duchess, Wally Simpson, in the richly wooded dining room.

Kevin met his father in the lobby, which was also ornately paneled. Robert Daulton was a heavy man, over two hundred pounds, but he had such an erect bearing and he moved so lightly on his feet that he never seemed overweight. His hair and mustache had turned pure white. He was more handsome now, his son thought, than when he was younger.

"Breakfast, Kevin? They have a fantastic Sunday brunch here."

"Not for me, Dad. I had something before I left — it's a long drive. But if you want to —"

"No, no, we'll sit outside. I can watch the girls on the beach."

The outdoor tables faced ranks of gardens, tennis courts, and expanses of white sand beach leading out to the ocean. The setting had the elegant ambiance of another world, Kevin thought, or another century. No poor or homeless in view.

They found a table, and Robert Daulton ordered breakfast. Kevin settled for a beer.

His father seemed amused. "So early?"

"I've been up since six o'clock. It's the middle of the day for me." He wondered if it was beginning to sound as if he were complaining about the trip to San Diego. "Besides, they're guzzling champagne with that brunch inside."

"So they are, so they are."

"How's Mom?"

"She's fine. You could get a full report if you called her more often."

Somehow, Kevin thought, he always fell short of his father's expectations.

They talked briefly about his father's navy reunion, which seemed to make the older man pensive. Finally, as if eager to change the subject, Robert Daulton asked, "So how's the law business? What's the name of your firm? I can never remember all the names."

"Bryant Forbes Lederer & Wyman."

"Is there really a Wyman?"

"I guess there was once. Bryant and Forbes are pretty much out of the picture, too."

"So it's Lederer's firm. Do you like it?"

"I'm not sure I was cut out to be a lawyer. It's my parents' fault. You and Mom taught me it was wrong to lie or cheat or connive." Kevin enjoyed his father's startled expression.

"Now you're exaggerating —"

"Like hell!" *Go ahead,* the inner voice prompted slyly. *Let him have it!* "We do a lot of corporate financial work, including preparing stock offerings, prospectuses, proxy statements and so on. You should read some of the ways we manage to turn the truth inside out and upside down, and get ourselves off the hook at the same time with neat little disclaimers at the end of the paragraph. And it's not just us. The underwriters play the same games, and the big auditing firms. Did you ever notice how, when one of those scandals breaks on Wall Street — Milken's junk bond hustle, the S&L thing, Keating and the rest — somehow the attorneys involved and the underwriters for all those big offerings and the so-called independent auditors, who just happen to work on other matters for the companies involved, never ever see anything out of line?"

Robert Daulton studied him, his eggs going cold on the plate. "That's quite a speech," his father said dryly. "But if you dislike it that much, maybe you should get out. I think you're selling yourself short. And you're selling the law short." He paused, searching for higher ground. "What are you working on, anyway?"

"Well, it's not the best example. I guess you can't really oversell Tyler Holdings —"

"Tyler!" Robert Daulton spat out the name. "What do you have to do with Reynolds Tyler?"

"Tyler Holdings is making a big stock offering — a series of them, U.S. and international."

"I hadn't heard . . ."

"I know, this is supposed to be confidential information and I shouldn't be talking about it. Which doesn't mean," Kevin added, "that a lineup of insiders don't already know and aren't taking steps to profit on the information. The stock is already going up. It'll go for a ride if you want to jump on board."

"You think I'd make a penny on that bastard's work?" Robert Daulton said harshly.

Kevin gaped at his father. "Uh . . . what . . . ?"

"Reynolds Tyler is a world-class son of a bitch! And any deal he's part of, no matter how good it looks on the surface, you can be damned sure there's something hidden under a rock."

Kevin stared at his father.

"Did you never wonder why I retired at fifty-eight?"

"Well, no . . . I mean . . . It's what everyone wants, isn't it? You told Mom it was time for some real golf, I remember."

"Yes, that's what I told her. It wasn't the whole truth. I was forced out. By your friend Tyler."

"What?" Kevin didn't realize he had exclaimed aloud. Some nearby diners glanced over at him, amused or curious. They were all wearing white tennis outfits, burnished tans, Nikes or Reeboks. "You never said anything . . . I mean, I knew your company was sold, but . . . I don't remember Tyler being part of it."

"His name didn't come up at first. He did it through one of his subsidiaries, a shadow company. His efficiency experts moved in, butch haircuts and sharpened knives. They got rid of more than half the company's management. I'd worked twenty-two years there. They had to pay me off, of course, me and the others who were kicked out." The older man was silent a moment. "I could live with it if Tyler's lean-and-mean management act was what the company needed. To cut expenses up front he got rid of top people who knew what they were doing. Then he bled the company of its assets and walked away. The company became a fire sale, what was left of it. That's what I can never forgive or forget."

"I'll be damned . . . I never knew."

Robert Daulton's smile was ironical. "You never really paid much attention."

Kevin Daulton had never felt so small and mortified. He couldn't think of anything to say. Even his mocking inner voice was silent.

"So, is there anything off-color about Tyler's megabucks offering?" his father asked after a moment. "Something about it bothers you, obviously."

"Well, it's not Tyler so much . . . it's just something that came up about Calvin Lederer, our senior partner. He and Tyler came over to the financial printer's offices one night. . . ." Kevin recounted Alison Carey's story about Lederer meeting secretly with a Japanese delegation on Guam earlier that summer. In the telling the incident didn't sound particularly sinister.

Robert Daulton stared thoughtfully across the strand toward the ocean. "Who's Alison?"

"One of the summer interns. We're both part of the working group on the Tyler Holdings prospectus."

"And you like her?"

Kevin nodded and glanced at the beach.

"Well, that Guam meeting is curious, but . . . that's all?"

"I don't know. Alison asks a lot of questions. She's new at this. She wonders about auditors certifying that they're not really certifying to anything. And the document being hedged all over the place with phrases like 'While no assurances can be given,' or 'Actual experience will vary and variations may be material,' and so on."

"That's normal legal waffling," his father said.

"I know. There are other things. For instance, Alison pointed out the other day how the notes being offered are subordinate to potential claims from third parties to the assets of Tyler Holdings' subsidiaries. Meaning that third parties come ahead of the company and ahead of the individual stockholders."

"That's not all that unusual."

"Yeah, but Alison says that unnamed operations of the company, called 'substantial' in the document, consist mainly of international operations conducted through various subsidiaries."

"Sounds more and more like Reynolds Tyler."

"Okay, so it sounds like business as usual. But we're very careful in the document not to make it clear that stockholders are subordinate to these unnamed subsidiaries."

"Mm. Your Alison sounds a bit more substantial than your usual girlfriends."

Your usual bimbos, he means, Kevin's inner voice tittered.

"The question is, what are those foreign operations? Where do they operate? Who are these third parties? We're talking about the flag-waving, bring American jobs home to America, Reynolds Tyler here."

"I don't quite see. . . ."

"Alison thinks the Japanese are involved. And Reynolds Tyler and Calvin Lederer are making sure no one knows it."

"Ah . . ." Robert Daulton studied his son with an expression that was, if not approving, at least neither critical nor disappointed. "Well, given what I know of Reynolds Tyler, what you tell me isn't surprising. But I'm sure it's legal. Calvin Lederer would see to that."

"I suppose. But it does make you wonder. I mean, Alison wonders whether there's more to it than just hiding a Japanese connection."

"I'd like to meet this Alison of yours," Robert Daulton said. His gaze followed a lissome girl in a thong bikini as she sauntered past the tennis courts toward the beach.

Kevin didn't reply. What could he say? Alison wasn't his girl, she was only his fantasy come to tantalizing life.

"Keep me posted, Kevin. If anything else comes up . . . let me know. One thing you can be damned sure of: Anything Reynolds Tyler is involved in, there's a good chance it's bent somewhere. I'd give a lot to know just where."

Kevin Daulton sat in a kind of glowing silence. It was as near as his father had ever come to taking him seriously.

Seven

Senator Elinor Woods dropped the question toward the end of the secretary of state's testimony Monday before the Senate Finance Committee. Until that moment the hearings had been predictably dull. The senators were getting ready to recess until after Labor Day. They didn't want to prolong a routine proceeding needlessly. Even the Japan bashing for the media by various members of the committee was not calculated to throw the secretary off his smooth stride.

Edward Grabow was unflappable. This administration, he intoned, was well aware of the shortcomings of previous trade talks. The lack of follow-through on previous Japanese commitments, or the belated discovery that the Japanese had different interpretations of agreements hammered out, was well documented. President Walton intended that any agreements reached at the summit would leave no wiggle room. Every *i* would be dotted and every *t* would be crossed, Grabow said, in a stiff attempt at injecting a little humor into the proceedings. Japan stood clearly indicted of unfair dumping practices in both consumer electronics and automobiles. Because of the president's firmly stated position regarding these unfair practices and the importance of opening up Japanese markets, Japanese leaders had finally recognized the need for concessions. That change in attitude was the driving force behind the Osaka summit.

Elinor Woods frowned uneasily as she listened. It was the same soothing pablum Grabow had dished out last Wednesday, and again in his Sunday *Meet the Press* appearance. Other administration spokesmen were serving up the same line. Either they're hiding something, she thought, or they just don't *know* this country is in an economic war with Japan that only one side is fighting. Was it possible that someone as sophisticated as Grabow remained ignorant or naive about Japanese intentions?

She caught Joshua Bodine's attention. "Mr. Chairman?"

The Georgia senator looked as if he was tempted to ignore her. But the Senate was sensitive these days to accusations of being a men's club. Even in Georgia there were rumblings. "The chair recognizes the senator from California."

"Thank you, Mr. Chairman." Elinor Woods smiled at Grabow, who sat back expectantly with a tolerant smile of his own. "I wonder if you could tell me, Mr. Secretary, about the O Fund."

The patronizing expression vanished from Grabow's face. "The O Fund?" he repeated.

"Yes. You're familiar with it, I assume?"

"Well, I . . . I've heard of such a fund, of course, but I don't see the relevance . . ."

That shook him up, Elinor thought. Not so smug now. At the same time Grabow seemed genuinely puzzled. He talked briefly to the White House counsel sitting beside him. An aide whispered something to him over his shoulder. Throughout the hearing room there was a buzz of interest. Reporters reacted, consulting each other or their notes. Two or three of them left the room in a hurry. Several of the senators were staring at Woods with varying degrees of curiosity.

Not Bodine, Elinor Woods realized. His beefy features had darkened into a very good imitation of a thundercloud. Within the folds where his eyes had retreated, lightning flashed.

"Then the O Fund is not part of the agenda to be discussed with the Japanese at this time?"

Grabow was reading a note thrust into his

hand by his chief aide. He glanced up at Senator Woods. "No, Senator," he said. "No, certainly not."

"Should it be?" Grabow was recovering quickly, she saw, perhaps recognizing that she was fishing.

"The O Fund was an emergency measure adopted by a number of Japanese banks and businesses to meet the severe economic conditions in that country immediately after World War II. It was, as I understand it, a temporary pooling of resources at a time of critical need. It has no relevance to current economic negotiations between our two countries." The secretary smiled, returning to the earlier note of indulgence that had so irritated her. "That war is ancient history, Senator. It would serve no purpose to dredge up old wounds in anticipation of the summit. It's the administration's view that mutual economic cooperation is the current goal of both countries. Our common purposes are more important than our differences."

"If the O Fund was an internal Japanese matter, why would it be a potential source of conflict, Mr. Secretary?" Elinor Woods knew at once that the question sounded lame.

"You misunderstood me, Senator. I meant to say only that any such postwar arrangement is irrelevant in today's world, and certainly to the Osaka summit."

The subject had shaken the unflappable Mr. Grabow, Elinor Woods thought. But she didn't know enough to follow up her original advantage.

Dammit, what *was* the O Fund?

And who had sent her that note under CIA letterhead?

The committee chairman caught up to her near the exit. He grabbed her arm and pulled her away from the doorway. Elinor Woods stiffened. Joshua Bodine hastily released his grip on her arm, but the storm clouds still darkened his florid features.

"Just what the hell do you think you're doing, Senator?"

Woods rubbed her arm where Bodine's thick fingers had bitten more roughly than he may have intended. Fire flashed in her blue eyes. "What do you mean, Mr. Chairman?"

"You know exactly what I mean — that sucker question about a mystery fund you threw at Grabow."

"With the chair's permission, I was asking the secretary a question he obviously didn't want to answer," she snapped back.

"The chair never gave you permission to dredge up old rumors and gossip, and make them the business of this committee's presummit hearings! When it's time for you to decide what is the business of this committee, I'll let you know! Maybe you think you made Grabow look bad, Senator. What's worse, you made this committee look like a bunch of clowns!"

Elinor Woods met his glare without flinching. Stay cool, she warned herself. Something's going on here.

"Is this about my stepping out of line, Senator? Or is this about the O Fund?"

Bodine's breath wheezed. His jowls shook as if she had slapped him. He reminded her of a basset hound, she thought, but the reflection brought no comfort. A mean basset could be formidable.

Before Bodine could reply the senior senator from Missouri stopped beside them, nodded politely to Elinor Woods and murmured, "If you'll excuse us a minute, Senator." He drew Bodine aside, and the two men engaged in a low-voiced exchange, heads together, hands draped over shoulders. Elinor heard something about a chamber of commerce luncheon and a conflict of dates. Bodine finally clapped his colleague on the shoulder and sent him away, apparently satisfied. Woods wondered if the two men were even aware how conspicuously they had excluded her.

The Georgia senator turned back toward Elinor Woods, the glower replacing a fading geniality. He stared at her for a moment. "The O Fund is old news," he growled. "If you know anything about it at all, you know that much. Which makes it a grandstand play. I guess you don't listen very well, Senator. I spoke to you about that."

"I wasn't —"

"Maybe you was and maybe you wasn't. Maybe you're Little Red Riding Hood lost in the woods, and you didn't mean any harm. Somehow I don't picture you that way, Senator."

"I'm just trying to do my job — the job I was appointed to do." Elinor Woods wasn't going to be bullied. "I'm sorry if that ruffles some feathers, Senator. But I don't much like what I know about this economic summit, I don't think the administration is being very candid about it, and I don't think anyone is taking seriously enough the possibility that there's more to it than the Japanese are letting on."

"I didn't know you were an expert on Japan."

"I'm not. But I am something of an economist, and the rosy picture being painted for us doesn't connect all the dots. What's more, what we're being told about Japanese intentions by the administration doesn't jibe with everything the Japanese have done for the past thirty years. If we're not even supposed to ask questions about that, what the hell are we here for, Mr. Chairman? And if the O Fund is such an unimportant piece of old history, why is everyone getting so upset about it?"

Joshua Bodine stared at her. Unexpectedly he chuckled. His jowls shook and his belly jiggled. "Well, now, we do have a hot little temper, don't we?" The chuckle erupted again. Within their deep sockets the small eyes glinted with what might have been amusement. "I reckon maybe it's time to back off a little bit here, less'n we have ourselves a real serious misunderstandin'. This isn't about any damned fund, Senator, it's about protocol. I thought I made that clear."

It was an attempt to lower the temperature of the exchange, Elinor Woods realized. Her common sense told her to accept the gesture for what it purported to be. "I believe I understand, Mr. Chairman. In the future I'll discuss any concerns I may have with the chair before I bring them up in public hearings."

"Well, now, I can't ask for more'n that, can I?" Bodine replied genially. "By the way, if you don't mind my askin', Senator, what put you onto that old alphabet fund, anyway?"

Elinor smiled. "It was just something I ran across in my research — reading up on our

101

economic ties with postwar Japan."

Bodine nodded. "Funny thing, I haven't heard about that fund since I was a freshman in the House. Long time ago, Senator — lot longer'n I like to admit." He walked with Elinor Woods into the bustle of the main corridor. There he placed a hand on her shoulder, as he had with his Missouri colleague. "No hard feelin's, Senator. We're gonna get along just fine." His blunt fingers squeezed. *Pressing the flesh,* Elinor thought.

They separated at the elevators. Bodine rolled on down the corridor, greeting friends, brushing off a persistent newsman. Elinor could still feel the imprint of his hand gripping her shoulder.

Eight

The composition room at the center of Enright
& Sons, the financial printers, did not enjoy
the expansive views through floor-to-ceiling
windows overlooking the city that Enright offered to its clients. The busy room was win-
dowless, crowded, noisy with the hum of a
dozen computer terminals. The screens on four
of the terminals were dark. Eight were active,
glowing at the typesetters sitting hunchbacked
before them, staring at the CRT displays. Production controllers snatched copy from the
operators as they finished changes on pages of
the Tyler Holdings prospectus, hurried to get
the new printouts as they crawled from laser
printers, and thrust the pages onto the desks
of the proofreaders at the far end of the composing room, two gray-haired men with thick
glasses and permanently rounded shoulders.
One had been in his prime a reporter for the
Los Angeles Times, the other had started his

career forty years ago setting hot metal type in an ad shop. End of the line.

"In house! In house!" a customer service representative brayed. He dropped a new stack of page changes into a tray on the controllers' table. "Are those last pages ready? Let's go, guys!"

"What are they doing now?" one of the typesetters asked wearily.

"They're ripping the document, starting from page one."

"These people are worse than Skadden, Arps. What's going with Tyler Holdings, anyway?"

"Ours is not to reason why. What do you care, Bowen? You gonna invest in some stock?"

"Yeah, I'm going to use my inside information and make a killing. I'll use the rent money."

The controller riffled through the new round of page changes from the attorneys for the underwriters and for the Tyler general counsel. It looked like another long night.

In the conference room on the west side of the building, lawyers from the underwriters conferred with their counterparts from Bryant Forbes Lederer & Wyman, who represented the interests of Tyler Holdings. At one end of the room Kevin Daulton was blissfully sitting next to Alison Carey. She turned toward him, holding a sheaf of pages from the prospectus. Her perfume rattled his concentration. "What are they doing? Have you seen these?"

"Sure. Piece of cake."

"That's not the point. They're changing every time we mention Tyler Holdings throughout the document to read 'The Company.'"

"That's about it."

"But we went through the whole thing Monday night and did it the other way around! We changed every mention of The Company to Tyler Holdings."

Kevin grinned. Nothing could mar his mood. Dexter Hilliard was his guardian angel. He had told Kevin to work with Alison until she got the hang of what they were doing. "Welcome to the world of high finance," he said.

The flurry of high-rise development in downtown Los Angeles during the frenzied 1980s had led to a glut of office space. That period had also seen heavy investment by Japanese developers in commercial real estate in major U.S. cities, including Los Angeles. The result was that more than 50 percent of the downtown skyline in the City of Angels now belonged to the Japanese, including the head-quarters of Bank of America, the Arco Plaza, such landmarks as the Bonaventure Hotel and the venerable Biltmore, and the twin towers of Pacific Plaza. The latter were properties of Jamieson Development, an American company. Jamieson Development was in turn owned by Miyaki Investments, a Japanese subsidiary of Miyaki Industries.

At fifty-four stories high, Pacific Plaza East was exactly eight floors and ninety-six feet shorter than its twin tower on the western side of the plaza. The top six floors had not been leased but were reserved for the use of Miyaki Investments. The two stories immediately below them were unoccupied.

During July and August regular deliveries of equipment rode the freight elevators to destinations on the forty-ninth to fifty-fourth floors. The modern offices — open, airy, divided only by glass partitions — revolved around a central core that included a secure, dust-tight and air-conditioned room housing a Sakai supercomputer. Adjoining rooms filled with rows of computer terminals, fax machines, high-speed laser printers, teletype machines and television sets. A satellite dish was mounted on the roof next to the helipad. Communications were established with New York, Washington, London, Geneva, Luxembourg,

Grand Cayman, Hong Kong and Tokyo. Direct links were arranged to the London, New York and Pacific stock exchanges. A satellite hookup was also made to a terminal in the private offices of Calvin Lederer, of the law firm of Bryant Forbes Lederer & Wyman, in Washington, D.C.

Over several weeks beginning in late July a growing number of serious young Japanese men and women began to arrive at the plaza each morning, purchasing bagels or croissants from Le Boulangerie or donuts at Mrs. Fields. They took the high-speed elevators to the upper floors. Most of them, the security guards at the plaza level noted, did not leave until dark.

By mid-August, everything was in place.

Nine

Joshua Bodine enjoyed eating well, a fact attested by the two hundred and twenty pounds he packed onto a five-foot-eight-inch frame. He also enjoyed the fawning attention he received when he dined at one of his favorite Capitol restaurants. He regarded that attention as one of the perquisites of his office. He was a United States senator, and he damned well ought to be treated right.

Among his favorite dining spots were Duke Zeibert's, which was like family for Bodine after more than twenty years in Washington, and the Jockey Club in the Ritz Carlton Hotel, which had what Bodine considered the best Maryland crabcakes in town. But today's luncheon hadn't been his call. Ken Chandler, a prominent lobbyist and attorney, had called him. He had made a luncheon reservation, Chandler said, for the John Hay Room at the Hay-Adams Hotel.

Bodine took a taxi there. As he emerged he looked over the sweep of green lawns toward the White House across the square. President Walton was vacationing at his summer home on Hilton Head, getting in a few rounds of golf before his summit trip to Japan. The vice president, a nonentity, was in Europe on a cosmetic trip designed to keep him out of harm's way. The store was being minded by a couple of Walton's closest friends, Gus Bonelli and Ed Grabow. Joshua Bodine had always wondered, when those two got into the back room alone, which one cracked the whip.

The Hay-Adams was a genteel, Tudor-style building erected in the 1920s. The John Hay Room strove for the atmosphere of an English country dining room, with its oak paneling, gilt-framed oil portraits and dark tapestries. Joshua Bodine, whose origins in rural Georgia were humble, always felt a bit uncomfortable in this room.

As the maitre d' greeted him and escorted him across the room to a corner table, chairs swiveled and heads turned. A murmur followed the senator like a wake. He basked in it.

The glow faded a little as he spotted Ken Chandler. Bodine had arrived right on time. The lobbyist was there waiting.

"Senator! Good to see you. Take a load off . . . I took the liberty of ordering a bourbon and branch water."

"I'm obliged," Bodine grunted, shaking Chandler's hand.

Unlike Bodine, Ken Chandler appeared perfectly at ease in this quietly elegant setting, with his thousand-dollar London tailored worsted suit in a light gray plaid, about the weight of a handkerchief, his styled hair, his gold cuff links, his comfortably thickening waistline. Though he looked like an effete dandy, Chandler had a grip of iron, which he never failed to demonstrate. Bastard must spend half his time working out in his health club, Bodine thought. Come to think of it, Chandler's law firm, Bryant Forbes Lederer & Wyman, had its own weight room. The firm occupied six floors of a modern building on M Street, with a private rooftop dining room for the partners, weight room, indoor pool and sauna, along with the usual libraries, offices and conference rooms.

Bodine sipped his bourbon. Over the rim of the glass he eyed Chandler with deceptive geniality. "Ah, that's nectar," he murmured.

The Georgia senator had a love-hate relationship with the Capitol's army of lawyers, particularly those who represented power and influence. "You can't live with 'em, and you can't live without 'em," Bodine would say, giving a personal spin to the old saw about women. He disliked the arrogance that rubbed off on those who associated with really big money. These attorneys had little to do with law or justice. What they were all about was political clout and whatever else major money could buy — which in Washington meant just about anything. Bodine resented them, and he was secretly afraid of them. They could change his life for the worse.

Kenneth Chandler was the stereotype. Partner in one of the big power firms. Influential lobbyist, representing a whole battery of special interests, including a labor union PAC in Georgia that had contributed handsomely to Bodine's last Senate campaign five years ago, a race that had been a very close call. He also represented the powerful Consumers of America Free Trade Association, or CAFTA. From his styled hair to his Italian leather shoes, he was what Bodine called a slick article. He also had that cool, faintly disdainful air that Bodine disliked.

CAFTA, Chandler said over the fresh Maryland crab salad, wasn't very happy with the Senate Finance Committee's current hearings. What was that senator from California up to?

"She's just getting her feet wet," Bodine

said. "And she's trying to make the six o'clock news back home, just like the rest of us."

"She's trying to sabotage this Japan summit, Josh."

"Well, now, that's goin' a bit far —"

"Hell, no, it isn't. Where'd that business about a special postwar fund come from? That's the sort of thing that makes taxpayers uneasy."

"I don't know where she got hold of that. It doesn't amount to a hill of beans."

"You know that, Senator, and I know that. But the people out there in Peoria don't know that. You get a senator making some wild statements and half the people will believe there's something wrong. Senator McCarthy taught us that."

"Senator Woods didn't exactly say there was anythin' wrong."

"She made it sound as if this O Fund was a problem."

"It's dyin' off already," Bodine said defensively. "The media took the bone, but they found there's no meat on it, and they dropped it."

"They haven't buried it," the attorney answered. "Where's she going with it? We don't know that. You need to put a muzzle on her, Mr. Chairman."

"I already spoke to her about it."

"We like to know about surprises like that ahead of time," Chandler said pointedly. He didn't say who "we" were.

"So do I," Bodine growled. "I let her know. I think she got the message."

"I hope so, Josh, I certainly hope so. This summit is important to our members. Like I said, CAFTA isn't happy about what's happened there on the Hill so far, turning the hearings into another round of Japan bashing. This isn't the time for it, with the Japanese prepared to make some real concessions."

"We don't know that yet. Not for sure."

"Take my word for it, Senator."

An unspoken message lay behind Chandler's confident assurance. CAFTA had an all-American name, and most of its members were Americans. But behind the association's devotion to free trade were some lesser known realities: a large percentage of the companies supporting CAFTA were American subsidiaries of Japanese companies. It had been formed by them, and it promoted their interests through effective lobbying and the influence of its well-financed political action committee. The free trade it promoted involved free access to American and European markets, not Japan's.

Ordinarily Joshua Bodine loved cold crab,

sweet and crunchy. Today he wasn't enjoying his salad as much as usual. When Chandler had called about a meeting, the senator had hoped the featured topic of discussion was to be *his* future.

As if perceiving Bodine's discomfort, Chandler smiled, displaying a row of perfectly capped white teeth, and changed the subject. Was Mildred still with the senator in Washington, or had she gone back home to Georgia? The weather was miserable either place in August. Georgia, Bodine said, had bigger bugs. Mildred was there, and he would be joining her for the recess to touch bases with the voters.

How were things with the voters, Chandler asked politely, knowing the answer. They were suffering, Bodine said. The peanut farmers were hurting. Unemployment in Georgia was over 8 percent, mirroring the average across the country. Workers were afraid for their jobs, and America's new breed of lean, mean CEOs were taking advantage of that fear, extracting concessions, cutting wages, siphoning off benefits. This was known as making American business more efficient. All of this, it went without saying, made it rough for political incumbents.

Joshua Bodine had come into the Senate when a four-term senator was set in office for life, or until he was ready to retire. That was no longer true.

"I saw that *Atlanta Constitution* poll," Ken Chandler said sympathetically. "The numbers weren't good."

Bodine's approval rating with Georgia voters was sinking like a stone. It was as if he was being held personally accountable for the miserable state of Georgia's economy — and the nation's.

"It's that knee-jerk throw-the-rascals-out syndrome," the lawyer said. "There's no rationality to it."

"Doesn't matter what you do for 'em," the Georgia senator nodded glumly. "It's what-have-you-done-for-me-lately?" His mood was becoming somber. Fortunately the crab was all gone, only a few leaves of lettuce still decorating the crystal bowl. He wouldn't have had any appetite for more.

"Well, election's still more than a year away. Things can change by then."

"Maybe." Bodine hesitated. Was Chandler leaving an opening for him? "If not . . . I won't run a losing campaign."

Chandler managed an expression of surprise. "You aren't thinking of stepping down?"

"I've given it some thought."

"What'll you do? Go home to the rocking

chair? I suppose that would make Mildred happy."

"She hates Washington. Always has."

"You don't."

"No." Bodine took a deep breath, procrastinated by waving at a senator from New Jersey just being seated at a table across the room, and said, "I figure I know my way around this pasture. Some folks might believe I could be useful to 'em. I might open an office. . . ."

"That's always a gamble."

"No payoff without risk."

"You could do yourself a lot of good without all the headaches, Josh. You have friends on the Hill. That counts for a great deal. You can pick up the phone, you know who to call, and they'll talk to you."

"I guess so. While I'm a senator . . ."

"You decide to leave office, you won't be losing all your friends. That means you can still be a player. And I don't have to tell you it can be much more rewarding financially than public office."

The words were what Bodine wanted to hear. Although a formal commitment hadn't been made, hints on both sides had been offered and acknowledged, cautiously but positively.

He decided to show his willingness to be

useful. "This O Fund Senator Woods brought up. Why is it important?"

"It's not important," said Chandler. "It's diversionary. It suggests a reason for taxpayers to start worrying when there's no basis for worry. And it undermines the president on the eve of the economic summit with Japan."

"Hell, he's not going over there to do any real negotiating. It takes the Japs two years to give an inch, and two days to take that back."

"That's negative thinking, Senator."

Bodine knew he had slipped up. "No, no, all I'm sayin', they're tough negotiators. I'm an old horse trader myself, I don't fault 'em for that." He pondered this a moment before deciding to take his concession a step further. "Fact is, I kind of admire their savvy. They know what they want and they go after it. I can get along with folks like that."

"I'm glad to hear that, Senator."

The attorney's cool tone brought the heat of anger to Joshua Bodine's neck. He checked it quickly. Kenneth Chandler had already made it clear he wasn't going to make a blind commitment. He might not even have that authority. But he and his principals now had been informed that Bodine was thinking of retirement from the Senate as a choice preferable to defeat. Chandler knew that Bodine wanted to stay in Washington, and that he could be a very useful man. For now that was enough.

Meanwhile, CAFTA wanted something from him. They wanted the Japan summit to proceed smoothly. A certain amount of the usual political posturing in Congress was acceptable, but nothing serious or disturbing to that small portion of the American public that listened closely. Senator Woods and her reckless questions had to be kept out of the limelight.

It was up to Joshua Bodine to demonstrate how helpful he could be.

"We'll have to do this again, Senator," Ken Chandler said. "Let's make it real soon."

Ten

Toshio Miyaki remembered the precise moment he knew that Yashi Nogama was an enemy to be watched.

Six members of the Sonno council had held an emergency meeting to consider a request by a major Japanese bank for special financial assistance. The falling stock market, and bad loans associated with plummeting real estate values in Japan, had created a crisis at many of the country's financial institutions, just as they had in the United States. Japanese investors, in fact, had participated painfully in the depression in commercial and recreational properties in California and the Southwest.

Miyaki was dismayed to find Nogama among those called to the meeting. Though only recently admitted to the Sonno Group, Nogama, with his aggressive style, was already exerting great influence.

After two hours of debate the decision was

made. The bank would be rescued. In return, the Sonno Group would acquire 25 percent of the bank's stock ownership. The meeting broke up.

Nogama suggested a visit to a *karaoke* bar in the Roppongi nightlife district. Miyaki objected, citing the late hour, but the other men were immediately enthusiastic. Members of the council rarely met away from Sonno's headquarters except in the course of business. But going out to drink with your peers was a way of life for Japanese workers. Young men working their way up could not escape the pressure to join in such carousing, especially when their superiors were involved. Participating cemented your role as part of the group. Refusing to go along stamped you as an individualist, someone suspect. Ironically, in these marathon drinking bouts, often joined with sexual escapades, Japanese men found release from the rigid conformity that ruled so much of their lives.

In the crowded bar a haze of blue smoke hovered over a small stage and the tiny tables arranged to fill every inch of floor space. Hostesses serving the guests had to squeeze by the tightly packed chairs. They were young, attractive women, many of them blond Europeans, who submitted with smiles and giggles to the squeezing, pinching and raucous comments that accompanied their progress to and from the bar. The general vulgarity competed with live *karaoke* singing by the more talented hostesses, or the blare of recorded rock music. Although Toshio Miyaki collected American jukeboxes and was fond of rock music from the 1950s and 1960s, the noise and smoke and drink gave him a headache.

Nogama, by contrast, enjoyed himself immensely. He seemed eager to prove himself one of the group. He drank more, laughed and joked more loudly, than any of his companions, many of whom had not been in such a bar since they were ambitious young men on the rise. Nogama, however, was well known at the bar. Several of the hostesses competed in an effort to please him.

One young woman tried to sit on Miyaki's lap. Miyaki demurred with good humor.

Nogama slapped him on the arm. "Relax, Miyaki-san! Drink up! Maybe you will sing for us before the night's over."

"It would be the sound of a hungry crow."

The hostess, a young Japanese, laughed with the other men. Nogama laughed loudest of all. As the woman tried to slip past his chair he reached out suddenly, grabbed her arm and pulled her toward him. She squirmed, but Nogama held her in an iron grip. His free hand fumbled under her gown. The hostess was startled, then frightened. Suddenly she shrieked.

Nogama withdrew his hand and held it up in a gesture of truce. The hostess retreated hastily, stumbling over another chair. Nogama roared with laughter and the other men all joined him. The *yakuza*'s eyes, as if sensing discord, found Miyaki's. And in that moment Miyaki's disapproval was naked, as naked as the hostility that leaped into Yashi Nogama's black eyes.

On a Saturday in late August, Miyaki remembered that moment, as he sat on the veranda of his father's house in Osaka's outskirts. He was an inordinately wealthy man, and he and his family enjoyed a villa in the hills outside of the city as their principal residence. It was situated on spacious grounds — the most visible evidence of Miyaki's wealth — with a view of both city lights and forested hills. But Miyaki had kept his father's house in town after the old man's death. It was convenient for business, and for those times when he needed to be alone. He had remodeled the house in the *shoin* style, with open rooms covered only in reed and grass mats, open not only to each other but also to the outdoors. With nothing between floor and roof but a few slender posts, and the wooden boards of the veranda repeating the parallel lines of the mats, interior and exterior were visually one. And these spaces in turn were linked organically with the garden that began at the edge of the raised wooden terrace. His father's garden and, for the past twenty years, Toshio Miyaki's private passion.

Although the price of such a property within the city would now have been astronomical, the garden space was not large — only twenty feet in depth, seventy-two feet wide. It was bordered by the veranda on the north and by white clay walls on the other three sides, topped with red tiles. The *niwa* itself seemed almost plain at first glance, devoid of color except for a single pink camellia sasanqua bush in the southwest corner that was just beginning to come into its autumn bloom. It grew between two rocks covered with dark green moss. The rocks and the bush thrust upward from the flat surface of the garden like a forested mountain rising above a plain, the effect separating this corner from the rest of the garden.

The main part of the garden was a *karasenzui*, a dry landscape. It had been created painstakingly over many years. Begun by Miyaki's father Shiro, it had been brought to its present state of perfection by Miyaki himself. A narrow rain gutter beneath the edge of the raised veranda was made of gray tiles and filled with black and gray stones. The rest of the surface was covered in white gravel, carefully raked so that its shallow furrows created the illusion of waves. The level white surface was broken only where buried rocks heaved upward, like islands rising from the sea. There was a single large rock near the western wall, worn and gray and seamed like a very old face. A cluster of three rocks in a triangular arrangement near the center was displaced enough to avoid an unnatural symmetry. And, near the eastern end, a flat rock extended over the sea of white gravel like a bridge, offering access to a final grouping of gray rocks.

The eye was drawn from the symbolic forest, with its splash of color, across the garden toward the final grouping. And here, as if growing out of a natural depression in the largest rock, was a single small Japanese white pine, set in an unglazed, purplish-brown earthenware pot. It was a bonsai. Sixty-two years ago it had been discovered by Shiro Miyaki in the mountains of Shikoku Island. When Shiro Miyaki spoke of such things at all, which was rarely, he said that the tree brought the mountains with it.

Its trunk, whose bark was a purple-brown matched by the color of the pot, coiled upward with sinewy strength, slanting to the right in the *shakan* style. About two-thirds of the way up it dipped and twisted back upon itself. The tree was thirty-one inches high, and the spread of its branches was over two feet. Almost hidden behind tufts of lustrous green needles, the longest branches reached out on the eastern side about eighteen inches, away from the slant of the trunk, as if the tree were leaning into the wind while the branches flowed out behind it. The white pine created an instant impression of strength, but the longer one looked at it the more one began to see the beauty in the muscular coiling of its trunk, the graceful composition of its tracery of branches, the green glow of its needle clusters.

Over a span of forty years Shiro Miyaki had cared for the tree with cautious devotion, seeking to bring out the essence of its natural form and beauty. From him Toshio Miyaki had learned both the art and the passion of caring for the tree and the garden.

The limited elements in the garden were part of its seeming artlessness. It contained only simple, natural materials, replicating nature in miniature. Each of its elements was real, but the whole was not realistic. In the Japanese hierarchy of gardens it was called *so*, because of its informality and the way in which it sought not to reproduce a scene in nature but to represent it symbolically.

As Miyaki sat in contemplation of his garden through the afternoon, a soft rain began to fall. The rain enhanced the mood of the garden. The gray rocks turned black. The white gravel darkened, much as the ocean turned gray under cloudy skies. In the far corner, the forested mountain withdrew into the mist, becoming both more mysterious and more real. And directly in front of Miyaki, droplets of moisture trembled on the needle tufts of the bonsai.

The effect of the garden was astonishingly tranquil. Zen-like, it opened the path to inner peace through contemplation of the simplest natural objects. Miyaki never tired of looking at it. It was always the same, yet always changing, as it did today in the rain. Here, where the world beyond the white clay walls ceased to exist, he found repose. It was here he came when he was troubled or uncertain, when he needed to cleanse his mind of anxieties so that it would open to the truth, or simply to lose himself in its quiet beauty. Invariably, after hours in his garden, Miyaki emerged refreshed in mind and spirit.

Not so today. He was troubled by the enterprise on which he had unwillingly embarked, but on this day his garden brought neither answers nor peace. At times he would lose himself in contemplating the purity of natural form and texture in the small pine tree, but each time his reverie was shattered by disturbing intrusions, like the memory of that moment in the *karaoke* bar. That too was a moment of truth, but a truth that brought only the perception of danger.

Thinking of these matters, feeling not refreshed but tired, Miyaki became aware of another presence. He turned quickly. A jolting shock ran through his whole body.

Yashi Nogama grinned down at him, pleased by the reaction. He stood in the open doorway facing the veranda. Behind him Miyaki saw the anxious face of his servant Toru who, with his wife Suzuki, were caretakers of the house. No one else lived there, and few visited. Toru's expression held more than a devoted servant's dismay over his lapse in permitting the unannounced intrusion. He appeared terrified. Miyaki wondered what Nogama had done to frighten him.

"Konnichiwa, Miyaki-san!" Nogama's polite bow was mocking. "You are surprised to see me here?"

"Irasshai, Nogama-san." Formally polite, Miyaki rose, the movement covering the fact that he did not specifically return Nogama's bow. His brusque tone did not match the welcome of his words. "How did you know

where to find me?"

"It was not difficult to discover." Nogama's gaze slowly took in the contents of the garden, his expression not admiring but amused. He was carrying a black umbrella. The roof of the terrace shielded him from the fine rain, and the umbrella was folded. He leaned on it lightly as if it were a walking stick. Water ran off the tip and pooled on the polished boards. "Your devotion to your garden is a well known part of your biography. Even the newspapers write of it."

"There was no announcement in the newspapers that I would be here today," Miyaki said dryly.

Nogama smiled. "It's my business to know such things."

"I wasn't expecting anyone. Perhaps you would like —"

"Nothing. It is business that brings me here. Urgent business."

Already alerted by the man's uninvited intrusion upon his privacy, Toshio Miyaki turned toward his garden, his expression impassive. The rain had ceased. A stillness lay over everything, broken only by a soft dripping from the edge of the roof into the stone gutter. "What business is this?"

"A question has been raised in the American Congress about the O Fund."

If Nogama had hoped to startle him, he succeeded. Miyaki considered the possible implications for the Sonno Group's plans. They were many, but only if the American inquiry led to answers. That seemed improbable.

"Why should the question arise now, on the eve of summit negotiations?"

"That's what we are all asking ourselves."

Miyaki suddenly realized that Nogama's unexpected visit, and his surprising revelation, carried other implications for Miyaki himself. "This matter has been discussed in the council?"

"*Hai*. The decision has been made that we must move quickly."

A decision had been reached, which implied discussion. On such an important matter, the debate would have been intense.

Nogama had been included. Miyaki, a senior member of the Sonno Group, had been left out. The ramifications were alarming. The decision to exclude him — who had initiated it? — said much more than that his opinion was no longer of value. It said that he was no longer trusted.

"I see. Is Shinji Sakai aware of —"

"He was the leader of our discussion," Nogama said, enjoying Miyaki's surprise.

The news about Sakai was disturbing, but there was no evidence of this in Miyaki's reaction. He stared out at his garden. They had cut him out of the decision-making process, but they still needed him. Not just his financial resources, although these were significant; the Fund dwarfed his contribution. No, they needed the cover he alone could provide. His U.S. contacts, his reputation, his personal role in the drama about to unfold. Nogama's attitude was arrogant, but in fact he had come as an emissary. His presence was an implicit admission that the all-powerful Sonno Group needed Toshio Miyaki.

"Our people are in place," Nogama said. "The resources are being transferred. We can't wait for an investigation by the American senators. The council's decision is that the timetable must be advanced. You will make arrangements to meet our American contacts as quickly as possible."

"As before?"

"Yes, on Guam. The arrangements were satisfactory."

Miyaki was silent. After a moment he said, "I will consider what you have told me."

Yashi Nogama scowled. A flush darkened his face. "There is no time for considering," he snapped. "You know what you must do."

"There is always time for thought." Miyaki smiled, unfazed by Nogama's anger. "That is what I come here for." He gestured toward the miniature landscape contained within the white clay walls.

"This famous garden of yours?" Nogama's survey of the *niwa* was cursory, his tone contemptuous. "There is little to see. No flowers, no trees —"

"It is a garden for the mind."

"For the mind? I see. . . ."

Nogama looked over the quiet scene, this time more carefully. The rain clouds had moved eastward, and there were even a few breaks in the cloud cover where the sun shone through. In the distance, beyond the garden, a portion of a rainbow appeared.

The *yakuza* was a blunt man, uncouth, poorly educated. Miyaki had no doubt that, like others of his kind, he had first gained access to wealth and business circles through criminal activities. At one time many legitimate Japanese companies had hired such men to quell the protests of unruly stockholders or provide other strong-arm services. Once gaining a foothold, gangsters had quickly learned of the huge profits available in stock speculation and investment, particularly to those with inside information. Sharing such information, illegal under SEC rules and regulations in the United States as it was on most of the world's exchanges, was an accepted practice in Japan.

But Miyaki's garden was a source of pride to him. It was simplicity itself. Even a man of vulgar sensibilities like Nogama, he thought, might find it beautiful.

So he was not surprised when Nogama suddenly stepped down from the terrace. But he was not prepared for the gangster's next action. Nogama plodded across the white gravel, heavy-footed, gouging a path across the skillfully raked surface. The lines of gravel were straight except near objects. They encircled the rock islands that rose from the gravel, like waves washing against beach and bluff. Nogama plowed across the garden like a bulldozer, scattering gravel with each step, stabbing the end of his folded umbrella into the ground. He headed straight toward the group of rocks on which rested the old bonsai.

Miyaki felt the first stab of alarm. It was inconceivable, but . . .

The heedless scattering of gravel angered and disgusted him, but to restore it as it was before would be a familiar labor of love. The bonsai was something else, irreplaceable.

"This tree," Nogama said, pausing before it. "It's stunted. I'm told these things may have great value." The umbrella stabbed toward the slanted shape of the white pine.

"Be careful — it is of sentimental value. It was my father's prize possession."

"Your father's tree? So old . . ." Nogama had his back to Miyaki, but there was amusement in his tone. "I had no father, so I know nothing of such trees."

He swung around. In the abrupt movement his arm whipped across the front of the bonsai. The umbrella slashed downward, seemingly by accident, as anyone carrying a folded umbrella might turn about and swing it casually, like a stick.

The tip of the umbrella snapped the end of the longest branch reaching out from the trunk. Four inches of tough old wood with its green needle clusters broke cleanly. The broken branch dropped to the wet surface of the rock and tumbled silently onto the gravel.

Miyaki's shout was a cry from the heart. *"Iie!"*

Nogama froze. *"Gomen nasai!* . . . an accident," he said. "Most regrettable, Miyaki-san."

Miyaki was speechless. Rage boiled inside him. All of his grief and loss had tunneled into that single cry of disbelief. No one would do such a thing deliberately, it was unthinkable. Not even this thug.

Before Miyaki could regain his composure Nogama was back on the terrace facing him. He stared into Miyaki's eyes. Miyaki saw no sign of remorse.

"You will consider what I've said. Don't take too much time. We must act quickly. The decision has been made. America must learn its lesson. The Sonno Group — and Japan — have waited long enough." When Miyaki did not immediately respond, Nogama became impatient. "*Wakarimasu-ka?*"

Miyaki nodded, containing his rage. He did not trust himself to say too much. "Sonno will have my thoughts promptly."

"It's regrettable about your tree. Old things . . . they become brittle." The words might have carried a hidden warning. "They break too easily."

Miyaki stared at him in silence.

Nogama gave a curt bow. "*Sayonara, Miyaki-san.* We will speak again soon. Oh, there is one other thing. I will accompany you to Guam . . . and to America."

Eleven

Robert Daulton had known Raymond Farrow for almost fifty years. They had met as freshmen roommates at Fordham University after World War II. Daulton, who had lied about his age to enlist in the navy early in the war, was twenty-two, freshly demobilized; Farrow was eighteen. A Catholic, Daulton had won a partial scholarship. Farrow was at Fordham because his parents admired the Jesuit reputation for discipline and intellectual agility. In spite of the disparity in their ages and backgrounds, they were instant friends. They remained roommates for four years. They studied, played, goofed off together. They even sought girlfriends who knew each other so they could double date companionably. They rowed together in double sculls, which required the rapport of Siamese twins.

After college their career paths had diverged. Daulton had gone straight into business, working his way up from selling to management positions in a successful career aborted early as a direct result of the takeover mania of the late 1980s. He told himself that he enjoyed travel and playing golf, which was true. He had no financial worries, especially now that his son was through law school and on his own. But Daulton remained bitter.

Raymond Farrow's career, from Fordham through Wharton's MBA program, and ultimately into international banking, had been much more public and even more successful. He was on the board of trustees of three universities. He was a Knight Sovereign of the Order of Malta. He had been with the World Bank. He had held appointments in three administrations, the last time on the president's Council of Economic Advisers. He knew all of the major power brokers in Washington and London. Now a consultant emeritus to the Brookings Institution, a Washington think tank, he was respected by leaders in both political parties.

Over the years the men had remained close, even when they didn't see each other for a year or more. Farrow had stood as godfather to his friend's son, Kevin. Robert Daulton had returned the favor as godfather to Farrow's oldest daughter, Denise. In late years they had dined together whenever business or pleasure brought them into proximity — which often meant when Daulton came to Washington. Though successful by any definition, Farrow could have enriched himself many times over had he not given so much of his time and energy to government service. His choice defined the man.

After his navy reunion in San Diego, and his meeting with his son, Kevin, Daulton flew back to his home in Connecticut. That Monday he caught a small segment of the Senate hearings on television. The California senator's surprising question to Edward Grabow about the O Fund startled him.

For the next few days Daulton thought often about Kevin's news of the huge Tyler Holdings stock offering, and particularly about the piece of the puzzle that didn't fit: Calvin Lederer's secret trip to Guam to meet some Japanese dark suits.

He also probed his memory for something about the O Fund. A fragment of memory kept eluding him, teasingly out of reach. The news media showed a flurry of interest in the question, but that interest quickly faded. There was no follow-up.

Daulton thought about his old friend's international banking connections, and about the two years Farrow had spent in Japan in the 1970s as part of a U.S. trade mission.

On Thursday evening Daulton dialed the familiar number in Chevy Chase. He felt a rush of warmth as Farrow's vigorous voice answered. "Hello?"

"Ray . . . it's Bob Daulton."

"Bob! Good to hear from you. How's the handicap?"

"That's what I called about. I'm going to be in Washington next week. I wondered if we could get together for a round."

Farrow chuckled. "Why do I get the idea golf isn't what you called about?"

Daulton laughed. "What makes you think I have something on my mind besides birdies?"

"Well, for one thing you usually do. And for another, you're in a hurry. Want to tell me anything about it?"

For a moment Daulton was silent. "It may not be anything, Ray. I don't want to build it up when I don't have anything concrete. It's just something my son mentioned the other day started me wondering."

"Kevin? How's he doing, Bob? Settling down? What firm is he with?"

"Bryant Forbes Lederer & Wyman. He's in their Los Angeles office."

"Ah," Raymond Farrow said.

He had met Calvin Lederer on several occasions at Capitol functions. Farrow didn't much care for him, but that was hardly important. The law firm, on the other hand, *was* important. In Washington, D.C., you were either connected or you weren't. Lederer's firm was connected. It also had a reputation for secrecy as well as political clout.

"It's a major firm, Bob. Kevin could do a lot worse."

"Right now he's working on something that has to do with Tyler Holdings. They're putting together a major offering."

"Uh-oh. Reynolds Tyler again."

"Yes, I thought you'd remember."

"He's on my list, Bob, for what he did to you. What's Tyler up to now?"

"I'm not sure. Maybe he just wants more money, or another conquest, which is what it looks like on the surface. Lederer is the puzzler. He's involved. The firm is handling the offering."

"Who are the underwriters?"

"All the major players. The principal representatives are Martin Fielding Associates, but it's too big a deal for anyone to handle alone. Bear Stearns, Smith Barney, Alex. Brown, First Boston, Morgan Stanley, PaineWebber, Lazard Frères — they're all committed to purchase big blocks of shares. This is a $3 billion offering for starters."

Farrow whistled soundlessly. For an instant

the thought flickered through his mind that he could probably make a substantial profit if he bought some Tyler Holdings stock before the word spread. He didn't pursue it. Acting on inside information was the name of the game on the Street — always had been — but Farrow had some old-fashioned ideas about integrity and the public trust. He remembered reading with amusement a scene in a best-selling novel about an all-American hero who, coming across an inside tip in the course of his adventures, had cashed in on it without a qualm. His action wasn't supposed to be dishonest, just smart. Raymond Farrow held a different view.

"Want to tell me about it, Bob?"

"Let's save it for Tuesday. There is one thing, though." Daulton hesitated. "You spent a couple of years in Japan. What do you think of this summit conference?"

"It scares the hell out of me. I'm afraid we're going to end up with our pants around our ankles." Farrow felt a little spurt of adrenalin. What had Daulton stumbled onto? "Does this have anything to do with Reynolds Tyler?"

"I'm not sure."

"This isn't about grudges, is it, Bob?"

"You know me better than that."

Farrow sighed. "It was a stupid question."

"No, just realistic. A banker's question. By

the way, didn't I read something about your country club being bought by Japanese interests?"

Another sigh. "You did indeed. Itaro Suchima bought it. Like that old joke, he's one of the three richest men in the world, and I'm not sure who the other two are. There was a great deal of initial trepidation among the members, but . . . so far he's done nothing but put money into improving the back nine."

"You can still get a starting time?" Daulton joked.

After Raymond hung up, the intuition that his old friend had something interesting and important to tell him came back stronger than before.

Twelve

That same Thursday evening, in the library of her leased Georgetown townhouse, Elinor Woods ate a solitary dinner off a TV tray in front of the television set. Originally built in 1876, the house was small by contemporary California ranchhouse standards. Elinor liked the meticulous detailing of the woodwork, the high ceilings and the warm intimacy of the rooms. It was a good house in which to take shelter, regroup and relax.

The telephone rang. She glanced toward the grandfather's clock visible in a corner of the hallway. Five after ten. She couldn't blame anyone for interrupting her meal at this hour.

"Senator! How's it going?"

"Lou? Is that you?" Her brain shifted gears as swiftly as the mute button silenced *L.A. Law.* She attached a name and face to the breezy voice. An attorney based in Beverly Hills, Louis Janowicz was a political activist and major contributor with potent influence in the California Democratic Party. He was one of those, Elinor knew, who had pushed the governor into appointing her to complete her late predecessor's term in office.

"Who else would be calling you at home? Not that husband of yours. Everybody knows doctors don't make house calls." Janowicz laughed cheerfully at his own joke.

"Doctors don't know the telephone has been invented yet."

She asked after Janowicz's wife, Ruth, who was recovering from her operation "beautifully." Janowicz inquired about her two sons. Richard, the older, was an environmental scientist at the University of California at Santa Barbara. His brother, Jason, who was enrolled in law school at the University of Virginia, was working with the U.S. Forestry Service in Oregon for the summer. "Hey, they're committed, just like their mom," Janowicz said. "That's great. Which one's gonna run for office?"

"Jason's going to be the lawyer. Is there anything special I can do for you, Lou? You don't ever need a reason to call, but —"

"I caught you on the tube Monday, doll. You looked and sounded great. Been getting a lot of play in the *L.A. Times*."

"That can't be all bad."

"Well, yes, that's what we say, just spell the name right, hey?" Janowicz didn't sound enthusiastic, which was out of character. Little alarm bells rang in her head. "You hear anything from Grabow or the White House over that mystery fund flap?"

"There was no flap, Lou, just a question that didn't get answered. And no, I haven't heard from the White House. Should I have? I don't think I'm that important to them."

"You will be, doll, you will be. Trust me. But it might not be a bad idea to go easy on that stuff, you know? I hear by the grapevine that you ruffled some feathers."

The feather ruffling must have been loud, Elinor thought, for Janowicz to hear it all the way out in California. "In the White House?"

"Where else? Walton is counting on Osaka to give him a boost in his approval rating. The summit gives him a chance to act presidential. You hear any other flack? How about Joshua Bodine? He wasn't very happy, am I right?"

"No, he wasn't," she admitted. "He thinks I'm getting ahead of myself."

"Bodine's a dinosaur, but he can throw his weight around pretty good when he wants to. You don't want him to get the idea you're trying to upstage him on his own committee."

What did Janowicz really want? Why had he called? Had Bodine got to him?

144

"Like I told you when you went to Washington, doll, you had three good years to make your mark. You've been doing fine. And it doesn't hurt that the media like you."

You've been doing fine, Elinor Woods thought. *Until now.*

"One thing you don't want to do, you don't want to build up media expectations when you're gonna come up empty, you know?"

"I'm not sure I do." *The O Fund,* Elinor thought.

"Sure you do, doll. Just don't give them a chance to turn on you, is all I'm saying. You send them off on a wild goose chase, you make them look bad, they have a million ways to come back at you."

She wondered if Janowicz had learned to call women "doll" through rubbing shoulders with the Hollywood movie people he mingled with. She had never noticed the habit before.

"You hear what I'm saying, Senator?"

"I think I do, Lou."

"Good, good, I knew you would. And if Bodine or anyone else gives you a hard time, you let me know, okay? I'm here for you, you know what I'm saying? This is California, and we have more electoral votes than anybody else, right? A hell of a lot more than Georgia."

"Right."

"Just don't let the old bastard get the wrong idea. Let Bodine think he's steering the boat." Janowicz chuckled. "You coming out to the coast for the recess? I wasn't sure you'd still be in D.C."

"I'm flying home tomorrow. I'll be there through Labor Day."

"That's great, you need some of our California sunshine. Maybe we can get together while you're here. Let's try, okay? Listen, I won't keep you, I bet you haven't even had your dinner yet, am I right?"

Janowicz's uncanny prescience gave her a chill. "I was just going to."

"I knew it, I knew it. That's what I keep hearing about you, Senator, that you're working hard, paying your dues, letting the old boys in the Club get comfortable with you. You're doing great. Keep it up."

"Thanks, I'll try."

"You'll do better than that, Senator, I know you." Lou Janowicz chuckled without apparent reason. "No more wild cards, right? They scare the hell out of people."

When he rang off, Elinor Woods sat for a long time without moving, letting her dinner grow cold, the courtroom drama on the television set still muted. She was no longer hungry.

Grabow. Bodine. Janowicz. They had little connection with each other, aside from being

146

in or near the corridors of power. They had one other thing in common. They didn't like having her asking questions in public about a Japanese fund that was old news a half century ago.

On Friday morning, when Elinor Woods collected her messages from the office before leaving for Dulles International, there were calls from the American Association for Global Trading Partnership, which was funded by the Japanese Ministry of Finance; from the House minority leader, a close friend of President Walton, who suggested lunch together as soon as possible; from a delegation representing steel workers in Columbus, Ohio, who were concerned about any possible glitch in the plans of Miyaki Industries to reopen a steel mill in Columbus; and from Norman Hollingsworth, the mayor of Fresno, California, who wanted an urgent meeting with the senator to discuss the vital importance to Fresno of the Sakai automotive plant, for which ground breaking was scheduled to begin in January.

Senator Woods placed the stack of messages on the taxi seat beside her. She stared out the window as the cab whisked her out of the city into the Virginia countryside toward the airport.

Thirteen

On a Friday evening late in August the Tyler Holdings prospectus was finalized in a ten-hour filing session at the offices of Enright & Sons. Figures and dates were plugged into the holes left for them in the document until the last minute. In a frantic rush the package was put together, copied and bound. A courier arrived at 11:00 P.M., in time to catch a midnight flight to Washington, D.C., where the package would be hand-delivered to the Securities and Exchange Commission for approval.

Kevin Daulton had not worked closely with Alison Carey during the long session. It seemed that Dexter Hilliard had other plans for her. And she seemed to have eyes only for Hilliard.

When the session finally broke up, Kevin Daulton lingered near the elevators, letting two groups go down ahead of him.

Alison didn't appear. Neither did Hilliard. As the crowd of lawyers thinned out, Kevin realized that both Alison and Hilliard had already left.

He rode an elevator alone to the lobby, feeling wretched.

Noise spilled across the plaza between the twin towers. Roddy's Place, a popular Thank-God-It's-Friday type of bar and restaurant, was jammed as usual on a Friday night. Few of the patrons seemed to be over thirty. They sipped margaritas or swigged from bottles of imported beer. A few teetotalers in the crowd were drinking expensive bottled water. Earlier in the evening there had been tables loaded with the free appetizers that helped to give Roddy's Place its happy hour reputation. You could nurse a drink and circulate, everyone said, and eat enough freebies to take care of dinner. The Buffalo chicken wings were supposed to be the best you could find downtown.

Kevin listened to the babble of talk and laughter as he headed across the plaza toward the elevators leading to the garage below. Everyone seemed to be having fun.

He saw them at an outside table off to his left. They were alone, sitting in semidarkness. Dexter Hilliard was leaning across the table toward her. Alison Carey laughed, tilting her head back.

Kevin felt as if someone had kicked him in the stomach.

He bypassed the elevators and stumbled down steps to the lower levels. Moments later he was roaring onto the freeway, bolting past a startled driver where the Fifth Street on-ramp narrowed to a single lane.

The hateful voice hissed in his ear. *Didn't I tell you?*

"She likes me," he muttered through clenched teeth.

In your dreams.

Alison Carey hadn't intended to stop at Roddy's Place with Dexter Hilliard. He had been unusually attentive and helpful to her during the filing session, however, patiently guiding her through the intricacies of preparing a final prospectus for the SEC. That night had been what Hilliard called a mop-up operation. The essentials of the financial document were already in place. The concerns expressed by the Securities and Exchange Commission over the preliminary prospectus, chiefly directed toward Tyler Holdings' financial statements for the past three years, had been addressed. The teams of lawyers grouped around the long conference tables in the financial printer's offices had been busy most of the night confirming figures supplied by the company and its myriad subsidiaries.

Even before the courier picked up the filing package, Dexter Hilliard assured the weary intern that her long day's work was done. He would leave with her. On the way down to the plaza in the elevator Hilliard said cheerfully, "It's celebration time, Alison. Is this your first Friday night at Roddy's Place?"

"Oh, it's late, I don't think —"

"You have to. It's a tradition after a filing. Most of the working group will be there." Hilliard grinned. "All except for the truly married ones, which is a very select list."

Quite a few of their colleagues were already there. The night air was still mild and most of them were clustered around the outdoor tables. Alison was a little disappointed not to see Kevin Daulton among them. He was probably inside at the bar. Before she could speculate further Hilliard steered her away from the others. He found a table off to the side, without asking her. She wondered about suggesting they join the others, but let it go. A girl in a scanty dress at a nearby table eyed Hilliard speculatively, as if he were alone.

"What'll it be? I'm afraid most of the appetizers are gone."

"Are you kidding? After all that feasting we did up on forty-four?"

Hilliard ordered stingers, again without asking her. Alison smiled. She hated stingers.

The party atmosphere swirled around them. A couple of the senior lawyers stopped by their table to say hello, and to congratulate Hilliard on his role in getting the prospectus pulled together. He introduced Alison, who hadn't formally met either of the men before. No one sat down, and none of the younger associates tried to join them. After a few minutes Alison realized there was a tacit acceptance of the fact that she was spoken for.

"So what do you think?"

"What do I think?"

"About the firm. Now that you've had a chance to get your feet wet. I'm not giving anything away, Alison — do your friends call you Alison? Or Allie?"

"Alison."

"Well, I'm not giving anything away, Alison, when I tell you the partners are impressed by your performance the past couple of months. We all hope you feel the same way about us."

"I haven't done anything," Alison protested.

"Not true. You've pitched right in, pulled your weight. You have a gift for language, you've shown that, and there's nothing more important in this business. The law is really all about language. And you've shown you can work with the team."

Alison groaned inwardly. She sipped her stinger, hoping the expression on her face would be attributed to the sourness of the drink.

"You can go a long way with this firm." Hilliard smiled, leaning across the table toward her. Off to the right, Alison thought she saw Kevin Daulton hurrying by on his way to the garage. "I think that's important to you. Am I right?"

"I'm not even an associate yet," Alison said carefully.

Hilliard's smile became conspiratorial, suggesting a just-between-us intimacy. "I can't say anything officially, of course, but . . . you don't have to worry about taking a long-term lease on your apartment, or even buying a condo. You probably should think about buying. The partners like that kind of commitment. It suggests stability, you know? And the firm helps its associates obtain favorable low-interest financing. You really should give it some thought."

Alison was suspicious. Not only was Hilliard telling her that she was going to be selected to join the firm as an associate at the end of the intern program. He was also hinting to her that he could help her get ahead. And he was coming on to her.

"Mr. Hilliard —"

"Dex! Mr. Hilliard is for the office, okay?"

"Dex . . . should you be telling me this? I mean, if it isn't official —"

"Don't worry about it, Alison. You're in. Just don't tell anyone else, not yet. They'll all know in a couple of weeks." Hilliard hitched his chair closer to hers, waved at a waitress to reorder, overriding Alison's protest. She wondered if she could manage to swallow a second stinger. She also considered the possibility that Hilliard was trying to weaken her defenses in the time-honored fashion. "Next week I'll introduce you to a couple of the partners you haven't met, men you should meet. It's time they got to know you. Like I said, you can move ahead with this firm if you get the right little push."

"I don't know what to say . . . Dex."

"Don't say anything." Hilliard sat back as the waitress arrived with the second round of frosty stingers. Alison felt an easing of the pressure, as if he had been physically leaning on her. "You're not in a hurry to go home, are you? It's early yet. We don't have to hang around here. This place will start to go dead in another hour."

"I think maybe I'd better, Dex. It's been a long day." She smiled brightly. "I'm not like the rest of you, you're used to these fif-

154

teen-hour days. I'm still in training."

"This is part of the training," Hilliard laughed, unfazed. "Relax, Alison. Did I tell you . . . even Mr. Lederer is impressed with you."

The transparent lie irritated her. Lederer didn't even know she existed.

Alison experienced a sudden mental shift. The photos! She reached for her purse, glad of the diversion, then remembered that she'd left them on her dresser. "That reminds me . . . I told you I was on Guam in June?"

Hilliard stared at her, his glass suspended a few inches from his lips. "No . . . you never said anything . . ."

"Oh, I thought I did. Anyway, my sister Kim lives there. I was visiting her before starting to work here. I knew I might not be doing any traveling for a long time, so I took the time out. Kim sent me some snapshots she took while I was there. I thought I had them with me but I must have left them in my apartment." She knew she was prattling, but she didn't care. Anything to divert him from the seduction scene. "And guess what, Dex. Mr. Lederer was there."

Hilliard shook his head in disbelief. "I don't get this. What are you talking about? You were on Guam?"

"Yes! In June . . . the same time Mr. Lederer was there."

"You . . . no, no, that's impossible," Hilliard answered. "You mistook him for someone else. I mean, that was two months ago. You'd never met Lederer before the other night. Someone who looked like him —"

"That's what I'm trying to tell you. I didn't make a mistake." Alison grinned. She lowered her voice, inviting him to share her secret. "My sister took some snapshots at the hotel. Lederer's in them."

Dexter Hilliard's whole body language changed. For a moment his expression was slack, mouth open. Where he had been edging closer, even crowding her, now he drew back. She had the distinct impression that he wanted to get away from her. "No, I don't . . . you took pictures?"

"Now you've got it. That is, Kim did — my sister. She sent me a batch of photos. I just got them." Hilliard's reaction piqued her curiosity. Was it possible that he didn't know of Lederer's trip? "What's going on, Dex? What are Lederer and Tyler up to?"

"Who else have you told about this?"

Alison hesitated for a fraction of a second. "No one. Why?"

"Don't."

Her delight at dropping the bombshell had

begun to fade. She'd just about knocked Hilliard out of his socks, all right. But he wasn't impressed, or eager for details, or even shocked that she had stumbled onto something Calvin Lederer preferred to keep under wraps. He looked scared.

No seduction scene tonight, she realized, relieved but a little disturbed by the impact of her revelation.

"What's so important, Dex?"

"It's not important — that is, it's something we don't want to become public just yet. It's business, Alison. Major business, okay?" Hilliard scowled. He had begun to get hold of himself, but he remained shaken. "I wish to hell your sister hadn't taken those pictures. I wish you hadn't gotten involved."

"Involved in what? Come on, Dex, no one's going to see them. What's the problem? I mean, they're personal snapshots, not something Kim is going to sell to the TV station or the *Guam Gazette*. And I certainly wouldn't."

"Yes, yes, you're right, of course. I get a little edgy about Lederer's plans getting out, that's all."

A trio of associates stopped by their table, grinning wisely, as if to acknowledge that Dexter Hilliard and the new girl were an item. A couple of young women Alison didn't recognize had joined the men from her working group. "Hey, we're going across the street to Stepps. There's more action over there. Wanna come along?"

One of the associates laughed. "Unless you two want to be alone . . . ?"

"Alison was just leaving. She's tired," Hilliard said abruptly. He forced a smile. "She's not used to lawyers' hours yet."

"That's right," Alison said quickly, picking up the cue. "I'm whipped."

"Hell, we're just going to have to whip you into shape," the other lawyer said. "How about you, Dex? You coming?"

"Not tonight," Hilliard said. He was already on his feet. The drinks were pay-as-you-go, so there was no need to wait for a bill. Hilliard seemed eager to get away. He drew Alison aside. "Listen, are you okay with this? I mean, about . . . what we were talking about."

"No problem." Alison grinned. "Hey, I'll burn them, okay?"

Hilliard didn't think it was funny. He said he had forgotten something at the office he had to go back for. Did Alison mind if he didn't escort her to the garage? Great. They would talk later. Everything would be okay. After all, one of the things an attorney had to learn about was confidentiality. He knew she'd gotten the message.

Alison watched him hurry off. She'd gotten the message, all right. And Dexter Hilliard wasn't the only one who was feeling a little shaken.

The hastily called meeting took place in the office of George Broward, one of the senior partners at Bryant Forbes Lederer & Wyman, who was in charge of the Los Angeles office. Broward was a compact, aggressive man with heavy features and iron-gray hair. Twenty years ago he had been a guard on the University of Southern California football team, and he looked the part. He was angry. He didn't like being brought downtown on an emergency late Friday night, and he didn't like what he was hearing.

The firm's chief of security, Daryl Rathman, was the only one in the office who seemed unperturbed. He was a retired federal agent of some kind, FBI or DEA or Treasury, Hilliard wasn't sure which. He was big, with the heavily muscled neck, shoulders and biceps of a man who worked out with weights. Hilliard had no trouble believing he was very tough, and mean. Rathman thought he had a great sense of humor, but his humor always involved making someone else look foolish or inferior. It was laced with malice.

Dexter Hilliard eyed the two men uneasily.

He was the bad-news messenger, and Broward seemed to be blaming him for the problem. Rathman always made Hilliard nervous.

"Has she talked to anyone else about the photos?" Broward asked. "Has she shown them to anyone?"

"She says no. She just got them."

Broward glanced at Rathman, who was leaning against the wood-paneled door to the office as if guarding it so no one could get out. Rathman said, "She hasn't talked to anyone at the office."

"You're sure."

"We always listen in on the rookies. That doesn't mean she hasn't talked outside the building. We don't routinely bug their apartments."

Hilliard, who knew that the offices were bugged, was a little shocked at how extensive the coverage must be if Rathman could be so certain that Alison Carey hadn't talked about the photos.

"Is she particularly friendly with anyone? Go out with anyone from the office?"

"I'm sure she doesn't," Hilliard said quickly. "You can't keep that kind of thing quiet here."

Rathman regarded him with sleepy eyes, as if to say, Children should be seen and not heard. "She's tight with that young guy we've been keeping an eye on, the one with the big mouth, Daulton."

"Kevin Daulton?" Hilliard was dismayed. "She's worked with him a couple of nights on the prospectus, but . . ."

Rathman said nothing as Hilliard's protest trailed off. His silence made Hilliard feel foolish, as if he had overlooked something obvious. He tried to remember whether or not he had noticed Daulton and Carey together other than when they were paired in the working group. Damn it, he had assigned them together himself a couple of times! He didn't like the thought that they might be close — that he might have thrown them together.

"I don't think she'll show the pictures to anyone. I think I impressed on her that wouldn't be a good idea. And she's real ambitious. She wants to get ahead, and she doesn't want to wait at the end of a long line. She won't do anything to damage her career with us."

"She already has," said Broward.

"She's not really to blame." Hilliard had given Carey a highly favorable rating on her first month's evaluation. If she looked bad, he looked bad. "They're just innocent family snapshots. It was a fluke."

"She's kept asking questions about Lederer," Rathman pointed out. "She's nosy.

And she brought up the subject of those photos with you. If she wants to get on a fast track, maybe she thinks those pictures will help her."

"It wasn't like that at all," Hilliard insisted. "She was just curious, that's all. She won't be a problem. I'll talk to her again, tell her to bury those pictures. Better yet, I'll ask her to bring them in and give them to me. She'll do it if she knows it's to her advantage."

"That's not good enough," Broward said. "You don't say anything else to her about them, Hilliard. Anything you said now would only make matters worse." He turned to Rathman. "We can't take any chances those photos might show up, even by accident."

Rathman looked pleased. "I'll take care of it."

Dexter Hilliard felt an irrational panic. Everything was spinning out of control. "You're not going to . . . ?" He couldn't finish the question.

The security chief grinned at him. "Whatever it takes, junior. Whatever it takes."

Fourteen

After five years in Washington, D.C., where few secrets survived, David Perez harbored a closely guarded one: he still found the view of the Capitol dome inspiring in the morning light. It symbolized history's most extensive effort at government subject to the will of the people. Capitol Hill, where he worked every day, was engulfed in its aura of power. The White House, home of presidents since the time of the second chief executive, John Adams. The Mall, thronged in the daytime with its parade of tourists. As much as when he first stood before them in awe, he continued to revere the Lincoln Memorial's massive, brooding silence, the glowing white beauty of the Jefferson Memorial reflected in the tidal basin by moonlight, and the Vietnam Veterans Memorial, less a monument to heroism than to grief.

He had trouble sharing these emotions. The

pervasive cynicism of his peers, the young men and women on the Hill who served as aides and assistants and secretaries to senators or representatives in Congress, recommended silence. And he was further constrained because he still felt like an outsider. Politicians might give lip service to the homogeneity of American society, but in Washington David Perez was still a brown-skinned Hispanic, and that made him different.

Even though it was Saturday, he was working late in Senator Woods's offices in the Dirksen Senate Office Building, thinking of a solitary stroll along the Mall before dinner, when the paneled door pushed open. A mass of shoulder-length blond curls poked into view. "Okay, Perez, you win — you get the prize."

David recognized her instantly. Lisa Gardner was a familiar face on Capitol Hill, where she seemed to be on a first-name basis with everyone who counted. She worked for Thomas & Witmer, one of the city's most influential lobbying firms. Its clients included at least a dozen Fortune 500 companies, and countries ranging from Taiwan to Turkey. The last Republican secretary of the Treasury was a principal in the firm. The former chairman of the Democratic party worked for Thomas & Witmer as a consultant.

"Prize for what?" he asked, more than a little intimidated by the young woman's striking looks.

"For being the only one left in this building doing real work on a Saturday in August, in defiance of all common sense."

"What's the prize?"

"A party. Free drinks, and all the food you can eat. And you get to take me, of course."

"How'd I get so lucky?"

"It must be your karma. Or maybe the fact that that son of a bitch, the honorable junior senator from Oklahoma, stood me up. It seems his wife wants him back in Ada." Lisa Gardner's blue eyes were amused. "Anyway, it's too early in the evening to know just how lucky you are. All I need is an escort."

"That's lucky enough for me." David began stuffing files into his desk, turning off lights. "Whose party?"

"The Japanese ambassador's."

It was the first inkling David Perez had that there may have been more to the invitation than luck. "Is the ambassador a client?"

"We have a bunch of Japanese clients, but . . . no, not the Japanese government." Lisa Gardner laughed, showing absolutely perfect white teeth. "The government isn't as important as our clients. Don't be so uptight, David. Nobody's going to corrupt you in public. In

165

fact, this gig is right up your alley. There'll be all kinds of VIPs there, including a bunch of trade specialists of every persuasion. You might even meet some people you ought to know."

"I wasn't really worried about it."

"Yes, you were." She linked an arm with his as they went out the door. David Perez had a limited knowledge of perfumes, but he felt that Lisa Gardner's must be something like Eternity or Escape or Passion, one of those exotic scents featured in enigmatic advertisements on television. "Relax, David. I think you're going to enjoy yourself."

David Perez had no doubt of it.

If anything, Lisa Gardner had downplayed the importance of the party, which was held in a ballroom at the Watergate Hotel, an enormous room dominated by huge crystal chandeliers. David Perez managed to retain his composure while he smiled and nodded at more important personages than he would have thought were left in the city in late August. In the crowd he glimpsed two network anchormen, Senators Ted Kennedy and Robert Dole, the secretary of defense and the president's national security advisor. Two of the capital's more famous hostesses vied for attention on what was presumably neutral territory. The imminent summit had to be the reason, he guessed. Two of the Japanese trade negotiators were present, surrounded by their American counterparts.

"What did I tell you?" Lisa asked, as they sipped champagne and eyeballed the room. "There's a who's who of the trade world in this room right now."

David Perez nodded. He had already spotted several deputy U.S. trade representatives on the White House staff. He recognized other trade specialists from State and Treasury and the Commerce Department's ITA, along with important congressional staffers from both the Foreign Affairs and Finance committees of the House and Senate. One staff man on the House Ways and Means Subcommittee on Trade failed to conceal his surprise at seeing David there.

"See the bald guy with the potbelly?" Lisa Gardner said. "The one talking to Barbara Walters? He's a former commissioner of the International Trade Commission. He's a registered lobbyist for MITI now. We tried to hire him."

"He works for the Japanese ministry?"

"Sure, why not? He has what they want."

"But he was involved on our side of the trade negotiations with Japan two years ago."

"Uh-huh. Which means he knows

America's game plan, not to mention plan B and plan C. So if you were the Japanese, who would you hire to flack for you?"

Spotting a client, Lisa abruptly deserted David, telling him to circulate. David wandered over to a long table with a life-size swan sculpted in ice, surrounded by heaps of hors d'oeuvres. He filled a glass plate with stuffed shrimp, pecan halves filled with cream cheese, miniature crab balls, crackers and some crumbly English Stilton cheese. Across the room Lisa Gardner talked animatedly with two Japanese men in regulation dark suits. She stooped a little, rounding her shoulders, to put herself at eye level with them. She laughed at something one of the men said.

"Well, Perez . . . what do you think?"

Beautiful, he almost said. He recognized Gerry Toomey, an attorney with the United States Trade Representative. He had met Toomey once when the attorney appeared at a Senate Finance Committee hearing. Toomey greeted him with the warm affection of an old friend.

"It's quite a party," David said.

"Wheelers and dealers." Toomey smiled in a way that suggested he and David were in on a private joke. "Good to see you here. You can do yourself some good in this company."

"I'm just visiting," David answered. "How

are things at the USTR? You guys must be busy getting ready for the summit."

"Oh, didn't you know? I left the USTR . . . I'm with Reeves and Summerton." Toomey named a prominent Washington lobbyist law firm with private and governmental clients in Denmark and Germany, as well as Kobiashi Electronics and Nakasone Steel in Japan. "Working the other side of the fence, you might say."

Perez gazed around the room, a sea of familiar faces and glittering reputations, and wondered aloud. "Half these people are still in the government. . . ."

Toomey laughed. "And the other half used to be. We get a new crew voted in next year, the first half will all be lining up at the foreign troughs. Japan alone is spending about $500 million lobbying in this country this year. That's half a *billion*, David. Where you have that kind of a money spigot turned on . . ." The attorney shrugged.

After a few minutes Toomey headed back to the bar for another drink. David Perez finished the shrimp and the stuffed pecan halves, and started on the crackers and cheese. The Stilton was delicious. He snagged another flute of champagne from a passing waiter, wishing it were an ice-cold Corona.

Lisa Gardner was flirting with a white-haired man who looked like the CEO of Standard Oil of New Jersey.

Another distinguished white-haired man joined David. Harold Henning had been the international trade commissioner when David first came to Washington. "It's Perez, isn't it?"

David nodded, bemused by the experience of being treated as an equal at this level of the nation's movers and shakers.

"I remember you from Senator Cranston's staff, am I right?"

"I was on the senator's staff one summer when I was still in school," David said. "That was seven years ago. You have a good memory, Mr. Henning."

"Well, yes, thank you . . ." Henning wasn't quite sure where that placed him now, David decided, and whether or not it was still important to stroke him. "And now you're with . . . ?"

David grinned, and let him off the hook. "I'm administrative aide to Senator Woods."

"Yes, yes, of course!" Henning beamed, relieved that he had not wasted his time. "Well. . . . the senator created quite a stir for a few days there, with that Japanese fund business. That's behind us now, I guess."

"I couldn't say."

"Naturally, discretion and all that . . . but the Senate's now in recess. By the time it's

170

back in session the president will be in Osaka signing a deal with our Japanese friends. I mean . . . your committee will be moving on to more pressing matters."

"I can't really comment on that, Mr. Henning. You understand."

"Yes, quite right." Henning patted him on the shoulder. "All that Japan bashing . . . we need to put that sort of thing behind us, Perez. We're economic partners, actually. You know, I'm representing Kirabashi Construction now. We're doing a number of major projects here in the U.S., including that new Sakai automobile plant in Fresno. The first phase will bring about eight hundred new jobs to Fresno, and there'll be more as the project develops. Everyone benefits."

Everyone benefits. It could have been the slogan for the evening's party, David thought.

"Are U.S. companies being allowed to bid on big Japanese construction projects?" he asked innocently.

Henning brushed the question aside. "I think you'll find a lot of those questions are going to be answered in Osaka. This economic summit can be a turning point, Perez. God knows, the U.S. economy needs some good news for a change. We're choking on all the negative things. That's what's eroded consumer confidence."

That, and being out of work, David thought.

"What are you two hatching?" Lisa Gardner asked.

The former ITC commissioner's shoulders snapped back and his stomach pulled in. "Lisa, my dear!"

"We were discussing construction projects," David said, wondering if any work had been done on Lisa's chest. It needed no enhancement, he decided. Unless, of course, that little brown mole really was an add-on beauty mark. He considered how he might ask her.

"Harold, don't try to steal David. I had my eye on him first."

"Well, all's fair," Henning said, beaming at David. "I can tell you, son, that Kirabashi would be very, very interested in talking to a young man who's been chief of staff to a member of the Senate Finance Committee. Those credentials are gold card in this city's job market."

"I still have a job. I'm very happy working for the senator."

Henning smiled. "Of course. But things can change very quickly, can't they? I mean, there's another election coming up next year. Senator Woods will be up for a new term, won't she?"

"Yes."

"There you are. You never know, do you?" Henning's touch was comradely on David's shoulder. "I'm glad we had this little talk. Think about it, David. And advise the senator to drop that fund matter, in her own best interests. Good to see you . . . and it's *always* good to see you, Lisa."

When the former commissioner moved off, Lisa Gardner grinned at David. "I guess I can't leave you alone, can I? You're quite the operator."

"Am I?"

"I leave you for a little while and when I come back you have job offers dangling from your lapel. From Kirabashi, no less!"

"It wasn't exactly an offer."

"Yes, it was. Big time. Kirabashi is part of the Sakai Group family, and they're tied up with Miyaki Industries."

"Is that good?"

"Miyaki is one of Japan's largest investors in the U.S. Real estate, auto parts, electronics . . . you name it. And you know about Sakai."

"I'm as ambitious as the next man," David said. "But I'm not looking for a job."

Lisa's blue eyes studied him seriously. She used her eyes the way movie actresses did, shifting them back and forth so they drew your attention. "You have to think of yourself, David. Henning is right, Woods might not always be there."

"I'll cross that bridge when I come to it."

Another congressman came by — he was either from Kentucky or Tennessee, David thought, kicking himself for not being sure — and seized Lisa by the elbow. "Settle an argument for us, Lisa, my girl. You don't mind if I steal her away for a few minutes, do you, sport?"

David minded, but he indulged the man. The representative carried her off to a group on the other side of the ballroom. Lisa seemed to know all of them, acknowledging each new greeting as if it were the single most important of the night. Her job, David told himself. She was very good at it. Thomas & Witmer was getting its money's worth.

He drifted, acknowledging greetings here and there, staring at faces he had seen only on television or on motion picture screens. Found himself with a group of his peers, staffers to assorted congressmen, mostly young men and women who are called Washington's invisible government. David hovered on the fringe of the group, listening to the gossip and shop talk, every once in a while searching the room for another glimpse of Lisa Gardner.

Billy Ray Johnson appeared beside him. He was Senator Joshua Bodine's chief of staff, a

Georgian in his late thirties, tall and lanky, with a prominent adam's apple and skin damaged by acne.

"Surprised to see you here, buddy boy," said Billy Ray.

"I'm kind of surprised myself."

"Not exactly your kind of company, you know what I mean? You and the senator, I don't mind tellin' you, I'm surprised you all would go in for that racist bull."

"What the hell are you talking about?"

"You know, trying to make the Japanese look bad."

"Senator Woods isn't anti-Japanese, she's pro-American."

"Save that for the media clods, buddy boy." Billy Ray drew David a few feet away from the others, retaining his grip on David's arm. "The chairman's really pissed at your girl."

"If you mean Senator Woods, I think Bodine is on the record."

"She didn't do herself any good. Y'all ought to know better than that. You still carryin' on that witch hunt?"

"Witch hunt?"

"Y'all know what I mean. I hear you've been rootin' around, tryin' to dig up dirt, like that O Fund. Woods pulls off another stunt like that, Senator Bodine will ride her out of this town on a rail."

"California voters will have something to say about that."

"Not a whole hell of a lot, buddy boy, not a whole hell of a lot." Billy Ray's small, shrewd eyes searched David's. "Y'all find out anything more about that fund? I hear you've been callin' around."

"No one wants to talk about it."

"It's ancient history, man! You better leave it buried." Billy Ray grinned slyly. "But maybe I don't have to tell you that, you bein' here at this hoedown tonight, am I right?"

"You never know," David said.

He considered how many people he had met tonight seemed eager to offer him good advice, which invariably included getting along with the Japanese. Well, it was their party, he thought.

He had always got along very well with in-dividual Japanese-Americans he had known, including several in his classes at Stanford. The same went for Japanese representatives of var-ious agencies or companies he had encoun-tered in his work with the Senate committee. That wasn't the point, David thought. The question wasn't whether we could get along with the Japanese people, much as we had learned we could like the Russians if we had the chance. The question was, what was the Japanese government after? What were the people in charge up to? For that matter, who was in control, the reactionary supernationalists, or the more moderate voices in the Diet?

What was the summit all about?

What did the O Fund have to do with it, if anything? It seemed to be a sticky subject with a lot of people.

David surveyed the food tables again, picked at some pure white chicken breast in a delicate white sauce, and decided he wasn't hungry anymore.

Nevertheless, he was impressed with the spread and the Japanese ambassador's party. This wasn't such a bad way to live. A long way from East L.A., David thought.

And here tonight, he didn't feel like an outsider at all.

They left together at midnight. David was a little surprised that Lisa Gardner was actually leaving with him. Lisa handed him the keys, and they drove off in her car, a sleek white Acura coupe (was Honda a client?).

She leaned back in the seat and closed her eyes. A spill of long blond curls drowned the headrest.

"Tired?"

"I'll recover." Blue eyes popped open, and the infectious grin hovered. "I'll answer the question of the night, just in case you weren't going to ask."

"I'll bite."

"I hope so. Let's make it your place, okay?"

David Perez decided he wasn't going to argue.

Fifteen

Vodka hangovers were supposed to be somehow milder than other hangovers. Beer hangovers usually ended up with the victim on his knees hanging over a toilet bowl wishing he were dead. Gin sickness actually turned your stomach inside out. And a bourbon morning-after left you unable to stand up, with a medieval torture ring binding your skull. Vodka, on the other hand, not only left your breath sweet but your morning sunny.

That was the Big Lie.

Kevin Daulton lay helpless in bed Sunday morning. If he could get up, he thought, without his brain slamming against his skull pan and the room reeling, he would seek out Brian Wilson, his neighbor, and confront him. He would plead manslaughter. No jury would convict him.

Brian had impressed him the night before, like an innocent snatched from the docks and thrown into the British Navy, for his party. He needed male bodies, Brian said.

Brian had an obsession with cute forms of vodka, and nothing would do but that Kevin should sample them all. There was a lemon-flavored vodka, one with orange, and one that tasted of licorice. They came in small sampler bottles; Brian never said where he got them. Kevin remembered sharing a small bottle late in the evening with a small, snuggly redhead. The vodka had had an apple flavor. The girl's lipstick was strawberry flavored. Kevin didn't know what had become of her. She wasn't in his bed or under it, which was a relief.

When the telephone started ringing Kevin swore at it weakly. It kept on ringing. He lost count of the rings. After they stopped there was a period of blissful silence. Kevin prayed that the phone wouldn't erupt again. After all, it was Sunday morning.

He prayed in vain. The jangling scream mocked him. This time, whoever was calling was determined. Kevin counted up to fifteen rings before he grabbed the instrument in desperation.

"Kevin? I've been trying to reach you."

It was a trick, he thought miserably. One of Brian's girlfriends had been assigned to torment him. Simple murder wouldn't be enough for Brian, he thought. There would have to be torture first.

"Are you all right? I need to see you."

Kevin managed to sit up. He held onto the edge of the nightstand because the bed kept going round and round. "Uh . . . Alison? Is that you?"

"Yes. Are you sure you're all right?"

"No . . . yes. I had too much vodka." He spoke as if offering the answer to the mystery of the universe.

"Oh. I see. . . ."

"No, no, I'm okay. I mean, I will be. What is it? Is something wrong?"

"I need to talk to you."

Kevin groaned aloud. This was a cruel nightmare, it couldn't be happening. Alison Carey needed him, and he couldn't even make it as far as the door of his apartment.

"Kevin?"

"Yes, I'm here. Listen . . . that is, when? Where are you?"

"At my apartment. If it's too much trouble, if you're not feeling well, forget it. I shouldn't have —"

"No!" Kevin cried out. "I mean, it's no trouble. Just give me time to get some clothes on, give Alka-Seltzer a try."

"Do you know where I live? I'm in Manhattan Beach."

"Ah . . . I'm sure the address is on our

working group list, right? I'll find it." The room had momentarily stopped swimming. He hung onto the nightstand grimly.

"Would you like breakfast? There's a place just around the corner — "

"Oh, no! That is . . . I may never eat again. Just some coffee maybe. Listen, I'll be there" — he cast about desperately for a time frame — "in an hour. Is that okay?"

"That's fine. It'll give me time to eat something. I have to get out of here. And . . . thanks, Kevin."

He stared at the phone after she hung up. It was a fantasy come true, and the worst moment of his life. He didn't pay attention to Alison's last words until, a half-hour later, he was sitting in his car, his heart and his head pounding, sweat beading on his forehead. Only then did he wonder why she had to get out of her apartment.

Alison Carey was waiting for him on the sidewalk outside her apartment building when Kevin pulled into the street, searching unsuccessfully for a parking space. She waved him toward a vacant space in the parking area beneath the building. "My next-door neighbor," Alison explained when Kevin clambered out of his car. "He doesn't use his space — doesn't drive."

"How can anyone not drive in this city?" Kevin stared at her. "You look great."

Alison studied him critically. "You look awful."

She had been poured into a pair of white-washed jeans and a knit top that displayed her figure far more advantageously than her work clothes. Her hair was casually brushed, and she appeared to be wearing no makeup other than a trace of lipstick. Kevin decided he liked the weekend version even better than the lawyer at the office. "What's up?" he asked.

"Have you eaten anything?"

"Don't mention food."

"That bad, huh. How about coffee?"

"We can try coffee."

"There's a café down on the oceanfront. We can sit outside. Or we can just walk along the beach."

"Let's try sitting."

The café consisted of a counter and a half-dozen tables under awnings. It was only a few steps from the sand. The day was already warm, and the beach was beginning to fill up. The usual early morning overcast was burning off rapidly, and the brightness hurt Kevin's eyes.

He squinted at Alison over his coffee mug. "You sounded upset on the phone."

Her lips tightened. "Not just upset. Mad. And . . . as if I'd been . . ." She stared across the beach toward the water. She had sounded close to tears. "They say when you've been robbed, it's like rape. You feel as if you've been violated. Like finding out you've been undressing while some creep has been peeping through a crack in the window shade."

"You've been robbed?"

"Yes . . . in my apartment."

"You were there? Did he — ?"

She shook her head emphatically. "It must have happened last night while I was at the movies. That new Costner picture."

"I've wanted to see that," Kevin said, wishing he had seen it with her. *She doesn't want to discuss movies,* his alter ego voice, which had been unnervingly silent, said caustically.

"That's the only time it could have happened. You see, they were there yesterday afternoon. I looked at them."

"At what? What did they take?" Kevin was becoming more incredulous as the story sank in. Alison — burglarized! Someone had broken into her apartment while she was away. He could have been waiting for her when she came back from the movie!

"That's just it, Kevin. This was no ordinary burglary. They — or he — didn't take my TV or the stereo or my camera, or any of

184

my jewelry. All they took were those snap-shots."

Kevin, whose head was still pounding, felt stupid. "What snapshots?"

"The ones I told you about — the pictures my sister sent me from Guam."

The shoe dropped. Kevin sat erect. He moved too quickly, and his brain crashed against the top of his skull. "Are you . . . that is, are you sure they're missing? You didn't just put them someplace? I'm always losing —"

He stopped when he saw the expression on her face. *You're a born loser,* his critical voice said.

"I didn't misplace them, Kevin." She spaced out her next words deliberately. "Someone — broke — in — and — stole — them."

"But who would . . . ?"

Alison watched the answer dawn in his eyes. "That's right. Who would want those pictures to disappear? Who in all the world would give a damn about some vacation snapshots?"

"Lederer." *Elementary, Sherlock.* "But why?"

"That's the question, isn't it? I'm gonna find out why."

"Uh . . . maybe you should take it easy, Alison. You don't know for sure. I can't see Calvin Lederer crawling through one of your

185

windows. Was there any sign of breaking and entering?"

"No, nothing. And it wouldn't have been Lederer himself," Alison said impatiently. "He'd have had it done. It would have been professional. They didn't want to leave any sign. They want me to think I misplaced those photos."

Kevin wished he didn't have a hangover. He was having trouble thinking clearly. He wished it was next Sunday, and Alison Carey had called him up to invite him over, and they would go strolling along the beach hand in hand. Maybe slip into their bathing suits and go for a swim, and he would admire her bikini while they lay on their towels to dry off and bake in the sun. His inner voice didn't even bother to scoff.

"Let's walk. I can't just sit here. This thing has really gotten to me. Can you walk?"

"Sure, I'm fine. Coffee was just the ticket."

He thought of himself as Sidney Carton going bravely to the guillotine for her sake. He would walk along the beachfront.

"I'm not going to let this go," she said after they had been walking for a while. Kevin was actually beginning to feel a little better, whether it was from the coffee or the exercise or the exhilaration of being with Alison. "I've been violated, and I'm going to find out why."

"I know how you feel, but . . . how are you gonna do that? You can't prove anything." He thought of something. "How would Lederer even know about those pictures?"

Alison glanced at him, her blue eyes holding something that might have been approval of his perceptiveness. "I mentioned them to Dexter Hilliard."

"Dex? You were with Dex?"

"I don't know why I told him about them. Maybe I just wanted to see if I could get a rise out of him. Maybe I just wanted to know why the secrecy. Anyway, after I mentioned the photos he couldn't get away from me fast enough — which wasn't what he'd had in mind earlier." She paused, her expression thoughtful. They had walked about a mile along the oceanfront by this time, and Kevin was feeling almost human. He knew what Hilliard had had in mind. "I think he had to report in a hurry. Does that make sense? It means that meeting in Guam really was important . . . and covering it up is just as important."

"Now they can simply deny it happened. Without the pictures there's no proof of anything. Even I didn't believe you when you first told me. They must have rigged the seminar. Lederer's live, in-studio performance

187

must have been on tape. That's a pretty elaborate charade, but . . . it wouldn't be hard to do."

"Not if you planned it carefully."

They turned back along the beach, walking more slowly. A bicyclist almost ran them down and, oblivious, raced on along the path. The sun was climbing toward its zenith, and Kevin was sweating. A volleyball match had started along one stretch of the beach, drawing a crowd of tanned, healthy young bodies. Kevin thought of his own untanned, unhealthy young body. He hadn't spent as much time at the beach this summer as he'd hoped. His workdays were too long. Maybe going for a swim wouldn't be the best suggestion, not yet. He would get out the sun lamp at night, start jogging in the morning, get back in shape.

"Have you been listening?"

"Uh . . . sure . . ." *That's right, go ahead, blow it! Your one chance, probably the only one you'll ever have with her.*

"Will you do it?"

Kevin considered the possibilities. Should he just say yes, regardless? Should he admit that he hadn't been listening, which was tantamount to saying he didn't take her situation seriously? She'd been robbed. She was mad as hell and wasn't going to take it anymore.

"If that's what you want," he said.

"Good!" Alison smiled up at him, and took his arm as they walked along, her hip brushing against his. "The sooner the better. They won't be expecting me to do anything right away. And they certainly won't suspect you."

"No reason to."

"It must have something to do with Tyler. That's the only thing that makes sense to me. We just have to get a look at those Tyler Holdings files and see if there's anything there."

Kevin Daulton felt as if the ground were dropping away under his feet. A chasm loomed. A pit into which his career was about to fall. The inner mocking voice whispered over his shoulder, *She's using you. It isn't* we *who are going to be sticking our necks out, it's* you.

Alison hugged his arm. "I can't get at those files, I don't even have a key to the offices. But you do. You're an associate, you're in and out of there all the time. It'll probably have to be after hours, though, don't you think? When no one's around?"

"Probably." He licked his dry lips. "It doesn't have to be anything sinister — what Lederer's up to, I mean. Just something he doesn't want to go public with."

"I know that. But I keep thinking . . . what if I'd been there? Or what if I'd come back when the thief was still in my apartment?

189

What would he have done?" She stared up at Kevin. "How big is this? That's the real question, isn't it? How far would they go?"

That's when Kevin knew that he really was going to do what she wanted him to do.

Three thousand miles away, on that same Sunday morning, David Perez awakened in his Arlington apartment to a remarkable vision.

The miniblinds over the bedroom window were in the open position. The window was open to a light breeze that stirred the curtains. Bars of light spilled across the sleeping Lisa Gardner.

David lay still for awhile, not wanting to awaken her, remembering their frantic coupling.

"I'm awake," Lisa said drowsily.

"Good morning."

She propped herself up on an elbow and regarded him with her friendly, infectious grin. "Do you serve breakfast to your conquests?"

"Scrambled eggs and bacon okay?"

David didn't feel like a conqueror. He had been overwhelmed. He felt grateful, and a little smug, but his satisfaction was not unalloyed. There was a nagging doubt at the back of his mind.

Over breakfast, wearing one of his T-shirts, Lisa Gardner chattered about the Japanese ambassador's party, supplying tidbits of gossip about the guests. She wolfed down a plate of scrambled eggs, bacon, warmed-over potatoes and two slices of raisin toast. A woman of splendid appetites, David thought.

"You even make good coffee," Lisa said. "How come you're not married?"

"No time."

"Too busy getting ahead? Tell me about it. Maybe you haven't met the right woman."

"Maybe I did last night."

Lisa grinned. "Don't get ahead of yourself. You ever hear about answered prayers? How you'd better be careful about what you pray for, because you might live to regret it? Well, I'm one of those prayers."

"I don't believe that."

"Trust me."

They sipped coffee in agreeable silence, Lisa's gaze amused, David's admiring the use to which his T-shirt was being put. He would never wash it, he decided.

The nagging doubt resurfaced.

"So where do you think the tip came from?" Lisa asked idly.

"What tip?"

"About the O Fund. You know . . . what we talked about last night. That really was far out, David, comparing me to an O."

He didn't remember making the comparison. He didn't think he would have forgotten. In fact, he didn't remember the conversation at all.

"It was an anonymous tip."

"Anonymous? And Senator Woods took it seriously enough to bring it up at the hearing?"

"We both took it seriously."

"Oh wow. She really stuck her neck out. You said it was a letter, right?"

David hesitated. "Yes."

"And you still don't have any idea who sent it? Any letterhead?"

"No. Why all the questions?"

"Just curious. Going public like that wasn't very smart, David. Of the senator, I mean. You know that."

"She tends to act in terms of what she thinks is right, not what's smart."

"How long do you think she'll last in Washington if she acts that way? This town eats people like that for breakfast."

David Perez was feeling very uneasy. What had he told Lisa last night? How much did she know?

"Why are you staring at me that way? Is it the shirt?"

"The shirt looks terrific."

"What's wrong?"

"I guess I should have known when you told me about the senator from Oklahoma standing you up. Maybe I did know. I just didn't want to believe it."

"Believe what?"

"You got what you came for, Lisa. I think maybe you should go."

"Do you think I came on to you just to get information? Oh, David, you don't even *have* any information."

"You didn't know that."

"I got stood up! What's so hard to believe about that? David . . . I like you. We were good together, okay? We're in the same business, so I ask questions. That's me. It's no devious plot to get David Perez to betray his sacred trust."

"We're not in the same business. We're on opposite sides of the fence."

She stood up, quivering in places, looking extraordinarily sexy and beautiful. "What's with you anyway? Are you getting it on with the senator, is that it? You think you're protecting her?"

"I'm sorry, Lisa, I really am. . . ."

"Don't be such a jerk. This is deal town, David. Don't tell me that's not why you're here. I took you where you could meet some people who could do you some good. Is that so terrible?"

"No. I . . . I'm glad you asked me. I really am. I did talk to some people — important people. It was fascinating."

Lisa Gardner began to calm down. "I need a cigarette. You don't smoke either, do you? I bet you don't smoke."

"No. I make dumb remarks, but I don't smoke."

She sat down abruptly and stared out the window. "You're not so dumb."

"A minute ago you wouldn't have said that."

"A minute ago I was Hurricane Lisa."

"You sure were."

Lisa turned to face him, blue eyes unflinching. "I might as well tell you . . . you were right."

"What do you mean?"

"When I stopped by your office yesterday. I knew you were there."

David Perez felt deflated. He hated to be right sometimes. He said nothing.

"Some of the people I work for, they're curious about that O Fund business . . . where it came from."

"I see. No senator from Ada, I guess."

"No."

"I didn't think a senator from Ada would have stood you up. I especially don't think so after last night."

She smiled crookedly. "Is that supposed to be a backhanded compliment?"

"Sort of."

There was a long silence.

"Think it over," Lisa said finally. "You can really go places in this town, David. Nobody's asking you to rob a bank, or sell your soul."

"What are you asking?"

Lisa shrugged. The T-shirt stirred. "Let me know what the senator is thinking, okay? Like with this fund. If you find out any more . . . or you know more than you're telling . . ."

"Okay, I'll think it over."

They rose, went into the living room, and Lisa began to collect her clothes from where she had dropped them. She went into the bathroom, as if she had had a sudden attack of modesty. David rinsed their dishes and arranged them in the dishwasher. Ten minutes later she was out, fully dressed, mass of blond curls shining, looking, David thought, as if no one had laid a glove on her.

At the door she grinned up at him. "Don't wait too long, David. This is deal town, but . . . deals are like people. You don't want to let the right one get away."

"I'll call you," David said.

The door closed. He felt physically sick. He had been duped, but that wasn't the worst of it. The worst was that he might have betrayed Senator Woods — and everything he had worked for during the past six years of his life.

Sixteen

Shinji Sakai's office reflected the many facets of the man. Smooth woods glowing with the patina of many layers of polish. Thick, elegant, light gray carpets with the softness of down. Modern steel sculptures juxtaposed with nineteenth century French impressionist paintings, both of which Sakai collected. Walls of glass open to the city, the Imperial Palace gardens and, in the distance, Mount Fuji, in an office accessible only through the most sophisticated security measures designed to ensure its privacy. Similarly, the man resisted categories. He was ruthless in business dealings, yet known for his generosity. A devoted family man who kept a mistress in a Tokyo apartment even his executives couldn't afford. Urbane and worldly, he was fanatically devoted to the emperor and to the purity of Japanese traditions.

Politically there was no ambivalence,

Toshio Miyaki thought. Sakai brought to mind what the American opposition used to call their President Reagan: a Neanderthal. A Neanderthal in a silk suit hand-tailored in Hong Kong, tapping a French filter cigarette against a gold case specially made to the measure of the long, thin cigarettes.

"It was necessary to act quickly," Shinji Sakai said, lighting one of the slender cigarettes. "You were in the country, I believe. An attempt was made to reach you without success."

"I would have made myself available, you know that. To change our plans now, so abruptly, without a complete exchange of views, seems impetuous."

Miyaki did not say what he was thinking: *Last minute changes are often foolish, always dangerous.*

The Sonno Group's plans had been meticulously developed and refined over many years, each step debated at length. Adherents had been recruited at every level, from students at the University of Tokyo to out-of-work steelworkers in Youngstown, Ohio, their roles as carefully blocked out as those of actors in a play. Lobbying measures had been crafted that would head off or soften the potential for angry reprisals. Billions of yen, converted into local currencies, had been electronically moved to banks and financial institutions in Hong Kong, Los Angeles, New York, London, Grand Cayman, Zurich. The timetable had been set as precisely as the battle plan for a military operation. The smallest detail of the conspiracy had been subjected to examination and reexamination. And now . . .

"Our plans have not changed, my friend. Only the timing. And that was always to a certain extent dependent upon the Americans."

"Not always."

The more fanatical nationalists in the Sonno Group had argued for action to coincide with the anniversary of the dropping of atomic bombs on Hiroshima and Nagasaki. The desirability of having the American president not only out of his country but on Japanese soil, and the ink still wet on an economic agreement, had forced the adoption of a more realistic agenda, adapted to President Walton's schedule for the summit.

Sakai's smile was a thin line of steel, like one of his elegant sculptures. "To act on the anniversary would have been an exquisite irony."

"But we chose not to do so for very good reasons. We did not act hastily or rashly. Why should we do so now?"

"Every possibility can't be anticipated. Who

would have thought the American Senate would suddenly begin to ask questions about the O Fund? This Senator Woods, a woman, has apparently initiated an investigation. The Senate is now in recess. Little will be done until it reconvenes. But we can't ignore the possibility that her inquiries, or the investigations of reporters, will bear fruit."

"It seems unlikely, after all these years."

"We can't leave it to chance. Of all people, Toshio-san, you know that."

The O Fund, Miyaki thought. Everything always came back to the fund.

Like Shinji Sakai and many others, Miyaki had received his opportunity to start in business and to thrive through his access to the Sonno Group and the virtually unlimited resources of the fund. *Gaijin,* foreigners, usually attributed Japanese gains in world competition to the extensive government support provided to target industries, to the great pool of capital created in personal post office savings accounts held by almost all Japanese families, and to the willingness of Japanese industry to look at long-term advantage rather than short-term profits. Obviously, these were significant factors. Less obvious was the secret financing made available to chosen enterprises by Sonno. Japanese business partnerships were triangular, not linear. There was the manufacturing leg, the government leg, and the financial leg. Each was vital, but capital made the difference. Sonno support through the O Fund had enabled Japanese companies to devote enormous resources to research and development of new products — often exploiting ideas that originated in America. The Japanese were not creative innovators, but implementing new ideas in functional products was their strength. American industry, profit driven, unable or unwilling to look beyond the next stockholders' meeting, time and again had failed to devote significant resources to products or developments whose potential was visible only on a distant horizon. Over and over, in everything from new, efficient, multivalve automobile engines to semiconductors and supercomputers, Sonno capital had offered Japanese firms a competitive edge.

"Even so, there was time for reasoned discussion." *And I should have been present,* Miyaki thought.

Sakai nodded, for the first time acknowledging that excluding Miyaki from the hastily convened council meeting had not been entirely by chance or the inability to reach him in time. "There are those on the council who felt that we had to act quickly and aggressively, and that you might be . . . hesitant."

Miyaki stiffened. He was not disturbed

about loss of face, but by the implication of disloyalty. "Haven't I agreed to do what was asked of me?"

"Yes, my friend. But there are some who say your heart is not with us. I know you'll be true to your word, that's never been questioned. But perhaps it's best if you are not burdened with the necessity of decisions about which you may be reluctant."

"Would I be wrong in thinking this suggestion first came from Yashi Nogama?"

Sakai took his time answering. He blew smoke toward the tall window behind his desk, the smoke forming a perfect ring — a distraction, Miyaki thought. "He is not your friend."

"No. He is a gangster."

"We can't always choose the paths we take," Sakai replied. "But we can choose our goal. In this respect Nogama is one of us."

Attempts in business circles to legitimize the presence of criminal elements were hardly news to Miyaki. Many of the extortionists known as *sokaiya* had bought their way to respectability. But Yashi Nogama was even more of a thug, part of a deeper layer of criminality, the underworld *yakuza*. In a justification of the function such men performed in Japanese society, it was said that *yakuza* walked on the shady side of the street so that ordinary citizens might walk in the sun. They controlled the inevitable vices, such as gambling and prostitution. Their presence virtually eliminated violent street crime, the everyday shootings, robberies, rapes and assaults that were so commonplace in America. The streets of any Japanese city were safe at night.

Toshio Miyaki found such reasoning specious and self-serving. Yashi Nogama remained a gangster. His very presence in the Sonno Group undermined its integrity. And to have him not only a member of the governing council but exercising undeniable influence was galling.

Shinji Sakai approached him. He was half a head taller than Miyaki, but his body language was deferential rather than dominant. His attitude was one of respect to an elder as well as a friend. "We've been friends for many years, Toshio-san. Nothing can change that. But you must understand that in great battles we can't always choose those who would fight beside us."

The continued use of Miyaki's first name was unusual. Though the lives of the two men were closely woven, in personal as well as business affairs, they were not intimate friends. Miyaki, who was ten years older, had been instrumental in bringing Sakai into the

Sonno Group. Sakai's wife was Miyaki's cousin. Their business ties were strong. Sakai was one of Japan's major automobile manufacturers. Miyaki Electronics provided services, parts and equipment for Sakai facilities as well as its products. And Miyaki Investments, which owned one of Japan's largest banks, controlling interest in a major brokerage house, and a 20 percent ownership in one of the largest United States underwriting firms, had provided financial liquidity for many Sakai enterprises as well as for subsidiaries in the Sakai Group.

"We have embarked upon a course from which there is no turning back," Sakai said. "It's more important than any one individual . . . more important even than friendship. It will bring glory to the emperor and honor to Japan. It will be the victory we have waited so long for, in which we will all share. Surely this was your reason for pledging your support."

The manner and tone were urbane; the words rang of fanaticism. Hearing them, Miyaki felt a chill.

"There's no question of my loyalty to Sonno's cause."

"Good, good. I never doubted it. But the timing is now urgent. That's why we're compelled to act quickly. The timing of the first strike has been moved up. You will leave for Guam as soon as possible. The American will meet you there. I trust there will be no difficulty in arranging your affairs to meet the advanced schedule?"

"None. And Nogama will be accompanying me?" Miyaki failed to hide his distaste.

Sakai hesitated. "He won't be flying with you. He is already in Guam — he was called there on urgent personal business."

Another abrupt change in plans, Miyaki thought. The change was plausible enough — Nogama was now a major investor in foreign properties, especially in Guam, Hawaii, Los Angeles, San Francisco, and downtown Manhattan. But once again Miyaki was being informed after the fact. He had not been included in the circle of discussion, as if he were not trusted.

"He will join you there, Toshio-san."

"I would feel better if I were to travel alone."

Shinji Sakai frowned. "The enmity between you and Nogama must be set aside. This . . . gangster, as you call him, is useful to us. He may prove to be even more useful in the days ahead."

Miyaki thought of the elaborately orchestrated chain of events in which he would soon play a vital part. Every step had been meticulously charted. In those plans there was no role for a gangster.

Why was Nogama going with him to America?

What part had been written for him, so secret that it had never been disclosed, so clandestine that, even now, it must be hidden from Miyaki's view?

Seventeen

The offices of Bryant Forbes Lederer & Wyman occupied four floors in Pacific Plaza East. Corporate had an entire floor to itself, the sixteenth, with its own secretarial and support staff, including paralegals and a librarian. The library was in the center, behind the receptionist's desk, which faced the elevators through locked glass doors. There were conference rooms to either side of the reception area. The general secretarial pool, paralegals, proofreaders, reprographics and other support services were in the smaller east wing, which also had a kitchen and space for the summer interns, who were grouped in two small offices. The offices occupied by associates and partners were in the west wing. The size and appointments of each office were a measure of rank and seniority.

The Indians wing, as it was called, was accessible to anyone who penetrated the glass entry doors to the reception area. The corridor leading to offices reserved for Chiefs was secured by a separate locked door of heavy paneled oak. Each office in turn had its own deadbolt lock. These security precautions had been introduced six years ago after a disgruntled client walked into the law offices one afternoon, marched down the hallway to the office of an associate who had been handling his product liability case, and shot him twice, screaming obscenities. The associate, wounded in the hand and shoulder, had taken disability leave and retired early. The heavy oak door at the end of the corridor was installed the morning after the assault.

Kevin Daulton had no need to fake a reason for working late Monday in his small office on the north side of the building. The frequent work sessions on the Tyler Holdings registration statement and prospectus had consumed huge blocks of time over the past two months, causing work for other clients to be set aside. He had a brief to prepare on a case involving a contractor accused of using defective materials, a routine partnership agreement to draw up that had become less routine because one of the partners wanted to anticipate every possible contingency of disagreement (Kevin didn't give the partnership much of a chance), and an environmental impact case involving a Palm Springs developer who was building a golf course over what were arguably ancient Indian burial grounds. Not to mention a three-foot stack of contracts and other papers to read or execute for Claude DeGraff, the partner to whom Kevin had been assigned as an assistant.

DeGraff was one of three partners, including George Broward, the senior partner in charge of the firm's Los Angeles offices, who were responsible for the Tyler Holdings account. DeGraff was a takeover specialist. Early Monday morning he hinted to Kevin that they could very shortly expect to be working sixteen-hour days and seven-day weeks. Kevin took that to mean something new was definitely in the wind with Tyler Holdings. Did that mean Reynolds Tyler planned to use some of the capital raised in his stock offering for new acquisitions, either friendly or hostile?

At five o'clock Kevin walked down the hall to DeGraff's office. He had DeGraff's secretary buzz him. Kevin knew that DeGraff had a dinner appointment that evening; he would be leaving early.

"Kevin! Glad you stopped by — I was going to call you."

"I've got the preliminary draft on the Oberst Construction brief done. I thought you might want to take a quick look at it."

"No need — I'm sure you've handled it. Go ahead and have the finished draft typed up. I'll look at it tomorrow." He offered a mechanical smile. "If there's time. We're going to be busy as hummingbirds starting very shortly."

Kevin, who had averaged twelve-hour days through most of the summer, wondered what busy meant.

"Tyler?"

"He never stays quiet for long, does he?" The words were barely out of his mouth when DeGraff winced, gasped, and nearly doubled over at his desk. His face went pale. He was a blond Dutchman, his complexion normally a light pink; now it was the color of dead flesh. The partner was a Christian Scientist, and there had been whispers in the office of several recent incidents of severe, painful attacks. It was the first Kevin had witnessed.

"Are you all right, sir?"

"Fine, fine . . . give me a moment." DeGraff forced himself to sit up. The cost of the effort was visible in beads of sweat on his forehead. "Out of sync, that's all . . . bit of indigestion. Let's see . . . where were we?"

"You said you were going to call me."

"Did I? Oh, yes . . . I want you to get some Tyler materials pulled together."

"The prospectus?"

"No, no, that's a done deed." Some color was returning to the attorney's face. He took a deep, cautious breath, his attention turned inward. The release of breath was a sigh of relief. He began to breathe more regularly. "I want extracts on all the financial statements for Tyler Enterprises and each of the subsidiaries. The material is all there." He indicated three stacks of documents on a long mahogany table under the window to the right of his desk. "The kicker in the deck is Century Pictures. We fudged it in the prospectus, but you know how these Hollywood people play accounting games. Wading through all the garbage to try to find some realistic bottom line, we might as well be digging in the jungle for Mayan tombs."

"This is everything on Tyler?" It was almost too good to be true, Kevin thought. *It is, you dummy. Nothing ever comes that easy.*

"Everything you need for now," DeGraff said without explanation.

"I wonder if we shouldn't keep all this together. I mean, here in your office," Kevin added quickly in response to DeGraff's raised eyebrows. "Especially if this involves some, ah, new Tyler activity that hasn't been cleared. No point in starting rumors, even in our own offices."

"Good point, Kevin — very good."

"I can work here. I'll need your key. That is, if I'm going to start on it right away. I suppose it can wait until morning, though."

"No, no, this is hot. I want you right on it. You'll have to let that Indian cemetery go for another week or so. Put everything else on hold, or farm it out. That's on my authority."

"Yes, sir."

"Now then . . ." DeGraff seemed to have more or less recovered from his attack, but as he paused his hands trembled visibly. "I told you I had a dinner engagement, didn't I?"

"Yes, you did. Are you feeling better, sir?"

"I'm fine," he answered stiffly. "Well, I'll leave you to it."

"Do you want to give me a key? I could get security to lock up behind me —"

"No, no, I have one right here." DeGraff slid a key off a large chrome ring holding half a dozen other keys. "Century Pictures . . . start on that. I wish Tyler had never got a bug about getting into the movies. As if those Hollywood accountants aren't bad enough, there was no need to go head to head with the Japanese. Like two collectors at an auction, they ran the price up too high. Century Pictures needs one hit after another just to service the debt. Anyway, you'll see the numbers. Try to make sense of them."

"Yes, sir." Kevin could hardly contain his glee. He could hear himself now, reporting in triumph to Alison, warmed by the glow of admiration in her blue eyes.

He went back to his office to finish up and to wait for DeGraff to leave. At six o'clock he told Linda, his secretary, to go home early, sending her into mild shock. He dialed Alison's office number. She had just left, the pool secretary said. Kevin decided she wouldn't be home yet. His news could wait. Besides, the less he talked around the office the better. Not that he was paranoid, but he had noticed that things spoken casually in the offices had an odd way of resurfacing later.

He had a pastrami and cheese on rye sent up from a deli on Wilshire a few blocks away, and waited for it in his office. He thought about DeGraff's sickness, and the religious need to deny its existence. Was he dying? Was blind faith worth dying for? It was a serious, troubling question for which he had no glib answer.

When he carried the sandwich and a mug of hot coffee down the corridor to DeGraff's office it was a few minutes after seven o'clock. Most of the doors were closed, especially toward the western end of the wing where the partners' offices were. One secretary smiled at him and said good night. The corridor was quiet.

He let himself into DeGraff's office with the key the attorney had given him. Obviously he had a spare, for he had locked the deadbolt behind him when he left. Kevin left the door open. *This is crazy,* his skeptical self muttered. *So maybe you don't want to be Alan Dershowitz. Do you have to flush the whole career down the tubes because one lawyer looks great in jeans?* Kevin ignored the jibe. He was too excited by the prospect of reporting his coup to Alison Carey.

An hour later he felt less sanguine. There was nothing new in the documents DeGraff had left for him. Most of the material was in the registration statement and prospectus, already public information.

In spite of DeGraff's admonition he had saved the Century Pictures files for last, but these seemed no more promising than the others. Unless DeGraff was interested in discovering how a movie could cost $40 million to produce, bring in $250 million at the box office, and still lose money, a conundrum that better men than Kevin had been unable to penetrate.

Someone coughed. Kevin jumped. He stared at George Broward, who was standing in the open doorway. "Working late, Daulton?"

"Mr. DeGraff wanted me to go over these Tyler financials before morning."

"Oh, yes . . ." Broward seemed to relax, or came as close as he ever did to relaxing. For some reason Broward reminded Kevin of his father, although Robert Daulton was a man of genuine good humor and Kevin had never heard Broward laugh. It's the Authority Figure, he thought. The judgment had once been recorded in one of his employee psychological tests: *Has an immature attitude toward authority figures.* "Was he feeling all right? That is, did you notice anything . . . ?"

"I don't think he was feeling well, sir," Kevin said carefully.

"I see." Broward frowned. "That's not for office discussion, Daulton. Is that clear?"

"Yes, sir." They know what's wrong with DeGraff, he thought. Or they guess. They've checked with the doctors DeGraff would never see.

"Well, don't burn yourself out," George Broward said. It was almost an expression of approval. "Good night."

You get Brownie points, Kevin told himself.

Until they find out you're a spy in the ointment.

He worked on the files for another hour after Broward left. Then he stepped out into the corridor. The silence was unnerving, like being inside a mausoleum. Empty corridor, closed office doors, no sound anywhere. Kevin tiptoed back into DeGraff's office. He closed the door, locked it behind him. His heart was pounding.

He checked the two file cabinets in a corner to the left of DeGraff's desk. One drawer was locked. The others held thick briefs and files, alphabetically arranged. Nothing under T for Tyler. He wondered about the locked drawer.

He carried the Century Pictures folder over to DeGraff's desk. He sat behind the desk and tried the drawers. Nothing important in the top or center drawers. The righthand drawers contained bills, correspondence, stationery and supplies. Only a file drawer on the left side was locked.

Kevin sat back in the high-backed, black leather chair and rocked gently, thinking. He'd done his best. Alison would recognize that. He couldn't very well pry open either of the locked drawers. That would be an immediate giveaway. There might not even be anything significant to find. DeGraff had dragged out all of the Tyler files for him to work on. There wasn't any smoking gun. *Everything you need to see for now,* he thought.

He rummaged through the top drawers again, searching for a small file cabinet key. Nothing. Had there been such a key on

DeGraff's ring? He couldn't remember. Would his secretary have a key? Probably. But her desk was out front, open to the corridor. Much too risky. Besides, that desk was almost certainly locked as well.

He stared down at the file drawer of DeGraff's desk. Solid mahogany, he noted. Beautiful wood. He'd have a tough time opening that drawer even with a crowbar.

A memory teased him. It took him a moment to chase it down. His father had an old desk in the basement, moved there from his office after he retired. He kept bills there, income tax records going back to his childhood. It had a locking file drawer, but on the right side.

On impulse Kevin pushed the chair back and bent to peer into the well of the desk. For a better view he got down on his knees.

The key was in its hole on the side wall, tucked up close to the top of the well, just as it was on his father's old desk. Too much trouble for DeGraff to grope under there, retrieve the key after each use, and slip it onto his key ring. Safely tucked out of sight, who would know it was there — or have the opportunity to use it if they guessed?

The grating of a key in a lock startled him out of his sense of triumph at the discovery. The door to the corridor flew open as Kevin launched himself from his knees into the black leather chair. His arm knocked the Century Pictures folder to the floor, spilling papers.

"What the hell do you think you're doing?" Daryl Rathman demanded.

"Rathman!" Kevin was alternately hot and cold. His nerves jangled from a sudden overdose of adrenalin. "You . . . you startled me."

"I asked you what you were doing under that desk."

"Nothing! That is . . . I dropped some papers." He bent over and began to scoop up the papers. He put them back on the desk, frowning at their disorder.

I knew it! the tiny, protesting voice shrilled inside his head. *Now you've done it! They'll never even find your body!*

"This isn't your office."

"Mr. DeGraff asked me to go over some files tonight before I left."

"Why'd you lock the door?"

"I dunno, just habit . . . hey, what's with all the questions?"

"Because you're sitting there looking like you got caught with your hand in the cookie jar, or maybe you just pissed in your pants. Because you don't belong here, junior. Because something's funny."

Rathman's voice was hard, suspicious. He

had been some kind of federal cop, Kevin recalled. Tough cop. He didn't care what he said to this yuppie kid lawyer, a Doogie Howser of the legal fraternity. He didn't sound at all like a security flunkie talking to a respected associate of the firm.

"Nothing's funny. Mr. DeGraff didn't want any of the Tyler files moved from his office, that's all. Back off, Rathman."

The security man didn't budge. His flat, hostile stare remained suspicious, examining Kevin as if he were a suspect hauled into the interrogation room. "Who you been talking to? You haven't been on the phone."

"Nobody. You can see for yourself. I'm alone."

I knew it! The phones are bugged.

"You in the habit of talking to yourself?"

"Hell, no . . . well, sometimes, I guess. You know, thinking out loud. I guess I'm not really conscious of doing it."

"Yeah."

Rathman advanced into the office. He glanced at the stacks of folders on the table, the file cabinets, the desk. Was he checking on the two locked drawers? Did he know about them? Where did he fit in the firm's hierarchy, anyway? One thing seemed clear: Daryl Rathman was no ordinary security guard.

"You just about finished here, Mr. Daulton?"

"Well, I still have one folder to go through —"

"I think it better wait till morning."

"I don't think so. Mr. DeGraff particularly wanted me to go over this Century Pictures file tonight so we can discuss it in the morning."

"We're closing up. It's after ten. Maybe you better come in early." Rathman's tone was unyielding. He was going to stand there, Kevin thought, until he left.

"Yeah, I guess I could do that." Kevin managed a weary smile. "I'm bushed."

He was conscious of Rathman watching him while he put all of the Tyler folders back on the table in orderly piles. He thought it was too late to insist on staying to finish what he had come for. Besides, what could he do with Rathman watching?

At the door Rathman's harsh voice stopped him. "Not so fast, Daulton."

No *Mister* this time, Kevin thought. He made his reply sound irritated. "What is it?"

"The key."

"It's Mr. DeGraff's key."

"I'll make sure he gets it."

Leaving DeGraff's office, not looking back as he strode down the hallway, Kevin felt

Rathman's eyes boring into his spine.

In his own office, turning off the light, picking up his briefcase, starting out the door, he suddenly thought, *You talk to yourself.*

Rathman had been *listening.* The office was bugged!

And if Claude DeGraff's office was wired for sound, one of the partners, that meant every office had to be bugged. Every conversation either listened to or, more likely, recorded.

He punched the elevator button, stood waiting. The thoughts tumbled on, spilling over each other.

Someone — Rathman or someone he supervised — either tuned in live or listened to tapes, keeping tabs on everything that was said inside the hallowed walls of Bryant Forbes Lederer & Wyman, guardians of the law. What kind of an outfit was this?

Where was the elevator? It was taking forever. Kevin glanced back through the glass doors into the reception area, half expecting to see Rathman there watching him.

Rathman knew he was lying — or he would know when he listened to the tapes more closely. He'd discover that DeGraff hadn't insisted Kevin work in his office on the Tyler documents, that it had been Kevin's suggestion, a cunning ploy to gain undetected access to the partner's office and files.

I told you so, the skeptical voice whispered, the voice that had been right all along. *Take another look back. You're finished here.*

A bell chimed, and a pair of elevator doors silently slid open. Stepping inside, Kevin turned to face the doors, and the entrance to his law firm's offices.

Rathman stood by the receptionist's desk, staring at him.

Kevin called Alison Carey as soon as he returned to his apartment. She had told him to call no matter what happened, no matter how late it was.

"Oh Kevin! That's terrible!"

"I did the best I could. I don't think there's any smoking gun there, Alison. At least not where I could get at it."

"I didn't mean that, I meant getting caught. That man gives me the creeps."

"He was pretty creepy tonight." Kevin laughed. "At least he didn't slap me in cuffs."

"I'm glad you can laugh, but . . . it isn't funny. You could be in trouble."

"Rathman can't prove anything. Maybe he's suspicious, but I think he was born that way."

"I hope you're right. I shouldn't have asked you to spy for me. I was just so damned mad about someone breaking into my apartment to steal those pictures."

"Hey, it's okay. I'm sorry I didn't find anything, that's all."

"You did great. Thanks, Kevin. I mean it. I owe you."

"You don't owe me anything."

"Yes, I do, and I won't forget it."

It was about as good as seeing the glow of admiration in her eyes that he had fantasized.

Anxiously Dexter Hilliard replayed his conversation with Daryl Rathman as he raced toward Los Angeles International Airport. He hoped to God the traffic wasn't its usual snarl at the airport. Maybe at this time of night he'd be lucky.

The poached salmon Hilliard had enjoyed for dinner had curdled in his stomach the instant he picked up the phone. Rathman's voice did that to him.

"I don't understand," Hilliard had said. "What did Daulton actually do?"

"He was snooping. That's enough."

"But you can't prove —"

"I don't have to prove anything. What you have to do is get your ass over to LAX."

"Why me? For God's sake, Rathman, it's nearly ten-thirty!"

"You'll have to catch up on your beauty

sleep later. Or do you want me to tell Lederer you couldn't be bothered?"

"I only meant . . . it doesn't seem all that urgent."

"That's not for you to decide, is it?"

"Can't you reach him by phone?"

"Sure, maybe he could use the in-flight telephone and the entire United States intelligence community can listen in." Rathman did not bother to conceal his disgust. "Do what I'm telling you, junior, and do it now. You're in Playa del Rey, so maybe, just maybe, if you haul ass you can get to the international terminal before Lederer's plane takes off. I'm downtown and I'd never make it. That means you're it."

"What'll I tell him?"

"Just what I told you. Daulton was snooping into Tyler files, and he lied about it. He's tight with that intern you've been sniffing after, the one with those photos. My guess is they're up to something together."

For once Hilliard was lucky getting into the airport. He found a parking place close to the international terminal and ran inside. No paging, Rathman had warned him. Lederer wasn't even flying under his own name. A friend of Rathman's in airport security would quietly alert Lederer to wait until the last minute before moving past the barrier that isolated travelers boarding international flights from their well-wishers.

Hilliard saw him at the gate, glancing at his watch, looking impeccably impatient. Hilliard broke off his run to avoid drawing attention, and strode briskly toward the gate. Lederer's sweeping gaze found him. *Cool it,* Hilliard told himself. *Don't let him see you rattled.*

"Mr. Le—" Hilliard saved himself just in time. "I'm glad I caught you."

"What is it?" Lederer snapped without preamble. "I've got five minutes to board my plane."

"Mr. Rathman thought you'd want to know something that happened tonight." He reported Rathman's words, leaving out the sarcasm and putdowns. Lederer began to frown as he listened. When Hilliard finished, Lederer glanced at his watch again. "It doesn't necessarily mean Alison Carey is involved —"

"Doesn't it?" Lederer's eyes bored into him like lasers. "You'd better be right. You recommended her."

Hilliard was stunned that Lederer even knew of his favorable review of Alison's application.

"Get rid of Daulton," Lederer said crisply. He bent to pick up a small carry-on bag. "I want him out of there by morning. Watch the girl. Tell Rathman I want to know everything she does, is that clear?"

"Yes, sir."

Lederer turned and walked away without a backward glance.

Eighteen

That same Monday evening, less than five miles north of Kevin Daulton's modest apartment in West L.A., the bedroom of Elinor and John Woods's Brentwood home was lit only by the dancing underwater glow from the swimming pool a few steps from their private patio. It was all the light Elinor and John needed for what they were doing, which was, in any event, being carried out largely by touch.

The house, on a half acre in a canyon a quarter mile west of Mandeville, was a sprawling rustic ranch designed by Cliff May in the 1940s. It featured the architect's characteristic post-and-beam construction, open rooms, wide overhangs and walls of glass. Like most homes in the area, it had been remodeled and expanded by previous owners, one of whom had added the swimming pool off the master bedroom. The pool was secluded enough for what John Woods still referred to as skinny dipping. Elinor and John were able to leave the draperies drawn back over the bedroom windows at night without worrying about their privacy.

John Woods collapsed onto his back with a heartfelt sigh. "Whoosh," he said.

"Whoosh is good?"

"Speaking personally, whoosh is as good as it gets."

"That's higher marks than I get from my constituents these days," Elinor said. "Not to mention my colleagues."

"I don't believe that for a minute, Senator."

They lay for a while in companionable silence. "It's good to be home," she murmured. "Even if it's only for a few days."

"It's good to have you home."

John Woods, his hair now almost completely white, pillowed his head on a folded arm. It was a moment when, years ago, lovers lit up a cigarette while thudding hearts returned to normal. He was still a handsome man, Elinor thought, his bone structure challenging the effects of age. "It's all gravity," John had complained. "Everything droops." At sixty-three he remained a passionate, if less frequent, lover. She wondered if their politics-driven situation, which stranded them on opposite sides of the country much of the time, actually worked to their benefit in some ways. John tried to get to Washington two or three times a month while Congress was in session, arguing that, as a first-term senator — appointed rather than elected — she should stay on the job. "I'll retire at sixty-five and we'll move to Washington, cats and dogs and all," he had promised her. That would only happen if she was reelected, she pointed out. "You'll be reelected. The people know a good thing when they see one."

Elinor was feeling less optimistic about her future.

"At my age," John mused, "you begin to wonder every time if you're up to it."

"I didn't notice any problem."

"Ummm. Did you ever notice how many expressions there are that seem to have that sexual connotation regarding male prowess? I mean, like being up to it."

Elinor giggled like a schoolgirl, rolled toward him, kissed the corner of his mouth.

After a moment John asked, "What was that about your colleagues?"

Elinor Woods considered the question soberly. She thought of Senator Bodine's harsh reaction, and the calls and telegrams from Lou Janowicz, Mayor Hollingsworth of Fresno, and others. She described the committee hearing briefly, touching upon the mysterious O

Fund and her relatively innocent question addressed to Edward Grabow, the secretary of state. "I'm not sure what it's all about," she admitted. "That's the real problem."

"You haven't been able to dig up anything about this fund?"

"Nothing substantial, only that it was some kind of postwar effort by some of the wealthy old Japanese ruling families and their big banks to help the country get back on its feet. Kind of like a do-it-yourself Marshall Plan. The United States couldn't afford to bail out both Europe and Japan at the same time."

"That doesn't sound very dangerous. Why would it worry Bodine now? Or anyone else, including Grabow and the Japanese?"

"I know. I think there's more to it, but . . ."

With a sigh she squirmed free of his arm and swung her legs over the side of the bed. Standing, her body still warm from their lovemaking, she scooped up her nightgown and drew it over her head.

"You okay, honey?"

"Yes . . . I just don't think I can sleep right now. Would you like some hot chocolate?"

"I'll keep you company," he said. "I'm up to that."

Over steaming cups of hot chocolate with miniature marshmallows floating on top,

Elinor Woods voiced her mixed feelings. "I suppose I should just be quiet and play the game the way rookies are supposed to. If I go along, don't stir things up or make any enemies, as Janowicz says, I'll have a good chance of being elected on my own. Then I'll have a six-year term and some legitimate clout."

John Woods studied her, warm affection in his eyes. "Doesn't sound like the woman I married — just going along, not making any waves."

"I don't have anything solid to go on, John, just . . . just this feeling. I'm like David Perez. I could feel the hairs rising on the back of my neck after I saw the expression on Grabow's face when I asked him that question. And now I'm getting all this other reaction. Janowicz was only the start. There's a delegation from Youngstown, Ohio, wanting an appointment. There are the Fresno people up in arms. Calls from a couple of big-time lobbyists, and one from an undersecretary at the State Department who said they were worried about disinformation misleading the public. Disinformation, for heaven's sake! All I did was ask a question!"

"A good one, apparently."

"Maybe. It's like the reaction is being orchestrated . . . and it's very far-reaching. It's coming from everywhere."

"So who's behind it? The Administration?"

"If I knew that . . ." Elinor frowned. "There's something about this Japanese summit, John, that doesn't ring true. They don't *need* to make any concessions right now. Why should they suddenly be ready to give us what we've been after them about for the past twenty years? *We're* the ones who are in trouble — this country is in trouble. Is MITI suddenly the good guys?"

"So what are your options, Senator?"

"I can sit back, play the game by Joshua Bodine's rules, be a good team player and possibly get reelected."

"Mmm. You got this job because the people of this state are fed up with all the old politicians' games — because you offered them something else. Intelligence, honesty, integrity, a mind of your own, common sense, a great body —"

"I got this job because my predecessor died of a heart attack with three years to go in his term."

"No," John Woods said emphatically. "That only created the opening. You were appointed because of who and what you are."

The junior senator from California sipped her hot chocolate, blue eyes watching her husband over the rim of her cup. "So you're saying, to mine own self be true, and to hell with the consequences."

"Exactly."

Elinor grinned at him. "Now I know why I married you, Doctor."

Nineteen

Alison's first thought was to quit. March straight in to George Broward's office and tell him she was leaving, and why. She rang the interoffice number and got Broward's secretary. Mr. Broward was tied up this morning, he had a luncheon appointment at one, and he wouldn't be back this afternoon. He would be unable to see anyone today.

Next she tried to reach Hilliard. He was in a meeting that was expected to last all morning. Alison left a message to have him call her as soon as he was available. She wondered if they were deliberately avoiding her.

At ten-thirty she took a coffee break. She rode the elevator down to the plaza, then an escalator to a lower level. Kevin Daulton was waiting at one of the small white tables next to a boulangerie. He looked unexpectedly cheerful.

"I had one of the cinnamon rolls to celebrate. Want one?"

"They're too much for me."

"They're too big for Godzilla, but I ate mine anyway." Kevin grinned. "Hey, don't look so down. It's not a wake. More like a party."

"I'm so mad . . . I don't know how I let myself talk you into this. It was stupid. I tried to get in to see Broward to hand in my resignation, but —"

"Now *that* would be stupid. Drink your coffee and shut up and listen. I wasn't cut out to be a lawyer. I mean, I am one, but it's not what I want to be. I think I went to law school to please my father. What happened this morning isn't a crushing blow to a budding career, Alison, it's a reprieve. I've been sitting here feeling about twenty pounds lighter. That's why I ate that whole cinnamon roll, so I wouldn't float away."

"You're just saying this —"

"No, it's the truth, the whole truth, and nothing but the truth, so help me God. So let's start from there."

"I don't know if I'm ready for this new Kevin Daulton."

"Masterful, huh? The point is, you have no reason to quit, not on my account. You *do* want to be a lawyer. And if you walk out on a firm like Bryant Forbes Lederer & Wyman, you might as well sew a big scarlet letter on your dress, because nobody in California will touch you. I got that message loud and clear from Hilliard."

"This morning? He did the dirty work?"

"Good old Dex. He was waiting for me when I came in. Had all my stuff already packed into cardboard boxes and stacked in the hallway outside my office. They were putting a new lock on the door. I wasn't even allowed to go in to see if they missed anything. Hilliard assured me I was persona non grata. When I made some noises about the Labor Relations Board, he assured me that if I caused any static at all, even a single blip, I would never work in California again, I had no idea of the clout this firm has, et cetera, et cetera."

"You seem almost relieved."

"Giddy is the word. That's what I've been trying to tell you. So forget about the sackcloth and ashes and doing penance. Put your lawyer's robes back on and go back up there and do whatever it is that attorneys do."

"I'm not so sure I want to keep on working for a firm that treats people the way they do."

"Why? Do you think there's another kind?"

Alison was silent for a moment, sipping coffee. For the first time she noticed that the tables on either side of them were occupied by groups of young Japanese men, speaking

Japanese. There had been growing numbers of them around the plaza in recent weeks. She wondered if a Japanese firm had moved into one of the towers. Had anyone told Reynolds Tyler?

Kevin grinned at her. He didn't seem to be able to stop grinning. "Are you ready to give up trying to find out what Lederer and company are up to? And don't you still believe they're behind the theft of those snapshots?"

"Yes and no. I mean, I'm not ready to give up. And who else would have any reason to steal those photos? Who else even knew about them?"

"There you are, you have to stay. Go along, keep your eyes and ears open, be a viper in their bosom."

"You have such a way with words." She studied him across the small enamel table, aware that she was looking at him with fresh eyes. "I suppose you're right. If I walk out, we have no chance of finding out what they're up to."

"Exactly. And something is going on, something they want to keep in the dark. Maybe it's nothing more than new Tyler corporate piracy. DeGraff hinted as much. He said I should drop everything else and clear the decks, we were going to be awfully busy with Tyler."

Alison stared at the new Kevin, liking what she saw. "I have to go back to work."

Kevin nodded. "Keep in touch."

He watched her walk toward the escalator, watched her calves tighten as she stood on the moving steps, saw her glance back at him over her shoulder. Her expression was . . . what? Curious? Speculative? What did that mean?

The snide little voice at his shoulder was ready. *It means she's going back to the arms of good old Dex, mentor and hatchet man.*

Kevin grinned. He knew better.

At the Ridgeview Country Club that morning, in the foothills of the Blue Ridge Mountains of Virginia, Kevin's father, Robert Daulton, two down after eight holes, found his ball in the short rough a few feet off the ninth fairway. He had hit a solid drive, a little over two hundred yards. Raymond Farrow was fifteen yards behind him but, as usual, in the middle of the fairway. Farrow was consistently hitting the ball ten to fifteen yards farther off the tee than he had the last time the two men played. It had to be the graphite shafts, Daulton thought. He had been resisting the trend toward graphites, but maybe he ought to try them. At least a graphite driver.

Japanese clubs, he thought idly. Raymond

Farrow, as Distinguished American as they came, was playing at his century old Japanese-owned country club using Mizuno woods and irons. Sign of the times.

Daulton waited while Farrow selected a seven wood, a utility club that Daulton didn't even carry in his bag. The shot was high and to the right. It bounced in front of an elongated sand trap, hopped once, and plopped into the sand.

Daulton sighted down the fairway toward the flagstick. The ninth hole, one of those damaged by flood two years ago, was now a work of art. The kidney-shaped green was protected by traps on the right and behind it. On the left, bordering the fairway and winding behind the green, a creek presented another hazard for a stray approach shot. Not an easy par four, even at 360 yards, but a chance to pick up a stroke on Farrow, or even two if Ray had trouble exploding out of the Sahara.

Under its new Japanese owners the course was immaculate. The sun shone on close-cropped fairways, emerald greens, sculptured sand traps, and the intermittent sparkle of the creek that came into play on nearly a third of the eighteen holes. The day was warm, but a refreshing breeze flowed down the flanks of Virginia's Blue Ridge Mountains, adding to the jewel-like perfection of the scene.

Daulton hit his five iron crisply. Jetting upward, the ball seemed to get a turbocharge that boosted its arc higher. It landed softly on the well-watered green, bounced twice and trickled within three feet of the cup.

"Beautiful shot!" Farrow, who had been waiting for him to hit, drove the cart up beside him and Daulton hopped on. "You're playing well, Robert."

"If that's the case, how come you're two shots up?"

"Not after this hole, it would appear."

Never a long hitter and losing yards as he grew older, Farrow retained a delicate touch around the greens, and was an effective sand player. He blasted out within ten feet of the cup, but missed the putt for a bogey five. Daulton tapped in his three-footer and grinned in relief.

"That puts us even after nine," he noted smugly.

"I think I'd better slow you down. How about a cold beer and a sandwich?"

"What about the foursome behind us?"

"They'll play through."

They carried beers and grilled cheese sandwiches to a table on the terrace and sat under a wide umbrella. Until then Robert Daulton had avoided the subject that had prompted him to call Farrow a week ago. It was Farrow who provided the opening.

"Have you seen the stories about the James-Yuki relationship and what it means to the Osaka meeting?"

"Yes. I guess the White House is promoting the idea."

James was James Arthur Walton, president of the United States. Yuki Nashido was the Japanese prime minister. The two men had hit it off during a previous summit meeting.

"We've seen this sort of thing before," Farrow observed. "When Reagan was in office, he and Yasuhiro Nakasone, who was the prime minister then, developed what seemed to be a genuine friendship."

"The Ron-Yasu thing."

"They became friends, and it was only natural for Yasu to ask his friend Ron for help occasionally, whenever U.S.-Japanese trade talks or other negotiations hit a snag. Reagan couldn't have been more obliging. He practically gave away the store, but all he ever got from his pal Yasu was feel-good stuff, promises of market openings that never happened."

Daulton grinned. "He got more than that after he left office."

"Mmm. $2 million for a couple of twenty-minute speeches in Japan. The Japanese have a way of taking care of their friends in that way, under the guise of a speech or a consulting fee or the like. They see their reward system as a perfectly logical way to conduct business."

"Perhaps it is, if it weren't so subject to abuse. What kind of man is Nashido?"

"Curiously enough, he seems to be much more independent than most of their political leaders have been. The Japanese have had a Western-style assembly for a hundred years, but until World War II it was a rubber-stamp group. The country was still run by their *genrō*, elder statesmen who were part of the old ruling oligarchy. MacArthur tried to change all that, and set up a true democracy. The Diet has acquired more real power over the past fifty years, but most of the prime ministers have been handpicked by the elders in much the same way they always were. Nashido is an exception."

"How does that affect the James-Yuki factor? Do you think President Walton is going to come away from Osaka empty-handed? Or worse?"

"I suspect there'll be something that sounds fine on paper, like a promise to conduct meaningful negotiations."

"If that's the case — and Walton is to be believed about the genesis of this summit —

why did the Japanese want it? Why do they want Walton over there at this time?"

"That's a puzzle, Bob." Farrow sipped his beer and watched a group of Japanese on the practice putting green. "What was it you wanted to talk about? Does it have anything to do with all this?"

"I'm not sure. It's about the Tyler Holdings offering." Daulton recounted his son's story about the young intern at his firm who had seen Calvin Lederer on Guam when he was supposed to be in Washington, and subsequent efforts to deny it. "Because of Tyler's well-known antipathy toward the Japanese, Lederer's firm has adopted a hands-off policy where the Japanese are concerned, even at the risk of losing Pac Rim business. So Kevin's young friend Alison Carey wondered what Lederer was doing meeting secretly with some Japanese businessmen, while his firm was actively working on the new Tyler prospectus."

Farrow sat for a moment, eyes thoughtful behind his dark glasses. "The stock market is reacting favorably to Tyler's filing. I see the stock is up more than six points already in anticipation."

"So I've noticed."

"The Street is looking for a saviour. Just as Walton is looking toward this summit to give our economy the morale boost it badly

needs. If he comes away with anything sub-
stantive that will immediately affect our balance of trade, the president might get his shot
in the arm. And Tyler's mammoth offering
may be what investors on the sidelines have
been waiting for."

"But . . . ?"

"Yes, that's where the scenario becomes
murky. The Japanese have no reason to relent
now — it would be completely out of character. And what if Tyler's offering fizzles? If
the summit is perceived as a failure, or little
more than political theater, and, if anything
goes wrong with Tyler's offering, you could
have a one-two punch our sick economy might
not recover from. Public confidence will hit an
all-time low. The economy is driven by consumer spending, and consumer spending is
driven by confidence, Bob. Without it . . ."

"Do you think this Lederer trip to Guam
is significant?"

"No way to tell. But it's certainly in-
triguing. There's one other thing, Bob . . .
did you hear about Ed Grabow's testimony
before the Senate Finance Committee? He was
asked about an O Fund. I believe the question
came from the senator from California, that
woman —"

"Senator Woods."

"Yes, Senator Woods. I tried to reach her

through her office, but she's back in California for the recess. Curious thing . . . I'd like to know why she dropped that little bombshell in Grabow's lap."

"What is the O Fund?" Daulton asked.

"It's an old story, one of those things that no one's ever been able to pin down, but one that would never go away either. Supposedly, some of Japan's wealthy families — part of that oligarchy that had ruled the country for a century — came out of the war with a secret hoard, spoils plundered from Manchuria and Southeast Asia, gold hidden from the Allies. Do you remember those stories about caves of gold that disappeared from the Philippines?"

"Yes, I've read about that."

"The Japanese, of course, denied that the spoils existed. But if even a small fraction of wealth surfaced during the Occupation, you can be certain General MacArthur's people would have been only too happy to take advantage of it. MacArthur was consumed by his vision of converting Japan to a true democracy. He might not have asked too many questions."

"You said a fraction of the total."

"Most of it would surely have remained secret. Controlled and managed by astute, powerful men, diehard supporters of the emperor, in a country ripe for the picking. Property being sold off for little or nothing by families that had lost everything else . . . a stock market opening up in 1948 that has since zoomed skyward . . . returns on invested capital of 2,000 percent and more, and property escalation at least that much. Imagine what such a fund would be worth today if it existed in 1946."

Daulton shook his head, unable to calculate the possibilities. "It would pay off our national debt several times over. Do you really think the fund existed?"

"I believe it's not only possible, but highly probable."

"What do you suppose put Senator Woods onto it after all these years?"

"It will be interesting to find out."

"Is there anything I can do, Ray?"

"You've already done a great deal, Bob . . . you and Kevin and his girlfriend. Now it's my turn. I'm going to ask the president for an appointment."

"You're going to try to see Walton?" Daulton was startled.

"Before he goes to Osaka. I know most of the people on his Council of Economic Advisors — that should help."

"There isn't much time. You may have trouble getting an appointment."

"I know, but that's the point, isn't it? There

isn't much time."

Raymond Farrow tired on the back nine, and Robert Daulton, hitting his irons solidly and sinking two "no-brainers," putts of twenty-five and thirty feet, came in with an eighty-seven after eighteen holes, sixteen over par but still defeating his friend by five strokes.

The price of defeat was dinner for two. They stopped that evening at an inn in the countryside on the way back to Washington. The time passed quickly, filled with reminiscences and current Washington news, but Daulton sensed that Farrow's mind was elsewhere.

"Are you worrying about what we talked about earlier this afternoon? Or is it those two long putts?"

Farrow laughed. "I never worry about acts of God. No, it's something I'm really not at liberty to discuss, not without proof."

"You're not going to get away with that."

Farrow hesitated, clearly reluctant. "I suppose you're entitled, Bob. When I was in Japan in the early 1970s, there was a rumor about the O Fund. That was the first I'd ever heard of it. The rumor that was circulating . . . I didn't want to believe it." A pained expression crossed Farrow's patrician features. "Do you recall a news item a few years ago, long after Nixon resigned in disgrace, about the Nixon camp receiving a secret contribution from Greece's military junta toward his 1968 presidential campaign?"

"Yes, I remember — there was a book about it. I believe it was said to be about $500,000. But by then people were so saturated in post-Watergate cynicism the story barely made a ripple."

"It was different back in 1968. Nixon was in a tough campaign with Hubert Humphrey, and his people were paranoid about losing. Nixon needed money, lots of it. One emissary visited Greece and flew back with a half million or so in plain brown suitcases. In Japan, the rumor was, another emissary arrived in the summer of 1968, and came away with a contribution more in the neighborhood of $2 million, a lot more than the Greek colonels had to offer."

Daulton whistled soundlessly. "If it happened, it wouldn't exactly be out of character."

"The thing is, that contribution supposedly came with strings attached. That's simply the way the Japanese do business. And if you'll recall, one of the first orders of business after Nixon took his oath of office was to return Okinawa to Japan. No charge for the American blood on the beaches."

Daulton was silent, turning over the implications of Farrow's story, both historically and for the present. At length he asked, "Do you think the story's true?"

"I believe it is plausible. And that's not all of it."

"What could be worse?"

"There have been other, more recent rumors. Once again, I'd prefer to believe they're completely false, but if they have any truth to them . . . the O Fund may have played a significant part in at least two presidential elections in this country. And it may have a great deal to say about whether or not we're going to survive this economic war with Japan."

"For God's sake, Ray — !"

"Exactly. Start praying . . . and since God helps those who help themselves, I think we have to do whatever we can to find answers to some of these questions."

Twenty

That night, for the first time since she arrived in Los Angeles, Alison Carey telephoned Alan Gillespie. It was nearly seven o'clock, which meant ten o'clock in Philadelphia. She wondered if he would be alone, and was pleased to note that she didn't give a damn.

"Hello?"

The familiar, clipped tone of voice released a flood of unwanted memories. Alison waited while they washed by, like a flash flood, dangerous but momentary. "Alan? This is Alison."

"Alison! My long lost love! I was beginning to think you'd forgotten me." His tone became playfully reproachful. "You've met some young hotshot, I suppose."

"You know better than that."

"Out of sight, they say. You're sure there's no handsome young renegade from *L.A. Law* enjoying your charms?"

"Hardly. We work twelve hours a day. There isn't time for anything else."

"Pity. I'd have thought better of the young studs in La-La Land."

But not of me, she thought. She found herself resenting his glib comments, which were demeaning.

"How are things at Bryant Forbes et al.?"

"That's really why I'm calling, Alan."

Faced with the necessity of putting her thoughts and suspicions in order, Alison had misgivings. Alan Gillespie was a notoriously demanding law professor at the distinguished Barnett School of Law, one of those teachers who would never let a student get away with slipshod thinking, an unexamined fact, a careless reference. He terrorized his students, but it was this clinically sharp, detached and uncompromising mind that first attracted Alison to him. As a teacher he intimidated her into doing her best. He stimulated her own single-minded determination not simply to succeed but to excel. When he began to single her out for special attention and grudging praise, halfway through a course in torts, she was drawn even more under his spell.

He became her adviser, mentor, friend. Entering into an affair with him seemed inevitable. It never occurred to her that others might think she was doing it to get good grades

251

— she would have got those anyway. It happened because she had never known anyone quite like him before. Because, through sarcasm, belittling, encouragement, wit, he forced her to dig deeper into herself, discovering resources she had not thought she possessed.

Only at the very end — even as Gillespie was pulling strings to get her the coveted summer internship at Bryant Forbes Lederer & Wyman — did she begin to sense that, rather than her using him, he had been using her. As soon as she started preparing to move out of his orbit, he was scanning the seats in his classes, auditioning her replacement. She had known there had been others before her — always the best students. She hadn't wanted to think about them, or to see herself as one of a procession of nubile, impressionable young women. There was an abruptness to their parting, a feeling that he was eager to have their affair behind him.

Alison remembered a short story she had read as a child about a boy who was being adopted — the story had been easy for her to identify with. The point of view was that of the foster mother who had come to love the boy. When he rode off with his new adoptive parents, and the puppy they had brought with them, he was so excited that he forgot to look back or wave goodbye.

This past spring, Alison was the one going off to start a new life. It was Gillespie whose attention had already found another object.

"Cat got your tongue?"

"No, I . . . I'm not sure I should even be telling you this." He despised conclusions drawn from flimsy evidence.

"Suppose you let me be the judge of that."

"The firm is everything you said it was, Alan. Very high powered. Major clients. I've been working on the Tyler Holdings prospectus for the past month. Everyone I work with has been very helpful."

"I heard about that Tyler offering. You should be able to handle that sort of assignment."

"Yes, I know, but . . . something strange has come up. I'm not absolutely certain it has to do with Tyler at all, it's just that . . . dammit, I don't know how to put this."

"I'm afraid you're losing me, my dear." Gillespie sounded the note of asperity when presented with ineptitude that made him dreaded at Barnett.

"There's something funny going on."

"In Calvin Lederer's firm?" He chuckled. "You're pulling my leg, of course. Because I've neglected you all summer. I apologize."

Distance, and the absence of that aura of

superiority and infallibility that enveloped students in Gillespie's presence, caused her to listen to him with an objective clarity she had not experienced before. He sounded pomp- ous, arrogant, disingenuous. Certainly he was all of those things, but in person, packaged with his careless good looks and Ivy League manner, they combined to create an undeni- able magnetism. For the first time Alison wondered if that appeal ever lasted for long — if it only worked on anxious students at a particularly vulnerable time in their lives.

"I saw Lederer when I was in Guam."

There was a pause. "That sounded as if it was meant to be significant."

"It was."

"I didn't think you'd met Lederer then."

"I hadn't. I didn't know who he was until later, when he showed up one day here in L.A. with Reynolds Tyler. But what makes this so strange is, everyone denies he ever left the country this summer. The man I saw was meeting some Japanese at a hotel, and every- one says it would never happen. Lederer ap- parently takes great pains to distance himself from the Japanese."

"Because of Tyler, of course. Are you sure of your facts, Alison? You could have been mistaken. I don't quite understand why you should find this disturbing, in any event —

there could be a hundred perfectly logical explanations — but . . . you're quite positive, I suppose."

"There isn't any doubt about it. I had photographs."

"Photographs? Perhaps you'd better explain."

Alison told him of Kim's pictures. When she described telling Dexter Hilliard about them, and the subsequent burglary, there was a prolonged silence.

"Alan?"

"I'm here. I'm just . . . flabbergasted. Nothing else was taken? You're certain of that?"

"Whoever broke in was after those pictures."

"So now there's actually no way to verify what you think you saw."

"What I *know* I saw, Alan. No, I don't have the photos anymore, but . . ."

Alison felt a new uneasiness. Even though the sequence of events had begun on Guam, that island seemed so far removed from the break-in at her apartment, so impossibly remote, that she hadn't seriously considered the possibility that the thieves might not be satisfied with stealing the prints in her possession.

"Your sister has the negatives," Alan Gillespie said, reading her silence.

"Yes, I'm sure she does."

"I see. Still . . . I'm afraid I don't quite understand why you were so keen on proving Lederer was there, or making an issue of it. It's hardly a matter worth sticking your neck out for, my dear, when you're trying to establish yourself with the firm."

"I didn't stick my neck out. A friend did, and got himself fired."

Reluctantly she recounted the snooping of Kevin Daulton on her behalf the previous night. "They didn't even ask him what he was doing. They just locked him out of his office this morning."

"Alison, have you been listening to yourself?"

"I think so."

"I thought I'd taught you better. I would've thought your own common sense would surface at some point in this shoddy little adventure. Do you realize what you and your friend have been doing?"

Alison bristled. "Maybe you'd like to tell me."

"For starters, what he did — what you encouraged and condoned — was unethical. It was improper. Worst of all, it was incredibly foolish."

"What about breaking into my apartment to burglarize it? Is that supposed to be proper and ethical conduct?"

"You don't know that the firm had anything to do with the burglary. That's an assumption. The thief might have left in a hurry — something might have scared him off. What you have isn't evidence, Alison, it's the wildest unsubstantiated conjecture. I can't believe you'd jeopardize your status with Lederer's firm over this. I'm beginning to suspect this friend of yours must have exercised far more influence over you than you're ready to admit. You were always so level-headed. That was one of your charms."

"I'm sorry to disappoint you," Alison answered stiffly. "But I've been lied to and robbed, a friend of mine has lost his job because of me, and I thought —"

"That I would be more sympathetic? When did you ever know me to countenance stupidity?"

The harshness of the judgment set her back on her heels. "I guess this whole conversation was a mistake."

"You made a mistake, all right, but it wasn't this phone call. That may be the first smart thing you've done. I recommended you highly to Bryant Forbes Lederer & Wyman. This escapade of yours not only makes you look bad, it reflects on my judgment."

"You don't have to worry," she snapped

back. "I'll tell them you had nothing to do with it."

"Stop being childish. What you should do is make it clear to your principals that *you* had nothing to do with this man Daulton's unethical conduct."

"But I did!"

"They don't know that, unless he's implicated you."

"Kevin wouldn't do that."

"Because he's smitten with you? My dear, you're being positively naive. I think it's time to take a long hard look at yourself and your reckless friend. You'd better decide once and for all what it is you want. I thought I knew. I'm sorry to see that I might have been mistaken."

Alison knew what he was saying. He had seen ambition in her, the determination to get ahead no matter what it cost, a toughness that would let nothing stand in her way. Even her compliant submission as a student to Alan Gillespie's routine seduction suddenly seemed calculating. She had never viewed it that way before.

"I guess I haven't been very smart."

"That expresses it nicely."

"What should I do now?"

Gillespie was slow to answer. *He thinks I've blown it completely*, she thought. *He's worrying how much of the debris is going to land in his yard.*

"This Hilliard fellow . . . the one you spoke to about the photos . . . he's also a friend?" The emphasis he put on the last word was sardonic.

"He's been very helpful."

"Let him know how upset you are over this whole situation . . . that you had no idea Daulton would attempt to pry into closed files. Distance yourself from it."

"Alan, that seems so self-serving."

"It is. We're talking about a career here — or hasn't that occurred to you?"

"Of course it has," she admitted.

"Then act accordingly."

"You're right, I know," she said, thoroughly disillusioned.

"I know Calvin Lederer personally. I'll see what I can do to repair the damage. As for you, get rid of that loser, Alison. You'd better get back to thinking about yourself and what you want for your future."

"Thanks, Alan."

"Don't thank me. Thank your stars this friend of yours was clumsy enough to get caught before he went too far . . . and brought you down with him."

When he rang off Alison looked down at the "G" listing in her little book of telephone

259

numbers. Gillespie's was the only number on the page.

She ripped out the page, tore it into long strips, then into smaller pieces. She dropped them into the wastebasket with a sense of finality, and of release.

Alan Gillespie had his list of personal telephone numbers in a Moroccan leather-bound booklet. One of the listings was for Calvin Lederer. It included office numbers in Washington, D.C., and Los Angeles, and another for Lederer's Georgetown residence. The number Gillespie dialed was an unlisted one. It would be routed through to Lederer wherever he was in the country.

While he waited, Gillespie weighed the potential damage. Like many of America's leading educational institutions, the Barnett School of Law, in an era of diminished returns and shrinking bequests, relied heavily upon corporate grants and endowments for its very survival. Japanese companies had endowed professorships and funded programs at some of the most prestigious colleges and universities in the country, from Ivy League universities to Corn Belt colleges to the seaside campuses of the University of California. They were particularly generous in supporting high-technology research. M.I.T. had a score of Japanese-endowed professorships. Even Washington think tanks welcomed funding from Japanese companies whose practices frequently came up for impartial analysis.

Barnett School of Law was no exception. Several Japanese firms, including the Sakai Group and Miyaki Industries, had endowed chairs at the school. One of the endowments funded Alan Gillespie's own professorship. It was Calvin Lederer who secretly controlled this funding.

Gillespie saw nothing improper in his relationship with or dependence upon Japanese largess. Nor did he find anything suspect in the generosity of the companies involved. American corporations operated in the same relationship to many schools. The difference was that American companies were not involved with Japanese universities, and exercised no influence upon the policies of their schools, or the minds and lives of their students. And gifts or funding from American companies were often tied to specific programs. Japanese firms were more farsighted. They were interested in influence. Establishing loyalties. Opening windows.

The possibility that he had jeopardized his connection with Lederer's law firm, and through it the money stream from Japan to the Barnett School, lay like a lump of ice over

Alan Gillespie's heart. He cursed his defective judgment. How could he have been so wrong about the girl?

She was so beautiful. One of the loveliest of them all. Ambitious, a little too impatient to make her mark, but these were attributes Gillespie did not find displeasing. When he had worked her up to the point of becoming his lover, she had been very inhibited at first, holding back, really incapable of losing control. That was a legacy of her childhood, he was to learn. Abandoned by her mother, never having known a father, she had promised herself as a child never to be dependent upon anyone else, never to yield control of herself, her body, her life. But she had a passionate nature she couldn't deny. Gillespie had brought her along slowly, until finally the dam burst.

She'd been one of the best, he thought regretfully. And one of the most promising students of the law.

"Mr. Gillespie? George Broward here. What can I do for you?"

"I'm trying to reach Mr. Lederer. It's quite urgent."

"I'm afraid that's not possible. You're with the Barnett School, aren't you? We've had very good reports about the school."

Gillespie remembered Broward now. A

blocky, humorless man. Head of the firm's Los Angeles offices. Gillespie, cold a moment earlier, was now sweating. How much did Broward know about Alison Carey's actions? Would any of the dirt from the affair stick to him because he had sponsored her?

"This is very important. I feel Mr. Lederer would want to speak with me if he knew."

Broward kept him waiting. Finally he said, "You're part of this firm's family of loyal friends, Mr. Gillespie. However, I can only tell you that Mr. Lederer will get back to you as soon as possible. I'll be sure to tell him you urgently wish to get in touch with him."

"Is he out of the country?" The question was impulsive, and immediately Gillespie wished he could take it back.

This time Broward's tone was no longer friendly. "What makes you ask that question?"

"I'm not about to cause trouble," Gillespie said quickly. "Far from it. I *am* a friend, Mr. Broward, and you can be certain of my discretion. I've come upon some information that I believe is very important to you and Mr. Lederer."

"Does it have to do with a former student of yours?"

Gillespie sighed. They knew.

"Mr. Lederer is out of the country for a

few days, Mr. Gillespie. I think you'd better tell me everything you know."

It was like turning on a faucet.

Twenty-One

"You'll be leaving Wednesday morning," Sylvester Runnels said. As secretary of defense, he had been briefed that morning on the plans designed to ensure the president's safety and security both aboard Air Force One and after his arrival in Japan. "You'll spend your first night in Tokyo before going on to Osaka."

"Damn!" President Walton said. "Rotten timing. I hate to miss Sunday's game. The Cowboys and the Redskins . . . it'll be the game of the year."

"We've arranged for live satellite transmission of the game. If you're tied up in conference, the videotape will be waiting for you when you get back to your suite."

"It's not the same as being there."

"You'll be where history is being made," Edward Grabow said. "You'll be making it."

"I know, I know." Walton brightened at another thought. "Does my suite come with geisha girls? After all, I'm the guest of honor."

The other three men laughed as the president chuckled. Sometimes he still acted like a college sophomore, Gus Bonelli thought without malice.

These were James Arthur Walton's favorite times, these moments when the Four Horsemen, as he liked to call them, took off their jackets, loosened their ties and sat around the Oval Office in shirtsleeves, drinking bourbon and kicking around the events of the day, the plans for tomorrow, the ups and downs of this roller-coaster ride that was the presidency of the United States. Runnels, Grabow, Bonelli and Walton: they had come all the way together, straight to the top of the heap.

"All these preparations for a ten-day trip," Walton mused. "It boggles the mind."

"They're essential," the secretary of state said. "Especially being prepared for anything the Japanese might spring on us."

"Oh, you don't have to convince me. I know it's all necessary." A gleam of reminiscence came into Walton's gray eyes. "Remember George Allen when he coached the Redskins? Talk about your attention to detail! People used to get down on him, reporters especially — you know how the media are, they always want to take someone who's on top and knock him down a peg. Well, old George, he'd have the players out there on the field before practice picking up scraps of paper or cigarette butts or anything else George could see. He'd have them tucking in their shirttails. He'd make damned sure the water pitchers were full and enough Gatorade was there, and there were plenty of fresh clean cups, and a barrel to throw the paper cups into so there wasn't any trash along the sidelines or blowing onto the field when it came time to work." President Walton paused for emphasis, leaning forward in that way of his, thrusting his face into the listener's as if it were a fist. "They laughed, but George did more with less than any coach we've ever had. He never had the players Joe Gibbs and Richie Pettibon had, never had a great quarterback in his prime. George did it with hard work, and attention to detail, and planning."

"And cheerleading," Runnels suggested. "Old George was a hell of a cheerleader."

Edward Grabow, the most serious of the group, came back to the question of Japanese surprises. "The big thing we have going for us this time around . . . well, you know what it is, Mr. President. The James-Yuki factor, as the media label it."

"We're on the same wavelength," Walton agreed. "We like each other, we understand each other, and that's important."

"You can say that again," said Runnels. He liked to feed selected lines to Walton, allowing him to sound presidential. "With the behavior of North Korea and China so unpredictable, the Pentagon doesn't want to disrupt our contingency planning for Asia. We need those Japanese bases, and we need the damned semiconductors. Without them our missiles are about as useful as those Easter Island statues."

"Well, you don't have to worry. Yuki and I have discussed the bases, and we're in complete agreement they're necessary to Japan's defense and to the stability of Asia. As for those semiconductors, well, hell, they want to sell 'em as bad as we want to buy 'em!"

Gus Bonelli sat on the brown leather sofa, puffing on one of his big cigars. He listened and said little. Not until Runnels turned to Grabow and said, "What about this O Fund, Ed? Any more on that?"

"It's a dead issue. Senator Woods is getting the word. If she wants to run next year — and what politician wants to bow out before he or she has really had a chance to be on stage? — she'll drop the subject like a hot potato."

"What if she doesn't?" Bonelli growled.

"Oh, come on, Gus, stop worrying," Grabow said. "Woods is back in California. The summit is already taking over the front pages and the opening segments on the nightly news. We're going to be in charge of what the American people are reading and seeing and hearing for the next two weeks." The secretary smiled. "No story lasts that long in this town without something to feed on. Anyway, there's nothing there that can really hurt us."

Bonelli did not reply. Alone of the men in the Oval Office that night, he knew better, but it was a private thing. There were some things even the Four Horsemen couldn't share. "I thought we were going to play some cards tonight," he said.

"Now you're talking," said James Arthur Walton, briskly rubbing his palms together.

They pulled chairs up to the handsome oak game table that was President Walton's addition to the furnishings of the Oval Office. Runnels got out the box with the stacks of different colored chips, and the president shuffled the cards. "My deal," he said.

"You're the president," Runnels chuckled.

"There's one other thing, before I forget," Ed Grabow said. "Do you remember a man named Raymond Farrow, Mr. President? Used to be on the Council of Economic Advisors, the World Bank? He's a consultant to the Brookings Institution now."

"Farrow?" said the president, who never forgot a name or a face. "Of course! I knew his family. That's old Boston money, you know, like the Cabots and the Lodges, long before Joe Kennedy came along. Farrow's the kind who believes in devoting his life to the public service, maybe to make up for the fact that he was born as rich as Croesus."

"He's been pulling strings, working the old-boy network, trying to wangle an appointment to see you. Insists it's important."

"Well, hell, I'd like to accommodate him if it's possible." The president chuckled. He was in a good mood. "You know me, I never like to stiff old money."

"There's no time," Gus Bonelli said.

"Well, Gus, Farrow's no town crier. If he says it's important, it must be important."

"We went over all that earlier tonight. Every minute's spoken for from now until you get on that plane. Farrow will have to wait." Bonelli spoke in a flat tone of finality.

Everyone looked at him during a moment of silence. It was a definitive moment.

"You sure, Gus?" asked the president.

"I'm sure."

James Arthur Walton turned to his secretary of state. "Let's send Farrow a note, my signature. Set up an appointment first thing when I get back from Osaka. Mention his mother. I think she's still alive, must be in her nineties."

"You've got it," Ed Grabow said.

"All right, enough about managing world affairs," Sylvester Runnels said. "Let's get down to some serious cards here."

Gus Bonelli was the last to leave the Oval Office. He caught up with Grabow and Runnels at the elevator. Gus carried the imprint of the president's hand on his shoulder, warming him.

Grabow and Runnels left together. Gus Bonelli's Cadillac limousine eased silently up to the south portico where Gus waited. He stepped into the rear and sank deep into the soft leather seat. The black car moved sedately along the winding drive and through the gates onto Pennsylvania Avenue.

"Home, Mr. Bonelli?" his chauffeur asked.

"No," Gus said.

He gave terse, explicit directions. The limo moved off into the night, leaving the White House behind.

Gus Bonelli wished that he had never heard of the O Fund. Contrary to what the others thought, it was not a dead issue. And it could hurt the president.

Gus thought about the economic summit that lay just ahead like a roadblock. He wouldn't do anything to hurt James Walton, or allow anyone else to do so. That was his mission in life — a higher mission than he'd ever dreamed he could aspire to. Now he was troubled. Gus had an instinct for danger, or duplicity, and all of his antennae were on alert. He suspected the Japanese were up to more than what showed in the summit agenda.

Gus Bonelli dealt in hardheaded realities. He knew there were maneuverings going on in financial circles that involved Reynolds Tyler and the Japanese, but he believed it was a side issue. He was totally convinced the Japanese government didn't dare do anything to seriously or permanently damage the U.S. economy. America was the largest market in the world for Japanese products and technology; Japan needed that market or its own economy would starve. Some Japanese diehards, as Gus understood it, wanted to get even, settle a score. Gus could relate to that.

But he remained uneasy. He'd heard a writer say one time that ideas sometimes hovered in the air if you were sensitive to them. So did danger.

The president liked to joke that it was Gus Bonelli's job to make certain no one sacked his quarterback. For Gus it was never a joke.

The black limousine cruised along Virginia Avenue until it turned into the Rock Creek Parkway, entering the long greenbelt of Rock Creek Park. The road wound deeper into the park, curling alongside the creek past the zoo-logical park, picnic groves, a nature center, changing names along the way to West Beach Drive and Beach Drive. It was past midnight, and the park was deserted. Though only a few miles from the White House and the U.S. Capitol, it might have been a wilderness area remote from civilization.

The drooping flagstick on the twelfth green of the Rock Creek Golf Course dispelled the illusion. The limousine eased onto a narrow service road and pulled to a stop. Another car was parked just ahead. The chauffeur switched off the Cadillac's ignition and the only sound was the ticking of the engine as it cooled.

Gus Bonelli sat motionless for five minutes, watching Beach Drive in both directions. There was no traffic at all.

The driver's door to the other parked car opened, and a man stepped out. There was no light when the door opened. The man's footsteps crunched on the gravel of the service road as he walked toward the limousine.

Gus leaned across to open the rear door on the left side. No light came on here either. The other man slipped onto the leather seat beside him and closed the door. Gus smelled garlic on his breath.

His name was Martin Wallach. Gus knew him as Marty. He had known him since they were kids, going to school together on Long Island. Marty worked for an investigative agency of the government, but Gus had once bailed him out of a situation involving a cheating girlfriend. Marty had lost his head and hurt her. He was looking at a felony conviction, a possible prison sentence, and certain loss of employment. Gus talked to someone at Justice, and he talked to the girl. He learned she was more interested in her own future than past grievance. They came to an agreement. She dropped her complaint, and Justice agreed to look the other way. Marty's gratitude was such that he would do anything Gus Bonelli asked him.

"So what's the story?" Gus asked.

"Perez — he's the senator's chief aide — admits she received an anonymous tip about this O Fund."

"Anonymous? How?"

"It came in over the transom. A letter, no signature. He claims there was nothing else, but I want to see the piece of paper. There's always something, even if it's not on a letterhead. I got into the senator's office and had a look at her files, but the letter didn't turn up. Maybe she took it with her, or maybe she put it in a safe place. We'll find it, but it may take time."

"That's all she's got, an anonymous letter? No follow-up?"

"Yeah."

Gus was silent a moment. The note, coming on the eve of the Japanese economic summit, was such a nasty piece of timing that it had to be deliberate. The question was whether or not the tipster really knew anything or was just a malcontent. Gus wasn't alarmed over an anonymous letter, but he still sensed danger.

"You said this Perez might be a problem."

"Yeah, he's digging. I mean, it's like he's going after the Holy Grail."

"I thought you were going to try to reel him in. He's an ambitious young greaser, you said."

"We made a move on him. It looks like that backfired. He's gone all holier-than-thou. Who'd figure? Kid on the make from East L.A., we offered him the whole circus. He was tempted — you should see the skirt we put onto him — but then he woke up thinking he'd committed the Original Sin and he has to atone for it to save the human race from evil."

"What's he doing?"

"What isn't he? He's calling every reporter in town. He's turning over stones all over the Hill. Who knows what he might stumble onto? And just as bad, he's starting to make other people curious."

"Shut him down," Bonelli said.

"All the way?" Marty sounded almost eager. He had that streak in him, Gus thought. He was one of those who could have walked on either side of the line. That he had ended up nominally on the side of law enforcement was an accident.

Gus considered his options. He was not a man who shrank from the truth, or hard decisions. There were no options. This David Perez was a loose cannon careening all over the deck. Left loose, sooner or later he would start to do damage. Serious damage. There were things Gus Bonelli could not allow him to find.

"I don't care how you do it," Gus said. "Shut him down."

Twenty-Two

When Alison called Guam, she wasn't paying attention to the calendar. She was simply anxious to reach Kim as quickly as possible. Kim had to know about the theft of the photographs.

A strange male voice answered. "Hello."

"Who is this?"

"If you're calling for Hank Goldberg, Sergeant, U.S. Army, I'm sorry I'm not able to talk with you just now, but if you'll leave your name and a number where I can get back to you . . ."

A recorded message on a telephone answering machine. For an instant Alison was startled. Then she remembered Kim's trip to England, while the strange voice simultaneously answered the question in her mind.

"If you're calling for Tim or Kim, you missed 'em. They're on their way to merry old England. You can reach them at this number along about next year, or leave a message and I'll forward it. Wait for the beep and sound off."

Alison debated with herself quickly. Kim and Tim must have leased the house, or lent it to a friend. No point in bothering Sergeant Goldberg about snapshots that meant nothing to him, but . . .

Beep!

The sound triggered her decision. "Sergeant Goldberg? This is Alison Carey, Kim's sister. I need to talk to you as soon as possible." She gave him her phone number, and told him to call collect. It was very important, she added.

Hanging up, she felt a mixture of relief and frustration. At least Kim and her family were safely off to England. Frustration lingered over the fate of the photographs, including the negatives, but as her concern for her sister ebbed away she began to think she was being more than a little paranoid. It was a bit too much to believe that Calvin Lederer would dispatch a burglar all the way to Guam to retrieve them.

England, she thought. Oh, to be in England. . . . "You deserve it, little sister," she murmured aloud. What a strange journey they had taken to reach this point in their lives. And as Kim, the eternal optimist, would be quick

278

to point out, they were just a little way out of the starting gate.

For some reason this made Alison think of Kevin Daulton.

In the doorway of the short hallway leading off the living area of the house on Guam, Yashi Nogama waited for the caller to speak. A woman, American. The sister of the one who lived in this house.

The message on the answering machine disturbed him, deepening the habitual scowl. So the owners of the house were on their way to England. For a whole year . . . it seemed an extraordinary vacation for the owners of such a modest house.

The message explained some things Nogama had already discovered in his first quick search. The uniforms in the closet of the main bedroom, and the absence of other clothes. The clutter of dishes in the sink, unwashed. The stacks of cardboard storage boxes in one of the bedrooms and in another room that apparently served as an office.

Nogama had watched the house for two hours, waiting for full darkness. He had been puzzled over the lack of activity. There were supposed to be three people in the house, a man and a woman and a child. None of them appeared. Lights went on, apparently set on

279

an automatic timer, creating the illusion that the house was occupied. But the house was empty.

It was the last house on the road, and the placement of the neighboring house, with carports between them separated by storage walls, meant that no one close by was able to look directly into the house, even though the interior was very open in its design and there were many windows. Once inside, Nogama had turned off the lights, waited for his eyes to become accustomed to the semidarkness, and conducted his search without using the flashlight clipped to his belt. He felt at ease. He would hear the occupants when they returned to the house, almost certainly by the car that was missing from the carport. He would have no trouble slipping away before they entered and discovered his presence.

Now he reassessed his situation. Who was Sergeant Goldberg? An American soldier who was to occupy the house in its owners' absence, or serve as a caretaker?

He had brought his clothes. He was staying in the house, and he would be returning.

Nogama thought about the sister's urgent message. She was the one from Los Angeles, he thought with surprise, as if the young woman's voice speaking so clearly from halfway around the world was a kind of miracle.

He could think of only one reason why she would wish to speak to the sergeant.

The photographs.

Her set of pictures had been stolen. She had thought of the originals in her sister's possession. Nogama did not know why the woman had become so interested in the photos, but she was obviously determined to have them.

He began to search methodically. There were several framed pictures of a young man and woman smiling at the camera, one of them a wedding photograph, the woman cheerful looking, short and a little plump, a figure that Nogama found appealing, the man thin and dark and self-important. Even more pictures of a small child, baby pictures and others marking her development to the age of two or three. In the bedroom Nogama found an enlarged snapshot of two young women, both in their twenties. One was the woman in the other photos. The second must be her sister. Nogama stared at it for a long time, matching it with the voice that was on the recorder. *The beautiful sister,* he thought.

The open rooms created few hiding places. There were no doors on the cupboards, and none on the closets, a feature Nogama knew came from the extreme humidity and warmth of the climate on the island, which encouraged mold in closed spaces. The living room and kitchen were quickly searched and dismissed. He opened drawers in the buffet in a dining area, but they contained only silverware and linens. He was careful to close the drawers and leave everything as he had found it.

Increasingly impatient, Nogama slighted the child's bedroom, which in any event offered few places to leave a set of photographs, other than a painted chest with a lift-up lid that was jammed with toys and stuffed animals. That left the main bedroom and the office, both of which included stacks of storage boxes.

He started with the parents' bedroom. According to the American who had ordered this search, the woman named Kim had taken the snapshots at the hotel. The husband was a professor, absorbed in his academic world. Nogama reasoned that the woman would have taken charge of the packet of photographs after they were developed. Where would she leave them?

It occurred to him, as it had earlier on, that she might have taken them with her to England. It seemed unlikely. They would have been unnecessary baggage for an extended trip. She had no reason to guess their importance.

He had been too long in the house. In assignments like this it was vital to get in and out quickly. Every minute the search dragged on increased the chance of arousing the curiosity of a friend or neighbor, or of something unexpected occurring.

He pawed through the dresser drawers, which were more than half empty. He checked the nightstands beside the bed, and a decorated box containing letters but no photos. Then, on a shelf of the open closet, he found a box filled with packets of snapshots, most of them still in the envelopes in which they had come from the developer.

He checked to make sure the draperies were fully drawn over the single window. Then he spilled the contents of the box onto the bed and flicked on his flashlight. Some of the collections of pictures were so old he quickly shunted them aside. He sorted the more recent packets and fingered through them, glancing quickly at the dates stamped on the outside of the envelopes. Some of them dated back three years. The latest had an April stamp of the current year.

Nogama stared at the pile, suppressing anger.

There were still the storage boxes to go through, a dozen of them in three stacks in this room, more in the office. And he had already been inside the house more than an hour.

Too long, he thought. Much too long.

The first thing Sergeant Hank Goldberg noticed was that the lights weren't on.

He had set up lights in the living room, office and bedroom on a timer. Kim had expressed concern about the house being empty so much, with Hank working late hours at the base. Actually Hank usually stayed out later than the eight o'clock time he had given her. Most nights he went for a couple of beers after work and got himself something to eat. Most nights he wouldn't get to the house until after ten, and he wanted Kim to feel comfortable.

Kim was a nice woman, Hank thought. And the professor had really helped him out with a crash course in using the computer that was taking over many of Hank's supply duties, particularly in inventory control. That was how Hank had got to know the couple, and how he had learned about the house being empty for a year while they were in England.

He'd set those lights up himself, and checked them out.

Someone had to have turned them off.

There were probably quite a few people who had learned the professor and his family were leaving the island on an extended trip. Maybe some of them weren't very honest, and maybe they hadn't heard that a soldier from the base would be living there.

Hank Goldberg was forty-four. Twenty-six years ago, when he was eighteen, he had left the States for Vietnam. He had been there, and in Laos, for the last years of the war, and for the pullout — the only time in his adult life he had ever cried. He had never been back home. He had no real home to go back to in the States, his only family an aunt he hadn't got along with and some cousins he didn't know. Hank had three decorations for bravery in action. He was an expert with a rifle or handgun, and he had been trained in hand-to-hand combat. He could also take care of himself in a knock-down, drag-out fight. You couldn't serve in this man's army for sixteen years without having been in a fight or two.

He crept up to the house the way he had once learned to creep through steaming jungles. The night was warm and humid, but nothing like Vietnam. Nothing would ever be as bad as Vietnam. He stayed away from the tall windows in the living room, and from the wash of light spilling over from the back-yard floodlight two doors down the street.

Hank crouched outside the kitchen for a time, listening. He heard nothing. There was no movement in the kitchen, no shadow stirring or changing shape where it shouldn't. He could see every part of the room but a utility corner in back where the washing machine was, and he didn't think anyone was back there. He could also see a wedge of the dining room.

If someone were stealing, he thought, they would be in the office or maybe the master bedroom. He thought of the storage boxes in both rooms. They would make it easy to cart valuables off, but in fact there weren't many valuables. The TV, a good stereo with speakers four feet tall that was almost too big to steal, some silverware. A petty burglar would have been in and out already, Hank thought, frowning.

He kept below the window line, lifting his head at a corner of each window to peer inside, showing as little of his head as possible. Like the other rooms, the professor's office was dark and empty. No movement inside. But as Hank waited, for the first time he caught a flicker of light. A moving light.

With all doubt removed, Hank circled back around the house to the side door off the kitchen. It opened into that corner utility area. Hank had a key and the lock turned silently. He eased the door open, holding his breath. It didn't squeak.

Hank was not wearing a gun. Most duty on the island didn't require it, including

Hank's current assignment as a supply sergeant. But he had little fear of a burglar. As likely as not it would be a teenager, a native who would be quick to run, or even one of the professor's students who knew he was leaving.

The bedroom door was ajar, but only an inch or so. The intruder had pushed it shut, and made certain the drapes were snug over the window, because he was using a light. What did he expect to find in the bedroom? In those storage boxes?

The sergeant straightened up, banged the door open and reached for the light switch he knew was beside the door. "What the hell are you doin' here?" he snarled.

Everything happened very fast. He saw that the intruder wasn't a kid, or a student from the university, or a soldier. The man looked Japanese. He was short but powerfully built. He was dressed in a black knit shirt and pants. He didn't panic, or look for a way out, or answer Hank's challenge. He just attacked.

Hank Goldberg was trained in combat fighting, but he had only a rudimentary knowledge of the martial arts. They weren't of much use in the jungle, even when it came down to hand-to-hand fighting, and they were irrelevant in a firefight. The burglar exploded across the room at him with a speed that took the soldier's breath away. Hank dodged a leg that shot toward his chest. He didn't escape a backhand blow that came out of nowhere as the Japanese flew past him and bounced off the wall. Hank reeled backward, hit the dresser and slid to the side. His ears rang, and there was a knot in his chest.

The intruder didn't give him time to collect his wits. He shouted — one of those militant "Hai!" yells — and he was all over Hank. The sergeant's fists flailed air. A kick numbed his left arm. Pistonlike fists hammered his nose and drove one of his teeth through his lip. Something that felt like a sledgehammer smashed into his ribs. Hank went down.

Rolling instinctively, he stumbled to his feet, hurt and angry. When the assailant instantly launched another attack, Hank didn't try to duck or evade the blows, he plowed right into them. And somehow got inside and smashed a fist into the other man's face, a quick one-two to his belly, and another shot to the head. The blows were all solid, and they brought a rush of elation. But the man didn't go down or even back up. The punches to his gut hurt Hank's hands more than they seemed to bother the Japanese. It was like banging your fists into a telephone pole.

But the intruder must have been hurt a little. He was more cautious. He didn't come flying at Hank like a human cannonball. He circled and watched, black eyes wary, blood streaming over his mouth and chin, dripping onto his shirt.

Hank felt woozy, but his brain was still working. For the first time he clearly realized that he was in a fight for his life. Without spelling it out he knew he couldn't fight this man by any known rules and survive. When the Japanese hurtled toward him again, Hank managed to get in one vicious kick with his heavy boot. It landed just below the knee, hard enough to tear the first hiss of pain from the intruder's mouth.

Not good enough, Hank thought. He picked up a small chair and met the next charge swinging. A chair leg broke against the intruder's rigid arm like a stick snapped across a knee. He snatched the chair from Hank's hands and flung it across the room. It sailed into the window. Glass exploded outward. Bits and pieces sifted into the bedroom. By then Hank was on hands and knees, his chest hurting and his vision blurred. He got to his feet again, because that was the only thing he knew how to do in a fight. One arm hung useless, and a sharp pain pierced his chest, and he sprayed blood when he shook his head. But he got to his feet, swaying, and he was conscious of the intruder glaring toward the broken window. And dimly, as if through a fog, Hank heard voices. A shout, a woman screaming.

The Japanese turned and came at him with a shine of hate in his eyes. Hank tried to meet him halfway. The man waded right through him. The sledgehammer caught Hank again, this time on the side of the head, and he went sprawling. The floor melted under him, turning liquid. It sucked him down, like some ancient tar pit, into a pool of blackness.

Yashi Nogama limped along an alley behind the row of houses. Behind him shrill voices pierced the darkness, brittle as glass. He tasted blood, and his left knee was swelling. He might need a doctor. He could not return to the hotel in this condition, clothes torn and spattered with blood, his own and the soldier's. His appearance would draw attention at once. That would become dangerous if Sergeant Goldberg survived. He would be able to provide a description of his assailant.

Curses pounded through Nogama's brain. He had been misinformed. He had expected to find a professor's family, careless and vulnerable. Instead he had confronted a trained and angry American soldier. Not a formidable opponent for Nogama in most circumstances, but in the close quarters of the furnished bedroom the American had proved to be tougher than expected. He had also been lucky, but Nogama understood that luck was a factor in such situations.

Moreover, Nogama had come away empty-handed. In addition to his injuries, and his sudden exposure to the possibility of police inquiry, there was the loss of face.

In spite of the pain in his knee, he ran along dark alleys and side streets until he was two miles from the scene of his disgrace. By then he had made a decision. He could not return to the hotel. He could not risk being identified by the soldier. He would leave the island at once, but not under his own name. Another would have to take his place, so there would be an official record of Yashi Nogama's departure under unremarkable circumstances. Arrangements would then have to be made for him to leave surreptitiously, his passage unrecorded.

The *yakuza* was most powerful in the islands of Japan. But Japanese interests were now extensive on Guam, as they were in Hawaii. Nogama had made serious investments in property on the island, both for himself and his associates. The organization's reach extended wherever its interests were significant.

Nogama found a gas station with a telephone. The night attendant was busy and gave him only a cursory glance. Nogama fumbled out some change and dialed a number. It was answered immediately.

Twenty-Three

The American attorney turned away from the hotel room windows overlooking the turbulent Pacific. Black waves as steep as walls rolled toward the deserted beach. Winds whipped across the poolside veranda, scattering forgotten cups and newspapers. Palm fronds tore loose from the tall trees fringing the beach and thrashed inland like fleeing animals. Except for a few thrill-seekers standing at the edge of the terrace to confront the storm, tourists had retreated inside the hotel. Far out to sea, thick black clouds rode close on the water, blotting up the evening light.

"A bad storm," Calvin Lederer said. "They say it will hit the Japanese mainland late tonight."

"We have survived many storms," Toshio Miyaki said enigmatically. He was uncomfortable with the American. Throughout their meetings, casual conversation had been difficult with him. Invariably he fell back upon traditional Japanese politeness.

Lederer was cold and arrogant, but Miyaki had known and dealt successfully with many Japanese businessmen who were equally self-important, equally ruthless. What was most chilling about this attorney was his single-minded focus. He was indifferent to the potential damage he was about to inflict upon his own countrymen. His attention was absolute: How would he benefit financially from the turmoil? Nothing else entered the periphery of his vision. Miyaki, a baseball fan, thought of a pitcher's focus upon the catcher's mitt as he prepared to throw. Blotted out were the raucous crowds, the hitter waving his bat back and forth to intimidate, the other players, the sun beating down, the beauty of the setting. There was only the ball, the glove, the taste of triumph.

"When will you act?"

"The initial steps have already been taken."

"How much of Tyler do you own now?"

Miyaki hesitated. It was typical of the American to cut directly to the core. He reminded Miyaki a little of his friend Shinji Sakai. Both were slim, elegant men who placed great importance upon clothes and appearances. Both concealed a steely personal ambition beneath a polished veneer. "The last figure I received from my accountants was 9.3 percent. That was, of course, before the purchases authorized for today." The Tokyo market was closed for the day, but America's Wall Street was just opening its doors. There, it was Wednesday morning.

"Then you have to announce soon."

"Yes. Friday, I think. Reynolds Tyler will have the weekend to regroup. American investors will have the weekend to think of potential profits."

For the first time Calvin Lederer smiled. "On Monday the Exchange won't be able to keep up with the buy orders. You would make a handsome profit, Miyaki-san, if you were to sell at this time next week."

Miyaki smiled in response. "We Japanese, as your pundits are always pointing out, don't think of short-term profits."

"These would be short-term, all right." Lederer glanced once more out to sea, then at his watch. "I'm not sure my plane will be able to leave on schedule with this storm, but I'd better be prepared. I have to be back in California when the news breaks. I'll see you next week, then, in Los Angeles."

Miyaki bowed. "I look forward with pleasure to visiting your city."

Lederer sniffed. "Not my city, I assure you. Nor yours, I believe. You'll find it a city of mongrels, fighting over scraps."

The contempt in his tone chilled Miyaki. Surely Los Angeles was one of the great cities of the world. Lederer's attitude was an emanation of the coldness of his heart, at one with his indifference toward a trusting client and a country he was about to betray.

Miyaki bowed politely again as Lederer turned to leave. *"De wa mata, Lederer-san."*

"Yes, yes," the American said. He nodded curtly, as if he could not bring himself to bend toward this small, white-haired Japanese. *"Sayōnara,* as you say in your country, correct?"

"Quite correct," Miyaki murmured.

But the American had already walked out the door.

While rain lashed the windows of his suite and the winds keened and thrummed, Toshio Miyaki watched on television as the American president, James Walton, strode purposefully across a sunlit green lawn from the White House toward a waiting helicopter. He turned, as American presidents habitually did, to shout a response to a reporter's question. At the helicopter he paused to smile and wave, instinctively staring directly toward the television camera that was recording this historic moment. It was morning in America, peaceful and sunny. The storm that was coming was not yet visible on its horizon.

A nagging question drew Miyaki away from the television set to the telephone. He rang Nogama's room. Once again there was no answer. The gangster had not appeared all day, nor had he left a message to explain his absence.

On impulse Miyaki called the front desk. "This is Miyaki-san in Suite 1210. I've been trying to reach Nogama-san in his suite, and there is no answer. He —"

"Mr. Nogama checked out this afternoon," the clerk said.

Miyaki was rarely speechless. It was a moment before he could respond. "You're quite certain?"

"Yes, sir. I was on duty. Mr. Nogama said he was trying to catch a flight to Tokyo before the storm grounded all planes."

"To Tokyo?" Miyaki repeated.

"Yes, sir. Is there anything wrong, Mr. Miyaki?"

"No, no . . . *arigatō*. Thank you."

But there *was* something wrong, of course. Nogama's abrupt departure was both puzzling and disturbing. Why had he remained in seclusion, after arrangements had been made for him to be present for the discussions with the American attorney? Why had he left Guam so hastily? Why had he kept Miyaki in the dark about his plans? And had he really returned to Japan?

Miyaki admitted to a certain relief that the *yakuza* might not be accompanying him to America, after all. But another sudden, inexplicable change of plans was alarming.

An aide entered the room and inquired if Miyaki-san wished anything else before retiring. Miyaki dismissed him. He gazed toward the rain-swept windows and the blackness beyond, wondering if Nogama's flight had outrun the storm. *"They say it will hit the Japanese mainland late tonight,"* Lederer had said.

Something on the television screen caught Miyaki's attention. He turned and stared at the screen. Yashi Nogama's face glowered at him.

Frozen in disbelief, Miyaki picked up the thread of the news report. It concerned a brutal attack the previous night upon an American soldier. The face on the screen was a police artist's rendering of the attacker's image. He had been surprised in the act of burglary when the soldier returned unexpectedly to the house where he was staying. The thief was described as a short, muscular, Japanese male. He was considered dangerous. An American officer was interviewed briefly by a TV reporter who asked questions without waiting for answers.

Sergeant Goldberg was in intensive care, the officer said, but his doctors were cautiously optimistic. He had remained conscious long enough to give a detailed description of his assailant. Authorities, civil and military, were anxious to hear from anyone who had knowledge of the attack, or who had seen the assailant in the vicinity. He might be injured and might seek medical assistance.

Sinking onto the overstuffed sofa facing the television set, Miyaki tried to make sense of the report. A coincidence, he told himself. Someone who looked like Nogama. But the attempt to reassure himself failed. The description was too accurate to be dismissed. And the incident helped to explain Nogama's failure to appear at the hotel all day. It accounted for his abrupt departure.

Miyaki called the front desk again. "This is Miyaki-san. I wish to speak to the clerk I talked to earlier about Nogama-san."

"That was me," the desk clerk said. A young American, Miyaki remembered. Incredibly naive and eager to please. It was as difficult to dislike such a young man as it was easy to despise Calvin Lederer. "Can I help you?"

"I wanted to make certain it was Mr. Nogama who checked out. Did you talk to him personally?"

"Oh, yes, sir!"

"He had been in an accident, and I am concerned. Was there any indication of his injuries?"

"No, sir. That is . . . he looked fine."

"Can you describe him for me?"

"Well, sure. He was well-dressed, you know, very polite. Not very tall, but heavy. Stocky, I mean."

"Do you remember . . . was his hair cut short, or long?"

"I remember that, all right." There was amusement in the young clerk's voice. "I guess I shouldn't say this, but . . . it was pretty obvious. He was wearing a piece."

"A piece?"

"You know, a hairpiece . . . a toupee."

Toshio Miyaki felt the tension of anticipation melt away. *"Arigatō,"* he said.

There could no longer be any doubt. Someone had left in Nogama's place. But where was Nogama now? Why had he flown to Guam so urgently, instead of traveling with Miyaki? And what had he been doing burglarizing the home of an American soldier?

Something teased Miyaki's mind. He stopped chasing the shadow, instead allowing his thoughts to focus upon the window, the rain weeping down its surface, the vibrations set up by the buffeting winds.

The burglar had broken into the house *where the soldier was staying*. It was not his house, Miyaki thought. Who were the owners? Perhaps the answer would provide a clue to Yashi Nogama's strange behavior . . .

Miyaki rang his aide. The annoyance in the young man's tone vanished instantly when he heard Miyaki's voice. Miyaki wished inquiries to be made concerning the burglary reported on the television newscast he had just watched, and the police search for a missing Japanese thug. He wished particularly to know the identity of the owners of the house where the incident took place. Most important of all, the inquiry must be absolutely discreet.

His aide said he would begin immediately. He said nothing about the storm raging outside.

Twenty-Four

"You've been missing out on all the news," Alison Carey said. "There's a rumor that someone's been buying up Tyler Holdings common stock. Tyler's been in the office, demanding to know where Lederer is. The stock started out Monday at 62 and it's up to 67-¼."

"So where is Lederer?" Kevin asked.

"Nobody knows. One guess is he's back in Washington. I heard one of the associates say he's at an Alaska wilderness lodge on a caribou hunt. Can you picture that?"

"No."

"I have my own version, but nobody's asked me. Then there's the news about DeGraff."

"What about DeGraff?"

"He's in the hospital. The gossip in the office is his wife called an ambulance and sent him to the hospital kicking and screaming. He doesn't believe in being sick."

"I know." Claude DeGraff was not a warm

person, but Kevin felt a genuine sympathy for him. He hadn't been all that hard on an inexperienced associate, and Kevin was almost certain that, whatever dirty tricks Calvin Lederer's firm might be up to, DeGraff was too much of a straight arrow to be part of it. "So how are things going for you? Are you getting any flack because of me?"

"No, why should I? There's lots of juicy gossip about you, though. One of the interns says you were caught embezzling. I straightened him out. One of the law clerks is spreading a story about you fooling around with George Broward's secretary, and let that be a lesson."

Kevin grinned at the idea. "I'm glad you're in the clear."

"I'm in a honeymoon period."

"What's that mean?"

"When Kim and I were kids, and we were going to be put in a new foster home, or placed with potential adoptive parents, there was supposed to be a honeymoon, a time when we acted like little angels. No temper tantrums, no defiant or unmanageable behavior, no stealing."

"No stealing?"

"Didn't you ever steal anything?"

Kevin thought about it. "Some Halloween candy from a store. Candy corn."

"Did you get caught?"

"No."

"We would, sometimes. Our therapist said we wanted to get caught. Either it was a cry for attention, or we wanted to act bad because it was expected of us. We wanted to give whoever it was the opportunity to reject us, since they were going to do it anyway eventually."

Kevin tried to comprehend what it must have been like to be abandoned as a child, to be bounced around between foster homes and group homes, to expect rejection as the normal condition of life. It was impossible. He thought of his own sometimes prickly relationship with his father, and the comparison brought chagrin. "So where does the honeymoon come in now?"

"I figure I'm under the microscope because of those photos. What I'm saying is, I know how to smile and act cheerful, give a performance that will make Hilliard think everything's just great and they don't have to worry about me."

"These people aren't playing games, Alison. Do you understand how much big money means to someone like Lederer? If he has to roll over my body and yours and anyone else's who gets in the way, he won't even notice the bump. This business with Tyler Holdings stock going crazy . . . do they have any idea who's buying?"

"I heard some talk . . . one of the partners and another man I didn't recognize. There's so much activity in the stock that anyone could be hiding in the bushes." She paused. "So what are you going to be doing, Daulton, while I go into the lion's den each day? What about DeGraff? Are you going to see him in the hospital? He's at Cedars Sinai."

"I doubt he'd want to see me. He's probably mad as hell."

"Think about it. He probably knows a lot about what's been going on with Tyler. And if he's been left out of the loop, he might not even know you've been sacked."

Kevin was dubious. "I suppose I could go see him."

"Not if you don't want to. I got you in enough trouble already."

"It wasn't your fault. Better me than you, anyway. You keep that honeymoon going at the office, okay? Don't let them catch you snooping. Remember what I said. They're watching and listening."

"Don't worry, I'm being a good girl. I can smile and smile, and be a villain."

"I've always said you'll make a great lawyer."

Alison laughed, a sound that had Kevin riding waves of euphoria higher than any comedy club comic. He was still in a glow when she said good night a moment later. He was holding the phone, reluctant to break the connection, thinking, *We're buddies,* when he heard a definite click.

Someone else had hung up.

The call from Guam came through at six o'clock in the morning, jarring Alison out of a deep sleep and a dream in which she was driving a car that was being pursued. She turned a corner and the street dropped away, like one of those steep hillsides in San Francisco, and she hurtled down the incline, trying to escape, but suddenly there was a black square hole in the street at the bottom of the hill, as large as an elevator shaft, and she rushed toward it, her pulse pounding —

"Hel . . . Hello?"

"Miss Carey? Is this Alison Carey?"

A stranger's voice. A man's voice, accustomed to being listened to. "Yes."

"I'm sorry to disturb you, Miss Carey. I'm not even sure what time it is in Los Angeles."

Alison was sitting up on the edge of the bed now. "It's six o'clock."

"I suppose I woke you up. My name is Abbott, Lieutenant Frederick Abbott, U.S. Army. I'm calling from Guam."

"Oh my God, what's happened?" But it

couldn't be Kim, she told herself. Kim had already left for England. Who was it who'd answered her phone the other night? Not Abbott . . . *Goldberg.*

"That's what I want to talk to you about. I'm afraid there's been a problem here. We're hoping you may be able to help us out. A soldier who was staying in your sister's house was attacked and severely beaten during a robbery attempt. There was a message from you on the answering machine at your sister's house. We think you must have called the same night the sergeant was assaulted. Do you recall when you phoned your sister and left your message?"

"Tuesday." Alison felt numb.

"That's about what we figured. Do you know of any reason why someone would break into your sister's house?"

"No . . . but if it was just a burglary . . ."

"It wasn't exactly routine, Miss Carey. Sergeant Goldberg received a very professional going-over. And as nearly as we can tell, nothing's missing."

The photos! Alison thought suddenly. They wouldn't notice missing photographs.

"Miss Carey?"

"Yes."

"Do you know how we can get in touch with your sister and her husband? We know they're on their way to England."

"Yes . . . they may be there by now. I don't know their schedule, but I have the address of the hotel where they were thinking about staying in London the first week. Let me get it."

She continued to move numbly, emotion suspended, as if she had to be very, very careful not to misstep. She found the name and phone number of the hotel on Russell Square. She wondered if Lieutenant Abbott was a military policeman or with Army Intelligence. He hadn't said. She told him she couldn't think of any reason for the break-in, but she hoped Sergeant Goldberg would be all right. The lieutenant was noncommittal. He thanked her and said he would try to reach her sister.

Alison sat for a long time on the edge of the bed after she hung up. She wondered if she had done the right thing in not mentioning the snapshots. But she had only her unsubstantiated suspicion, the fact that her apartment had also been broken into, no real proof of anything. Not enough to tell an arm of the U.S. government that the prestigious law firm of Bryant Forbes Lederer & Wyman was involved in petty theft and aggravated assault.

Kim! she thought. She had to reach her sister. Maybe Kim was at the hotel by now.

Kim might have been home that night instead of Goldberg. Kim and Tim . . . and Jenny.

The anger came then, the raw feeling she had been holding back. Her hand shook as she picked up the phone and tried to dial. She was so agitated that she had to hang up and start over again.

She had learned about more than false honeymoons during her years in foster homes. She had learned about defending herself and her sister, and sending a message to anyone who bothered them. She had learned about getting even.

Twenty-Five

Marty Wallach had been watching the Senate staffer all week, and he now had a pretty good idea of his habits. For one thing, he was a workaholic, routinely putting in twelve- to fourteen-hour days. He was in his office in the Dirksen Building by seven or seven-thirty every morning. Most nights he didn't leave until after dark, which meant eight or nine o'clock. In between he was either on the phone or he was out running all over town, looking into old records, buttering up secretaries and clerks in various government offices with his Latin gigolo looks, trying to buttonhole people, always asking questions. Once he met an ordinary-looking man on a park bench near the National Academy of Art. The man held a bag of peanuts he was sharing with hungry pigeons. Marty tabbed him right off as a Fed, probably from the Bureau. Another time Perez met an unidentified man in a hotel coffee shop near Dupont Circle. The man had a careful way of looking around before he walked quickly to the nearby Metrorail station and disappeared.

Perez was digging, is what he was doing. The way Marty saw it, he was trying to dig up dirt.

Marty had obtained a copy of a questionnaire David Perez had submitted to a young assistant to the undersecretary of state for foreign affairs, with the plea that it be delivered personally into the hands of his boss. Apparently the aide had got cold feet over answering some of Perez's questions, and insisted on having them in writing. Marty had Perez's questions memorized.

1. Are you aware of the existence of a file on the O Fund?
2. When did you first learn of the fund?
3. Have you reviewed the file and its contents at any time?
4. Has the undersecretary or anyone else discussed them with the president?
5. If the fund was discussed with the president, what was his reaction?

To Marty Wallach the questionnaire was a record of treason. He couldn't believe Perez had put it on paper. Marty's view was that he had been commissioned to represent the government of the United States. Gus Bonelli had laid it on the line. David Perez was a threat to the stability and integrity of that government. He was trying to hurt the president. That made everything cut and dried. Marty didn't have to wrestle with moral scruples over what he had to do. Not that he lost much sleep over such questions. Perez was, after all, the chief aide to a United States senator. If something happened to him, there were bound to be questions raised.

After leaving Gus Bonelli in the park that night, Marty had spent about an hour considering the possibilities before him. Should he put Perez in the hospital for a considerable period of time, until presumably he would no longer be a threat to his president and his country? Or did the solution have to be more permanent? Marty hadn't really needed a whole hour. Gus had made it clear that the threat Perez presented wasn't going to go away by itself. It was ongoing and serious, not a temporary irritation. There really wasn't anything to argue about.

Once his mind had been cleared of extraneous concerns, Marty was able to concentrate on following Perez through his daily routine, assessing his vulnerable moments, working out different scenarios.

Because darkness was always an ally, Marty first took a long look at those periods when the staffer left his office late at night and headed home. There were problems. Perez drove to and from work, and Marty quickly rejected the notion of hitting him on the steps of the Capitol before he got to his car. That prospect, even if it had been feasible, offended Marty's patriotic sensibilities. Invariably Perez stopped at some fast food outlet on the way home, if he hadn't had something sent in to his office. Then he went straight to his place in Arlington, the only stops along the way being at a minimarket and once at a supermarket, where Marty had pushed a cart along the aisle behind him while Perez picked up some coffee, cereal, eggs, cat food and cat litter. These nightly journeys told Marty several things. One was that Perez apparently wasn't fooling around with some bimbo from one of the offices he visited, or a housewife looking for a little action on the side. Another was that Perez had a cat. Marty had serious questions about any man who lived alone with a cat. It bore out his observations over the years that traitors usually had other quirks. The English weren't the only ones.

An accident while Perez was driving home was the next possibility, or as an alternative, one of the popular new carjacking attacks that could so easily end in tragedy. But Perez was a careful driver. He buckled up, locked his doors, used the air conditioning or cracked his windows but didn't leave them wide open. In particular he kept the driver's side window rolled up; that open window was a carjacker's best friend. The staffer's apartment building had secure underground parking, a gated garage with card-key access. Marty could have let himself in easily enough, but there was no place in the well-lighted garage to hang around inconspicuously. Moreover, there was no predicting how late the hard-working Perez would be. Some nights it was ten or eleven o'clock.

All of this was routine preparation for Marty Wallach. He was not a sloppy operator. The only time he had ever acted really sloppily was that time with Gail, when he had come close to trashing his career and Gus Bonelli had had to bail him out. He knew without asking that Bonelli wanted this operation to be neat and clean, with no spillover. The White House had to be totally insulated from it. If anything went wrong, Marty would take the heat alone. That was understood.

In the end Marty decided against taking the target (it was useful to begin thinking of him that way) in his garage, or waiting in his apartment for him to come home. In either situation

314

it would be hard to guarantee neat and tidy.

David Perez made the decision almost too easy. Three or four times a week he ran several miles, always in the early morning, along the jogging trails and footpaths of Rock Creek Park. There were any number of fitness enthusiasts out at that hour, of course, but it was a huge wooded park and the runners were not always in sight of one another. Marty could easily join them, an inconspicuous figure like dozens of others.

And even here David Perez was a loner. He liked to get off on side trails by himself. There were many places along the way where he would be alone, pounding along a narrow path surrounded by trees, huffing and puffing, a lean young man in his designer sweatsuit, keeping in shape, living the American dream he was so anxious to trample on. Jogging after him one morning, Marty worked himself into real anger.

Perez had skipped Thursday, so he was due to run on Friday. But when Marty reached Foggy Bottom early Friday morning there was a fine rain falling. Marty was afraid Perez would cancel his morning run. The day was gray and cheerless, and there were only a few joggers out braving the wet weather.

Perez favored Key Bridge over the Potomac on his morning drive from Arlington. It brought him into Georgetown, and from there he worked his way over to the Dumbarton Oaks area, where he looked for a parking place. If he found one he walked down the Lovers Lane Walkway into the park, stopping along the way to do stretching exercises, a routine Marty noted with approval. Otherwise he drove into the park.

At five minutes past six o'clock Marty was sitting in his car in the park where he had a view of a portion of the Lovers Lane Walkway. He felt a solid jolt of excitement. A slim, lithe figure in purple-and-yellow sweats paused along the path. He seized the guardrail for a moment while he squatted and stretched. Then he stood, lifting his face up into the soft warm rain, as if he found it beautiful.

Marty Wallach, opening his car door, felt the same way.

He was getting close. David could feel it. The senator might laugh at his back-of-the-neck itch, but David trusted it.

Not only was the O Fund real, it had someone in the White House scared to death. Everywhere David turned he found people running for cover. Old files were missing. Microfilmed records were lost or damaged. People who had always talked to him, at least off the record, suddenly developed laryngitis.

Friends gave him funny looks in the corridors of the Dirksen Building, or found a reason to be busy talking when he walked by. By now David was convinced there had been a conscious, heavy-duty effort to bury the fund, to erase any knowledge or evidence of its existence.

He hadn't heard from Lisa Gardner since the night of the Japanese ambassador's party at the Watergate Hotel. He hadn't really expected to, but that perception didn't do anything to fill the empty space she had left behind. David had liked her.

In his research David had adopted a new tack, not going after the O Fund itself but the identity of the anonymous informant who had sent Senator Woods the note about it on CIA letterhead. Langley was a very closed operation, even to a senior Senate staffer, but inevitably in such a large, paranoia-driven agency there were factions. That meant ex-agents with axes to grind, current agents who had been passed over for promotion, agents who had bet on the wrong horse in the periodic upheavals that occurred with a change in power at the top of the Agency, from Casey to Webster to Gates. In addition, there was the well-known rivalry between the Agency and its domestic counterpart, the FBI, where David had a number of friends. He hoped to exploit one of those divisions. Somewhere in that shadow world there was a man with a grievance, waiting to be found.

David fell into a rhythm as he jogged, a mystical music syncopated this morning by a more distinctive slap as each Nike hit the wet asphalt. He veered off onto a dirt footpath, losing the intrusive sound.

He liked running in the rain. The best moments running in any kind of weather were those in which you withdrew into a kind of envelope where there was nothing but you, your pumping legs and drumming heart, where you blended into the rhythm and there was no sense of time and place, only the harmony of the effort. The rain enhanced those moments. It muffled sounds. Most mornings it was impossible to escape completely the blare and hum of morning traffic as the city came alive. But the rain brought a hush to the park, especially in the wooded areas. Traffic noises ceased to exist. The surrounding cityscape disappeared. The loudest noise was the dripping of raindrops from the trees onto the grass.

A running figure appeared on the path ahead of him. Slim legs, no waist or hips. A young woman, running easily, blond ponytail whipping back and forth under a scarf. David drew steadily closer, until he could hear the soft fall of her steps on the path. She glanced back over her shoulder, then resolutely turned her eyes ahead. At a fork in the trail, as she swung right, David deliberately veered to the left, freeing her from anxiety. He sensed her watching him through the trees as he ran on.

Usually he ran about two miles into the park before turning back. This morning he was feeling so alive, jogging in the rain, that he decided to extend his run. He let his thoughts float, taking him wherever they would. He thought about the unknown man who had raised the question about the O Fund in his anonymous letter. What was his motive? He must know something significant about the fund. It had to be something that had been covered up, perhaps buried long ago, something that, if it came out, would be damaging to the current administration. But how did that figure? Only Edward Grabow, Mr. Clean himself, had been close to the centers of power through several administrations.

Surely the informant wasn't going to stop with that single enigmatic communication. He wanted the truth to come out. Why had he been so secretive? What was he waiting for?

Was he afraid? Of whom?

David had to find him, one way or another. Or if not him, then another disgruntled bureaucratic lifer, or patriotic whistle-blower, with the same crucial knowledge.

David reached a loop where the jogging trail turned back upon itself. The two sides of the loop were separated by a small wooded knoll. On the far side of the loop, through the screen of black trunks and drooping branches, David caught a glimpse of another runner in gray cotton sweats following the same trail behind him. David's nylon jacket and pants shed water. The other runner's outfit must be thoroughly wet by now. Even though the rain was light, it would gradually have soaked through the cotton. David wondered how far the man planned to run. His suit would become an extra weight to carry, the wet fabric dragging at tired legs.

As he found his own familiar envelope once more David forgot the stranger. After a few minutes, however, the illusion slipped away from him. He had the sense of no longer being alone. A quick glance over his shoulder confirmed it. He thought of the young woman he had inadvertently frightened. The man in gray was about fifty yards behind him, plodding steadily along in his wake.

David broke into the open as he passed through a picnic ground. He increased his speed. Just before he entered another tunnel of trees he had another look back. The other runner was keeping pace. If anything he had gained a few yards.

David accepted the challenge. He estimated that he had run about two-and-a-half miles. Later in the day it would be warm and humid, but at this early hour the rain had cooled the air. He still felt fresh. How far had the other guy run? No way to tell. David hadn't noticed him until they passed on opposite sides of the loop. Was his wet cotton suit feeling heavy about now?

Curiosity got the better of him after a few moments, prompting another over-the-shoulder glance. He felt a mild astonishment. The man in gray was only twenty yards behind, running without apparent effort. David's glance recorded other details: the runner wasn't some kid from Georgetown University. He was an older man. His hair was plastered to his skull, dark with rain, but the gray in it was visible. He was in good shape, David thought. For the first time he wondered if the man meant to show him up. Flash by and make David eat his spray.

David had started running to keep himself fit and continued because he had come to enjoy it, even the punishing parts, like now, when each breath became a knife in his lungs and the blood hammered in his ears and his legs were heavy. He had never run in competition. But there was an exhilaration in confronting the challenge his fellow runner offered.

Mentally David shifted gears, willing himself to step up a notch in speed. For a moment his legs seemed to hesitate, protesting. Then he broke through the wall of resistance and was running free.

For a quarter mile he didn't look back. The jogging trail entered a dogleg turn. The track immediately behind him disappeared behind the trees. David found himself grinning. He wondered about the other runner. Was he doing this out of arrogance, or for fun? Was he keeping up? Gaining ground?

Glancing back once more, David unconsciously broke stride, slowing his pace.

The trail behind him was empty.

David was struck by the oddity of it. The man had simply vanished, as if he had been a figment of David's imagination. David continued jogging, but much more slowly now, the knowledge of fatigue assaulting him from every part of his body. His chest heaved as he sucked air. Odd, he thought again. Why had the challenger given up?

For some reason his mind flipped back to his earlier speculations about the O Fund. Army intelligence files on the subject had been closed to him. Classified. Why would files, some of them presumably nearly a half century old, still be labelled *Top Secret: Sensitive,* no

foreign distribution. He needed to find someone willing to risk being the can-opener. He
needed to find the mysterious informant from
the Agency who wanted to —

The gray figure burst out of the trees to
his left. David had an impression of a square
face, unshaven, wet hair like a skullcap. David
veered to his right to avoid a collision. At the
moment before their momentum hurled them
together David thought, *What the hell* — ?

Two jarring images flashed before him: the
wolfish grin on the stranger's face, lips pulled
back; and the white shine of steel from the
switchblade in his right hand.

David reacted instinctively. He made a desperate leap for his life. He vaulted from the
jogging trail into the first stand of pine trees
beside the path. Clusters of wet needles lashed
across his face. The grip of his Nikes, so sure
on asphalt or dirt or gravel, skated like
rollerblades on the carpet of wet grass and
pine needles. David slithered out of control,
and banged into the sturdy trunk of a pine
tree.

The man in gray was on top of him in an
instant.

Turning, striking out blindly, David experienced an unreasoning terror. *Why? For God's
sake, why?*

The knife struck deep just below his rib

cage, penetrating until he felt the crunch of knuckles driving against his flesh. As the knife twisted and a hard white-hot pain exploded, suddenly he *knew*.

Twenty-Six

"Kevin, we have to talk."

"We have to talk."

Their words tumbled over each other, and they both stopped. There was a moment of silence.

"You first," Kevin said. He was calling from a pay phone. He no longer trusted even the phone in his apartment.

"Some things have happened that you don't know about," Alison said.

"Don't tell me now. I mean, they can wait till we get together."

She was silent for a long moment, obviously puzzled. She was in her cubbyhole of an office at Bryant Forbes Lederer & Wyman, where she had been working on one of a half-dozen briefs that had been dumped on her. "Any particular reason?"

"Yeah." He didn't elaborate, hoping she would understand.

"Where should we meet?"

"How about the usual place?"

"The usual . . . ?"

"The coffee's great." They had only met one place for coffee, the little café facing the beach. Kevin didn't think anyone had been watching them at that time. Or listening.

"Okay, that'd be fine. The usual time?"

They had met on the strand late in the morning. Is that what she meant?

"Uh . . . what about tonight? This is important."

"I'll be working late tonight. I have another brief to finish . . . and I have a date afterward."

"A date?"

"You know, like when you go out to dinner with someone?"

"Alison, this isn't supposed to be a *real* honeymoon!"

"Don't be childish, Daulton. I'll see you tomorrow. Have you been watching the news?"

"No."

"I think maybe you should."

The story was featured on the financial news. Kevin caught it on the Cable News Network and again on Channel 28, the PBS network station in Los Angeles. A company identified as Jamieson Investments had filed the required Form 13-D with the Securities and Exchange Commission that morning, confirming that it had acquired more than 15 percent of the outstanding common stock of Tyler Holdings.

The shark was under attack by a predator of unknown resources. The attacker's purchases had been made through a variety of prominent brokers and investment firms on both the London and New York stock exchanges. No one seemed to know much about the company, and in the early scramble to acquire more information the impression gained credibility that Jamieson Investments was a shadow company, fronting for a player of the first magnitude.

At three o'clock in the afternoon, its computers and the printers at the trading posts on the floor falling behind the frenzy of trading, the New York Stock Exchange suspended trading in Tyler Holdings common stock an hour before the normal closing bell. By that time the stock had jumped to 89-½, up nearly twenty points for the day.

Some of the country's largest pension and insurance funds, which had been investing heavily in Tyler futures, were busy congratulating themselves. Their managers were planning late-night sessions where the decisions would be made about investing in more stock index futures or in the stock itself.

One analyst, summing up a panel discussion on Channel 28, predicted that within three months, certainly before the release of Tyler's mammoth new stock offering, Tyler Holdings common would double in value.

On the general euphoria set off by the bull rush for Tyler Holdings, the DOW average closed ninety-five points higher for the day, on heavy trading of more than 220 million shares. One of CNN's guest experts, who held a position with Morgan Stanley's bond department, suggested that the events of the day might be the spark needed to jump-start the faltering U.S. economy.

Kevin Daulton watched the progression of the story, fascinated.

Reynolds Tyler was holding a glass of Jack Daniels on the rocks, jiggling the ice cubes angrily, glaring at Calvin Lederer. The two men stood at one end of the long covered patio facing the pool at Lederer's Palm Springs estate. It was late evening, but a pale light lingered in the night sky, outlining the dark bulk of the mountains that heaved upward from the flat desert floor.

Bubbling voices and a shriek of laughter drew their attention to the pool, where several shapely young women in skintight bodysuits or miniscule string bikinis frolicked in and around the pool. The scene seemed more appropriate for the Playboy mansion than Lederer's secluded desert retreat. One of the women, in fact, had been a Playmate of the Month in 1992.

"If the bastards think they've been in a fight before," Tyler said, "they're gonna learn different."

"Don't sweat it," Lederer said in his familiar oil-smooth tone. "All this will work to your advantage."

"Will it?"

"The smart money is already jumping on the bandwagon. They know in any shootout over a company the size of yours, the stakes will drive the price up. You're going to be a very rich man, Reynolds."

"I'm already a rich man. And I don't like being mugged in the dark. Who the hell are these people? I never heard of Jamieson Investments. Where is it incorporated?"

"In Delaware, naturally. And the principals of record are also people you never heard of."

Tyler rattled the ice cubes furiously. "It's a damned blind. Who's behind it? Someone's out to sabotage me."

"That's a little far-fetched. Who has that kind of capital to throw around these days?

There's a good chance someone is out to make a killing at your expense, though. Start a war, run up the price of the stock, and then let you buy him off."

"Greenmail?" Tyler had already worked this possibility over. The term referred to the unsavory practice of mounting a hostile raid on a stock with the specific intent of forcing a buyout at an inflated profit. "It doesn't smell right."

Although the desert air had started to cool, Tyler was still dressed too warmly for August in Palm Springs. He was wearing his trademark outfit of boots, jeans and a heavy cotton twill shirt. He hated the desert. This kind of desert, anyway, which was more like a movie set than anything real.

"Relax, Reynolds. Enjoy yourself. You can't lose."

"I'm in debt up to my neck," Tyler answered. "How much higher do you think I should pile it up before I drown?"

Lederer smiled. "As high as it takes. That's the way you've always done it. You can't stop now."

Tyler resented the smile and the soothing reassurances. Calvin Lederer had been very valuable to him during his turbulent rise over the past decade. His firm's Washington political connections had cleared away obstacles to some of Tyler's wheeling and dealing, had caused local political and environmental threats to Tyler's development projects to melt away. Lederer's experts could thread a safe path across the most dangerous legal minefield. And Lederer himself had been able to provide surprising access to the financing Tyler had needed for the highly leveraged takeovers upon which he had built his empire.

With all that admitted, Lederer remained a man Reynolds Tyler did not completely trust. In the old cowboy saying, he wasn't a man to cross the river with. When you pushed into really dangerous waters, you had to know your sidekick was someone you could count on, without having to wonder, when you looked his way for help in a crunch, if he would still be there.

"Where the hell have you been, Lederer? I can't have you disappearing on me when something like this blindsides me."

"Don't worry, I'm not going anywhere. I was away on client business. But from here on out I'm yours."

Tyler wasn't completely convinced. Lederer had a habit of disappearing without notice, and then evoking the lawyer's mystique of client privilege so he didn't have to say where he had been or why.

"What about DeGraff? I may need him."

"He's doing fine," Lederer lied. "He'll be back with us long before you need him."

Originally a defensive takeover specialist, Claude DeGraff had proved his agility in offensive maneuvers during some of Tyler's past skirmishes. Tyler felt more comfortable with him than he did with Calvin Lederer.

"I never could understand that Christian Science stuff. How could anyone as smart as DeGraff keep telling himself he's not sick when he is? He could've killed himself."

"Who can understand matters of religious faith?" Lederer answered. Now that Tyler's anger had cooled somewhat, the attorney's attention was wandering. "What say we find a couple of suits and join the girls in the pool? We're going for a ride, Reynolds — isn't that what you really love? And how about freshening up that drink?"

"Yeah," Tyler grumbled. "I may need it."

One of the nymphets grinned across the sparkling pool at the entrepreneur. She lowered her eyes, then glanced up quickly. Oldest look in the world, Tyler thought, but he grinned back.

"I want you to find out who these people are," he said. "I want to know what I'm up against."

"We're already working on it."

Tyler grunted skeptically. "I tell you this,"

he said. "It's gonna be a brawl."

The eleven o'clock news on Channel 7 included a brief camera shot of a man's body, covered in canvas, being carried out of wooded brush in a Washington, D.C. park. A picture of a handsome, dark-haired young man appeared on the screen in a window. He was identified as David Perez of East Los Angeles, chief aide to California's United States Senator Elinor Woods.

A television reporter, standing bareheaded in a drizzle in Washington's Rock Creek Park, said that David Perez had apparently been attacked by a mugger while jogging in the park early that morning. His body had been discovered by a young woman who had also been out jogging. Her name was being withheld.

The camera watched an ambulance pull away through the flanks of subdued spectators. Its lights glittered in the rain. Then coverage switched to a camera crew camped outside of a small frame house in the Boyle Heights district of East Los Angeles. It was identified as the home of Perez's mother and younger sister. Watching, Kevin hoped the older woman would not come outside to confront the inevitable question, "How do you feel, Mrs. Perez, about your son's murder?"

Briefly Kevin pondered the irony of someone surviving the warrior childhood David Perez must have experienced in the barrio, and escaping it only to meet a violent death in the nation's capital, within jogging distance of the White House.

Then he went back to CNN, searching for more news of Tyler.

Twenty-Seven

Elinor Woods caught the United Airlines red-eye flight from LAX to Dulles International. She flew first class against her natural inclination. On this flight she welcomed the extra space and privacy. The section was more than half empty. The few business travelers sharing first class kept to themselves, or dozed. The flight attendants were quiet and discreet. One man drank steadily. Elinor refused even the compulsory champagne. Champagne was for celebrations.

She was still in a state of shock. David alive was so vivid in her mind. How could he be dead? He wasn't even thirty years old, his whole life was ahead of him! The senselessness of his death — victim of a random mugging — appalled her. She knew there was a trace of elitism in her reaction, as if the murder of a promising young man of exceptional talent and intelligence in Washington, D.C., was more tragic than the snuffing out of a nameless youth in a drive-by shooting in Watts, the sort of thing that happened every day. But the Greeks — and the Elizabethans, for that matter — had been insightful in telling their high moral tales about kings rather than commoners. The sense of horror was magnified.

And she had *known* David Perez. Loved him as she did her own sons. Cherished his humor, admired his caring, appreciated his loyalty. David with his Big Macs and fries making the office reek of grease. David of the junkyard desk, from whose paper disorder he could always pluck exactly the note or memo or file that was needed. David the handsome bachelor, sublimely ignorant of the covetous glances of many of the young women on Elinor's staff. David the shrewd operator, already a better politician than she was, with unerring instincts for what was important and what was smoke. Like that hunch of his about the O Fund, based on nothing more than an anonymous scribble.

She huddled in her seat, turning her face toward the window, crying silently and unashamedly. When a worried flight attendant came to hover over her, Elinor waved her away.

Somewhere over Kansas, her grief finally exhausted, she slept fitfully and fearfully, as if she might awaken to see one of Rod Serling's gargoyles clinging to the aircraft's wing. . . .

The chauffeured Buick Park Avenue sedan, not a limousine but nevertheless a luxury, whisked her silently through the early morning traffic from the Virginia countryside into the heart of the Capitol. On the way she used one of the luxuries she did appreciate, the car telephone, to place a call to police headquarters. Her call was expected. Lieutenant Adam Walker, the homicide detective in charge of the case, was not at his desk. Elinor guessed that he had been up half the night dealing with the paperwork such a case generated. She said she would be at her office in the Dirksen Building.

She rode the rest of the way in numbed silence, staring through the tinted windows. Everything seemed changed, as if the shock to her system had subtly altered her angle of vision. The woods along the parkway were darker. Apartment and office windows were blind, impenetrable. When the parkway swept over the Theodore Roosevelt Bridge she glanced down at the deserted, heavily wooded island and shivered.

On a Saturday morning she expected Capitol Hill to be deserted except for tourists. Her steps made a hollow echo along the corridor to her office. Her staff was off on Saturday, but she was surprised to see the door open and lights turned on. Her secretary, Julie McConnell, jumped up quickly as the senator entered the office. She had been at her desk, and she had been crying.

"Senator, I . . . I thought you might be back. I'm so sorry about David. If there's anything I can do . . ."

Julie was bright and diligent, a strawberry blonde, more gamine-cute than pretty. She was one of those whose yearning glances David Perez had failed to recognize.

"Thanks, Julie, for coming in. But you don't have to stay. I'm not sure there's anything either of us can do."

"No, I'll stay for a while."

Elinor regarded her with sympathetic understanding, then nodded. "Okay, you field any phone calls. I'm not available, but use your judgment. No reporters until I've had a chance to write a statement. Do you know about anything special David was working on?"

"No, he didn't say . . . but he's been working late every night. He was really intense."

Elinor Woods frowned. The O Fund? It was odd even for David, to be working long hours during the summer recess. Unless he'd gotten a lead on something. . . . "I guess I'll have to go through his desk and try to make some order out of it," she said reluctantly.

"Well, you won't have to do that, Senator. I mean, David left things pretty organized."

"He did?"

When she saw David's desk Elinor stared in surprise. He *had* been busy while she was away. There were still stacks of files, newspaper clippings, correspondence, scribbled memos and messages with queries scrawled in the margins. But there was a semblance of order to the piles. You could even see the top of the desk here and there. Elinor couldn't remember ever having seen the wood before. It was as if David had been putting things in order in case something happened. That was nonsense, of course, but it left Elinor feeling unsettled. One more thing out of kilter. . . .

She made a start at going through some of the stacks on David's desk, not putting anything away, just gaining a sense of the unfinished business he had left behind. As she went through the accumulated papers her curiosity grew. There was nothing on the O Fund. No record of phone calls or interviews, no messages, no files or notes. That wasn't like David, who scribbled notes to himself about everything, and notes about the notes, often stuffing his pockets with scraps of paper.

"Senator Woods? There's a Lieutenant

Walker to see you. He said you were expecting him."

"Thank you, Julie. Yes, send him in."

She talked to the homicide detective in her office. She sat behind her desk, and Walker sat on the edge of the leather chair facing her, as if he didn't intend to stay long. He was black, about forty, with curly gray hair clipped short. He wore a summer-weight gabardine suit in a light olive color. He could easily have passed for a government bureaucrat or a lobbyist working the halls of Congress.

"What can you tell me about Mr. Perez, Senator? Did he —"

"First . . . can you tell me what happened? All I know is what was on TV."

"There isn't much more," Walker said.

David Perez had been found in a relatively isolated area of the park. No one had witnessed the attack. Because it had been raining that morning, there were fewer joggers than usual in the park. He had been found by a young woman who had seen him earlier — he had passed her along one of the trails. She had observed several other men out running, but she hadn't paid close attention to any of them. She had learned it was best to avoid eye contact when she was jogging, the detective said in a tone of irony.

"How did he . . . . how was David killed?"

The weapon had been a thin, sharp, long-bladed instrument — probably a switchblade knife, Walker explained. It was the weapon of choice for muggers because it was easily hidden. The assailant had apparently been well aware of the internal damage such a blade could inflict, Walker said, causing Elinor to wince. While the evidence at the scene of the crime was not conclusive, it appeared that the mugger had come through the woods to the left of the trail, probably earlier that morning, and had been waiting when David came along.

Elinor felt sick. After a moment she managed to speak. "Then it . . . it could have been anyone. I mean, it just happened to be David."

"Kind of looks that way, Senator. Yes. I would like to ask you some questions, though, if you don't mind. Do you know if Mr. Perez was a regular jogger?"

"I think he ran three or four times a week. In the morning before he came to work."

"Would he be in the habit of carrying much money with him? I notice he was wearing a good designer running outfit."

Elinor shook her head. "I don't think so. David liked clothes, but . . . no one on a senator's staff is going to get wealthy. I imagine David had his wallet, if he drove to the

341

park, but his murderer certainly didn't strike it rich, Lieutenant." There was bitterness in the comment.

"No wallet was found," Walker said, jotting a note with a ballpoint pen. "Did Mr. Perez have any enemies?"

"He was the nicest young man I've ever known. Everyone liked him."

"Any special girlfriend that you know of?"

"No. Not that there weren't quite a few who wanted to be."

"Boyfriend?"

Elinor smiled without humor. "No, Lieutenant."

"A little unusual, isn't it? A good-looking kid like that, you figure there would be somebody."

"He wasn't very gregarious, Lieutenant Walker. He was friendly, but a little reserved. I think he was shy, really."

"Uh-huh. What did he do in his spare time?"

"I didn't give him very much, I'm afraid," Elinor said. "I mean, he was very conscientious, he worked very hard. His job was his life. It wasn't unusual for him to work twelve, thirteen hours here at the office. In fact, it was unusual when he didn't."

"I didn't mean to upset you, Senator. You understand, we have to ask these questions."

Walker sighed. He pushed his hands against his knees and stood. Like any Capitol Hill lobbyist, he looked to be about twenty pounds overweight. "Was he working on anything unusual?"

"No," Elinor said too quickly. Except that mystery fund. She dismissed the thought. "No one had any reason to harm him."

"Thank you for your time."

At the door to her office Elinor asked, "Are you going to catch him, Lieutenant?"

The detective's expression was weary. He had heard that question too often before, and too often had to give the same answer. "We'll do our best, but you understand . . . there's very little to go on. Most serious crimes, you look to someone the victim knows, or knew. But in something like this, with no witnesses . . ." Walker shrugged. "The farther away we get from the event in time, the longer the odds."

Elinor asked when the body would be released for funeral services the family planned in Los Angeles. Walker indicated that immediate release might be possible. Elinor said she would make the arrangements.

When the detective had left Elinor noted that Julie McConnell appeared more grief-stricken than before. Elinor sent her home, overriding her protests. Julie gave her a short stack of what she had selected as the more important messages for the senator. Then she left. Elinor was alone in the office.

She tried to return to the puzzle of David's semiorderly desk. He had probably been looking for something, forcing him to straighten out the confusion. Then she remembered that she had been searching for David's notes and files on the O Fund when the homicide detective arrived. There was nothing. Odd, she thought. Unless David had taken them home.

The answer brought an exaggerated relief. She was uptight, she realized, overwrought, prone to make mountainous anxieties out of molehill suspicions.

Elinor carried the small stack of messages back to her desk and shuffled through them. Most were expressions of condolence, several from other senators and one from the White House. The chief of protocol, or whoever was responsible for such things at the White House, was on the ball.

At the bottom of the stack was a phone message from Raymond Farrow, urgently requesting that she return his call as soon as possible. Everything was urgent on the Hill, Elinor thought. Who was Raymond Farrow? Had he known David?

Suddenly the name clicked. *That* Raymond Farrow! It was a name synonymous with

Eastern Establishment, money, privilege, government service, like an Averell Harriman. What could Farrow want? To express his sympathy over David? Why would he feel the obligation? Elinor didn't recall ever meeting him.

She considered putting the message aside with the other condolences. They could be acknowledged later. She had to begin making arrangements for shipping David's body to Los Angeles. She had to telephone David's mother, whom she had spoken to briefly about the funeral services Friday night before her flight. She'd forgotten to ask the detective if she could have access to David's apartment. She would need to send his clothes, look for his notes —

Her eyes stung. No eye makeup today, she told herself wryly. She looked awful enough without mascara draining down her cheeks.

Composing herself, she punched up the number given on the Farrow message, recognizing the prefix for Chevy Chase. A woman's voice answered, and a moment later Farrow was on the line. "Senator Woods? I appreciate your calling. I know this must be a difficult time for you."

The tone of good breeding, self-confidence, impeccable manners. The voice of a man whose conversation would shun four-letter words because they trivialized the language.

"It is difficult. If you're calling about David —"

"Please accept my sympathies, Senator, but I think you should know I was trying to reach David Perez before his death."

Elinor Woods was startled. She had started to regret making this call. Now she changed her mind. "What about, Mr. Farrow?"

"I hope you won't mind my being so blunt. I believe it's important. Was David making inquiries about the O Fund on your behalf?"

"I'm not at liberty to discuss —"

"I'm looking into it myself," Farrow said. "I believe something very significant may be happening, and the Japanese and the O Fund may have some relevance. Is that not also your thinking, Senator Woods? I know you set the secretary of state back on his heels asking him about the fund. In my inquiries I've found that David Perez was usually ahead of me. A very resourceful young man. I'm sure you'll miss him a great deal."

"I already do," Elinor said softly.

"Do you mind my asking one more question? What put you onto the O Fund?"

Elinor made her decision. She liked the sound of Raymond Farrow's voice, and his straightforwardness. He also had a reputation for integrity rare in the corridors of government. She told him of the anonymous, handwritten letter she had received, under CIA letterhead, of David's hunch that it might be worth investigating, and her decision to broach the matter with Edward Grabow. She added that, starting with the chairman of the Senate Finance Committee, Joshua Bodine, there had already been considerable political pressure brought to bear to cause her to drop her inquiries into the fund.

"I'm not surprised. Would it be possible for me to see that letter, Senator?"

"Yes, but I'm afraid it doesn't tell us much. Just a moment . . . I have it filed away." She fished her key ring from her purse and unlocked the wooden file cabinet behind her desk. She fingered through the current files in the top drawer, stopping at the Os. She stared for a long moment. Thinking hard, she returned to her desk. "It's not in the file, Mr. Farrow," she said slowly. "David's notes are also missing. He must have taken everything home. He sometimes made calls from his apartment."

"He had access to your file?"

"Yes . . . he was the only one besides myself."

"I believe it's very important to retrieve anything he had related to the O Fund, Senator. If it's possible, I would appreciate meeting with you —"

"It will have to wait," Elinor said firmly. "I know you feel this is urgent, Mr. Farrow. I'm inclined to agree with you. But I have to return to Los Angeles as soon as possible for David's memorial services, and I have a great many arrangements to make. It will have to wait until I get back."

There was a long pause. Raymond Farrow said, "I understand, Senator. Will you call me as soon as you return to Washington?"

Elinor agreed, and rang off. A gracious man even when blocked, she thought. She sat in the silence of the office, feeling its emptiness, knowing that part of it would never be the same. She was reluctant to leave, as if any action she took would begin the final, inevitable journey that would take her away from David Perez.

After a while her thoughts returned to a question Lieutenant Walker had asked. Was David working on anything unusual?

David and Raymond Farrow, she thought. *"In my inquiries I found that David was usually ahead of me."*

For the first time since the terrible news of David Perez's murder, doubt crept into Elinor Woods's mind. She sat motionless in the empty office, listening to someone's footsteps echo along the corridor outside, fading away from her, and she felt a chill that brought gooseflesh to her arms.

Over the loudspeakers the first boarding call came for her flight to Los Angeles. Senator Elinor Woods listened to the rings. Eight . . . nine . . . he was out. Dammit! David's funeral was Tuesday; she would be back in the capital Wednesday. But this call couldn't wait.

"Hello?"

"Mr. Farrow? Thank heavens! This is Elinor Woods."

"Senator Woods!" Farrow hadn't expected her to call before her flight, and there was urgency in her tone. Something had come up. "What's wrong?"

"I'm not sure. I went to David's apartment to pick up some of his clothes. I looked for his notes. They weren't there."

"I see. Was he in the habit of making notes, or did he keep things in his head?"

"He once joked about joining Notemakers Anonymous. It's the only way he functioned. He was investigating the O Fund for two weeks, and there's no evidence of it, either at his apartment or at the office. And from what you said, he was very busy while I was out on the Coast."

"And the letter?"

"It's also missing."

She heard the last boarding call for her plane, but she waited. Then Raymond Farrow said, "I'll see what I can learn on my own. I think we need to meet as soon as you return to the Hill."

"I'll call you Wednesday."

She hung up and ran toward the gate.

Twenty-Eight

Sitting under an umbrella on the strand facing the beach, a cup of coffee on the glass-topped table in front of her, Alison Carey fancied watching her law career sail out to sea, first the internship at Bryant Forbes Lederer & Wyman dropping slowly out of sight beyond the horizon, then the promised position as an associate, finally the bar itself.

She thought about what she was risking. Alison had never dreamed of becoming society's pro bono champion at righting wrongs, or a public defender dedicated to lost causes. The law was a province of winners. But in an ugly turn, the success and achievement at which she had aimed didn't seem as desirable a goal anymore. What she had really promised that abandoned child all those years ago was that one day she would make herself safe and secure, dependent on no one. But there was no absolute security. You could be hit by a car, or get AIDS, or accidentally see something you weren't supposed to see . . . and what did you have to show for all your glittering promise?

She hated this kind of thinking. This was Kim's way. Kim the do-gooder would have loved to hear her now.

A Santa Ana wind had pushed all the haziness out to sea, bringing a dry desert heat to the coastal areas that normally enjoyed cool sea breezes. Alison could feel the heat radiating from the sand, which was rapidly filling up with tanned young bodies. She glanced at her watch. Kevin was late. Had he misunderstood their absurd, cloak-and-dagger references to time and place? What had made him start that, anyway?

She finally saw him, far down the strand. He was wearing a ridiculous pair of plaid shorts, a Hawaiian shirt overhanging the shorts, Keds without socks, big aviator sunglasses and a blue Dodgers baseball cap pulled low over his forehead. She wondered if it was an amateurish attempt at disguise. It was his walk she recognized, before he was close enough for her to identify the features under the low bill of his cap.

He eyeballed the beach crowd as he approached. *Ogled* was a better word, Alison decided, as his gaze appeared to linger on a pair of bikini-clad teenagers.

"If you're through taking in the view," Alison said cheerfully, "why don't you sit down?"

Kevin slipped into a chair opposite her. He stared at her openly. She was wearing a pair of white cotton shorts, an oversized T-shirt and a wide-brimmed, floppy straw hat that shaded her face.

"Morning," he said. "Have you eaten anything?"

"Hours ago."

"I haven't." He flagged a waitress and ordered a cinnamon roll, heated, and coffee. "No more than ten seconds in the microwave for the roll," he said.

They studied each other in silence for a moment. There was something different about him, Alison decided. An edge.

"How was your date?"

"You don't really want to know."

"Yes, I do. I'm serious. How has Hilliard been acting? How did you two get together again?"

Alison shrugged. "They've been keeping me busy, piling briefs on me. I kind of like it. It's better than flopping periods and commas, or changing columns of figures to read from right to left instead of left to right. At first I thought Dex was avoiding me. Then a couple days ago he asked how things were going, and he hoped I wasn't upset about the photo thing last Friday. I told him they were only snapshots. Why would I be upset?"

"How did he react?"

"He hoped I'd give him a raincheck."

"So you said yes."

"I want to know what's going on, Daulton. He's my best source."

"Did you learn anything from him?"

"No," she admitted. "Except there's going to be a big powwow at Lederer's place in Palm Springs this week, I guess to fight off this take-over. Lederer and Tyler and the whole brain trust will be there."

Kevin mulled this over while he broke off sugary pieces of cinnamon roll and chewed them. She guessed that he would have liked to ask more about her date, but was worried about the answers. She wasn't going to let him off that hook, even though Hilliard had stayed at a cautious arm's length all evening.

"Where did you get those shorts?" she asked.

"You don't like them?"

"They're a surprise, that's all. What were you going to tell me that you couldn't say on the phone? I mean, before you got all mysterious."

"You first. Why did you say we had to talk?" His glance strayed past her, scanning the beach and the strand.

"I had a call from Guam." She described the startling call from the army investigator. When she finished and Kevin said nothing, she said, "Don't you see? Someone was after the originals of those snapshots of Lederer and the Japanese."

"I suppose it's possible . . ."

"There's no supposing about it, Daulton. It's too much of a coincidence. Someone broke into Kim's house! Just like someone broke into my apartment."

"Any way of knowing if he got the pictures?"

"He didn't. Kim has them. She's having another set made, five-by-seven enlargements of the pictures from the hotel, and she's mailing them to me from London."

Kevin glanced around again, moving his eyes back and forth under his cap almost surreptitiously. Alison began to feel annoyed. The least he could do was pretend to pay attention.

"So what was so important you had to tell me?"

Kevin caught the sharpness in her tone, and he had the grace to appear dismayed.

"Your phone is tapped."

She actually felt her jaw drop. "You're kidding!"

"No. Do you know if you were followed over here?"

"No — why should I be?"

Suddenly the question sounded foolishly naive. They had burgled her apartment, reached halfway around the world to break into Kim's house, put a soldier in the hospital, trashed Kevin's job. Why wouldn't they follow her? *That's why he keeps looking around.*

"I didn't want to say too much on the phone. I didn't want them to realize I knew about the phone being bugged. Did you know they bug the phones in the office, too? And the offices?"

"No," she whispered.

"They know we're seeing each other and talking to each other, which means they may not be buying your honeymoon act. They probably told Hilliard to keep an eye on you."

He watched her expression change. A closed, determined stare matched the tight line of her lips. "I don't know what's going on, Daulton, but someone's violated my space. Now they've done the same thing to Kim. I'm not just going to forget it." She sat back, allowing her gaze to wander over the crowded beach. "Do you think we're being watched now?"

"Maybe. They want to keep tabs on us . . . or maybe just on you. Otherwise why bother to tap your phone?"

Alison was angry, and she felt the same sense of violation she had experienced when she discovered the burglary of her apartment. At the same time Kevin's suspicions — even his assertion about the phone being tapped — were too incredible. Sinister clicks on her phone line? Eyes watching them? Who? That burly man covered with black hair? The fat one with the newspaper over his face, hiding his eyes? The rollerskater? None of it was believable.

She shivered in spite of the heat. "I can't go back to my apartment."

"What?"

"You heard me, Daulton. I'm not going to have strangers peeping in my windows, listening to everything I say, feeding their dirty little reports to that creep Rathman."

"Where will you go?"

She looked at him with a tolerant expression. "I guess it'll have to be your place."

His apartment had a small, high-walled patio that provided a welcome degree of privacy. The heat of the day, baked into the stucco walls, lingered in the enclosed space. Alison lay on the webbed chaise, still wearing her white shorts and the loose T-shirt, her long tanned legs stretched out toward him.

Kevin sat in a plastic Kmart chair, nursing a cold beer. An empty pizza box lay open on the table between them.

"I think you should stay out of trouble," Kevin said, breaking a relaxed silence he was reluctant to disturb.

"What's that supposed to mean?"

"There's nothing you can do, Alison. What can either of us do?"

"Just let it go? Let them walk all over us?"

"Be realistic. We don't have any idea what's going on, or who's involved."

"Don't we? We have this Tyler takeover attempt coming out of the blue. Does that seem like another coincidence to you? We have Lederer secretly meeting some Japanese types on Guam, and breaking the law to cover it up. We have the president in Japan for the economic summit — okay, so maybe that *is* a coincidence — we have you being fired for no good reason, and my phone tapped. That may not add up to anything specific, but *something's* sure as hell going on. Someone's pulling the strings — Lederer, maybe, or Tyler, or the Japanese. And we're all supposed to dance." She sat up on the chaise, and he saw that fiercely determined expression again. "Well, nobody pulls my strings, Daulton! Not anymore!"

Kevin bit off his objection. She obviously

wasn't going to listen to common sense.

"What happened to the new Kevin Daulton?" she demanded. "I thought you were ready to fight back."

"I don't want you getting into trouble. Or getting hurt. Have you forgotten that soldier on Guam?"

"No, I haven't forgotten." The hostile challenge faded from her eyes. "You're really worried about me?"

"Yes."

"Don't be. I can take care of myself." After a moment she speculated aloud. "What if this thing is bigger than Lederer and Tyler? What if it's something the Japanese are up to?"

"That's a reach," Kevin said.

"Not such a long one. Anyway, I think whatever is going to happen will come soon. That's why they're so paranoid, even about you and me. I'm going to see if I can get an invitation to Palm Springs from my good friend Dexter Hilliard. Do you know I've never been there? It's supposed to be beautiful."

"It's hotter than sin."

"There's that way with words again."

"I don't like your going down there alone."

"With Dex, you mean?"

"Yeah, with Dex. And Lederer. And Tyler. You don't know what you're getting into. I don't think you should go."

"It's not your decision. What about you? Are you going to just stand by and watch? What about Claude DeGraff? Have you talked to him?"

"I called the hospital. He wasn't receiving visitors."

"Maybe you should surprise him."

"I don't know . . ."

"Do it, Daulton. If he knows anything, you can get it out of him. I know you can."

The confident assertion both elated and disturbed him. All he knew for certain was that he couldn't say no.

"Ask him about the Japanese," Alison said.

They stayed out on the patio until long after dark. Kevin was loath to shatter the sense of complicity that drew them together. He could almost feel grateful to Lederer and Hilliard and their unholy crew.

When he saw Alison stifle a yawn and hug her chest with her arms, as if chilled by the night air, he said, "What are you doing about tonight? And clothes for tomorrow?"

"I'll get some clothes in the morning." She stared at him sleepily in the semidarkness of the patio. "Are you going to kick me out?"

"No, no, I didn't mean that!" He began to have trouble breathing. "What'll the watchers think if they're out there?"

"It'll just confirm that you were craving my body."

"Well, it's true. I do crave your body." *Now you've done it!* the disbelieving voice wailed over his shoulder.

"I know," Alison said. "But I'm not ready for that yet, Daulton, okay?"

"Uh . . . sure. You can have my bed. I can sleep on the couch."

"That won't be necessary. I don't mind you holding me, Daulton. I think maybe I need that."

Twenty-Nine

As Toshio Miyaki moved closer to the continental United States, media interest in the Japanese business tycoon picked up. Growing curiosity forced Miyaki to hold a brief press conference in Honolulu, where he stayed for two days after his arrival from Guam. He confirmed that he was scheduled to give a speech before a gathering of important American businessmen the following Thursday at the Century Plaza Hotel in West Los Angeles. He declined to discuss its subject.

Miyaki also refused comment on proposed plans for reopening a steel mill in Youngstown, Ohio, saying that any such announcement would be premature.

Reporters tried to browbeat him about the Youngstown plan. "Aren't you backtracking on your pledge to the steelworkers of Youngstown?" one demanded.

Miyaki smiled. "I have neither advanced nor

retreated. I simply said that any statement at this time would be premature."

"Are you going to visit Youngstown while you're in the United States?"

There was a slight hesitation before the answer came. "I will have a statement to make next week."

"In your speech Thursday?"

"In due course."

The elderly Japanese businessman who, according to his biography, had built a financial and industrial empire out of the rubble of a defeated Japan after World War II, obviously was not going to be stampeded by aggressive American journalists. He said that plans were going forward for the Sakai automotive plant in Fresno, California, but that any statement on that subject should more appropriately come from his friend Shinji Sakai, who was the driving force behind the development.

As Miyaki started to leave the podium in the hotel conference room where he had agreed to meet the press, another reporter shouted at him. "Why are you visiting America now? Is there any reason you're coming here just when the president is in Japan for the economic summit?"

Miyaki turned back. His plans for his trip to the United States had been made long before the agenda for the economic summit was agreed upon by the leaders of the two countries, he said. Then he dropped the first of the bombshells that were, during the next seven days, to rock America's financial markets and shake public confidence. "I see no beneficial purpose in the summit meeting at this time. America's economic difficulties are of its own making, and it may well be too late for the Japanese government, however willing it may be, to extricate the United States from its severe deficit and trade problems, and its declining industrial base, given the unwillingness of either the American people or its leaders to make the necessary sacrifices."

With that, as pandemonium broke out among the assembled television and print journalists, Miyaki walked briskly out of the room.

Yashi Nogama barged into Miyaki's suite unannounced. *"Omedetō!"* he said. "A very effective performance."

"Ah, so desu-ka?"

"Hai... the reporters were very impressed. There is already much talk about what you meant, as if your words weren't perfectly clear and obvious. This will increase the speculation over your speech in Los Angeles. The timing will be perfect."

"Yes."

Miyaki drew no satisfaction from the impact of his press conference or from Nogama's congratulations. During the long flight from Guam to Hawaii, after satisfying himself that Nogama himself was not on board but that one of his agents had been assigned to follow Miyaki and observe his movements, the old man had struggled with the heaviness that had descended upon his spirit. He told himself that he must do what honor demanded, but the sands upon which the fragile edifice of honor rested were shifting.

Miyaki had not been surprised to find Nogama waiting for him in Honolulu. Since then the *yakuza* had remained secluded in his room. His facial injuries, especially a swollen nose and fading discoloration around one eye, explained his desire to stay out of sight. He had been injured in a minor auto accident, Nogama had explained when Miyaki inquired politely about his well-being. His bruises were superficial, but they were the reason for his abrupt departure from Guam ahead of schedule without meeting the American Calvin Lederer.

By this time Miyaki knew most of the truth of what had happened on Guam. What remained unexplained was Nogama's purpose in breaking into the house of an obscure mathematics professor who was currently in England with his family. Miyaki had extensive personal resources on Guam and in Los Angeles to call upon. It had not been difficult for his aide to obtain the name of the owners of the house Nogama had burglarized, as well as a copy of the police report. The latter included a reference to a phone call from the housewife's sister in Los Angeles. His curiosity piqued, Miyaki had asked for an inquiry into the sister. Upon his arrival in Honolulu he had received the report he had requested. The sister's name was Alison Carey, she was a recent law school graduate now living in Manhattan Beach, California, and she was employed by the law firm of Bryant Forbes Lederer & Wyman.

This information did not answer the mystery of Nogama's actions, but it provided a rational link. Whatever the gangster had been after was related to Calvin Lederer . . . and therefore to the Sonno conspiracy. And it was something else that had been concealed from Toshio Miyaki.

As Miyaki remained silent, Yashi Nogama's expression darkened with suspicion. A gregarious bulldozer of a man, Nogama did not comprehend silence or discretion as being innocent of motive or malice.

"It's important that you do not waver," the *yakuza* said.

Miyaki was startled. Nogama's lack of subtlety made it easy to underestimate him. He had penetrated Miyaki's heart and mind, sensing his misgivings, with a street criminal's cunning instinct.

"I don't need to answer such doubts."

"Perhaps . . . but I will be watching."

"Watch, then," Miyaki said coldly. "But try not to have any more auto accidents."

Nogama stiffened, anger flashing in his eyes. "What of the devil Reynolds Tyler?" he demanded. "You didn't speak to the reporters of him."

"It's not yet time."

"When?"

"His fate will also be determined by the end of the week."

Nogama's habitual suspicion appeared to ease. His trap of a mouth twisted in a smile, and his tone registered a gloating satisfaction. "Friday there will be panic. The American president and most of his advisors will be in Japan, far removed from the center of power. America will be a ship rudderless in a storm. There will be no time to get back on course by Monday."

"*Iie,*" Miyaki said, surprised by Nogama's attempt at metaphor.

"Friday will be America's economic Pearl Harbor. Monday will be its Hiroshima!"

Toshio Miyaki said nothing.

He did not wish the gangster to sense the depth of his self-doubt and despair.

Robert Daulton had moved to a small farm near the Housatonic River in the southwest corner of Connecticut after his forced early retirement. The house had been built in the 1870s, and he had spent six years slowly restoring it, coming to take pride and satisfaction in working with his hands and heart. His wife, meanwhile, had planted an herb garden behind the house in the first year. She now had a thriving small business selling herbs. The tiny garden had expanded tenfold.

We ought to be grateful to Reynolds Tyler, he thought.

It was Sunday evening. Sitting on the long porch, he could smell a fragrance in the warm evening air. Lemon basil, he thought, though he was far from being an expert. He had the portable phone with him, Reynolds Tyler on his mind.

He dialed the familiar Chevy Chase number of his friend Raymond Farrow. For several days Daulton had been unable to reach him. This time Farrow was at home.

"Sorry, Bob, I meant to call back. I've been on the go." Farrow's voice lacked its usual bounce.

"So I gather. You sound tired."

"Tired . . . and worried."

"What's happening? I can't believe this takeover attack on Tyler Holdings. It doesn't add up."

"Unless someone's on a personal vendetta."

"Yeah," Daulton said. "I guess I could understand that."

"Have you heard anything more about Tyler from Kevin?"

"That's one of the things I wanted to tell you . . . he's been fired."

"Fired! For heaven's sake, why!"

Daulton explained the circumstances. "It would appear he had no business doing what he did, trying to investigate another attorney's files. The firm was within its rights. Still, it makes you wonder what they're so sensitive about. Then along comes this takeover blitz by someone unknown."

"Not completely unknown," Farrow said. "Jamieson Investments is a United States company, but it's owned by a Japanese businessman, Toshio Miyaki."

Robert Daulton stiffened. "Miyaki . . . didn't I just read about a flap over a speech he gave in Honolulu, castigating us for our failure to address our deficit and trade problems?"

"It was at a press conference. The story was

on the front page of the *Times* today. Nothing really new there. Other Japanese leaders, from Sony's chairman Akio Morita to that maverick Ishihara, have said some of the same things. What's interesting is that Miyaki said them at the same time we learn he's on his way here . . . and he's attempting a hostile takeover of one of our major corporations. Morita and others have been critical of our takeover frenzy in the 1980s, remember."

"Where are we heading, Ray?"

"Unless I'm badly mistaken — and I hope I am — it's like that joke about the light at the end of the tunnel. It's another train . . . a Japanese bullet train."

"Not very funny," said Daulton soberly.

"No, it isn't."

Farrow revealed that he had been unable to arrange an appointment with the president before Walton left for Osaka. Someone in the White House had blocked him. Since then he had intensified his efforts to develop hard information about the O Fund, and also about any recent activities on the part of the Japanese government or major Japanese companies or individuals that seemed unusual. Toshio Miyaki's name was the first to surface. Oddly enough, Farrow observed, Miyaki didn't have a reputation as being anti-American, or even a hard-line Japanese nationalist.

"Were you able to talk to Senator Woods about the O Fund?"

"I did," Farrow said, "but under unhappy circumstances. The senator's chief aide was on the same hunt — our trails kept crossing. The young man was always a couple of steps ahead of me. Unfortunately, he was mugged in Rock Creek Park the other day."

"I hadn't heard. Was he badly hurt?"

"He was stabbed to death."

Daulton was jolted by the revelation. Violent muggings had become a commonplace item, hardly sensational enough to warrant more than a minute or two on the local evening news. But in the context of the aide's investigations into the O Fund, his murder was particularly unsettling. It created an uneasy notion that everything might not be what it seemed. *Our national conspiracy paranoia,* Daulton thought. That triggered another popular joke of the times: *It's not paranoia if it's happening.*

"Were you able to find out how Senator Woods tumbled onto the fund?" he asked.

"Someone sent her an anonymous tip, suggesting that she ask Ed Grabow about it. That's why she clobbered him with it during the Senate hearings. Since then the Administration has done some nifty footwork to pretend the question was never asked, much less answered, and the media have been distracted by the summit. I gather the senator is getting some heavy political pressure to back off. Neither she nor her young assistant were buying that. I wish I'd had a chance to talk to him."

"Woods sounds like someone I'd like to vote for."

"You can always move to California."

"I don't want to go that far." Daulton gazed across the herb garden in the fading summer twilight. *Never,* he thought. "Any chance of finding where that tip came from?"

"This gets interesting," said Raymond Farrow. "That letter has disappeared from the senator's files, along with any notes or information her aide had made."

Daulton inhaled sharply.

"So far I haven't a clue as to who might have wanted to open up the O Fund to public scrutiny," Farrow continued. "I have friends in the CIA and the FBI, but no one can tell me anything. Can't or won't. The intelligence community is about as homogeneous as the Serbs and the Bosnians, but let an outsider stick his nose in and they close ranks in a hurry."

"You're hardly an outsider."

"I was never a spook, Bob."

Daulton had a sudden thought. "Maybe I can help. I've got an old friend in Navy Intelligence who owes me. Dan Hallerman. Those people tend to know each other — Army Intelligence, the Navy, Treasury agents, the Bureau, the Agency, the DEA and the rest. Like you said, they have their rivalries, but there's a lot of overlap. They all hear things. Besides, Hallerman and I go way back. I'll call him tomorrow."

"How about tonight?" Farrow said.

Thirty

Watching on CNN as his old friend James Arthur Walton approached the diminutive figure of the Japanese prime minister, a broad smile on his face, Gus Bonelli felt a mixture of anxiety and satisfaction. The president was facing rough times, but he would survive them. Yuki Nashido, the prime minister, bowed. He smiled as he stepped forward to accept the traditional Western handshake, his hand swallowed up in Walton's large-knuckled grip. Bonelli saw Ed Grabow hovering in the background. Undoubtedly Runnels was also present, though not visible.

Bonelli didn't mind not being there. In the view of the White House press corps, and in Gus's own view, he was minding the store. Technically the vice president was on hand for any crisis, but if there were any hard decisions to make, short of the transfer of power mandated by a presidential assassination, Gus would make them.

He made them even when the president was in Washington. Three years ago he had made the tough decision to acquire the capital infusion Walton desperately needed for his campaign — he wasn't yet president — the only way he could get it. He hadn't liked it, but he had done it. Now he had to ensure that that decision didn't destroy everything he had helped to create. The secret had to stay buried.

The televised coverage of the summit opening ceremonies shifted to a turbulent street scene. A crowd of white-shirted students demonstrating outside the American Embassy in Tokyo. It was not necessary to understand what the students were screaming. Their faces spoke for them. Faces and fists.

Gus Bonelli scowled. Why did the media have to show such garbage?

Cable News Network coverage of the national scene resumed after the president and prime minister entered the latter's limousine and drove away together. The opening day was all ceremony, Gus knew from his briefing. Formal negotiations were to begin Tuesday morning. The scenes he had witnessed had been filmed earlier. It was the middle of night now in Tokyo, morning in Washington, D.C. Gus watched the national coverage briefly, his interest fading. The market had opened higher this morning, buoyed by soaring prices for Tyler Holdings stock and the Street's expectations of the Osaka summit. Hurricane Felix was threatening the Bahamas. The Mets had traded for a pitcher for the September pennant drive.

He checked his watch — a Seiko, not a Rolex. Gus was not of the "if-you've-got-it-flaunt-it" school. He had no desire to be noticed. Especially today.

He knew the residue of the press corps would be curious about his activities if he left the White House. For that reason he had agreed to speak at the graduation ceremonies for the new class of FBI agents. Going down to Quantico enabled him to get out of the city and away from scrutiny on an excuse that was plausible, but not interesting enough for anyone to follow him closely.

From the Beltway he rode south on I-95 in the direction of Fredericksburg in the hushed silence of his chauffeured limo. The land was flat, wooded, dry and brown. About twenty miles south, with little traffic on the highway behind him, Gus had his driver divert onto a side road heading west. At the first crossroads he told the chauffeur to pull over and stop. They sat in silence for five minutes, watching the intermittent flow of traffic. Finally satisfied, Gus directed the driver south once more along a little-used state highway. After another twenty minutes he spotted a roadside café ahead. "That's it," he said. He stepped out of the car onto gravel and into ovenlike heat. "Keep the air conditioning going," Gus growled. He didn't have to tell the chauffeur to stay in the car.

Marty Wallach's dark blue Ford LTD was parked to the side of the restaurant. Marty liked large American cars with big V-8 engines. Gus was sweating by the time he reached the café, which was as icy cold inside as the September day was hot. The interior smelled of grease and beer. Marty was sitting in a booth at the far end of the counter area, facing the entrance.

Marty lifted his glass of draft beer and an eyebrow. Gus shook his head. "Coffee," he said. "I'm giving a speech at Quantico in a couple hours."

Marty grinned. "Sounds like fun."

They had not discussed the solution to the David Perez problem. They never would. Marty was superstitious about such things, and Gus Bonelli was glad to put it behind him. It was something that had to be done, not something he was proud of.

"Do you have the letter?"

"Yeah. The kid's notes, too."

Gus studied the handwritten scrawl. Shaky,

he noted, not firm. What did that mean. Was the writer old? Sick? Scared?

"CIA stationery," he muttered.

"Doesn't mean he's with the Agency," Marty said, "but it's a probable. They don't sell their paper stock at swap meets."

The waitress came with Gus's coffee and another beer for Marty. Gus waited until she had returned behind the counter, where she removed a filter full of wet coffee grounds and inserted a fresh packet. Piped music pounded through the long, narrow restaurant. A Garth Brooks number, hot and loud. Gus said, "Anything in the notes?"

"He was going at it right, but he hadn't come up with anything, either on the fund or this songbird."

"You've gotta find him before anybody else does."

Marty looked at him. "If he's current, and he's with the Agency, this isn't a jog in the park."

"I know. I'm asking a lot."

"You know I'll do what I can. What I'm saying is, this could get messy."

"Just find him," Gus said. "Then tell me. I'll figure what to do from there. I need to know who the son of a bitch is, and what he's after."

"You think he's after the president?"

"If he is, he's gonna be one sorry son of a bitch."

Marty glanced at the single sheet of CIA letterhead with its terse message. "If he's a spook, and you've got to figure he is, and he doesn't want to be found, it won't be easy."

"If you can't find him, maybe nobody else can. But I can't take the chance. Besides, he might not stop with this note. Why should he start this if he's not gonna finish it?"

Marty sipped his beer, glanced out the window at the hot, dusty highway, listened to Garth Brooks wail. "You don't have to tell me, Gus, but how bad is it?"

Gus held his mug of bitter coffee in both hands as if to warm them. The beige pottery mug had a chip on the edge. He thought of rich Colombian coffee served in china cups in the Oval Office.

"He can take the president down, Marty." For another moment he was silent. "He can take me down."

Marty finished his beer in a long, chug-a-lug swallow. He banged the frothy, empty glass on the plastic-topped table. "You make your speech to the tenderfeet, Gus. I'll find that son of a bitch for you."

A little less than an hour's drive east by northeast from Washington, Raymond Farrow slowly climbed the steps of a football stadium. About halfway up he came to the long bench seat where a burly man, elbows on knees, watched the navy football team run through conditioning drills on the green field below. Farrow sat beside him, hatless in the sun. Beyond the end of the stadium he had a glimpse of tree-shaded promenades and ivy-covered buildings in one small corner of Annapolis.

"Good of you to meet me, Commander."

"Bob Daulton vouched for you, Mr. Farrow. That's good enough for me."

Hallerman was a granite-jawed man in his fifties, gray hair in a stiff brush cut, razor creases in his pants, flint in his eyes. Raymond Farrow had the immediate impression that Hallerman had agreed to meet him reluctantly.

"I'm looking for a man."

"You'll have to be a little plainer than that."

Farrow wondered how to break through the barrier. "I'm looking for a patriot. A man who has information vital to his country's well-being, but who doesn't know how — or is afraid — to reveal what he knows to the right people."

Hallerman grunted. "A whistle-blower."

"You could say that, I suppose. I prefer to put it another way. Paul Revere was a whistle-blower. What he tried to do was warn his fellow countrymen of imminent danger."

"Imminent danger?" Hallerman smiled with his mouth. "You don't strike me as a melodramatic type, Mr. Farrow."

"I'm not. Let me put it plainly. I have reason to be seriously apprehensive about the current Japanese initiative. I tried to meet with the president before he left for Osaka, but I was unable to. There are layers of jealously guarded turf you have to cross to reach the Oval Office personally."

"Tell me about bureaucracy."

"I've been working with Senator Elinor Woods of the Senate Finance Committee," said Farrow, exaggerating slightly. "We've been investigating a secret Japanese fund that may have had a significant impact upon events affecting our country in the past, and could be even more important in the immediate future. There are hard-liners in Japan, Commander, extremists fanatically devoted to the emperor and to Japanese superiority, who may control that fund. The senator received an anonymous tip about the fund on CIA letterhead — unsigned. Her chief aide was trying to investigate the fund and the identity of the informant. He was murdered last Friday morning. His notes and the reports of his investigation — and the anonymous letter — have disappeared." Farrow saw that he now had the navy man's attention. "This is not melodrama, Commander Hallerman. Someone doesn't want the facts about the fund to become public. We have the possibility of a conspiracy involving Japan that even the president of the United States is ignorant of — at the very moment he's negotiating new trade and technology agreements in Osaka."

"You think the president might be sandbagged."

"In a word, yes."

Hallerman's formidable navy jaw jutted out a little farther. After a moment he said, "What can I do?"

"You've worked in intelligence for many years. I need to find that whistle-blower. I think he's CIA. He could be anyone, of course, but we don't have much time and we have to concentrate on the probable here. That would be an older man, old enough perhaps to have personal knowledge of the fund. Probably a former or retired agent. I believe the fund's origins go back to the postwar occupation of Japan. Someone who was there would be my age, or older."

Hallerman's flinty gaze appraised the white-haired man beside him. "That narrows the field considerably."

Farrow smiled. "That's a nice way to put it."

"This is the kinder, gentler navy." Hallerman gazed down at the field below, where burly linemen were engaged in blocking drills, crouching and driving forward against each other. The collisions were clearly audible up in the stands.

"You think this man, probably one of the Agency's old Cold Warriors, is scared to come out in the open."

"With good reason. I believe if his identity is discovered before I can find him, his life is in danger."

Hallerman rose. He paced the length of the aisle, his back ramrod straight. His walk was stiff-legged. A knee injury, Bob Daulton had said, had put Hallerman behind a desk. Probably hated it, Farrow judged. Hallerman struck him as a blunt, forceful man of action, impatient with the paper blizzard of teaching or administrative duties.

Returning along the narrow aisle, Hallerman stopped before Farrow, hands on hips in a challenging pose. "We're talking the security of the United States here."

"I believe so."

"I'll see what I can find out. I know some of the old-timers who used to work on the Farm. There aren't too many faces left from those occupation days — not in our trade. If it's some scared clerk who saw a memo, I think you're out of luck. But if it's someone with firsthand knowledge from the old days, we might have a chance. Intelligence isn't a calling where you think too much about living to enjoy your old-age pension — unless you happen to get stuck behind a desk."

"This is a good chance to get out from behind that desk," Farrow said.

"Yeah." Hallerman grinned. "That's what Daulton said."

Thirty-One

In his comfortable hotel suite in the old city of Osaka, President James Arthur Walton was briefed Tuesday morning on the news headlines from *U.S.A. Today*. He roused himself from his morning lethargy on hearing that the Dow average ended forty points higher on Monday, led by a surge in Tyler Holdings stock, which had broken one hundred in the last hour of trading.

The president interrupted Edward Grabow, who was reading him the headlines. "What do you suppose that's all about?"

"It could be very good news, Mr. President. It may be an early favorable reaction to the opening of the summit meetings."

Sylvester Runnels turned away from the view windows, where he had been impressed for the dozenth time by the juxtaposition of ancient wooden buildings cheek by jowl with modern skyscrapers.

"I kind of wish we were back home," Walton said wistfully. "Yuki is friendly enough, but all this bowing and scraping, it gets on your nerves. Besides . . . do you get the feeling some of them don't mean it at all?"

In a span of three days Kevin Daulton had plunged from the highest of highs to the lowest of lows. One night he was holding Alison Carey in his arms, nothing between them but the cotton nightshirt she had borrowed from him. He could feel every lean and tender curve through the thin knit fabric. When she breathed, his body moved in gentle unison with hers. Listening to each soft breath, he tried very hard not to make his excitement too obvious.

"Are you cold?" she asked him once.

"No," he whispered, trembling.

"This is nice," she murmured drowsily.

She slept, hours before Kevin was able to drift into an uneasy slumber.

In the morning, though cheerful and affectionate, Alison was more distant than the night before. And she had decided that she wasn't going to let anyone scare her away from her own apartment. They had breakfast together at Coco's, and afterward Kevin drove her to Manhattan Beach. She had him drop her off two blocks from her building. That was the last time he had seen her.

That Saturday night was so euphoric that he had banished his skeptical voice to the farthest reaches of his mind. Even when he played devil's advocate with himself, arguing that this one night didn't mean anything special, confirming only that she liked and trusted him, he didn't believe a word of it. But from that weekend peak he had now, on Tuesday evening, descended to the desolate bottom of hearing her say over the phone, "I don't think we should see each other for awhile, Daulton. Not until this is over."

"Not until it's over? We don't even know for sure there's anything there to be over!"

"Yes, we do," she said very firmly.

"Why can't we see each other?"

"You know why. For the same reason I'm calling you from a pay phone. Because they're watching, and I'm tired of playing hide-and-seek. I think Hilliard wants to believe I'm ready to be a dutiful girl and not make waves. If he keeps getting reports about us, he might have second thoughts."

"You're still going to Palm Springs with him?"

"Stop sounding possessive, Daulton," she answered coolly. "It doesn't become you. Besides, what are they going to do, kidnap me?"

The suggestion seemed preposterous on its face, but Kevin was unwilling to give up. "I don't like it. How can you trust him? How can you trust any of them?"

"I don't, of course. But how else are we going to learn what's going on?" She paused. Kevin could hear traffic noises in the background. "You weren't able to talk to Claude DeGraff, were you?"

Kevin had been hoping she wouldn't ask. "He was having tests done all day. CAT scans, infrared scans, audio scans and so on. I hung around there for over an hour tonight after visiting hours until they kicked me out. I'm not a relative, you know. The head nurse at his station was ready to call security." Listening to his lame excuses Kevin thought, *You didn't get it done, that's all. You think she doesn't see through your excuses?*

"I'm about out of change. This is crazy, isn't it? I mean, using public phones, talking in secret, looking over our shoulders to see if anyone's hiding behind the telephone pole. It's like we're hiding an illicit affair or something. I've got to go."

"Alison —"

"I'll try to call you from Palm Springs if I hear anything. Hilliard and the others are really excited, so something's about to happen. I can feel it. There are meetings all day, the partners all looking grim as ghosts. Oh, one other thing . . . I got those pictures from Kim. She sent duplicates. I've mailed you a set. See if you can make anything of them, okay?"

"I miss you —"

She had hung up, and he didn't know if she had heard him.

Kevin was determined that, the next time he talked to Alison, there would be no empty excuses. He waited for the morning mail before going out on Wednesday. The package of photographs didn't arrive. There was a polite letter of regret in response to one of the résumés he had sent out. His qualifications did not meet the firm's immediate needs, but his application would be kept on file, et cetera, et cetera. Kevin tossed it.

If it weren't for Alison, he could always go back to the family farm in Connecticut. Wasn't that what sons and daughters were doing in droves? But he would never put a continent between himself and Alison, even if his dwindling bank account soon relegated him to the ranks of the homeless. Besides, at the end of this week he would be able to pick up his first unemployment check.

Partly because he was feeling impoverished, he splurged on a hamburger at the Hamburger Hamlet on Beverly Boulevard, a short walk up the street from the hospital. Then he made his way to the third-floor wing where he had located Claude DeGraff's room. To his relief the disapproving head nurse at the station wasn't on duty, or was away from her post. The other nurses were too busy to pay attention when Kevin walked by without slowing. The door to DeGraff's room was partly open. The room was dim, blinds drawn over the single window.

Claude DeGraff lay on the contour hospital bed in a sitting position. A tray beside the bed held the contents of a liquid lunch, most of it untouched. He stared unblinking at Kevin, as if his appearance in the room were the most natural of events. "Kevin!"

"I thought I'd stop by and see how you were doing," Kevin said heartily, despising himself.

"The office sent flowers." DeGraff's gaze swung toward a large but tired bouquet in a plastic vase on a bedside table. His voice was drained of energy, and Kevin was shocked by his pale, drawn appearance. He looked shrunken, as if he had lost twenty pounds almost overnight. "Good of them."

Kevin didn't think it was particularly good of them at all. He wondered if George Broward or any others among the firm's partners had been to see DeGraff. That brought up an awkward question. Did DeGraff know Kevin had been fired? That he had been more or less accused of prying into DeGraff's desk?

"Has anyone been by to fill you in on what's happening?"

"No, but I have the TV there. I've heard about the Tyler takeover fight. Knew it was coming. A strange business, Kevin. He's our client, after all."

It was an opening Kevin had hardly dared to hope for. "Yes, I thought that was odd. Which side are we on, anyway?"

"Oh, I think we can mount a strong defense, if I can just get out of this hospital. I never thought I'd see the inside of such a place. My wife's well intentioned, you know, and she was frightened, but . . ." He seemed at a loss to defend her actions.

"Maybe she just didn't want to lose you."

DeGraff was silent for a long time. His eyes were closed, and Kevin began to think he might have dozed off. Then he said quietly, "That's it, of course. Meant well. We shouldn't try to . . . change the truth about ourselves, Kevin. Better to . . . stick to your guns, you know."

"I agree. That's why I couldn't see you selling out your own client to the Japanese."

DeGraff's eyes opened. He stared at Kevin

for a long moment. "You know about the Japanese?"

"Yes."

"Hmm. Odd, that. Surprised. Kept it under wraps, you know. Lederer's very . . . secretive." He spoke in brief spurts, like someone out of breath.

"Lederer's made a deal, hasn't he?"

"What are you doing here!"

The battle-axe nurse loomed in the doorway, tall as a linebacker, fearsomely indignant.

"Uh . . . just visiting —"

"You will leave at once! Mr. DeGraff is not supposed to have any visitors. I told you that!"

"That was last night —"

"It's all right," DeGraff protested feebly.

"It's not all right!" The nurse glared at Kevin. "You've deliberately tried to circumvent the doctor's orders. You'll leave *now*."

Kevin turned to DeGraff. "He's made a deal, right?"

"It's no use, Kevin. Too late . . ."

The battle-axe came between them. "Out," she snapped. "I don't want to see you near this room again."

"It might not be too late," Kevin said desperately. "Who's involved? Who's behind it?"

But DeGraff had fallen back against his pillow, exhausted. The chance was lost.

Thirty-Two

"We'll let her think the government is doing it," John Woods had said to Elinor in the moments before her flight left Los Angeles International Airport for Washington.

"Do you think she'll believe that?"

"Why not? The checks will come from your office, bearing your signature. The only difference is they'll be drawn on your personal account. Even if she doesn't completely believe it's money owed to David, this way she doesn't have to feel she's accepting charity."

"I wish I'd known David was supporting his mother and sister completely."

"Would it have made any difference? He was doing it on his own. We're just going to make sure David's mother keeps the house, and that girl gets the same kind of chance at an education her brother had."

The 11:00 A.M. flight, leapfrogging through three time zones, was not due in at Dulles national until six in the evening. Another day. The uneasy sense of urgency Elinor Woods had experienced for weeks stayed with her throughout the flight, as if she were chasing a clock that kept speeding ahead of her. David's death, and the uncertainty surrounding it, added to her restlessness. The mood of the nation, spelled out in the three newspapers and several magazines she scanned en route, reflected her own uncertainty. The stock market, oddly, flew in the face of other markers such as high unemployment, a relentlessly stubborn deficit and rising interest rates. The Dow average had climbed nearly sixty points in two days. A White House press release attributed the Street's optimism to the talks under way in Osaka. As usual Wall Street was a long way from Main Street. The market had soared throughout George Bush's last two years while the nation plunged into recession. It was doing the same thing now.

The capital was startlingly cooler than Los Angeles. The temperature was in the fifties, with a brisk breeze blowing, as the senator rode in from Dulles. The first hints of autumn sprinkled the leafy fringes of the expressway with yellow and gold.

Sudden image of David jogging through the woods, violence bursting out of the rain-dark foliage. She shook it off, grieving.

Elinor directed her chauffeur to the Capitol rather than going directly home. Her office was empty. She leafed through her piled-up correspondence and messages. Nothing that couldn't wait until morning. Except for Raymond Farrow.

She was dialing his number when she heard the echo of footsteps approaching along the corridor. The steps faltered as they neared her office. Stopped entirely. Elinor hung up, waiting. A woman's steps, she thought.

She's beautiful, was Elinor's first thought as a young woman paused in the doorway. The face was vaguely familiar, framed by a mass of blond curls.

"Yes?"

"Senator Woods? I was hoping to find you. They said you might be returning late today."

"I just got in. Can I help you, Miss . . . ?"

"Lisa Gardner. I was . . . a friend of David's."

Elinor felt a little lurch of surprise. She tried to analyze it. They would have been stunning together, she thought, but the picture seemed out of focus. Lisa Gardner was a little glossy for David — or was she doing him an injustice?

"I have to talk to you, Senator."

For the first time Elinor heard the pain in

the young woman's voice. "Maybe you'd better come in."

In the senator's office, with the door closed, a gratefully accepted gin and tonic in her hand, Lisa Gardner said, "Do you know any more about how David died than was in the newspapers?"

"Very little, I'm afraid."

"I've been over and over it. I know these things happen, and maybe I'm imagining things, but . . . it doesn't feel right. I keep thinking that maybe I'm responsible. I know that's crazy, but I can't sleep nights. I just lie there wondering . . ."

"Maybe you'd better tell me about it."

As Lisa Gardner described the night of the Japanese ambassador's party, Elinor felt anger rising. The young woman did not meet her eyes. Elinor tried to keep the distaste out of her voice. "You were supposed to recruit David? Is that it?"

"Not exactly. Just sort of let him know what was out there. It's done all the time."

"I know," the senator said in a level tone.

"But that wasn't all. My boss . . . *somebody* wanted to know what David was working on. I think that's what bothers me the most. It's like there was more to it than seeing if maybe he'd be interested in working our side of the fence if, you know, his situation changed."

"Like if I wasn't reelected."

"Whenever the guard changes in this town, there's a scramble to see where you can fit in. David found out he wouldn't have to send out any résumés."

"I see."

"Listen, I leveled with him," Lisa Gardner said with a trace of defiance. "I stayed with him that night. We even had a big fat argument in the morning, but I didn't stay because I was told to. That was me, okay? I sleep with who I want to."

"Go on, Lisa."

"David liked going to that party. It was like he really liked seeing what was going on at that level, meeting all those high-powered people, and having them butter him up. But he didn't buy into any of it. It rolled right off him."

"Did he tell you what he was investigating?"

"Nothing I didn't already know. My firm . . . its principals like to know what senators are thinking, like with this O Fund you brought up at the hearings. And they knew David was asking around, trying to get information about it."

"So you were supposed to help recruit him, or if that didn't work to find out how much he knew."

"It doesn't sound good, I know, but . . . it's only business."

"But this time it's bothering you."

"What bothers me is he's dead! Why? Dammit, why?"

"The police think it was a random attack. He happened to be in the wrong place at the wrong time."

Lisa Gardner stared at Elinor through huge, tear-filmed eyes. "Is that what you think, Senator?"

For a long time after Lisa Gardner left her office, Elinor Woods sat motionless behind her desk, still confronting the young woman's question. She had given pat, reassuring answers. Whatever guilt Lisa Gardner might carry from her night with David Perez, she wasn't to blame for what happened to him. David must have liked her a great deal. She should try to remember that.

Alone, Elinor did not feel reassured.

It was almost nine o'clock when she reached Raymond Farrow at his home. He sounded solicitous. The senator should get some needed rest. Farrow had the impression that events were closing in on them. He shared Elinor's questions about David's death, but he voiced other concerns as well. He had been putting out feelers to old friends in the financial world.

There was unexplained activity in the global markets affecting U.S. stocks. Rumors, their sources unnamed, were even more rampant than usual. Major investors were becoming jittery. In the European markets, some investors were retrenching their U.S. capital investments. The dollar was dropping.

"I thought the market was bullish here . . . It's way up."

"That's an aberration. The optimism is very fragile. The bubble can burst in an instant. The worry is that those who are selling dollars may be jumping the gun."

"You mean they know something we don't know."

"There is that suspicion. I don't know if you're aware, Senator, how close we came to the complete collapse of the American stock exchange back in October of 1987."

"Black Monday, you mean. October 19."

"Everyone thinks about Monday, with good reason. The Dow lost over five hundred points that day, by far the largest single-day loss in the history of the exchange. But on Tuesday we started to see a repeat of that same free-fall. We came very close to the total collapse of the market. By noon the market had lost a quarter of its value. Trading had virtually halted.

"We were damned close to the point of no

return," Farrow continued, in language as strong as he ever used. "Then, at almost the last possible moment, some positive things started to happen. The Fed promised credit support for lending banks, so stock dealers could stay in business. And the Major Market Index unexpectedly rallied. I believe some journalists summed it up by saying the market actually died that day. Then it rose from the dead."

"You're scaring me," Elinor Woods said.

"I mean to. One of the keys to our survival that day was the actions of the Japanese, who were of course heavily invested in our market. On Monday they stopped buying, which was clearly prudent. But the amazing thing is that, while U.S. investors lost their nerve and embraced panic selling, the Japanese sat on their stock, even though by Monday night they had lost billions of dollars. The same thing happened on Tuesday. They didn't buy, but they didn't sell either. They were a stable element. The obvious question is, what would have happened, given our precarious situation Tuesday morning, if Japanese investors had chosen to pull out and go home? I need hardly tell you that lesson was not lost on the Japanese. Some pundits blamed them for contributing to the crash by failing to buy our treasury bonds. The fact is, they saved our bacon."

"What makes you think such a scenario is possible now?"

"A number of things. I don't like the way this Tyler takeover has been manipulated. Something's going on there, and I know of a Japanese connection. I'm suspicious of these rumors floating about the dollar. Where are they coming from, and why? Today, as I said, there were signs that foreign investors in Europe and Asia may be bailing out of their U.S. market holdings, just as they did in October of 1987 even before the crash. Then there's the O Fund surfacing — another Japanese connection. You put it all together with an economic summit in Osaka that doesn't make sense, and the fact that hard-liners have become more vocal in Japan recently, and you have a very disturbing picture."

"And David's murder is part of that picture."

"I don't like coincidence either, Senator." Farrow paused for a moment of somber silence. "I believe we're heading for disaster. How deeply are the Japanese involved? And if we have another serious crash, manipulated or otherwise, will Japan's investors react the same way they did the last time? Or will they bail out, and push us over the edge?"

Farrow's doomsday summary shook Elinor

Woods. At the same time she recognized that it was speculative, insubstantial. She said, "We need something solid to go on, Mr. Farrow."

"Senator, for heaven's sake. You're right, of course. Perhaps the O Fund will give it to us. We don't have anything else."

"Have you learned anything new about the fund?"

"No . . . but I believe we're getting closer to your mysterious informant. Give me a couple of days."

"Do we have a couple of days, Ray?"

Farrow's prolonged silence was more disturbing than any possible response. Then he said, "I don't know."

Thirty-Three

The diminutive, white-haired figure was unimposing, almost lost behind the long speaker's table. He spoke quietly, without the gutterals associated with the Japanese language, in a version of English that was correct but stilted. Even with the microphone in front of him and large speakers amplifying his voice from the corners of the large hotel conference room, his listeners had to strain to hear him.

Outside the Century Plaza Hotel in Century City, not far from the Westwood campus of UCLA and the gracious estates of Bel Air, a small number of demonstrators paraded back and forth, bearing placards that cried, AMERICA FIRST!, SAVE OUR JOBS and, anachronistically TOJO GO HOME!

As he spoke, the room became quieter. The clinking of glassware and china, the scraping of chairs, the muted buzz of bored conversation died away to a stunned silence. The business leaders, politicians and investors in the room might have been the same ones who had once assembled here at $1,000-a-plate dinners to hear former presidents Reagan and Bush speak. Although a few were curious about apparently sharp statements this mild-looking Japanese businessman had made in Hawaii, most had come expecting to hear generalities, familiar complaints about being misunderstood, and platitudes about the necessity of global partnership for the twenty-first century. Instead they were treated to a litany of their sins, and a prediction of their demise. Long before Toshio Miyaki had finished, one red-faced CEO of a Fortune 500 company had ostentatiously stalked out, followed by a handful of others. Most remained, however, unable to tear themselves from their seats.

The gist of Miyaki's speech was concentrated in his closing remarks. "America's problems are not Japan's problems. The steel industry is a good example. Japanese steel mills were rebuilt after World War II, using the most modern technology. But America's steel mills, then the greatest in the world, were all built in the nineteenth century. And it was the choice of your steel manufacturers not to invest in new equipment and technology for the future, bringing your steel plants up to twentieth century standards, but to invest in such things as soaps and circuses, in immediate profits for their stockholders, and in extravagant rewards for managers. The result has been that Japan's steel industry is now the world leader, and America's steel mills are a wasteland of deserted buildings and unemployed workers.

"This was to become the pattern for American business. You did not look to the future. You did not plan even ten years ahead, but looked only to today's profits and perks, to your silver linings and golden parachutes. In the 1980s Americans sought to make money not by research and production of new goods, but by playing money games. Your money was used to enrich bankers and speculators. One man might make hundreds of millions of dollars in a single year, while through his efforts many companies went bankrupt. You forgot what American industry once taught the world: how to make the best products that sell because they are the best, at the best prices."

Miyaki paused to take a sip of water from the glass beside him. He was aware of the anguish his words brought to his listeners, and of the few who had walked out of the room. At a table off to the left side of the room Yashi Nogama glowered at him, his expression revealing nothing of the satisfaction he must feel.

"The end of the Cold War should have been a time for American industry to reassess its future. Instead you spoke not of making new and better products, but of converting America to service industries, which produce nothing. You forgot that societies that do not make products do not prosper for long. This has always been true.

"Recently, while I was in Hawaii, I said that America's leaders and its people are not willing to make the necessary sacrifices to regain your place in the world. I have been much criticized in your newspapers for these words. But it does no good to become angry at the truth.

"Today America's leaders have traveled to Japan as beggars. They wish us to save you from your mistakes and excesses. This is not possible. The time has come for Japanese leaders to tell Americans the truth. That we will no longer invest in America in order to save it. That your time as a great country leading the world has come and gone, just as it ended for the British Empire." The little man paused, and in the awful silence concluded, "You must save yourselves, or you will perish like the dinosaurs."

He sat down. Someone coughed, and the sound was like an explosion. In a far corner of the room there was a sharp oath. Then another prolonged silence. Miyaki sipped his water. Suddenly a man rose from a large table near the dais and shook his fist. "You son of a bitch! Go back to Tokyo!"

The shout released the collective pent-up anger and outrage. Men rose in unison throughout the room, yelling and pounding on tables. Toshio Miyaki sat motionless as the fury washed over him. His expression revealed nothing of his emotions — of the humiliation that rose in him like a tide.

Staring out at the montage of screaming, angry faces, Miyaki's gaze swung inexorably toward the far table where Yashi Nogama watched, his eyes narrow. *Only he knows,* Miyaki thought. *Only he sees the truth inside.*

At Calvin Lederer's estate, Alison Carey drifted into a large room referred to as the cantina. It served as a lounge, dining and recreation area, facing the veranda and the pool. Outside, the desert air was still warm at eleven o'clock. A number of strikingly beautiful young women reclined on chaises, cavorted in the warm water or, like extras in a movie, strolled in their string bikinis across the veranda in front of imaginary cameras. Several of the partners of Bryant Forbes Lederer & Wyman had spent much of the evening clowning at poolside or making egregiously sexist conversation with the young women, apparently with no self-consciousness, Alison thought, about the fat bellies hanging over their trunks.

The cantina had a Mexican tiled floor, a large wet bar, numerous beige leather sofas and chairs, a pool table and a sunken television viewing area dominated by a Mitsubishi TV set with a forty-inch screen. Momentarily alone, Alison switched on the eleven o'clock news.

She had ridden out from Los Angeles in the afternoon with Dexter Hilliard in his Acura Legend coupe, a sleek vehicle that, he assured her, was capable of cruising at 150 miles per hour. The California desert was initially disappointing — not sculptured sand dunes but flat, dusty terrain covered with scrub brush and sorry-looking cacti. Palm Springs itself resembled an open-air mall.

Calvin Lederer's estate, however, was spectacular. It was situated miles from any other structure on an isolated ridge overlooking the valley floor, with mountains immediately behind it rearing almost vertically to a height of ten thousand feet. The house was a sprawling pink building of Spanish design. There were walled gardens, saunas and a pool, tile-floored terraces and decks on several levels. Its endless rooms were filled with an eclectic variety of lavish furnishings, Indian pottery, rugs and artifacts, and paintings.

Left on her own, Alison had browsed through the open rooms, admiring the paintings and objets d'art, and wondering why Hilliard had seemed eager to have her come to the desert with him. He had disappeared soon after their arrival. Neither Calvin Lederer nor Reynolds Tyler had appeared. "They want you out of circulation," Kevin Daulton had warned her darkly in a brief phone conversation that morning. She smiled at the memory of the desperation in his voice.

One part of the huge house had been blocked off. Lederer's office and bedroom suite, she guessed. She had met Daryl Rathman outside those rooms. He had nodded, leering, giving her a dirty look. Not just an ordinary dirty look, but a *dirty* dirty look. She had retreated to the main part of the house, feeling soiled, as if he had touched her.

Something on the huge television screen caught her attention. Angry demonstrators outside the Century Plaza Hotel in Century City. A small, white-haired Japanese man being hustled toward a waiting limousine. "Toshio Miyaki," the news anchor said over the picture, "is one of Japan's leading business tycoons and richest men. Miyaki Electronics, one of his many companies, is involved in the projected Sakai automobile plant in Fresno, California." The newsman appeared on the screen, smiling cheerfully. "His message for America today was, our time as a great country has ended, just as it did for the British Empire. Reaction to the Japanese businessman's speech was highly vocal and angry." There was a snippet of an interview in the hotel lobby with one of those who had attended the dinner and heard the speech. He angrily demanded to know why the president of the United States was going to Osaka while Japanese spokesmen were coming to America to tell us the Japanese weren't going to give us any more handouts. Once more on screen, the anchor turned, still smiling, to his co-anchor, a beautiful young Asian woman, and said, "Susan?"

Beaming at the camera, Susan said, "I think it's important to note, Bob, that Mr. Miyaki said Japan will no longer invest in America in order to save it. It remains to be seen whether he meant that literally or not." She glanced down at the sheaf of papers before her and said, "In other news, a woman was seriously injured in downtown Los Angeles today when she was struck by an RTD bus. . . ."

Alison stared at the screen, not really seeing the image of a woman lying on the sidewalk while paramedics attended to her, and people in the background gaped or waved at the television camera.

Toshio Miyaki, she thought, wondering why the name seemed familiar. Why would such a man deliver such a speech at this moment in time?

"He's cute," a voice said behind her.

Alison glanced up at a young woman with a thick mane of glossy black hair that spilled down her back almost to her waist. The lush figure in the skintight bodysuit made Alison consider retreating to her room in despair. Instead she smiled. "The Japanese billionaire?"

"No, no . . . Bob. The anchorman."

"Oh, the anchorman. Right."

"I was at a party where he was once. He's real tall."

"You can't tell that on the screen. I'm Alison Carey, by the way."

"Oh, hi. I'm Linda." She said it as if she had only one name, like one of those single-name models or celebrities. She sat on an arm of the beige leather sofa, extending a tanned leg that was about six feet long to inspect it. Alison was convinced she wouldn't find any flaws.

"Have you been here before?"

"Uh-uh, this is the first time. It's kind of . . ." Linda glanced over her shoulder to survey the room, while lowering her voice to make it even huskier. "Boring, you know?"

"I drove out with one of the attorneys," Alison said, "but he's been busy somewhere. I guess most of them are in meetings."

"So, are you and this lawyer, uh, together?"

"No, not that way. I'm also an attorney. I work for Mr. Lederer's firm."

"Oh, wow." Linda studied her with new respect. She had dark brown eyes about the size of large walnuts. "That must be something, being a lawyer."

"It's not exactly what I expected," Alison said truthfully.

At that moment she glanced up to see Dexter Hilliard, Palm Springs-attired in a white *guayabera* shirt and pale blue duck shorts, weaving his way across the cantina toward her. Alison brightened with a sudden inspiration. "Oh, Dex! . . . there's someone here who would like to meet you. Linda . . . this is Dex."

Hilliard appeared startled, then awestruck as Linda unfolded her six feet of legs from the sofa and rose to meet him.

"Linda!" Hilliard said.

"That's me, Dex." She slipped an arm through his and leaned against him. "How would you like to go for a moonlight swim?"

Over Hilliard's shoulder Linda winked at Alison.

★ ★ ★

In Lederer's spacious office suite, the chairman of Bryant Forbes Lederer & Wyman sat quietly in an oversize leather chair while Reynolds Tyler paced back and forth.

"So what are you telling me?" Tyler demanded, blue eyes bright with anger. "This one Jap is trying to buy me out, and you can't figure out how to stop him? Where the hell is DeGraff? He'd have tried *something*."

"He's in the hospital. They've found colon cancer."

Tyler stopped pacing. "How long's he had it?"

"Too long, I imagine."

Tyler went to the bar and freshened his bourbon over ice cubes. He carried the drink over to the sliding glass doors of the office, which looked out upon a private deck and sauna, and the stillness of the desert night. The doors were open to the soft breeze. Without turning he said, "What kind of game are you playing, Lederer?"

"I don't know what you mean."

"Sure you do. You're the smartest son of a bitch I've ever met, and you don't see anything funny in this Miyaki character making a run at me, at the same time he shows up in Los Angeles to read the riot act to greedy American speculators? Give me a break!"

"Obviously he's a very shrewd man. I still say he'll surprise you with an offer to sell back his shares at a price."

"That what he told you on Guam?"

Surprise flickered across Lederer's face.

"Yeah, I know about Guam," Tyler said. "I know that's where you've been on your last couple of junkets. Maybe you'd like to tell me about it."

Lederer gave a patient sigh. "Reynolds, Reynolds . . . when are you going to grow up?"

"You're stalling. Is that where you met Miyaki?"

"I met some entrepreneurs from Hong Kong there, some people who want to have legal representation in the United States. It's business, Reynolds. I can't ignore the Pacific Rim forever, no matter how you feel."

Tyler stared at him, his suspicion only partly allayed. "This Jap's pushed me right out on the ledge, and you're telling me it's business as usual with the whole damned Asian continent?"

"Calm down, Reynolds. Listen to what I'm saying —"

"No, you listen! I'm going into town tomorrow. I'm gonna find this Toshio Miyaki, and the little bastard's gonna give me some answers! And if you've been screwing me around, Lederer, I'm personally gonna wrap you naked around one of those fancy cactus in your garden!"

Daryl Rathman had been quietly observing the scene from a corner of the room. Now he rose from his chair. "Take it easy, Mr. Tyler. You don't want to be making threats."

Reynolds Tyler blew his stack. "You call off your ape!" he yelled at Lederer. "You try to pull that shit on me, I'll hand you his balls for breakfast!"

Tyler started toward the door, ready to challenge Rathman, who was in his path. He didn't see Lederer wave his security man aside.

The heavy door with its carved panels slammed behind him. Rathman raised an eyebrow at his boss. Lederer said, "You'd better send somebody to watch him."

"You want me to — ?"

Lederer shook his head. "He's finished, he just doesn't know it yet."

In another one of the many small patios that opened the rambling house to the outdoors, this one outside Alison Carey's bedroom, she stood in the shadows, listening. She had stepped outside to enjoy the feel of the desert at night, for the first time sensing its appeal as she gazed up at a billion stars and heard the soft whisper of the desert wind. Reynolds Tyler's harsh words had come to her clearly. *"I'm gonna find this Toshio Miyaki, and the little bastard's gonna give me some answers."*

Suddenly Alison regretted not bringing her set of the photos Kim had mailed to her. Traveling out to the desert with Dexter Hilliard into what Kevin called the lion's den, she'd been afraid to carry the photos with her. She had hidden her set, and mailed the duplicates to Kevin. She had had only a televised glimpse of Toshio Miyaki leaving the Century Plaza Hotel tonight, but the big-screen image had been clear, and now she was able to make a match with her memory of the white-haired Japanese at the hotel in Guam. The photographs would prove it.

Tyler was right. Lederer had met Toshio Miyaki on Guam. How did it all tie together with the hostile takeover attempt against Tyler? With Miyaki's speech?

Alison shivered, though the air was warm.

The desert night no longer seemed peaceful and still.

Thirty-Four

He would write a novel, Kevin Daulton had decided. Every lawyer in the country was trying to bang out a courtroom novel in his spare time, working a hundred hours a week at one of the high-powered firms and squeezing in an hour in the predawn chill, like Hemingway in Cuba, or locking the door to his office during his lunch hour so he could sneak in some private time at the word processor. Well, hell, Kevin had an advantage over all of them. For one thing, he had all day and night with nothing else to do. For another — a prerequisite for a best-selling lawyer novel — he had decided that he honestly hated lawyers. Some of these other guys had to fake it.

Friday morning, while he was waiting for the mail to arrive — one of the highlights of each day — he started reading one of the six lawyer novels he had bought the night before at Crown Books. Two were hardcover, the others paperback. He would probably have to stick to paperbacks in the future, particularly if he was going to write in a garret, presuming that he could find a garret that wasn't too far from the ocean and, even more importantly, Manhattan Beach.

He got through three chapters before the mail arrived. By then he was a little suspicious of the author's credentials as a lawyer. He actually wrote fairly well.

The manila envelope jumped out of the mailbox at him. He tore open the top with his finger, and pulled out four five-by-seven glossy photographs. The pictures all featured the same subject, viewed against the same background. There was a pool with chaises scattered around, palm trees and tropical flowers, a corner of a modern hotel, and assorted tourists in swimsuits or colorful shirts and shorts. The tableau that caught Kevin's eyes, as it had the photographer's, was similar in each photo. It showed a tall white man in gray slacks and an embroidered white shirt talking with a group of Japanese men, half a foot shorter than the Caucasian, all of them fully dressed in dark suits and ties. In one of the snapshots one of the Japanese, a slender, white-haired man, was bowing toward the white man. He was evidently the leader of the group, because another of the shots showed him turning away and the others all following.

Kevin rummaged in a drawer of his desk until he found a magnifying glass. He held it over each of the photographs. Calvin Lederer's image leaped up at him. Lederer smiling at the group. Lederer inclining his head slightly as the white-haired Japanese bowed. Lederer glancing at a girl in a bikini poised on a diving board, as a couple of the Japanese suits laughed. Lederer watching the group leave.

Alison had been right all along.

So who were the Japanese? And why did the white-haired guru of the group seem familiar? Kevin studied him under the glass. Sixties or seventies, handsome features, like a Japanese movie star in his later years. He would have to use his novelist's imagination to conjure up a plot that would place Lederer in Guam at a secret meeting with an aging Japanese movie star playing a millionaire. *Ha!* his private voice sneered. *How can you write? You can't even tell a good lie.*

Kevin set the photographs aside for later study. He picked up the lawyer novel. He wondered how good a liar the author was. Good enough, he hoped, to take his mind off Alison and Palm Springs.

Toshio Miyaki was up long before dawn,

overlooking the activities in his command center on the six upper floors of Pacific Plaza East. The European markets were in full swing, and electronic orders went out to financial flashpoints in Frankfurt, Zurich and London. New York was three hours later than Los Angeles, so Miyaki did not have to wait long for the bell that announced the opening of the New York Stock Exchange. Miyaki's small army of technicians were ready at their computer terminals and fax machines. Through scores of company and individual cover names, and a legion of brokers, the orders were the same: sell Tyler Holdings.

The trickle became a wave, the wave a torrent. By nine o'clock that morning at the Pacific Stock Exchange, noon in New York, the market was in turmoil. Tyler Holdings stock was in free-fall, and it was carrying the market with it. The remarks made by the Japanese industrialist, Toshio Miyaki, in a Thursday night speech had awakened widespread fears in the financial community. The bad news about Tyler reinforced those fears.

At precisely noon in Los Angeles, with the Dow average down over ninety points, an announcement chattered out of the teletype and fax machines, and appeared simultaneously on financial network computer screens, in investment houses and brokerage offices and on the floors of the exchanges across the country. Bank of the Pacific, which had guaranteed most of the loans supporting Tyler Holdings, was exercising an obscure clause in the loan agreements requiring immediate payment in full if, in the bank's sole judgment, Tyler stock had fallen substantially below the minimum acceptable levels defined in the agreements. The bank was calling in the loans.

Within the hour another blow fell. At a brief press conference at the Bonaventure Hotel in Los Angeles, Toshio Miyaki announced that he was reconsidering his commitment to re-open a dormant steel mill in Youngstown, Ohio. He also revealed that an announcement would be forthcoming from Shinji Sakai in Japan regarding the Sakai automotive plant in Fresno, which had encountered significant environmental impact and design problems. Immediately after the press briefing, Miyaki went into seclusion.

The announcement battered the reeling market. It seemed to confirm Miyaki's earlier warning: Japan was bailing out of America, leaving the nation to solve its own economic woes.

Program and institutional selling by the huge insurance and pension funds, all of which had gone overboard for Tyler stock, was later blamed for the chaos that engulfed the stock exchanges. Orders backed up as computers on the floor, unable to keep pace with the volume of trading, fell more than an hour behind. There was no way of telling exactly where the market was at any given moment. Futures trading, which larger traders had embraced as a reliable hedge against calamity, became impossible.

It was Black Monday all over again.

At three-thirty New York time, a half hour before the normal closing bell, trading was suspended on the New York Stock Exchange. Tyler Holdings common stock stood at 33, down more than 70 points. Confidence was shattered. Blue chips had tumbled across the board. The market had recorded its second highest loss in history, 235 points for the day, a loss calculated in the neighborhood of $300 billion.

And the panic had only begun.

When the news broke, it was night in Osaka. President James Arthur Walton had returned from a dinner hosted by Nakafumi Tokito, the Japanese minister of finance. The president had reluctantly nibbled at at least two unidentifiable dishes, and his stomach was unsettled. "They don't serve those poisonous fish at these dinners, do they?" he had asked his secretary of state three different times.

"Those are blowfish, Mr. President, and they were not on this evening's menu."

Sylvester Runnels, accompanied by a nervous, white-faced undersecretary of the Treasury whom Runnels had summoned, was waiting with sheafs of tickertape reports in his hand, and a translation of a coded telegram from Gus Bonelli that read:

TO PRESIDENT WALTON/CONFIDENTIAL: SEVERE STOCKMARKET CRASH STOP POSSIBLE JAPANESE MANIPULATIONS STOP RECOMMEND SUSPEND SUMMIT TALKS IMMEDIATELY STOP HAVE ISSUED STATEMENT FROM PRESIDENT TO READ OUR UNDERLYING ECONOMY IS STRONG AND THERE IS NO REASON FOR PANIC STOP URGENT ADDITIONAL ACTION NEEDED STOP BONELLI.

James Walton was bewildered. "I don't understand. What's happening? What does Gus mean — urgent action needed? What can I do?"

Runnels, who had had longer than the others to assimilate the bad news, said, "I think we've been double-crossed. It's just like Pearl Harbor. They initiate talks to get us to let down our guard, and then hit us without warning."

"Let's not go overboard until we know

more of what's going on," Ed Grabow said.

"I want to talk to the prime minister," Walton said, surprising everyone by his decisiveness. "Get Yuki on the phone."

"He's on his way to his country estate," the undersecretary said timidly. "He goes there on weekends."

"Get hold of their negotiators. We'll use these trade talks as leverage," the president said.

"There are no talks scheduled again until Monday."

The men all stared at each other. The same thought struck each of them. Monday might be too late.

James Walton felt really ill. He didn't know if it was from the stricken expression on Ed Grabow's face, or those unidentified Japanese delicacies he had eaten at dinner.

Alison Carey was annoyed but not concerned when she asked Dexter Hilliard to drive her into downtown Palm Springs for "a little shopping" and Hilliard put her off till later. "Too much going on," Hilliard said before rushing away. "The shit's really hit the fan. Oh, by the way," he added. "The phones are out."

She stared after him. So much for calling Kevin Daulton from town, as she had planned, or from the house as a last resort. Odd, the phones in the house being down. She had heard one ringing earlier that morning, before Reynolds Tyler left the compound — a departure that didn't surprise her after the outburst she had overheard last night.

Hilliard's comment sent her to the TV set in the lounge. She stayed there through the afternoon, fascinated, as the story of the Tyler Holdings collapse played out on CNN against the larger drama of the stock market's plunge. The president issued a statement through the White House that all was well, the economy was basically sound. The chairman of the Federal Reserve Board weighed in with more reassurances. By the end of the day it was clear those placebos weren't working. The patient needed intensive care.

Alison tried to make sense of it. It looked as if Reynolds Tyler had been set up. Was that the explanation for Lederer's trips to Guam? Had he made a devil's bargain with the Japanese to bring Tyler down? For a lawyer such a betrayal of a client was appalling. But why do it? For the Japanese, it meant getting even for the Century Pictures debacle. If the conspiracy seemed elaborate for so small-minded a goal, it was at least a plausible explanation. But why would Lederer be party to it? Why trade one client for another?

And then the larger picture intruded. It was not only Reynolds Tyler who was being brought down. The market had crashed with him. The U.S. economy was the target.

Was that the answer?

The outlines of a monstrous conspiracy became clearer. But the implications were so staggering it was hard to accept them.

Alison checked the telephones in the lounge and in her room. The lines were dead. She needed to talk to Kevin. She realized that, after what she'd heard the night before between Lederer and Tyler, she had information no one outside Lederer's compound possessed. That's what those photographs were all about. That was why Lederer had been so anxious to destroy them. They established a secret link between Lederer and Toshio Miyaki, long before the carefully orchestrated takeover fiasco. Somehow or other she had to let Kevin know. She wasn't sure what he could do, but there must be something. Ironically, she could do nothing from inside Lederer's compound, which she had been so eager to penetrate, but Kevin was free to act. He could take the photos to a newspaper — the *Los Angeles Times* would be interested. Expose the conspiracy, let investors know they'd been manipulated. Let the president know, for God's sake!

At seven o'clock a buffet spread was set up

in the cantina. Huge trays of Mexican food — carnitas, enchiladas, sweet corn tamales, chicken fajitas, chile colorado, taquitos, rice and beans and bowls of chips. A mariachi trio set up on the patio and began to play. At the bar there were pitchers of icy margaritas. The young women drifted in from the pool area. When Calvin Lederer and George Broward finally appeared, along with most of the other partners, supper became a festive party, another Palm Springs event. There was no hint of impending economic disaster. *They're celebrating,* Alison thought. They'd pulled something off, something tricky, and now it was over.

The party was becoming lively when there was a commotion down the hallway near the front entrance. Someone shouted. Footsteps pounded along the tile floor. Reynolds Tyler, wild-eyed with rage, burst into the cantina. Daryl Rathman was right behind him.

"You bastard!" Tyler screamed. "I'll have you disbarred! You set me up! You knew about Miyaki — you knew that was Japanese money!"

He hurled himself toward Calvin Lederer. A girl screamed. One of the partners blocked Tyler's way, and he shoved the man aside. Then Rathman was on top of him. He was heavier and stronger than Tyler. Tyler's hard-soled boots slipped and slid on the polished tiles as he struggled. Rathman got a hammerlock on him.

"Get him out of here!" Lederer snapped.

"Traitor!" Tyler raged. "You sold out your country! You and the Japs — you knew it all along!"

The men in the room had been reacting to the melee with varying attitudes of apprehension and shock, the bikini-clad women with open-mouthed wonder. When Tyler began to choke, everything changed. Fear became a physical presence. Tyler's struggles to free himself from Rathman's grip ceased. He sagged, and Rathman had to brace himself against a suddenly dead weight. Tyler's face turned gray, drained of color.

"Oh my God!" George Broward said. "For God's sake, Rathman, let him go. He's having a heart attack!"

Thirty-Five

It was nearly midnight before Alison was able to talk to Dexter Hilliard. "I'm going back to Los Angeles," she announced.

Shortly after the ambulance and paramedics — summoned by a car phone — had left, it was announced that Mr. Lederer's guests would be driven back to Los Angeles that night. The party, obviously, was over. The atmosphere was subdued. No one knew for certain if Reynolds Tyler was dead or alive.

"That's not a very good idea, Alison. I can't go right now."

"You don't have to. I can go with the others. There's room in the cars for one more."

"Mr. Lederer wants to talk to you."

"I don't think I want to talk to him. I'm leaving."

"Don't be unreasonable, Alison. You know that's not possible."

She stared at him, suddenly remembering

her offhand remark to Kevin: *What are they going to do, kidnap me?*

"Come along to Mr. Lederer's office. We can talk there."

"That's off limits."

"Not anymore."

Alison realized that she *did* want to confront Lederer himself. He was the architect of the destruction of Reynolds Tyler and his enterprises, setting off shock waves that had produced chaos in the stock market.

Lederer and Toshio Miyaki, she reminded herself. Lederer and the Japanese. Who were the real architects? And what were they after?

She followed Hilliard down the main hallway to Lederer's suite, which occupied an entire wing of the house. At a nod from Hilliard the security guard in the hall made no attempt to stop them. Once inside, Hilliard visibly relaxed. Too late Alison realized that he had been worried about a scene in the cantina in the presence of others. She had given away her one trump card.

Alison's mouth tightened. She *still* wanted to face Lederer.

"Want a drink?" Hilliard asked cheerfully from the wet bar.

Alison surveyed the office. It was very large, and apparently the only section of the house with deep plush carpeting instead of Mexican tiles on the floor. The furnishings were all oversize — a huge crescent-shaped modern desk with nothing on it but a telephone and a sculptured lamp, sofas ten feet long, deep leather chairs, a painting of a desert scene that covered much of one wall, another entire wall of bookshelves. There was nothing personal in the room — no mementoes, trophies or photographs. It might have been a showroom floor display instead of one man's retreat.

"Drink?" Hilliard repeated, smiling as he watched Alison. He'd mixed a martini for himself.

She shook her head emphatically. "Is Tyler dead?"

"He was alive when they carried him out of here. If not, he died with his boots on." Hilliard found this amusing.

"How can you stand there and gloat? You betrayed a client's trust."

"Our client was an ass."

"What difference does that make? You were supposed to be looking after his interests. That's what he was paying you for."

"Oh, come on, Alison —"

"And what about all those investors who were taken in? You betrayed them, too. I suppose they're all asses who deserve whatever happens to them."

Hilliard's smile vanished. "I'm not responsible for them. I took an *EST* course once, Alison, and I *got* it. I got the key thing: I'm responsible for myself, no one else. You ought to know that better than anyone. You've looked after yourself since you were a kid. You don't owe anything to anyone."

Alison flinched at the implication, scared that there might be truth in it. "It's not true," she said after a moment. "There are people I care about, and people who care about me. And I thought the reason we live in a society of laws is we care about each other."

"What? Oh, spare me, Alison! What do you think this is all about? Mother's milk and cookies?"

"I wouldn't know," Alison snapped back. "My mother treated me the way you treated your client, as if nothing mattered but looking out for number one. God forgive me if I started thinking the same way. I won't do it again."

Behind Alison someone chuckled. She whirled about. Calvin Lederer had entered the suite without her hearing him. He brought his manicured hands up and mockingly applauded. "A very pretty speech," he said. "But like most pretty speeches, it has very little to do with the real world."

Lederer crossed the room to his desk, though he did not sit down. He was elegantly dressed as always, in a lemon pastel silk shirt and white slacks. He wore a tolerant smile. She realized he had been the only one in the cantina who had shown little emotion when Reynolds Tyler collapsed.

"I want no part in what you've done. I don't want to work for your firm. I want to get out of here."

"I'm afraid that won't be possible immediately."

"Am I being held prisoner?"

"Now you're being melodramatic, my dear. You're my guest. Just for a few days . . . by Monday night it'll all be over. You can go anywhere you want. You'll be free to say anything you want. It won't matter, because no one important will be listening."

Lederer's arrogant self-assurance was more frightening than anything else Alison had seen or heard. "That's kidnapping. It's a federal offense."

"Oh, I hardly think that will hold up. You came here of your own free will — on a date with one of my other attorneys, I believe. It was a weekend business party. No one has assaulted you. No one has harmed you in any way, and I assure you no one will. Transportation is not available tonight, but you may leave of your own accord on Monday."

"I'm being held against my will! Do you

really think that doesn't matter? That you're above the law?"

Lederer smiled. "I think your small cry will be a very faint sound in the general wailing. But you're welcome to try."

Alison glanced from Lederer to Hilliard. Their cool, smiling indifference affected her strangely. It calmed her. It enabled her to distance herself from what she had witnessed over the last few hours. It put the enormity of what Lederer had done into perspective.

"You think you've won," she said quietly.

"My dear, I don't *think* anything. It's all over but the shouting. There are always winners and losers. I make very certain that I'm on the winning side. The ethics of the profession, the morality of the pulpit — they have nothing to do with it."

"Dammit, you've sold out your own country! No one will ever trust you again. What do you think your firm is going to be worth when this is over?"

"You can't possibly imagine. Countries are artificial institutions, my dear, like fraternities. In the end they're meaningless. Bryant Forbes Lederer & Wyman will be, as the saying goes, sitting pretty come Monday night. We'll be with the winners, helping to pick up the pieces."

"You'll be lucky if someone doesn't shoot you."

Lederer laughed. "Reynolds Tyler might have . . . but I think not now."

The coldness finally silenced her. What she was hearing was a form of psychopathology, she realized. The total absence of any sense of guilt or remorse, right or wrong, responsibility or human concern.

"I think you might escort Alison to her room now, Dex. Just for tonight, my dear. And don't worry too much. You're a clever girl. You might even keep your job. My colleagues admire cleverness."

"Your colleagues?"

"You couldn't know, of course. Our firm has been a part of the Sakai Group for many years. So you see . . . there was never any question of betrayal." He chuckled. "You might say . . . we were just following orders."

An hour later Alison slipped over the low wall of her patio. The air was cool on her bare shoulders. Hilliard, with the help of a security guard, had taken all of her clothes except the sundress she had worn that afternoon and evening. She could have them back in the morning, Hilliard said.

The ground sloped gently away from her.

There was no moon, but the stars were so bright she was readily able to make out the squat shapes of cactus and mesquite brush. She moved cautiously through the darkness toward the outer wall of the estate. Behind her the sprawling house was silent. Something caught at her bare leg. Panicking, she squirmed free. She saw a dark line on her calf where the spine of a cactus had sliced through the skin, drawing blood.

A car door slammed, and Alison froze. The sound helped her to orient herself. It had come from her left, behind the long, low sprawl of the house. That meant the main driveway to the entrance gates was also to her left.

She crept down the slope, keeping low, angling toward the gravel drive. After a moment she was able to make out the gates ahead of her. They were closed. Wrought iron with an elaborate crest, and electronically controlled, she remembered from her arrival at the compound. Maybe there was a manual switch at the gates. Or if a car was leaving, perhaps she could slip through unnoticed before the gates closed behind it.

She was half running when she neared the bottom of the slope. A dark figure stepped out of the shadows directly into her path. Alison blundered into him. For an instant she fought, striking out blindly. Then she realized that the guard was making no attempt to subdue her.

She stumbled back, panting. Her heart raced from the shock of adrenalin.

"Sorry, miss. Nobody leaves without permission. It's for your own good. You wouldn't want to walk across that desert at night. It's dangerous out there."

She didn't recognize the security guard. He was young, about her own age, earnest, his guileless face untouched by doubt.

"All right, Hamill, I'll take it from here." Daryl Rathman materialized on the driveway a few yards away. "Go back to the gate."

"Yes, sir."

Rathman stared at her for a long moment. Even in the darkness she could see the insolence in his expression. "The gates lock automatically," he said. "You couldn't open them. And in case you wondered, you tripped an infrared beam when you left the perimeter of the house, and you stepped on a pressure-sensitive alarm beside the road. You might as well have been sending up flares."

"I'm a prisoner, right?" Just for the record, she thought.

"If you have any complaint, you'd best talk to Mr. Lederer. I suggest you go back to the house. It might not be a good idea to come out again. We turn the dogs loose on the grounds after the last car leaves."

"Dogs," she muttered to herself as she walked back to the house alone. Dogs and alarms, and a small army of thugs. How was she going to get out of here?

She was concentrating so hard she almost walked into the long white Lincoln limousine waiting in the curve of the driveway at the front entrance. A tall woman with long black hair emerged from the entry, carrying an overnight case.

"Linda!" Alison exclaimed.

"Oh, hi, Alison!" the young woman said. "Hey, aren't you coming?"

Alison rejected the temptation. She would never get past Rathman. If she made a scene, he would simply imprison Linda too. "I'm with Mr. Lederer's law firm, remember? I have to stay for meetings."

"Oh, hey, that's too bad. This has been a real bummer, huh?" Linda handed her bag to the chauffeur, who threw it into the spacious trunk and slammed the lid. The door was open, and Linda turned toward the limousine. Alison glanced down the driveway, searching for Daryl Rathman.

"Linda, listen . . . could you do me a big favor?"

"Well, I guess . . ."

"I'm gonna be stuck here, so I can't get back to L.A., and I've got a date. I wonder if you could help me out."

"Oh, I don't know. My boyfriend wouldn't like it."

Alison didn't pursue the question of how her boyfriend felt about her junkets to Lederer's desert parties. "I didn't mean that," Alison smiled. "I don't think I'd want him to get a good look at you."

Linda glowed at the compliment. Rathman appeared in the driveway, approaching the house.

Alison had Kevin's phone number in the pocket of her dress, where she had put it earlier that afternoon when she still hoped to go to Palm Springs. She shoved the slip of paper quickly into Linda's hand. "Just call Kevin for me. Tell him I couldn't leave, but he should go to the Bonaventure Hotel where Mr. Miyaki is staying — that he's the man in the photographs. Okay? You got that?"

"Uh . . . sure. I guess I can do it. What does that mean — the man in the photos?"

Alison practically pushed Linda into the waiting limousine. "I think he's smart enough to figure it out."

Linda giggled, seemingly delighted with her role as go-between. It gave her speaking lines, Alison thought. She wasn't just an extra strolling past the imaginary camera lens.

Linda folded her long legs into the car, smiled and pulled the door shut. The long white vehicle started down the driveway. Its taillights flared briefly when the limousine slowed, where Daryl Rathman stood beside the drive. Then the lights moved on, vanishing around a curve in the drive.

Rathman stepped back onto the gravel road, staring toward the house.

Alison turned and ran inside.

Thirty-Six

Kevin Daulton hadn't shaved in three days. He hadn't even showered since Thursday. Staring at the apparition in his bathroom mirror Saturday morning, he shuddered. He could be the poster boy for the new America, he thought. The America of riots in the rust belt. Of thirty thousand unemployed workers starting to march on Washington, D.C. late Friday, joined by such a massive outpouring that by noon Saturday morning — nine o'clock on the coast when Kevin turned on the TV — the crowd was estimated at between ninety thousand and one hundred thousand. The America of lost hopes and shattered dreams.

Two days and not a word from Alison. Two days in the enemy camp, Tyler Holdings down the tubes, Tyler himself undergoing bypass surgery at the Eisenhower Medical Center in Palm Springs, and not a call, not a whisper, not even a weather report.

In desperation Friday Kevin had tried to obtain Calvin Lederer's phone number in Palm Springs from the operator. It was unlisted. Then he had actually pulled off the impossible by calling a receptionist at Bryant Forbes Lederer & Wyman, identifying himself to the new girl — there was at least one new receptionist per week — who was unaware that he had been fired, and asking her for Lederer's private number at his desert retreat. She hadn't hesitated. When Kevin punched in the number, however, there were some squeals and squawks, and an operator broke in. The phones were temporarily out of order. Alison was isolated.

He debated driving down to the desert. Would he be able to get inside Lederer's estate? What was going on?

Kevin tried attacking the third of his new collection of lawyer novels, but his heart wasn't in it. Anxiety was undoubtedly quenching his creative fires.

The phone rang. He knocked it off the end table in his haste, grabbed the instrument and said, "Hello!"

"Kevin? Is this Kevin?" A stranger's voice, very husky, very sexy. Like one of those late-night-television come-ons for a 900-number companion. $3.88 per minute.

"Yes, this is Kevin."

"Hi, I'm Linda. I'm a friend of Alison's."

"Linda? Alison? Is she all right?"

"She's great. She just wanted me to tell you, she couldn't get away for your date tonight."

"Uh . . . she couldn't get away?"

"Yeah, you know, they're having meetings or something. But she said you should go ahead and go to the Bonaventure Hotel without her."

Kevin was bewildered. "You're sure that's what she said?"

"That's it, okay?"

"Yeah, sure, but . . . did she say anything else?"

"Oh, that's right," Linda said. She laughed sexily. "She said that's where Mr . . . Uh . . . Mijaki is staying. Oh yeah, she said that he's the one in the pictures. Okay? Hey, listen, I gotta go."

As he replayed Linda's message in his head, Kevin's excitement faded into perplexity. What was Alison getting at? *Don't be dumb,* his alter ego pleaded, for once on his side. *It's something Alison knew you could figure out. She's got faith in you.*

Then it hit him. Miyaki, not Mijaki. The Japanese millionaire businessman whose speech set off tremors Thursday night. Who was involved in the takeover of Tyler Holdings. Who was, according to a *Los Angeles*

Times cover story this morning, a majority shareholder in Bank of the Pacific, which was in turn, unbeknownst to its hundreds of thousands of California depositors, an American subsidiary of a Japanese bank. Who was the man in the photographs meeting Calvin Lederer on Guam.

Who was staying at the Bonaventure Hotel.

Kevin wasn't sure exactly what Alison wanted him to do, but one thing was clear. He was going to the Bonaventure, and one way or another he was going to see Toshio Miyaki.

At the same time Kevin Daulton was stepping into the shower, Elinor Woods, Raymond Farrow and Dan Hallerman were trying to fight their way out of the heart of Washington, D.C. The huge mob of marchers who had descended on the capital overnight now occupied the Mall from one end to the other, and filled Pennsylvania Avenue from Capitol Hill to the White House, which had the appearance of being under siege.

Farrow was driving. No one else was to be involved in today's trip, not even a trusted chauffeur or assistant.

Taking a roundabout route, Farrow escaped the congestion and crossed the Anacostia River on the Eleventh Street Bridge. From there he connected to I-295 south to the Beltway. Everyone began to breathe easier.

"How the hell do you suppose they did it?" Hallerman wondered aloud.

"Did what?" Elinor Woods asked absently.

"Organized that many people so fast. That whole mob scene wasn't spontaneous. It was organized. No way you could pull it off otherwise. Not overnight."

He had Elinor's full attention now. She had met the navy man for the first time an hour ago when Farrow picked her up at her house in Georgetown. She knew only that he was in navy intelligence, that he had a comforting solidity about him, and that Farrow trusted him. "What are you saying, Commander Hallerman?"

"It's fairly obvious. You have the stock market going through the floor, with a whole lot of evidence that Japanese speculators were behind the manipulations that set off the crash. And overnight a hundred thousand Americans who've lost their jobs or are scared of losing 'em suddenly find a way to get together in the nation's capital for a protest march so organized you haven't even had any arrests. Hell, they might as well be Japanese demonstrators, they're so much in step."

"I see what you mean."

"There's much more," Raymond Farrow

said as he drove. "The economic summit has been suspended this morning, with both sides crying foul. There is talk about the Japanese getting ready to dump American stocks and sell dollars Monday morning, which will deliver the coup de grace to the market if it's able to open at all. And don't forget the seed sowing ahead of time. You can't underestimate the impact of Toshio Miyaki's recent speeches, and his press conference Friday. Here's a man you've hardly ever heard of, even though he's one of the richest, most successful men in Japan, and all of a sudden he's making pronouncements one after the other that have been carefully calculated to unsettle, frighten and finally panic American investors, leading up to what happened to the market yesterday."

"And what's almost certain to happen Monday."

"Yes. Unless this tardy administration and the financial community can find a way to stop it."

"What you're describing," the senator said soberly, "is a carefully scripted Japanese conspiracy to destroy the U.S. economy."

"I don't think there can be any doubt of it now," Farrow replied. "The only thing we don't know is, is this an action on the part of the Japanese government, or at least with its support, or is this a coup being pulled off by a powerful, traditional group, some of the old-line Japanese imperialists? Whoever is behind it, it's been very carefully planned over a long period of time. I remember a story I heard about one of the major Japanese companies moving its administrative headquarters to a new location. The operation was planned for a full year ahead of time. Every detail of the move was meticulously blocked out. Nothing was left to chance. If there was a single paper clip on a desk, the place for that paper clip in the new location, and the timing and method of moving it there, was plotted. That, on a much grander scale, is what we're looking at here." He paused. "One paper clip fell to the floor unnoticed. The O Fund came to your attention, Senator. It wasn't supposed to."

They rode for a time in silence. Neither Farrow nor Hallerman had said exactly where they were going. It was a former safe house, Hallerman had explained briefly. It was now used as a hospice for members of the intelligence community, primarily the Central Intelligence Agency, who were either terminally ill or in need of full-time care. "It's small, secluded, privately funded, and it does not officially exist," Hallerman had said.

Elinor broke the silence. "Tell me about

this man we're going to see. How did you find him, Commander?"

"It wasn't easy. His name is Richard Zehlke. I'd met him once, as it turns out, but I thought he was dead. Everyone else did, too. He wanted it that way. For good reason, apparently. Someone else is looking for him."

"You're sure?" Farrow demanded sharply, turning so quickly that he nearly veered off the road.

"Yes. And if I know that person is looking, then he knows about me."

Elinor Woods digested this. Alarm mingled with a rising eagerness. Maybe they *were* getting close to something important . . . close enough to cause someone to panic.

"Is Zehlke terminally ill?"

"Lung cancer. He's lasted longer than expected. Some of the treatment is quite drastic. It's destroyed his motor system, and confined him to a wheelchair. He's living on pills — pills to energize, pills to calm him down, pills to enable his stomach to tolerate food, pills for pain." Hallerman paused, his mood turning somber. "This hospice is a way for the intelligence community to take care of its own. Some agents have enemies; others simply want to disappear, and go out on their own terms. Career agents tend to be loners, and Zehlke is one of them. He's also aware that the knowledge he has is dangerous. Being thought dead was a good way to disappear from anyone's wanted list."

"So how did you find out about him?"

"Luck, really. I talked to some old-timers I know, and finally ran down one who was in the OSS in Japan during the Occupation. He was on the staff of Colonel Frank Schuler, who was parachuted into Japan in 1941 and spent the war there in hiding, sending gobs of vital information to MacArthur's command. Schuler surfaced after the war and was added to MacArthur's staff. The man I talked to worked for him. He'd heard of the O Fund but didn't know much about it. But he did come up with another name from the OSS . . . Zehlke. Zehlke spoke Japanese, and he was attached to SCAP's finance division during the Occupation as a liaison with Japanese financial interests. My contact thought if anyone knew anything about the O Fund it would be Zehlke. Only trouble is, he thought Zehlke was dead."

"Excuse me," Elinor Woods said with a smile. "But you'd better define SCAP for me."

"Sorry. Acronyms are a military habit. General MacArthur's command was called Supreme Command for the Allied Powers — SCAP for short."

"So how did you track Zehlke down?" Raymond Farrow asked, bringing the discussion back on target.

"Once I had a name, it was easier. Quite a number of people knew he had gotten cancer. Most thought he'd died. I heard whispers about the existence of the safe hospice, and I played a hunch that it might be a good place to find a dead man."

"Have you talked to him?" Elinor asked.

"Yes. He was surprised I'd found him, but a little relieved, I think. I believe he's been keeping himself alive long enough to tell his story. After this he can let go. No one can hurt him then."

They had been driving northwest for some time, following Hallerman's directions. In the foothills of the Blue Ridge Mountains they turned off the state highway onto a two-lane road that immediately began to switchback into the hills, climbing steadily. Farms and villages fell behind them. They drove into the tree line. Only an occasional cabin was visible from the road.

"I guess no one could find this place without being seen coming," Elinor Woods suggested.

"That's the idea of a safe house."

"Did Zehlke indicate that he knows how the O Fund is being used against us now? Does he know anything about the people behind it?"

"He knows something about the fund he wouldn't tell me," Hallerman said with a frown. "He'll only tell you, Senator. I believe it's . . . politically sensitive. I'm not sure I even want to know."

"I believe we're looking at two different questions here, Senator," Farrow said. "If the O Fund is what I believe it to be, it plays a part in every decision many of the major Japanese corporations make, as a source of virtually unlimited capital and influence. But having questions about the fund surface here in Washington at this crucial time couldn't have been part of the conspiracy we're talking about. That wasn't in the plan. If, as I believe, David Perez was murdered to protect a secret related to the fund, it was a separate issue from this economic blitz we're facing. I hope Richard Zehlke can tell us what it is."

In the silence that followed Elinor Woods felt a tension in the car that hadn't been there when they set out. She peered ahead at the isolated canyons and forested hills that held their secrets so well.

"We'll be there inside an hour," Hallerman said.

The frail old man sat in a bentwood rocker on the lawn behind the house. Only his eyes moved in their deep, dark sockets. He was hunched over, shriveled, his neck so scrawny it seemed inadequate to support his head. The skull was protected by a few strands of hair left from what had been a bushy thicket. The day had been warm, and he had asked to be put out in the sun while he waited. The sun would soon be behind the thrust of the mountains, and the first hint of autumn coolness was in the air. He sat enveloped in a knitted afghan, huddled within its folds as if he felt the cold.

The cabin was set in a clearing. The outer perimeter of the lawn was defined not by a fence but by the first stand of pine trees. At this time of the day and year the shadows were long. They reached out across the lawn toward him, and they filled the hollows and spaces in the woods. Even so, he saw the man in black some time before he reached the edge of the clearing.

Richard Zehlke observed the man without surprise. He had known that, once one of the hunters found him, others would follow.

He watched the man in black with professional interest. He had observed the cabin long enough to record the minimal level of activity. There were only three other residents besides Zehlke, and two were bedridden. There were three caretakers who functioned as nurses, cooks and bottle washers — and guards. One had driven off to the nearest town to buy the week's supply of groceries. He always stopped for a couple of drinks, Zehlke knew. He wouldn't be back for another hour.

The second caretaker was in the kitchen preparing supper. The third had checked on Zehlke earlier. Now he was with Givens, the other ambulatory patient, for his physical therapy session.

No one worried about Zehlke. There was nothing they could do for him, and they knew he liked sitting alone out back until the sun set.

The man in black had circled along the fringe of the woods until he was close to the house on the north side, almost opposite Zehlke. From there he could see into Givens's room, and he had a view of the kitchen window as well.

He must have been satisfied with what he saw, for he started across the lawn, moving quickly, making no sound. A pro, Zehlke thought with satisfaction. He would have been offended if they'd sent an amateur thug.

The man knelt beside Zehlke's chair, placing it between himself and the house. Zehlke didn't recognize him, but he hadn't expected to. It wouldn't be anyone from his generation. Most of them were gone. Not a youngster, though. Lot of gray in the matted hair. Seasoned eyes, appraising.

"I guess you know how it is," the man said in a low voice. "You takes your chances . . ."

Zehlke's eyelids blinked slowly. Watching, Marty Wallach took the movement as a nod of assent. It took the curse off what he had come to do. Probably the man couldn't even talk. He'd be relieved to get it over with at last.

Marty knew he was only a short jump ahead of the opposition. Frustrated in his efforts to identify the informant who had sent the anonymous letter to Senator Woods, Marty had discovered that someone else was in the hunt, an old navy spook. Touching all bases as usual, Marty had decided to see what the navy guy found out. Friday morning he had followed Commander Dan Hallerman when he left Annapolis. Marty was sure he hadn't been burned, but Hallerman pulled some evasive maneuvers, probably as a precaution, and lost him.

Marty had to wait. The only thing that kept him from losing his cool entirely was that he'd accessed Hallerman's vehicle the night before and checked the mileage. He hadn't risked planting a beeper, but the mileage figure — if he could read the odometer on Hallerman's return — would give him something to go on.

Hallerman didn't return until after dark. A longish trip, Marty figured. Hallerman lived off base in a pleasant old house near the Chesapeake Bay. He had three kids still living at home, and the garage was full of family junk. Three cars were parked in the drive, one of them Dan Hallerman's. About an hour after the house was dark, Marty eased the driver's door open and peeked inside with a tiny pencil light, noting the mileage.

Later, in his room, he divided Hallerman's mileage for the trip in half to get a radius and, using Annapolis as the base point, drew a semicircle on a map, a line that extended north into Pennsylvania, swept down across Maryland and ended south around Point Lookout, where the Potomac fed into the bay. Then he drew a second, shorter semicircle allowing for diversions Hallerman might have made to be sure he wasn't followed.

Marty studied the map with a magnifying glass for a long time. He was almost ready to give up when he noted a familiar spot in the Blue Ridge Mountains that fell within the two curved lines. He remembered a safe house there.

Now Marty looked into the haunted eyes of the dying man he had come to hasten on his way. Marty had a hypodermic needle in his gloved hands. Very thin black gloves.

Richard Zehlke hoped the assassin could handle the needle efficiently while wearing gloves. Zehlke was used to needles. He'd had needles poked into every possible surface of his skin — even between his toes to inject an experimental drug into his glandular system. Needles no longer bothered him.

"This won't hurt," the assassin said.

He pushed a fold of the afghan aside to expose the old man's left arm. Zehlke turned away, almost as if he were resisting. But he didn't attempt to pull back his arm.

Marty positioned the needle over a vein. Not that it mattered, really; the poison would kill no matter where it was injected. It would simply work faster inserted directly into the bloodstream.

As he thrust the needle into the wizened arm, the man in the chair turned toward him, smiling faintly. The right arm under the afghan moved, and Richard Zehlke fired the Beretta automatic pistol he was holding. He fired three times before the gun became too heavy, and his arm dropped. The hot metal of the barrel seared his thigh.

By then the fluid that had been injected into him was already working. He felt a strange lassitude, a heaviness in his limbs, and he had trouble focusing his eyes.

Through a mist Zehlke saw the man in black

flopping in the grass on his back like a fish out of water. Zehlke's lips drew back over his yellowed teeth. "Join me," he whispered, one professional to another.

One of the caretakers was running across the lawn toward him when he finally let go.

Thirty-Seven

Kevin Daulton stared at the scowling Japanese who blocked the way to Toshio Miyaki's suite.

"I've got to see Miyaki-san," Kevin said, using up his full command of Japanese. "It's very important."

"No English," the Japanese said.

Kevin didn't believe him. He didn't think the man was simply a bodyguard either; he was too self-assured and authoritative for that.

"I'm not leaving until I see him."

"Miyaki-san not here," the man said, his black eyes narrowing as he took a step toward Kevin. "You leave now."

"I thought you couldn't speak English."

"You go. No reporters. No speech, not tonight."

Kevin didn't really have any options to consider. It had taken him much of the afternoon just to find out where Miyaki was staying in the hotel. He'd finally managed that through bribery — not of a bellhop but one of the reporters camped out in the lobby, who had talked freely for the price of a couple of drinks. Miyaki was in the hotel, all right, but he wasn't talking to anyone. No phone calls, no visits, nothing. And the reporter knew Miyaki hadn't left; there were too many alert media people watching.

"The bastard as much as declared World War III, and now he's got nothing more to say."

"Does he have guards in the corridor?"

"Just one guy's with him, but he looks like a gangster. You might as well try to get by a tank."

He *did* look like a gangster, Kevin thought. Or a wrestler. Not one of our actor-wrestlers, and not a *sumo* wrestler. He wasn't fat enough for that. He was square and muscular, and he had about the coldest eyes Kevin had ever peered into.

"I'll be back," he said. *Great,* his inner skeptic said. *That'll really have him shaking in his boots.* "Give Miyaki-san a message for me . . . tell him I know about Guam!"

Something flared in the Japanese sentry's eyes, but Kevin missed it. He had turned away toward the elevator, wondering what kind of diversion he could rig to lure the gangster away from his post.

Elinor Woods and Raymond Farrow stopped for dinner on the way back to the capital. The senator wasn't hungry, but Farrow insisted she needed to eat something. In a small town in the Virginia countryside he found the Blue Heron Café. It had mullioned windows, lace curtains, an Amish quilt hanging on the wall, some old redware platters, ceramic cows and other country decorations. The menu featured such staples as meatloaf with mashed potatoes and gravy, liver and onions, and baked Virginia ham with raisin sauce. They both ordered the ham, Elinor without enthusiasm. When the platter was placed in front of her, however, she discovered she was ravenous.

"Thanks, Ray," she said after a while. "This really was a good idea."

"When you feel like talking," he said, "I'm listening."

Two hours earlier, when they arrived at the remote hospice, they had confronted the worst possible case: Richard Zehlke was dead, apparently from a lethal injection, though the certainty of the cause of death awaited an autopsy. And the man who had come to murder him was also dead. He had been found by one of the caretakers near Zehlke's feet, moments after three shots were fired.

Horrified by the scene, the senator had been equally dismayed by the realization that the information Zehlke had promised had died with him. The assassin had succeeded, even if it cost him his life.

Farrow and Hallerman took over the situation immediately after their arrival. Hallerman conferred by phone with navy brass. Then calls were put through to the CIA for a cleanup squad, and to the FBI as a matter of protocol. The assassin had carried no identification. If he was in the trade, Hallerman said, someone would recognize him.

Elinor wandered outside, needing fresh air. She stood behind the cabin, staring at the empty bentwood rocker where Zehlke had died, and at the dark woods ringing the clearing. She asked herself why the old man had waited until he'd been given the lethal injection before he fired his weapon. The answer was obvious: He had chosen this time and this way to accept the inevitable. There must have been an ironic satisfaction for the old spy, effectively dying in action.

While she stood there in the darkness, she felt a presence on the porch behind her. She turned quickly. A white-haired man stood watching her, wrapped in a frayed terrycloth

461

robe. "I'm Givens," he said. "Are you Senator Woods?"

"Yes, I am, Mr. Givens. Were you a friend of Mr. Zehlke's?"

"Guess you could say that." From a pocket of the robe he drew a sheaf of pages torn from a spiral notebook and folded in half. "He wanted me to give you this if anything happened." Givens stared briefly at the empty rocking chair. "I guess he figured he might not get the chance to talk to you in person."

Elinor's heart started to pound as she took the note pages.

She left the hospice with Raymond Farrow shortly thereafter. Hallerman stayed behind to sort things out with the agency officials who were racing through the night toward the cabin. While Farrow drove, Elinor had kept the reading light on in the car and silently read what amounted to the last official report of Richard Zehlke.

Now, in the café, Farrow sat back. "Summarize it for me, Senator. I know quite a bit about the O Fund, but I'd like to hear the eyewitness version."

"The core of the O Fund was gold. It was controlled by a handful of powerful old families, members of the core of *zaibatsu* that General MacArthur broke up, who joined together as the Sonno Group. Much of the fund was the spoils of a decade of war by Japan against its Asian neighbors. Even more was mined in Manchuria and elsewhere during their occupation. Korea was the main collection point. In August of 1945, $2 billion in gold kilo bars was crated and flown from Korean vaults — Zehlke says this is on the record, nothing secret about it. It was sealed in steel containers and dropped into Tokyo harbor.

"When Edwin Pauley was sent to Tokyo by President Truman to assess the situation in Japan, he reported back that Japan's gold holdings were no more than $200 million. He didn't know about the fortune buried in Tokyo harbor, or the even larger fortune in gold still hidden away in vaults and caves in the Philippines, Korea and Japan, or secretly deposited in branch drops of Swiss banks."

Farrow grunted. "Gold was essential, of course. There was no foreign exchange available in Japan for the enormous costs of rebuilding. Without gold, there was nothing to back the yen. Go on, Senator."

"One of the key members of SCAP's finance division was Zehlke's immediate superior, a Colonel Jack O'Meara. He was contacted by someone in the Sonno Group, who hinted that a large sum of gold was available. O'Meara learned about the containers buried in Tokyo harbor. He took the news to General Mac-

Arthur. The general had a mandate from President Truman to bring Japan back to economic parity by hook or by crook. Those gold bars solved the greatest crisis the Occupation faced in rebuilding Japan and converting it into a fall-fledged democracy. MacArthur gave the order, and in the spring of 1946 the harbor was dredged. $2 billion in gold bars was deposited in the central Bank of Japan. It provided the backing needed so banks could provide business loans and generally pump money into Japan's economy."

"And that $2 billion turned out to be like a circus clown's car," Raymond Farrow said softly. "It kept coming and coming, inexhaustibly."

"That's what Zehlke says," Elinor Woods concurred. "Colonel O'Meara was the go-between for SCAP with the Sonno Group. That's why the fund came to be called after his initial 'O', as a convenient shorthand. No one knows how much was actually poured into the Occupation — its phenomenal success in getting Japan back on its feet might give us a clue. Zehlke suggests it was more like $6 billion. And what is equally clear is that the Sonno Group only funneled to O'Meara as much as they wanted to provide. The fund itself was much larger than anyone fathomed."

They fell silent. Farrow studied the senator

shrewdly as she finished the last of her tea. "There's more, isn't there, Senator? The second half of this puzzle."

Elinor nodded. "The trouble is, I don't know what to do with it. According to Zehlke, a member of President Walton's election campaign staff traveled secretly to Tokyo during his campaign for the nomination. He obtained an illegal contribution of $2 million from the Sonno Group. Zehlke theorizes that the current economic summit is a payback for that donation." She paused, troubled. "That assumes that Walton knew about the contribution."

"Not necessarily," Farrow said. "In fact, I'd be surprised if he did. Walton is a political animal, but an easy mark, really. It's very possible he didn't and doesn't know what's going on. I can't believe he would authorize David's murder, if that's what you're thinking."

"Then who did?"

"I've an idea. Gus Bonelli masterminded Walton's campaign. That Sonno contribution couldn't have happened on his watch without his knowledge. Perhaps when Zehlke's killer is identified, we'll have an arrow to aim. In the meanwhile, unfortunately, that doesn't answer our main problem. I'm afraid what Zehlke's told us in those notes about the O Fund isn't enough ammunition to derail the economic juggernaut the Sonno Group has loosed against us."

Studying him closely, Elinor realized that he looked suddenly older. There was defeat in his tired slump.

"I'm not giving up," Farrow said, answering the question in her eyes. "I've asked for a meeting with the Economic Security Council, and I've put in calls to the chairman of the Fed, the president of the World Bank, who's a personal friend, and the secretary of the Treasury, who isn't. The secretary wouldn't talk to me before," he added grimly. "I believe he will now."

Elinor felt some of his depression. "I can't believe this Sonno Group would wait nearly half a century to attack us like this. I've heard about the Japanese taking the long view, but this is ridiculous!"

"To understand what they've done you have to understand the people involved. In America they would be called hardliners, extremists who embrace rigid isolationist or jingoist attitudes. Japan has its own such hardliners. They're fanatical followers of the emperor and believers in Japanese nationalism. I've done some research on my own. The slogan *Sonno joi* goes back to the nineteenth century, to samurai who fiercely opposed the barbarian invasion of Japan. There was also a group after

World War II who called themselves *Sonno joi gigun*. They were bands of soldiers who roamed the countryside, wearing white headbands and refusing to surrender even after the Occupation. They called themselves the Righteous Defenders of Imperial Rule and dedicated themselves to driving out foreigners. Whether they were supported by the Sonno Group, we don't know. But they clung to one common, bitter belief: The war wasn't over. It would never be over . . . not until Japan won."

Elinor pressed her lips into a stubborn line. "We've got thirty-six hours before Monday morning, Ray. I'm not giving up either. We haven't lost this war yet."

"I know," Farrow answered quietly. "But to win, we're going to need a miracle."

Thirty-Eight

For most of the day Saturday Alison was ignored. She was free to move about Calvin Lederer's desert playground — though once outside she discovered that she immediately came under surveillance. The estate was like a country club prison, she thought. Every amenity provided, hotel-like accommodations, a pool, tennis courts, gardens, recreation, television — everything you could ask for to fill the emptiness of days without purpose. Everything except freedom.

She coldly turned down an invitation to play tennis with Dexter Hilliard, and she had no wish to subject herself to the poolside stares of the members of Bryant Forbes Lederer & Wyman who had remained behind after the Friday night exodus.

Television was no refuge. She found herself unable to watch the scenes being played out across the country. Marchers in Washington. Angry demonstrations — some of them anti-Japanese, others frightened cries against government neglect — in Fresno, Detroit, Youngstown, Cleveland, New York. A parade of government officials and financial gurus offering solemn but empty reassurances. Riots in front of the American embassy in Tokyo. The president of the United States holed up in an Osaka hotel, apparently helpless to do anything but watch his nation crumble.

By the end of the day Alison was glad to retreat to her own room. The mood in the cantina was like New Year's Eve. She wondered how she could endure two more days of this, watching and waiting helplessly. Was Lederer right? Was it all over? Would America face disaster Monday morning when the markets opened? What could anyone do now to stop it?

She stood on the tiny patio outside her room as darkness filled the desert floor like pools of ink. She thought of Kevin Daulton with unexpected pain. Had Linda delivered her message? It was unfair of her to ask Kevin to accomplish what was so obviously impossible, but he was her only hope. For the first time in her adult life she felt entirely dependent on what someone else might do. And she didn't reject the feeling.

Toshio Miyaki, secluded all day in his suite at the Bonaventure Hotel in downtown Los Angeles, took no pleasure in the predictable turmoil his words and actions had unleashed across America.

Friday had been the scheduled monthly meeting of the Sonno Group, the first he had missed in more than a year. He imagined a scene of jubilant celebration. The exultation over their triumphant strike would mirror that of Admiral Yamamoto and his staff at his naval headquarters in Tokyo in 1941 when he received the first reports of the devastating *shokku* of Pearl Harbor, when the half-century-old conflict really began. But now, as then, celebration was premature.

Miyaki believed in his heart, as Yashi Nogama had perceived, that the Sonno conspiracy was doomed to failure.

His colleagues, friends of so many years, assumed that, presented with a financial first strike of the magnitude that America was about to endure, Americans would respond as the Japanese typically would: they would stoically accept the reality of defeat. Just as most Japanese had passively accepted the occupation of their country by American soldiers, Americans would accept an inferior role because there was no other choice. But this conviction was demonstrably ignorant of America's past and the tendencies of its people. Like the British, when faced with overwhelming odds and imminent defeat, Americans fought harder, more tenaciously, with a quixotic faith in themselves that had little to do with rational assessment of the odds against them.

No, Miyaki thought, staring from the windows of his suite at the high-rise towers of Los Angeles' financial district, victory was not assured. For one thing, America had many friends. Japan had few, if any, either in Asia (where her neighbors were afraid) or in the West. Moreover, even if Monday saw the total collapse of America's financial infrastructure, the triumph would be a hollow one, disastrous not only for America but for Japan. Shinji Sakai and others among Sonno's leaders spoke eagerly of vast new markets in China and Russia, but these were still dreams without substance. It was to a friendly America that Japan's economic miracle had been linked. But America's wrath would be terrible and lasting.

Twilight spread over the great city. Miyaki thought of the darkness to come with a growing sense of dread. Japan's victory would bring no honor to the nation or to the emperor, for it would have been won through duplicity and deceit. But it was honor that held Miyaki prisoner, helpless to act against a policy he deplored, bound by his lifelong obligation to the men he now saw as the real enemies of Japan.

Nogama burst into the room behind him, as usual without knocking. "I've made arrangements for you to join the American attorney Lederer-san until the battle is over. His estate in Palm Springs is said to be magnificent. It's also very secluded."

"I have no wish to leave."

"The *gaijin* reporters will not leave us alone. It's Lederer-san's wish that you join him. It is also the wish of the Sonno council. You'll be safer away from this city on Monday. It's a violent place."

Miyaki stared at him. Now Nogama spoke for the Sonno council, giving him orders.

"I'll divert the attention of the reporters. They're hungry for the smallest morsel to chew on. Your car and driver will be waiting in the garage across the way. There's a bridge over the street from the hotel to the garage roof. There you'll find a stairway — you can see it here from your window. Take the stairs down to the tenth floor. That's only two flights."

"You're not coming?" Miyaki asked hopefully.

"I'll follow later."

At least he wouldn't have to ride with the *yakuza*, Miyaki thought. "When do I leave?" he asked with resignation.

"In thirty minutes exactly." Nogama smiled with satisfaction. "I will see to it that no one follows you."

Kevin Daulton stared across the street at the three bronze glass-and-steel cylinders that formed the unique architecture of the Bonaventure Hotel. He had crossed the street by way of a pedestrian bridge that linked one of the mezzanines of the hotel with the seventh level of a huge parking structure across the way, and with an adjoining terrace leading to several fast-food restaurants. Kevin had just glumly devoured a western barbecue bacon cheeseburger. Standing on the terrace, he sucked at the bottom of his container of coke through a straw.

A young couple in formal dress emerged from the garage and started across the bridge. Saturday night party time. The man wore a light blue tux with a yellow bow tie. Kevin hated bow ties, especially yellow ones. His father, on the other hand, favored bow ties. *Isn't that why you hate them?* his mocking inner voice wondered.

Kevin scowled, ready to argue with himself. At that moment a stocky figure shouldered past the young couple and, partially screened by two other men walking ahead of him, started across the bridge. The figure seemed familiar. Standing at the parapet on the terrace overlooking the bridge, Kevin suddenly recognized the man as the glowering bodyguard who had been stationed outside Toshio Miyaki's suite. He hurried on by, not glancing up, and entered the garage.

Kevin gave up on the icy dregs of his soft drink.

Why was the guard leaving the hotel? Was Miyaki planning to slip out?

Out of curiosity Kevin trotted down a short flight of steps and entered the garage. The Japanese was not in sight, but the doors of one of the elevators closed just as Kevin appeared. He watched the lights that marked the passage of the elevator. It stopped at ten.

And stayed there.

Kevin thought of taking the other elevator up to the tenth floor. Then, there was a sudden commotion outside. Two young men dashed down the steps from the restaurant terrace, heading toward the bridge and the hotel. Kevin recognized the reporter he had talked to earlier. "What's up?" he called out.

"Miyaki's gonna have a press conference!" the reporter yelled back. "Downstairs — gotta beat the stampede!"

He ran across the bridge into the hotel. Kevin started after him. He paused at the edge of the building. Down on the street a car pulled up and a man spilled out, carrying a camera. Another man joined him as they ran into the hotel. More reporters, Kevin guessed. The word spread fast. He ought to go too, at least hear what one of the generals of the Japanese economic army had to say.

But that wasn't what he wanted. That wasn't what Alison wanted. He had to get to Miyaki alone, one on one.

He thought of the burly bodyguard again.

Why would he be leaving the hotel just when his boss was to give a press conference before a mob of screaming, hostile reporters?

Kevin stood irresolute, actually asking himself what Alison would do in this situation. He saw movement out of the corner of his eye and glanced upward.

There was another pedestrian bridge off to his right and a fall five stories higher. The lighting was poor, but Kevin saw the head and shoulders of a white-haired man hurrying across the bridge toward the roof of the garage.

He squinted. The white-haired man glanced down at him, an instant before he disappeared beyond the edge of the roof.

A jolting charge of energy shot through Kevin. The press conference was a ruse —

Miyaki was trying to sneak away!

Kevin raced back into the garage. The elevator the Japanese tough had taken was still stuck at ten. Two remaining elevators were on five. Kevin jabbed the up button. Nothing happened. He jabbed the button again, furiously. What was going on? Why weren't the elevators moving?

He bolted over to the nearby stairway, flung the door open and pounded up the metal stairs.

Thirty-Nine

Toshio Miyaki felt exposed on the pedestrian bridge that vaulted above Flower Street. He glanced down once, then hurried off the bridge onto the roof of the garage structure across from the hotel.

A narrow cement stairwell, dimly lit, led from the roof level into the garage. A door at the bottom of the enclosed well opened to more stairs, these of naked steel. Miyaki started down to a landing. His steps rang on the metal. A door at the bottom of the second flight of stairs bore a large painted number eleven.

The stairwell was damp and cold as Miyaki continued down. It smelled of urine, and it was littered with discarded paper cups, beer and soft drink cans, discarded advertising flyers, a section of Friday's *Los Angeles Times*. Miyaki frowned in disapproval. He regretted the necessity of sneaking out of the hotel and down neglected stairways like a thief, though he recognized the pragmatism of Nogama's arrangements.

At the next level, marked ten, Miyaki opened a steel door into a small connecting passage. The door stopped halfway. Something was blocking it. Easing past the door, Miyaki saw a man crumpled in a corner of the passage. He wore a faded knit shirt, soiled cotton pants and sneakers. Unshaven and threadbare, he had the appearance of one of the legions of homeless who littered empty nooks and doorways and alleys in downtown Los Angeles. But something about him gave Miyaki a chill.

He hesitated. Another steel door faced him. It was connected to an alarm system, Miyaki saw. Presumably the alarm was not activated until later.

He opened the door. Yashi Nogama smiled at him. His right hand held a dark blue automatic pistol, aimed at Miyaki's chest.

"*Wa!*" Miyaki exclaimed softly. Understanding exploded in his mind. "This is why you came to America!"

Nogama's smile evaporated, as if Miyaki's lack of surprise or dismay affronted him. "You don't seem surprised."

"Many things become clear when the light shines on them."

Everything fell into place. Shinji Sakai's insistence that Nogama must accompany him to America, the timetable that placed all of Miyaki's essential actions at the beginning of the dark enterprise, the secret councils to which he was not invited. But if the pattern of betrayal was clear, the explanation was not. "Why?" he asked in an almost conversational tone. "The conspiracy is not complete. Without me it may yet fail."

"You can't be relied upon. You act like a woman. That was known from the beginning."

"I don't understand."

Miyaki wondered about the absence of any activity on this level of the garage. He thought of the unnatural stillness of the man lying at the bottom of the stairwell. Looking past Nogama at the cement alleys of the garage, he saw no movement. A few cars were parked, but no one was in sight.

"*Baka!*" Nogama's grin resurfaced. "Fool! You were useful in our plan, but you've done your part. Now you'll play a more important role. You will become a martyr. America is a violent place, and overnight you've become a hated man, the destroyer of the pirate Tyler, the visible architect of the American economic failure. It will surprise no one if one of our enemies strikes back at you. Your death will unite the people of Japan behind our victory. Your children will be proud, Miyaki-san."

"I am to be killed by an American assassin?" Miyaki suddenly understood the reason for the man at the bottom of the stairs.

"*Hai*. This is an American weapon, obtained in this city, the criminal capital of America. The man on the floor . . . his fingerprints will be on the gun. Naturally I will find it necessary to kill him, but unfortunately too late to save you."

"This building has security guards." Miyaki spoke almost idly, knowing that words were impotent.

Nogama's smile became insolent. "Our friends own this building. The guard who should be patrolling is a friend. The elevators are temporarily delayed. We will not be disturbed until it is time. But we've talked long enough. . . ."

"Not everyone will follow you on this dishonorable path. There are reasonable leaders in Japan, men of honor —"

"They'll come over to our side in time. They will have no choice." Nogama gestured abruptly with the pistol. "Back into the stairway — quickly!"

"*Getsuyō-bi* . . ." Miyaki murmured, more to himself than Nogama. "Monday it will be over." He was appalled by the final betrayal in the conspiracy he had joined out of misplaced loyalty and obligation. What debt could be owed to men so obsessed that honor was without meaning?

"Monday Japan will withdraw from America," Nogama said harshly. "We will sell their treasury bonds, sell dollars, withdraw our capital. America will collapse into chaos — and it will all be legal. No bombs will fall, no war will be declared. There will be nothing for Americans to do but lament." He stepped threateningly toward Miyaki. "Open the door!"

The old man stumbled backward. He read hatred and death in Nogama's black eyes. He fumbled for the panic bar that released the door.

Without warning the door burst open. Miyaki felt himself pushed aside. He saw a startled face, Caucasian, guileless and open.

Nogama's composure shattered. In the instant in which his attention wavered, Miyaki hurled himself at the *yakuza*'s gun.

Miyaki was in his seventies, and he had neither the quick reflexes nor the strength of youth. But Nogama had been startled by the unexpected intrusion. He was slow to react. Miyaki seized his arm and slammed it against the concrete wall behind him. The gun spilled free, and clattered across the cement floor.

Miyaki spun away from his enemy into the stairwell passage.

The young American gaped at him, then at Nogama. "Uh . . . quick! Up the stairs!" He pushed Miyaki ahead of him.

The infuriated Nogama grabbed the American from behind and threw him against the door. The young man's head cracked against the steel panel. His knees buckled.

Nogama shoved past him as Miyaki ran up the stairs. In his rage the gangster hadn't taken time to retrieve his gun. He would not need it. He was quicker than Miyaki, and he caught the old man at the landing.

Behind the blocky Japanese, Kevin Daulton, head still spinning, wobbled toward the stairs. The scene had unfolded too swiftly for him to sort it out, but it was Toshio Miyaki he had come to see, Miyaki who was being attacked. The guard had him by the throat and slammed him against the wall. Stumbling up the stairs, Kevin seized the attacker's leg.

With a snarl Nogama spun around. His foot lashed out in a vicious kick at Kevin's head. Kevin's lurching ascent saved him. The kick grazed his skull. Instinctively he grabbed at his assailant's foot and caught it with both hands. He pulled with all his strength.

What happened next was not planned, but it followed an elementary principle of martial arts: Kevin's reflexive grab and flip turned the momentum of the Japanese thug's kick against him. Off balance and moving forward, Nogama flew effortlessly into the air.

He landed on his back, spread-eagled across the stairway railing, and somersaulted onward. He crashed onto the metal stairs below Kevin.

The white-haired old Japanese had pushed to his feet. There was blood on his mouth where he had been hit. But his eyes were clear, penetrating. When Kevin took his arm and hustled him up the stairs, he didn't resist. Both men listened apprehensively for the thump of pursuing steps.

A moment later they burst into the open at the roof level. From behind them came a scream of rage.

"He tried to kill you!" Kevin gasped.

"*Hai* . . . we must be quick. He may not be badly hurt." The old man's English was clear and precise.

"I have a car — this way." Kevin still held Miyaki by the arm. He urged him toward Hope Street, where he had earlier parked his car.

"*Iie*," Miyaki said, resisting. He felt a wonderful sense of relief. The bond was broken. Now he could act freely. "The hotel . . . there are reporters waiting to hear me."

"Dammit!" Kevin shouted at him, suddenly

angry. "I don't know what this is all about, or what you people are trying to pull —"

"You must trust me," Toshio Miyaki said sharply. He started toward the pedestrian bridge leading to the relative safety of the hotel. Kevin hurried after him. "I will speak to the reporters . . . then I must speak with someone important in your government. It is of the greatest urgency."

Kevin felt a surge of hope. Something in the old man's eyes and attitude was at odds with all that he had feared. His judgment was a leap of faith in their common humanity. "The government? I think my father may know someone."

Together they raced across the bridge.

Forty

Kevin Daulton drove down to Palm Springs at dawn. He had been up all night but, running on adrenalin, he felt wide awake.

The events of that night were a blur. He had spent most of it in Toshio Miyaki's hotel suite. There had been endless telephone conversations, to Connecticut and Washington, D.C., Palm Springs, Tokyo and Osaka, among other destinations. There had also been one prolonged visit from the Los Angeles police. Yashi Nogama was now the object of a police inquiry. What Kevin remembered most clearly from the night was the ring of approval in his father's voice the last time they talked.

When Kevin drove up to the gates of Calvin Lederer's secluded estate overlooking the valley floor, the sun was climbing over the blue-gray mountain wall behind the ridge. The desert air was clear and brilliant, and every shadow was etched with the sharpness of cut glass.

The gates stood open. Kevin drove up the gravel drive. Alison came running out of the long, low Spanish house at the sound of the car. Her face lit up.

They stared at each other in silence for a moment. "Where is everybody?" Kevin asked.

"They cleared out during the night. We've got the place to ourselves."

"Until the reporters converge."

"How long's that gonna be?"

"The full story wasn't released, including the role of Bryant Forbes Lederer & Wyman, until after the president's statement. They'll come any time now."

He followed her into the house. He couldn't take his eyes off her. In the cool silence of the tiled foyer she turned and slipped naturally into his arms. They kissed for a long minute. It seemed to him that they had been doing this for a lifetime, even though it was the first time.

"Have you had breakfast?"

"No, just coffee."

"I found some frozen cinnamon rolls and defrosted them. I popped them in the oven after you drove in and I closed the gates."

"You closed the gates?"

"The control panel's in the cantina. I didn't want us to be interrupted just yet."

They carried the hot cinnamon rolls and fresh coffee into the cantina. It was a huge room overlooking pink terraces and a turquoise swimming pool. The room seemed empty with only the two of them. There was a forty-inch television screen in one sunken area with a circle of beige leather upholstery facing it.

Kevin reached for the remote control, saying, "Senator Woods is on Dennis Loughery's show." The newsman's top-rated interview program was a Sunday morning fixture.

The program was in progress. While they waited through a series of commercial interruptions Kevin filled Alison in briefly on events subsequent to his midnight phone call. Then he said, "Where do you suppose Lederer's gone?"

"Somewhere in the Caribbean would be my guess. Some place that doesn't have an extradition treaty with the United States."

Dennis Loughery's pugnacious bulldog's face reappeared on the big screen. He thrust it at Senator Elinor Woods, who was seated in a chair beside him.

"What you're saying, Senator, is that a right-wing cadre of Japanese extremists mounted an attack against our economy without the knowledge of the Japanese government or its corporate establishment."

"I think the joint announcement by President Walton and Prime Minister Nashido speaks for itself. The conspiracy has been exposed and denounced by both our governments. Japan is taking steps to increase, not decrease, its capital investment in the United States. And the summit trade talks are now going forward with a new determination on both sides to achieve real agreements."

"Spoken like a politician," Loughery said. "But just between you and me, Senator, what the hell went on here? How close did we come to the edge?"

Elinor Woods smiled. "Just between you and me and your thirty million viewers?" Her expression sobered. "A handful of financially powerful fanatics, the Sonno Group, pushed both Japan and the United States to the brink of economic chaos. That conspiracy was stopped by a few courageous people on both sides, including the prime minister and Toshio Miyaki. Mr. Miyaki's revelation of part of the conspiracy Saturday night, and his pledge to reopen the Youngstown steel plant, was the turning point. Mr. Nashido's quick response in contacting the president and pledging his wholehearted support was the beginning of the end for the conspirators."

"And that's it?" Loughery demanded belligerently.

"I'm sure there will be other aspects of the affair that will come out in time. I should also add that my good friend Raymond Farrow, a great and patriotic American who was instrumental in bringing the truth about the Sonno Group to light, has been in touch with the chairman of the Federal Reserve, the secretary of the Treasury, and other leaders in the banking and investment communities here and in Europe, and in Asia as well. He assures me that America's financial markets will open tomorrow morning on a very positive note. The crisis is over."

Loughery appeared skeptical, or possibly disappointed. Pablum didn't get high ratings. "What about this Sonno Fund? What put you onto it? I know your late assistant, David Perez, was digging into it."

"Another patriotic American came forward," the senator said. "His name was Richard Zehlke. Unfortunately he has passed away. He had lung cancer of long duration. He first wrote me anonymously about the fund. When I managed to find him, he was able to give me the full story of the fund's origin."

"How did Zehlke know about it?"

"He was on General MacArthur's staff, attached to the financial division, during the postwar occupation of Japan."

"Did he know about the Sonno conspiracy? Is that how you learned about it?"

"Mr. Zehlke's knowledge was historical. He wasn't aware of the current misuse of the fund by the Sonno conspirators. The Japanese government, as you know, has launched a full investigation."

Loughery had been holding one question back. Now he seemed to pounce. "Gus Bonelli has just resigned as the president's chief of staff — within moments after the joint statement was released in Osaka. Does his resignation have some connection with this sorry adventure?"

Elinor Woods took a deep breath before replying. Then she spoke evenly. "I believe that any statement on that subject should come from Mr. Bonelli or the administration."

Loughery feigned the exaggerated incredulity that was his trademark response to an answer he found less than candid. "Isn't this a case where 'no comment' is an implication that there's something there?"

"You don't expect me to answer that."

"Are you suggesting that Gus Bonelli was part of, or had prior knowledge of, a conspiracy against the United States?"

Elinor stared at him. The bulldog did bite. "No, I'm not, Mr. Loughery. I don't believe

Mr. Bonelli was part of the conspiracy, or that he did anything with the intention of causing harm to this president or to the United States. He has chosen to resign, I'm sure, for his own good reasons. I don't believe his resignation is directly connected to the Sonno conspiracy."

"Not directly?" Loughery shot back.

"You're a reporter, Mr. Loughery. Find your own story."

The newsman rewarded her with a tolerant smile. Then he tried to catch her off-guard with an abrupt change of subject. "Are you planning on running for president, Senator Woods?"

She laughed with an engaging lack of pretension. "A fine politician with whom I've worked on the Hill offered me some very good advice: Don't get ahead of yourself. I plan to follow that advice."

Loughery turned toward the television camera, which moved in for a close-up until his face filled the screen. "This is Dennis Loughery. Until next week, remember . . . you heard it here first."

In Calvin Lederer's cantina in Palm Springs, there was a sudden loud electronic rasping. "The barbarians are at the gate," Alison murmured. "Should we let them in?"

491

"I suppose," Kevin said, still watching the television screen. "Senator Woods is engaging, isn't she?"

"She's intelligent and honest, and she may have played a big part in saving this country from ruin."

He turned away from the television set and focused on Alison. "In any respectable melodrama, this should be the scene where the guy gets the girl."

Alison grinned.

With the cameras off, Loughery complimented Woods on her adroit bobbing and weaving during the interview. She reached over and laid her hand gently on his wrist. "If I were in your seat, Mr. Loughery, I would be less interested in yesterday's events and more intrigued by the brief story on page A-26 of today's *Post*."

Loughery raised an eyebrow. "Tell me more, Senator," he said, and leaned forward.

"A Japanese cargo ship, the *Akatsuki Maru*, pulled into Tokyo harbor this week with nearly two tons of plutonium in its hold. The load originated in France, and there's more where that came from — thirty tons in all that the Japanese plan to purchase in the next twenty years. You'll be interested to know that the buyer was a business consortium

called the Sonno Group. They're also negotiating with the Russians for plutonium from
dismantled nuclear weapons. They say it's for
a string of nuclear power plants across Japan."

"You don't believe that?"

"I'm no expert on plutonium, but I've just
completed a crash course on Japan. Perhaps
we've only won the latest battle, not the war."